STORY HAMUO

ART MO

HELL MODE

The Hardcore Gamer Dominates in Another World with Garbage Balancing

jnc
New York

HELL MODE 5

The Hardcore Gamer Dominates in Another World with Garbage Balancing

STORY **HAMUO**

ART **MO**

Translated by Taishi Edited by Seanna Hundt

Yen Press
150 West 30th Street, 19th Floor
New York, NY 10001

Visit us at yenpress.com
facebook.com/yenpress · twitter.com/yenpress
yenpress.tumblr.com · instagram.com/yenpress

First JNC Paperback Edition: August 2024

JNC is an imprint of Yen Press, LLC.
The JNC name and logo are trademarks of J-Novel Club LLC.

Library of Congress Cataloging-in-Publication Data
Names: Hamuo, author. | Mo (Illustrator), artist. | Taishi (Translator), translator.
Title: Hell mode : the hardcore gamer dominates in another world with garbage balancing / story, Hamuo ; art, Mo ; translated by Taishi.
Other titles: Hell mode. English
Description: First JNC paperback edition. | New York : JNC, 2023. | Identifiers: LCCN 2023015021 | ISBN 9781975368494 (v. 1 ; trade paperback) | ISBN 9781975368500 (v. 2 ; trade paperback) | ISBN 9781975368517 (v. 3 ; trade paperback) | ISBN 9781975368524 (v. 4 ; trade paperback) | ISBN 9781975368531 (v. 5 ; trade paperback)
Subjects: CYAC: Graphic novels. | Fantasy. | Internet games—Fiction. | Video games—Fiction. | Reincarnation—Fiction. | Adventure and adventurers—Fiction. | LCGFT: Fantasy fiction. | Action and adventure fiction. | Light novels.
Classification: LCC PZ7.1.H36344 He 2023 | DDC [Fic]—dc23
LC record available at https://lccn.loc.gov/2023015021

ISBN: 978-1-9753-6853-1 (paperback)

1 3 5 7 9 10 8 6 4 2

TPA

Printed in South Korea

HELL MODE

The Hardcore Gamer Dominates in Another World with Garbage Balancing

Chapter 1: Returning to the Academy

Ten days had passed since the No-life Gamers departed Rohzenheim, and it was now late March. The group was currently eating inside a private booth at one of Academy City's high-end restaurants, sharing their table with the slender son of Count Hamilton, Rifol. One of the reasons Allen had invited Rifol today was to ask him what House Hamilton knew about the war's progress on the Central Continent, as its forces had been dispatched as a part of the Ratashian contingent. In return, Allen was catching him up on the current situation in Rohzenheim.

Rifol whistled softly. "Wow, so much happened."

"Well, that's the gist of it, at least." Allen shrugged. "It shouldn't be all that different from what you already know, right?"

"Yep. My father told me how surprised he was when he found out two million monsters were attacking."

According to Rifol, the Empire of Giamut—one of the major powers of the Five Continent Alliance—had declared victory against the Demon Lord Army attacking the Central Continent. The forces from Ratash who had been redeployed when one of the few fortresses came under attack had now begun returning to the fortresses they had been manning originally.

Rifol's information network is as impressive as always. I see, so things are going back to normal for Ratash.

When Keel saw that Allen and Rifol's exchange was finished, he spoke up. "By the way, thank you for taking care of my family while I was away, my lord."

Rifol waved a hand. "Come on, you don't need to address me by my title. We're classmates, Keel."

Back when Allen's group had hurriedly departed from Academy City for Rohzenheim, they had only had less than a day to get things in order. During that limited time, they had approached Rifol and asked him to take in Keel's younger sister and their servants; Rifol agreed on the spot. House Hamilton was the parent family of both House Granvelle and the now-defunct House Carnel—Cecil's and Keel's households, respectively. Just like her older brother, Nina had lost her family name, but the Hamiltons still treated her like any noble daughter. In fact, today's lunch with Rifol was in part to thank him for everything he and his family had done.

Allen lowered his eyes to the table. Among the many plates in front of him, there was one loaded with confections around half the size of a fist that looked like a cross between bread and cookies. A small flying squirrel was currently holding one in his tiny hands and nibbling away at it.

Right, Rohzen switched so that he's contracted with Sophie instead of the queen now. Ha ha, so even the God of Spirits needs to eat.

After the war in Rohzenheim ended and Allen's group had indicated they were leaving, Sophie and Volmaar had asked to join them. And despite Sophie being the crown princess and next in line for the throne, when she expressed her intention to accompany Allen, her mother had given her blessing, saying, "Go. Stay by Lord Allen's side and fight for the sake of the world."

"Many thanks for catching us up on the situation on the Central Continent, Sir Rifol," Sophie told him warmly, gently inclining her head in gratitude.

"O-Oh, of course. The pleasure is all mine." Although Rifol had just corrected Keel about using a title with him, he could not very well say the same thing to a princess.

"Now, my turn," Allen said. "Like I said before, the war in Rohzenheim is almost completely over. To go into more detail..."

Allen proceeded to give an account of what he and his companions had just experienced. He described the elves defeating seven million monsters in just under three months, glossing over the specific details of his own group's contributions. Rifol seemed deeply curious as to how the elves managed to pull off such a feat, but Allen had no intention of telling him the truth.

"Sir Keel was able to focus on helping us in no small part thanks to you and your household's generosity in accepting his family." Sophie made a small gesture. "Volmaar."

"Yes, Your Highness." Volmaar stood up and carefully fetched a wooden box that had been sitting on another table.

With questioning eyes, Rifol asked, "Um, what is this?"

"Basically, a thank-you present from Rohzenheim," Allen replied. "Go on, open it."

"O-Okay..." Rifol gingerly lifted the wicker lid of the box and found ten red, peach-like fruits lying within.

"These are elven elixirs," Sophie explained. "I'm afraid we could not prepare *too* many. I hope you accept them even so."

The puzzle pieces fell into place in Rifol's brain. The elven elixirs that Rohzenheim sent to the Central Continent had displayed efficacy that was simply mind-blowing. Not only did they heal physical injuries—even going so far as to regrow lost limbs—they also restored MP and erased fatigue. What was more, they could heal many within a massive area all at once. This was a miracle beyond what even a Saintess's Healing Magic could achieve. Thanks to these elixirs, the number of casualties on the Giamutan front this year was the lowest in recorded history, despite the Demon Lord Army attacking with record-breaking numbers. Taking this into account, the worth of just one of the fruits in this box was unfathomable.

Rifol was so touched he could only manage a simple "Thank you."

"You'll continue taking good care of Keel's family, yes?" Allen asked in a tone that sounded more like confirmation than question.

"O-Of course. However, the war's over now and the school year is about to begin. Wouldn't they prefer to return to Academy City and live together?"

It was easy to forget, in light of everything that happened so far, but Allen and his group were still only second-year students. As the Academy's curriculum was three years long, they still had one more year to attend.

"Nah, we'll be graduating." *We no longer have any time to waste attending school.*

"Huh? What do you mean?"

"We're asking the headmaster to let us graduate early."

The question "Is that even possible?" was on the tip of Rifol's tongue when he noticed the total lack of concern on the rest of the group's faces and started to doubt himself instead. He had initially intended on asking about the squirrel on the table once there was a lull in the conversation, but he had much bigger things to think about now.

When the meal was over and Rifol had left them, Allen turned to Sophie. "Do you think they're done talking?"

"I believe so, Lord Allen."

"Let's go, then."

With that, the group boarded a magic train headed for the heart of the Academy. Then they walked straight into the campus, still wearing their street clothes.

I feel like an alumnus revisiting the ole alma mater. I remember when I did this back in my previous life.

Before long, the Gamers reached the building where the headmaster's office was located. Allen knocked on the door.

"Sir, it's Allen."

A voice that Allen was extremely familiar with but did not belong to the headmaster answered, "Come in."

The group walked in to find the headmaster not behind his desk but at the conference table. With him sat two other elves, one of whom Allen had met in Rohzenheim—Field Marshal Lukdraal.

Headmaster Theodojiil's eyes widened when he saw Sophie. Apparently he was very surprised to see her back safe and sound.

She smiled at him, then turned to the field marshal. "How went the talks?"

Lukdraal bowed his head without getting up. "We're finished, Your Highness."

"Meaning we can graduate now, right?" Allen asked plainly to make sure.

"Indeed," the other elf answered as he picked up one of the papers on the table with a wrinkled hand. "The Five Continent Alliance charter does not specify that Academy students must complete three full years of attendance before graduating. There is even a precedent of those who have graduated early. As such, your diplomas have already been ordered."

This was the Elder in charge of Rohzenheim's internal affairs, Filamehl. Because he and Lukdraal were already on their way to have an audience with the king of Ratash, they had stopped by Academy City to help the Gamers sort out their school affairs.

Though to be honest, I don't really care whether we graduate or not. Neither do Dogora nor Krena, I bet.

Sophie and Volmaar had graduated from the Rohzenheim Academy once already, so they had no need to do so again. This left Cecil and Keel, whose situations were different from the rest. Cecil was a noble of Ratash and therefore needed to graduate by all means. Keel was not currently a noble, but he was working hard to restore his house someday, so the same went for him.

In light of this, before they left Rohzenheim, Allen had asked the elven queen to help his friends get their diplomas, no matter the method. That request was why Lukdraal and Filamehl were now here. Theodojiil had not pushed back against it either. Perhaps he thought there was no longer anything for the Gamers to learn at the Academy.

"Thank you for the confirmation, Elder." Allen lowered his head in thanks. "By the way, how goes your request to meet with our king?"

"To think you can handle politics as well..." Filamehl smiled at Allen. "Of course, we have already sent the official missive, and Ratash has no pretext to turn us down."

Allen grinned. "Would you mind if we joined you?"

Eventually, it was decided that the No-life Gamers would accompany Rohzenheim's Elder and field marshal to their audience with the king of Ratash.

"When is the audience scheduled for?" Allen asked.

"According to the response we received, ten days from now," Lukdraal replied.

Ten days, huh?

This time frame seemed somehow affected by the official proclamation that Rohzenheim made to the world the other day through the Five Continent Alliance. Namely, it had declared its defeat of the Demon Lord Army force attacking the Northeast continent and that Rohzenheim was no longer at war. Furthermore, the proclamation detailed that the attacking force had been seven million strong and included one Demonic Deity, and that by the end of the war, this number including the Demonic Deity had—with help from Hero Helmios—been almost thoroughly eradicated.

Rohzenheim kept one fact to itself—that Demonic Deity Rehzel had been a dark elf. The way the elven queen put it, this was a matter between the elves and dark elves; resolving it would require a lot more than simply winning the war. The dark elves currently lived in a reclusive country located on Galiat, the continent to the south of Rohzenheim. The queen was planning on reaching out to set up diplomatic talks with them in the near future.

What was it—"I want to settle our differences and restore relations with them under my reign"? Allen looked at Sophie while recalling the elven queen's words. He then turned back to the elves at the table. "Ten days it is, then. We'll make sure to arrive at the capital by the day before."

Lukdraal and Filamehl nodded in acknowledgment.

Cecil poked Allen. "You make it sound like we're going somewhere else before that. What're we going to be doing for the next ten days?"

"Dungeon delving, of course. We can't very well charge into the royal palace with all of you still at Lvl. 1 now, can we?"

"And just what is it that you plan on doing to His Majesty that would require us to level up?"

"That'd depend entirely on him. Oh, right, Headmaster, can we borrow one of those panels used for the Appraisal Ceremony?"

"Hm? Is there someone you wish to Appraise?" Theodojiil did not know that the Gamers had received class upgrades and were now back to being Lvl. 1.

Allen nodded. "Yes, sir. May we use one for about an hour? This year's exams should be beginning soon, so you should have a few Appraisal stations all set up already, I believe."

"I don't see why not." Without ado, the headmaster got up and left the room to ask one of the teaching staff to prepare for an Appraisal.

Gotta properly determine just how our stats are going to develop, after all. That kind of thing can really affect the strategies we'll use.

The Gamers could have done their Appraisals back in Rohzenheim, but Allen had decided that they ought to return to Ratash as soon as possible. And because they had only arrived the night before, they were finally getting around to it just now.

Before long, the headmaster returned. He informed the group that preparations were complete and directed them toward the room.

"In that case, Field Marshal Lukdraal, Elder Filamehl, let us meet again at the royal capital." With that, Allen then led his companions out of the office.

We probably don't need to attend the commencement ceremony, since we're not graduating the normal way anyway.

The "normal way" to graduate from an Academy was to finish three years of classes, clearing the curriculum the charter required of all Alliance Academies. At the end of each school year, the graduates would gather in the auditorium for their commencement ceremony, where the headmaster would directly confer their diplomas.

Allen, however, would much rather his party use their time to level up in a dungeon. He had already asked his companions ahead of time whether they wanted to attend the ceremony, but even Cecil had waved it away with a wry "It's a bit late for that." The Gamers had all left common sense far behind by now.

When the No-life Gamers entered the room the headmaster told them about, they found an instructor waiting for them alongside a pitch-black board and crystal ball.

"Thank you for doing this for us, sir," Allen said.

"My pleasure," the teacher replied. "Now, who's going first?"

All of the No-life Gamers were Appraised in turn, with the teacher doing a double take each time.

Name: Krena
HP: S
MP: B
Attack: S
Endurance: S
Agility: A
Intelligence: B
Luck: A
Talent: Sword King

Name: Cecil Granvelle
HP: A
MP: S
Attack: C
Endurance: C
Agility: A
Intelligence: S
Luck: A
Talent: Archwizardess

Name: Dogora
HP: A
MP: C
Attack: S
Endurance: B
Agility: B
Intelligence: C
Luck: B
Talent: Berserker

Name: Keel
HP: B
MP: S
Attack: C
Endurance: C
Agility: B
Intelligence: A
Luck: A
Talent: Saint

Name: Sophialohne
HP: B
MP: A
Attack: C
Endurance: C
Agility: B
Intelligence: S
Luck: C
Talent: Spirit Wizard

Name: Volmaar
HP: A
MP: C

Attack: A
Endurance: B
Agility: A
Intelligence: C
Luck: B
Talent: Bow Master

"All our readings seem to have improved quite a bit," Cecil noted.

"Mm-hm! We have so much room to grow!" Krena beamed.

Dogora and Keel also looked pleased as they took in their own results. Everyone's class promotions had come with a noticeable boost to their stats.

Allen told Cecil, "Your stats now look like what mine had been until I reached Lvl. 60."

"Really?" The girl's eyes glittered with curiosity.

The boy opened his grimoire and turned to the page where he had copied down the Status that Elmea sent him after his Appraisal Ceremony.

Name: Allen (5 years old)
HP: A
MP: S
Attack: C
Endurance: C
Agility: A
Intelligence: S
Luck: A
Talent: Summoner

"Wow, you're right. That reminds me, Lord Helmios also said something similar."

"Yeah, he said that my Status looked like an archwizard's. He was right on the money." *He probably knew because he had an archwizard or archwizardess in his party.*

"Hm? Did you just say, 'until I reached Lvl. 60'? What do you mean?"

"Well, keep watching."

Allen then placed his hand on the crystal ball. It shone with a light so bright it verged on blinding. Then, silver text appeared on the pitch-black board. Just as before, all of his stats were still 'E.'

"There's no change."

"That's because these letters are indicators of how fast someone can grow each stat. Based on the actual stat bonuses I'm getting from leveling up, this is what my Status became when I hit Lvl. 61."

Allen flipped to the page displaying his current Status.

Name: Allen (Lvl. 61 onward)
HP: S+
MP: SS
Attack: A
Endurance: A
Agility: S+
Intelligence: SS
Luck: S+
Talent: Summoner

"What the hell, man?!" Dogora exclaimed. "Y'mean there are stats that're even higher than 'S'?!"

"Before, whenever I leveled up, even my best stats only went up by 40 points at most. Once I passed Lvl. 61, however, aside from Attack and Endurance, all my stats started going up by more than that."

Dogora whistled softly in appreciation. "*Fweeet!* You really are incredible."

To put it another way, after Allen reached Lvl. 61, each level-up boosted his stats at double the rate compared to before. This was clearly due to him surpassing the level cap of Normal Mode.

I bet that when I surpass the Extra Mode level cap, these numbers will only get bigger. In other words, I still haven't even tapped into the potential of Hell Mode.

The thought of how much fun there was to be had in the future brought a smirk to Allen's face as he chuckled to himself. Krena, in turn, watched him with a smile.

"You look like you're having fun, Allen."

"Hm? Oh, Krena. I sure am—it feels like things are only just getting started. You all work hard so you can get promoted again and get even stronger!"

"You bet!"

Krena was eligible for one more class promotion. Allen wished to see her become just as strong as Helmios had been when he was a five-star Hero, and he hoped to make it happen as soon as possible. For comparison's sake, he opened to the page where he had written down Helmios's Status—during his entrance ceremony, he had managed to finagle the Hero into showing it.

Name: Helmios
HP: S
MP: A
Attack: S
Endurance: S
Agility: S
Intelligence: A
Luck: A
Talent: Hero

I now know that Krena's stats can get at least as high as this. All that's left is to confirm whether someone in Normal Mode can have a stat surpassing 'S.'

So far, Allen had yet to see anyone gain more than 40 points in a stat from leveling up—other than himself after he reached Lvl. 61, that is. If possible, he wanted to confirm the veracity of this limitation as well.

"All right, guys, let's head back to our hotel. We'll be heading into the dungeons first thing tomorrow!"

After having graduated without any issues, the No-life Gamers took their first step in the next phase of their lives.

* * *

Nine days had passed since the No-life Gamers cleared up all the red tape for their graduation. They were now inside one of the best hotels in the capital of Ratash, an establishment usually reserved for members of royalty or nobility.

Every time I see this cityscape, I can't help admiring how much history it has.

Allen was standing at a window by himself, looking down at the city illuminated by the rising sun. He had learned from his history class at the Academy that Ratash had not once moved its capital since the nation's founding. As a result, the buildings here looked somewhat dated, even for a world that bore such great similarities to medieval Europe. In contrast to the Ratashian Academy City, which had been built within the last fifty years, there was no magic train here. Instead, horse-drawn carriages could be seen lumbering in between the streams of pedestrians here and there.

After they had wrapped up a dungeon-crawling session the other day, the No-life Gamers arrived at the royal capital late the night before. They checked into this high-class hotel before meeting back up with Lukdraal and Filamehl; the elves informed them that the audience with the king would take place later that afternoon.

Allen left the window to groom himself, then headed down to the lobby on the ground floor. There, he found Keel sitting alone.

"Good morning. You the first one down?" *Did he have a bad night's sleep?*

Keel looked up at Allen. "Oh, hey, morning. Um…are we really bringing what we made last night?"

The previous night, after the Gamers briefly met with Lukdraal and Filamehl, they had worked together to create a certain something.

It had been for Keel's sake, but apparently Keel himself still had qualms about it.

"Why not? It's not like there's any evidence to the contrary."

"I mean, yeah, but..."

"Considering it's King Invel we'll be facing, we can never be too careful."

"You say that so glibly... It's *my* future on the line."

"I really couldn't care less about nobles, after all." *Not interested even in the slightest.*

"Seriously, how the hell can someone born a serf have *no* interest in becoming a noble? Is this because of your memories from your past life?"

"Maybe, who knows. Regardless, I hope your wish comes true."

Originally, Keel had come to the Academy intent on restoring his household in order to create a place for his younger sister, Nina, and his servants to call home. The reason he had gone along to Rohzenheim was to fulfill the requirements set out by the previous king. So, Allen had asked to accompany Lukdraal and Filamehl because he wanted to take this opportunity to bring Keel's achievements on the battlefield to the current king's attention.

Everyone's got their own dreams and goals.

Krena and Dogora, respectively born as serf and commoner, had played make-believe knights throughout their childhood. Even now, they looked up to the knights.

Sophie, the crown princess of Rohzenheim, was doing what she could for the sake of her subjects. And Volmaar, one such subject, always put his life on the line to protect her.

Even though the No-life Gamers were heading in the same direction together as a party, each member had wildly different backgrounds, social statuses, and aspirations.

"Allen, Keel, good morning. You two sure are up early." Cecil had come down, looking graceful and elegant in noble attire.

"I can't very well be late, can I?" Keel clutched his stomach. "Ugh, I'm so nervous."

Speaking of goals, I wonder what Cecil's is. Is it revenge for Mihai?

She did make this really dark face sometimes when we were fighting the Demon Lord Army.

Cecil was absolutely delighted about having become an archwizardess, but this apparently had not been her ultimate goal. Nor did she seem all that obsessed about defending her homeland or helping develop it financially—those duties belonged to Thomas, Cecil's older brother by two years, who was currently employed at the royal palace. He was the one who would be inheriting the household.

After a bit of idle chatting between the early birds, Sophie, Volmaar, Krena, and Dogora made their way down to the lobby as well. Allen did a quick head count. "All right. Looks like we're all here, so let's mosey. To the Adventurer's Guild we go!"

There was one thing that the Gamers had to do before visiting the king. It only took them a few minutes walking down the main avenue outside the hotel before they reached the Adventurer's Guild. They approached one of the counters and told the receptionist that they were there to pick up the items they had won from the auction the other day.

The group was then led to a private room and asked to wait there. Eventually, one of the guild staff pushed a cart loaded with something bulky into the room. The squeaking of the cart wheels hinted at how heavy the item was.

"That's pretty big. Are you sure you're gonna be fine?" Keel asked worriedly.

"Should be," Allen answered.

"Uh, I was asking Dogora," Keel returned.

The actual person in question proceeded to lean over the cart and grab the handle of the item with both hands. He took a deep breath, then lifted the large adamantite shield with a sharp exhale.

"Looks like you can lift it," Allen observed. "You gonna be able to use it with your greataxe?"

Dogora nodded slowly. "I...I think I can handle it. Though it is pretty heavy." He switched the shield he was holding to his left hand, then grabbed the greataxe that had been propped up against the wall with his right. The muscles on both his arms bulged as he strained to hold up both.

So it depends on his strength. It should get easier for him once his level's higher.

While reviewing his party's fight against the demons and Demonic Deity in Rohzenheim, Allen had identified something they sorely needed: someone to stand up front and focus on protecting everyone else—in short, a tank. Allen, Keel, and Sophie had ways to buff everyone's Endurance, but that was not enough. This had become all the more obvious as the opponents they faced grew stronger and stronger.

According to Helmios, inside the Rank S dungeon that awaited them, Rank A monsters were a dime a dozen. During the war in Rohzenheim, the No-life Gamers had only faced at most three Rank A monsters at the same time, and those situations had definitely not been easy to handle. Yet things were going to be even more demanding inside the Rank S dungeon.

In light of this, Allen thought he needed to be more intentional about balancing offense and defense in his party. Krena's main weapon was a greatsword that she needed two hands to wield, making her a pure attacker. That left Dogora to take up the shield and with it the burden of protecting the rest of the party. Even though he could barely lift it up along with his weapon at the moment, once his stats increased and he gained more levels in Shield Mastery, he ought to be able to wield it properly.

Allen told Dogora reassuringly, "It might be heavy, but you've got this."

Dogora replied with a simple "Mm-hm."

"Do you have any issues with the product?" the guild staff member asked.

"None at all," Allen confirmed. "How much was the bid for this?"

"Including service charge, 3,600 gold."

Wow, less than five grand.

Allen handed over the stated amount without hesitation. As it had not been all that long ago that everyone received rings that boosted their stats by a thousand, they were still quite low on cash. After discussing the matter, it was agreed that Allen would pay for anything that would bolster the party's fighting potential as a form of initial investment. In exchange, the members of the party were to accommodate each other to the best of their abilities.

In the Rank S dungeon, they would very likely be picking up extremely rare weapons, equipment, and items. However, there was no guarantee that what each party member needed would appear at a fair, even rate. And so, the agreement was that they would compromise whenever exceptionally rare items appeared in an effort to keep each other's fighting strength more or less balanced.

The guild employee did not look surprised when she accepted the money from Allen, even though the boy had just produced a staggering number of gold coins despite not even being fifteen years old yet. She knew full well that this party had already cleared five Rank A dungeons.

"I confirm that I have received the full amount. Is there anything else that I can help you with?"

"I want to gather as many Rank E, Rank D, and Rank C magic stones as possible. Can I put in a request now?"

"Of course."

Good, good. Let's see how many more I can get on top of the orders I've already got going on in Academy City.

Allen had resumed posting magic stone gathering requests when he returned to Ratash since he had expended quite a substantial number of stones and recovery items in the war in Rohzenheim. He was not likely to face monsters ranked C or lower going forward, so he was utilizing every opportunity he could to buy what he could.

And thankfully, the market price doesn't change no matter how crazy I get with my spending, even in a small country like Ratash.

The biggest exporter of magic stones among the members of the Five Continent Alliance was Baukis. It had a ton of dungeons and thus a ton of adventurers constantly bringing magic stones out from those dungeons. Consequently, the market price of magic stones remained very steady globally.

On the other end of the spectrum was Rohzenheim, the world's greatest importer of magic stones. It possessed very few dungeons and therefore regularly bought a large number of stones from Giamut as well. This made Giamut a rather significant exporter too, though it was still far from being Baukis's equal.

Allen himself bought tens of thousands of magic stones at a time. And when he could not come in person to pick up the orders, he would pay a bit more to have them delivered to Viscount Granvelle's mansion.

Allen turned to his companions. "All right, let's finally head to the palace."

Now that they had picked up the shield and put in new orders for magic stones, there was nothing left to do but go to the royal palace. The No-life Gamers therefore returned to the hotel to regroup with Field Marshal Lukdraal and Elder Filamehl.

Chapter 2: Royal Audience

The No-life Gamers, Field Marshal Lukdraal, Elder Filamehl, and ten other elves all boarded the luxury horse-drawn carriage that came to pick them up at the hotel. When they arrived at the Ratashian palace, they were greeted by a large lineup of officials, then led to a room so plush and sumptuous that it made Dogora, a commoner who had only first ventured outside his village a few years ago, quite ill at ease.

"*Psst.* Allen, you sure I should be here?"

Compared to this opulent chamber, the royal palace at Rohzenheim had not been so gaudily decorated. Even the throne room had been rather plain; its design, like that of nearly all elven architecture, had been focused on bringing out the natural beauty of the wood grain. Having visited these two locations back-to-back, the Gamers could not help but compare them.

"Huh? Why not?" Allen replied. "The king's probably only gonna notice Sophie, the field marshal, and the Elder anyway. Won't make a difference whether the rest of us are there or not."

Allen shrugged and reached for one of the fruits from the basket on the table. He took a big, juicy bite, the sight of which prompted Krena to do the same.

"We *just* had lunch." Cecil sighed. "Where on earth do you two find the stomach space to eat so much?"

Some time passed before there was a knock at the door. An official wearing a fancy, perfectly pressed uniform walked in. "I'm terribly sorry for the wait. His Majesty is ready to see you now. Kindly follow me, please."

"All is well," Elder Filamehl reassured him, waving the apology away as he slowly got to his feet. "Rather, we thank you for the swift reception."

Rohzenheim and Ratash did not have official diplomatic relations. In light of this, the fact that the Ratashian side managed to arrange an official audience ten days after receiving the request Filamehl had sent meant that they truly had reacted as fast as they could.

"However, I'm afraid that what your entourage is bringing is..." The official shot an awkward look toward the Gamers. His gaze lingered just a bit longer on Dogora, who was holding his greataxe and the large shield he had just picked up.

As I'd thought, they really won't let us in fully armed. Same rules as the ceremony after the tournament.

Allen once had the opportunity to meet then-Crown Prince Invel after winning the Ratashian Academy's martial arts tournament. Back then, he had been forbidden from bringing weapons into the meeting, same as now. This time, however, Allen's group had intentionally arrived in full armor expecting this to be the case.

"Oh, how embarrassing!" Filamehl chuckled apologetically. "I was not aware that it is customary in Ratash for both sides to disarm themselves for an audience."

"Huh? Uh, that's..." The official looked confused.

Looks like old man Filamehl's already got his diplomatic chops in full swing. No wonder he's tasked with dealing with Giamut.

According to Sophie, Elder Filamehl handled all of Rohzenheim's diplomatic dealings himself. He was in frequent contact with Giamut, the neighboring superpower across the sea, and often represented Rohzenheim at the regular Five Continent Alliance summits. Put simply, Filamehl was a man with enough authority and influence that his words could move the world.

Although Rohzenheim's queen was the official head of state, its affairs were actually handled by its Elder Council. Twelve Elders served in this Council, each in charge of a different aspect of the country's management; for example, there was someone in charge of infrastructure such as canals and roads, another in charge of finance, and so on. It was these Elders who gathered to decide the policies of the nation.

Each Elder was an expert in their respective field; however, Filamehl was somewhat different from the rest in that he was one of the few who dealt exclusively with diplomatic, not domestic, affairs.

Naturally, Ratash was already aware that Filamehl was now in the country.

"Filamehl, don't trouble them too much," Sophie chided. "There's no way Ratash would be so disrespectful as to greet a peaceful foreign delegation fully armed."

Of course, Sophie did not mean what she said. She kept her eyes trained on the official to see how he would react.

"It is as you say, Your Highness." The Elder also turned to the official. "I apologize for my disrespect."

Seeing this, the official gasped a little and asked for a bit of time. He then ducked out of the room. Thirty minutes later, he returned to say that everyone in the audience chamber would be armed only to the bare minimum and once again asked Allen's group to disarm themselves.

Sophie and Filamehl had no intention of wasting any more time on this issue, so they obliged and followed the official out of the room.

And the God of Spirits is still asleep on her shoulder.

Allen looked at Sophie's shoulder where a flying squirrel was currently perched. This was none other than Rohzen, the God of Spirits himself. Perhaps the official had been so occupied with disarming the group that he failed to notice the creature.

The official led the group down corridors lined with ostentatious decorations and ornately designed carpets that stretched on forever. Allen was marveling over how this palace was so unlike anywhere else he had been before when they approached gigantic double doors framed by knights standing on either side. The doors opened inward, revealing the audience hall beyond.

A red carpet ran the length of the hall, all the way to the throne at the far end. Ministers and nobles wearing resplendent clothing lined both sides of this pathway, who all began furiously muttering to each other the moment they laid eyes on Allen's procession.

Sophie entered first, flanked by Field Marshal Lukdraal and Elder Filamehl. The rest of the No-life Gamers followed behind, and the ten or so elves carrying a variety of gifts and tribute brought up the rear.

I wonder if Viscount Granvelle is— Oh, I see him.

Allen scanned the crowd of nobles while walking and spotted Cecil's father. He was positioned quite close to the door—that is, far away from the throne—either because he was considered a minor noble as a viscount or because he belonged to a different political faction from the king.

The aforementioned king, who had only been crowned just that year, sat reclined on his throne. Royal guards stood before and behind his throne, all looking wary and vigilant. They had had their eyes trained on Allen's party from the moment they entered the hall. The one stationed closest to the throne seemed to be their commander. Next to the king sat the queen, and beside those two were others wearing extravagant clothing, likely also members of royalty. None of them matched the description of the princess whom Keel had almost been forced into protecting.

I see, so the newly ascended king wants to make a show of his authority.

A royal audience could either be held in a smaller conference room with only the king and a few important ministers present or in a flashy, public way like today's setup. However, given how widespread news of the arrival of Rohzenheim delegates had been, perhaps this was not a choice—it had been simply impossible to choose the former.

Sophie walked half of the length of the room before coming to a stop. The king shot a look at the minister standing closest to him, who nodded then walked down the carpet to approach the delegation. Seeing this, the other nobles ceased talking all at once.

In a voice that carried through the silence, the minister declared, "Delegation from Rohzenheim, we thank you for making the long journey to our country. We welcome you. I am the prime minister of Ratash. It is my pleasure to meet you all."

As everyone watched on, Elder Filamehl replied, "King of Ratash, Prime Minister, and all esteemed parties—your presence does us much honor. I am Filamehl of Rohzenheim. Today, before anything else, I wish to offer thanks to the Kingdom of Ratash myself, but a mere citizen of Rohzenheim, for sending your *invaluable* fighting strength to our aid."

The elf made a show of slowly looking to his left and his right, then turned back to the king and bowed deeply. Regardless of King Invel's intentions, had he not sent the No-life Gamers to Rohzenheim, Tiamo would have fallen and the queen could have even died. Worst-case scenario, the Demon Lord Army might have wiped out the entire elven race and the entire Northeast Continent would have been under their control right now instead.

"I-Indeed. Both of our countries are fellow signatories of the Five Continent Alliance. It is only natural to assist one another." The prime minister said, somewhat flustered as he had not expected such a forthright and exaggerated display of gratitude.

"Now, Your Majesty and all other esteemed persons, there is someone I need to introduce you to," Filamehl said.

Catching his look, Sophie gracefully stepped forward with her back straight and her head held high. She did not appear nervous in the slightest. Everyone in the room seemingly forgot to breathe for a beat.

Filamehl continued, "I present to you Her Highness Princess Sophialohne of Rohzenheim. She is with our delegation today as proxy for her mother, Her Majesty the Queen."

The fact that Sophie was serving as proxy for the queen of Rohzenheim meant that she was here today with the full authority of the head of state of one of the major powers of the Five Continent Alliance.

Sophie smiled softly. She addressed everyone present while keeping her eyes fixed on the king's face. "I, Sophialohne, on behalf of all of Rohzenheim, wholeheartedly thank the Kingdom of Ratash for your wise decision to send us aid. Our people will never forget the favor that you have shown us, and our country will forever walk beside yours. If Ratash is ever in need, you can count on Rohzenheim to answer your call."

When Sophie was finished speaking, King Invel stood up from his throne. He returned her gaze and said, "As the one who bears the Kingdom of Ratash on his shoulders, I accept your words with grati— Hm?" The king cut himself off when he finally noticed the flying squirrel, now awake, on Sophie's shoulder. The small creature was staring directly at him, so Invel stared right back.

A strange silence hung heavy in the audience hall.

"What is the matter, Your Majesty?" Sophie asked.

Invel replied to her question with his own. "Do all members of royalty from Rohzenheim keep small creatures on their shoulders?"

"Not all." Sophie turned to the flying squirrel. "Lord Rohzen, the king of Ratash wishes to speak with you."

"'Rohzen,' as in..." A look of astonishment came over King Invel's face. "...*The* Rohzen?!"

The king's cry prompted all the nobles to turn to stare at the flying squirrel. Every one of them, be they graduates of the Academy or of the Noble College, knew the name of the being that the elves worshipped. A buzz sprang up as they resumed whispering furiously among themselves.

"The God of Spirits is here?"

"That tiny animal is the God?!"

"Are you crazy?! Don't point! What would you do if you were to anger him?!"

As the noise level in the room continued to swell, the flying squirrel on Sophie's shoulder—who was indeed Rohzen, the God of Spirits—slowly floated up into the air. As he continued rising—first above Sophie's head, then Lukdraal's—the voices in the room died down. When all were silent again, the God of Spirits spoke.

"Children of man, I am Rohzen, the God of Spirits. I thank you for saving the elves whom I hold close and dear to my heart. Ha ha."

The king of Ratash gulped as he stared up at the deity. Even after

Rohzen returned to Sophie's shoulder, the audience hall remained deathly quiet. Everyone was dumbfounded, including the king.

"As I hope you can tell from how we have brought Lord Rohzen with us," Filamehl said, breaking the silence, "Rohzenheim truly is here to express our gratitude. And of course, we have not come empty-handed. Please accept these as our thanks."

Filamehl's request for an audience had mentioned that he and his delegation would be presenting gifts on this occasion. The Elder's words served as the signal for elves standing behind Allen's group to step forward with the wooden boxes they had been carrying. Officials who had been standing behind the nobles then hurried forward to receive these boxes from the elves.

"After the onslaught of millions of monsters and suffering many casualties, I'm afraid we do not have much to offer. And so, we present you with these—our nation's treasured items, elven elixirs."

Each box was packed with ten elven elixirs. Filamehl's words sent the nobles abuzz once again.

"What're elven elixirs?"

"You don't know? They're miraculous recovery items."

"Did you just hear him say 'millions of monsters'? Talk about padding a story."

"I imagine we'll know soon enough whether it's true or not."

As it turned out, Ratash had yet to finish its own verification of the official proclamations Giamut and Rohzenheim had made.

After confirming the contents of the boxes carried over by the official, the prime minister said, "On behalf of His Majesty, I thank you for the valuable gift."

"We are glad you are pleased with it." Filamehl's facial expression shifted ever so slightly. "Now, let us get down to today's main business, shall we? We, on behalf of Rohzenheim, sought this audience for three purposes: information, a proposal, and a request."

The prime minister blinked a few times in surprise. "Three purposes… And what would they be?"

"Indeed, three. The proposal and request, I shall leave for later. I shall start with this: Rohzenheim is making a personnel appointment in light of the events that transpired during the war with the Demon Lord Army. We are informing you because this is a decision that involves your country."

"I-Is that so? What are the details of this appointment?"

Instead of answering the prime minister, Filamehl turned to give Sophie a look. She nodded, prompting one of the elves standing at the rear to come forward and hand the Elder a rolled-up scroll of parchment. When he unfurled it, the nobles in the room fell silent.

He cleared his throat. "Hear the words of Her Majesty the Queen: to recognize the heroic achievements of Allen of the Kingdom of Ratash in the previous war and to acknowledge how crucial his continued aid to Rohzenheim's future will be, we hereby appoint him the position of grand strategist."

As the Elder slowly rolled the parchment back up, the murmuring in the room started buzzing again, louder than before. The king of Ratash and the prime minister exchanged looks. The former nodded, prompting the latter to turn back to the Elder and clear his throat.

"Ahem. Sir Filamehl, may we inquire as to the specific nature and status of the position of grand strategist in your country?"

Field Marshal Lukdraal stepped forward. "As it is a military position, I shall be the one to explain." When he confirmed he had the king's and prime minister's attention, he continued, "In the military structure of the forces of Rohzenheim, the grand strategist is second only to the grand marshal. This is a position that has the authority to speak to the grand marshal on matters of military strategy. On the battlefield, the grand strategist also has the authority to give orders to the generals. This position has remained vacant in our forces for a long time, but the need for it has been made apparent in our recent war with the Demon Lord Army, and someone appropriate for the position has appeared. As such, the Elder Council decided to bring this position back."

The longer the general went on in his brisk tone, the more the blood drained from the prime minister's face.

"Th-That's preposterous! The position second to the grand marshal?!

That's above the generals, even! How could you give the authority to mobilize your forces to a teenager who has yet to even graduate from the Academy?!"

"A clarification: this position ranks above *field marshal*—my position, that is. That is how highly we hold his achievements in esteem."

The nobles' chattering climbed a decibel. All they could see was a boy who, apart from his black hair, seemed perfectly normal. Sure, he was probably a pretty good fighter, considering that he had been dispatched to help in Rohzenheim's war. But if he was that capable, he would have been properly recognized in Ratash. Suddenly being appointed to be the second-in-command of the military for one of the Alliance major powers was absolutely unheard of.

"Lord Allen's request did have some bearing on this decision, but it was made with the unanimous agreement of the Elder Council and our queen. We all think this reward commensurate with what Lord Allen has already done for our country." Filamehl continued. "I am sure your own country will have further opportunities to reward Lord Allen for his future contributions. When you do so, we ask that you remember our military ranks are comparable to your noble ranks. We are sorry for the inconvenience, but know that this is already a forgone decision."

"Ugh..."

That's right. Early bird gets the worm.

Allen thought back to when, right before he left Rohzenheim, the queen had approached him and insisted on thanking him for his contribution against the Demon Lord Army. He had replied, "Please give me a status similar to nobility in Ratash; any would do." The reason for this answer was rooted in the explanation regarding nobility that Viscount Granvelle had given him back when he was looking for ways to restore Keel's status.

According to the viscount, the nobles of this world were in general given their position as a reward to people for serving their country or making significant contributions. No matter how the person arrived at such circumstances, their investiture had to be sanctioned by a head of state. Furthermore, for the same reason, one person could only be appointed by one country at any given time.

And now that I'm technically another country's noble, Ratash can't make me one and order me around like how Invel dispatched me to Rohzenheim this time. Heh heh heh.

It was not clear whether this had been a part of the queen's considerations, but the end result was that she and the Elder Council had decided together to revive the position of grand strategist and appoint Allen to it.

Rohzenheim did not have a noble structure like Ratash had because they believed that everyone was "equal before the spirits." However, they did have positions like "general" and "Elder" for those involved with national self-defense and government, and these were acknowledged by other Five Continent Alliance nations as being equal to noble ranks.

The queen had told Allen that no particular duties came with the position of grand strategist. In turn, Allen told her that he would do everything he could should they ever need his help.

In short, this was how Allen managed to secure the freedom that he had wanted. This alone was worth the trip to Rohzenheim.

"The official proclamation will be sent to you on a later day. We are only informing you ahead of time today for your understanding."

"I-I see. Your consideration is much appreciated."

"Now, may we move on to the proposal?"

"Very well. What, uh, is it that you are proposing?" The prime minister looked very apprehensive about what the Elder would say next.

"Currently, our countries do not share official diplomatic relations. We would like to take this opportunity to do so formally and establish embassies in each other's countr—"

Before Filamehl could even finish, the prime minister blurted out, "Is that true?! We would be more than happy to!" The apprehension on his face disappeared in the blink of an eye as the nobles in the room burst into cheers. Even King Invel leaned forward with sparkling eyes.

As Elder Filamehl had pointed out, of the major powers of the Five Continent Alliance, Ratash currently only had official relations with

Giamut. While it was still trading with the other four, there were no mutual embassies or diplomacy. Because of this, Giamut often threw its weight around to make unreasonable demands, and Ratash did not have the national power to keep dodging these demands. If it was able to officially form relations with Rohzenheim, however, things might go differently.

This time, Ratash had received a bunch of elven elixirs as remuneration; next time, they just might be able to request an elven squad dispatch. And if Rohzenheim was willing to permanently station an ambassador at Ratash, this would give the impression that Ratash had Rohzenheim's backing and therefore keep Giamut in check. This proposal was one that could drastically change Ratash's standing within the Five Continent Alliance.

They seem so smitten with the idea that they've clearly forgotten having Rohzenheim as a backer means they also become susceptible to Rohzenheim's own demands.

On a personal level, there were many things about Invel ascending to the Ratashian throne that worried Allen. That said, he had zero interest in playing politics, nor did he want to take the throne for himself. If Rohzenheim and Ratash were to establish official relations, however, he could simply go through Rohzenheim if he ever needed to influence Ratash on any matter.

Nodding with satisfaction at the response he received, Filamehl said, "That leaves us with the last matter: the request."

"Ah, yes. What would that be?" The prime minister tried to dispel the fog of elation in his head so he could think straight.

"Please help Princess Sophialohne and Lord Allen."

"Help…them? What do you mean?"

"Well, during the previous war, the Demon Lord Army destroyed many of our fortresses and cities in its advance."

"I imagine so, yes."

Even Fortenia got destroyed. The Demon Lord Army seriously went too far.

"Now, we are firmly committed to fighting the Demon Lord Army.

As a part of this effort, our queen has ordered Princess Sophialohne to travel outside Rohzenheim to obtain further strength."

"By which you mean...?" The prime minister shot a look at Rohzen. To his knowledge, Sophie was the only person who held the right of succession to Rohzenheim's throne, and there was only one God of Spirits. In other words, this princess was practically confirmed to be the next elven queen.

"To fulfill the task bestowed upon her, Princess Sophialohne intends on challenging the Rank S dungeon in the Empire of Baukis."

"Wha—?! The Tower of Tribulation?! Are you referring to that temple in Yanpany that Hero Helmios also attempted?!"

"The very one. She will need companions to aid her in this venture, and she has chosen, besides Lord Allen, other classmates from her time at the Ratashian Academy. Our request, therefore, is for official permission for them to head to Baukis."

Krena, Dogora, Keel, and Cecil had been with Sophie as much as Allen during her Academy days. This was why they had also been dispatched to help Rohzenheim. However, unlike the previous time when the No-life Gamers were responding to a request for aid, they required a permit to travel overseas now that the war was over. While Sophie, Volmaar, and the newly appointed grand strategist of Rohzenheim could do so with permits from Rohzenheim, Cecil and the rest needed theirs from Ratash.

"I-I see. When will they be making the journey? To my knowledge, Her Highness still has one more year at the Academy, does she not?"

"All of them have been conferred official diplomas. As such, they will depart as soon as possible."

The prime minister failed to reply immediately, leaving an awkward silence in the room. He turned to look up toward the king to ask for his decision and found the monarch with a difficult expression of his own.

What's the holdup? Just give us the permit already. You did it pretty quickly the first time when you sent us to Rohzenheim knowing they were on the verge of annihilation.

Eventually, King Invel raised his head and looked at Sophie.

"Princess Sophialohne, your companions include a valuable asset of ours, a Sword Lord. At the same time, Yanpany is well-known for being the site of death for many an accomplished adventurer. I have heard that no one has *ever* cleared this dungeon, not even Hero Helmios, despite his certain efforts. As ruler of Ratash, I am loath to send someone so important to us to such a dangerous place. I hope you understand."

Oh, right. Helmios said, "Dygragni can't make MP Recovery Rings," with a knowing smirk, but it's not like he'd cleared the dungeon yet either.

Without missing a beat, Sophie replied, "My foray into the Tower of Tribulations is for Rohzenheim's sake as well. In order to do so, I need all of my companions who are with me here today. If we cannot receive Ratash's cooperation in this matter, we will have to seek other recourse. I'm afraid we would have to pause the diplomatic talks between our countries until we can resolve this predicament."

"Hmm, as I'd thought." Invel rubbed his chin for a few seconds as if he was deep in thought. "We cannot allow this opportunity to foster amicable relations between our countries to go to waste. Very well. We will issue permits for everyone here to go to Baukis. Do note, however, that this would take some time."

Did he just want to act like a king?

Sophie bowed deeply. "I thank you truly, King Invel. Now I can head to Yanpany with peace of mind and heart."

Invel nodded with satisfaction. "Until the permits are ready, it would be our pleasure to host you and your delegation in our capital, Your Highness. Without ado, we shall arrange a ball tonight; may we expect your presence? It would be the perfect opportunity for those from our countries to become better acquainted with each other. For now, however... Welcome to Ratash."

The king's words of welcome served as the cue for the nobles lining the red carpet to echo his sentiments as they began clapping enthusiastically.

After waiting for the noise to die down, the prime minister declared, "This audience is hereby concluded!"

Just as King Invel was about to stand, however, Keel blurted out in a shout, "W-Wait, hold on a moment, please! Are you really ending it there?!"

The prime minister gave him the stink eye. "What is the meaning of this? Are you not aware that this is a royal audience?!"

So they skipped over talk of Keel's reward.

Allen gave Keel a look. The other boy returned it and nodded.

"My deepest apologies," Allen said. "Keel here raised his voice in indignation because he had been given a promise by the previous king—may he rest in peace—but no mention was made of the matter."

When Allen walked up, passing Sophie to stand at the very front of the group, a sense of alarm shot through not only the king but also the royal guards. The captain even took a step forward to position himself between Allen and King Invel. The nobles gave Allen their full attention so as to not miss even the slightest gesture from him.

"What promise was that?" The prime minister's voice was tinged by a healthy dose of fear. He was recalling the match he had witnessed between Allen and Helmios.

"The previous king promised that if Keel went to the battlefield on Ratash's behalf, his family name, the dissolved House Carnel, would be restored. You ought to be aware of this agreement, prime minister."

These were the terms that had been written down at the time:

The Promise Between the Previous King of Ratash and Keel

- Keel is to fight on the battlefield for a minimum of five years under the dispatch of Ratash or the Five Continent Alliance.
- Achievements made during service will be grounds to consider shortening the mandated service time.

Allen continued, "While with us, Keel performed numerous feats of remarkable merit on the battlefield in Rohzenheim. Would these feats not meet the requirement for the consideration of his service being shortened?"

The prime minister frowned. "We are indeed aware of this

matter. However, whether to consider shortening your companion's period of service is something that His Majesty will be contemplating at a later time."

"Hm? There's a chance that His Majesty would decide to not do so? Would that not be going against the wishes of the previous king, my good man?" Allen made sure to enunciate properly so that his lack of an address would be all the more obvious.

Sure enough, the prime minister flared up, turning so angry that his face became flushed. "How dare you forget my address?! Just what on earth did they teach you at the Academy?!"

Allen immediately clapped back with, "I am currently talking to you as the grand strategist of Rohzenheim."

"What?!"

"Did Field Marshal Lukdraal not explain this just now? I kindly remind you to consider what I just might say to the grand marshal when he seeks my input regarding future requests from Ratash, such as for, say, elven forces or elven elixirs. Are you sure you do not want to reconsider your reply?"

The idea to do this just occurred to me, but hey, that was a pretty good comeback if I do say so myself. I did think the grand strategist title was a bit too big for me, but... I see, so this is how useful it can be in situations like these.

"Y-You can't just..." In a fluster, the prime minister turned to look at Sophie, Lukdraal, and Filamehl. However, the three simply returned his gaze without saying anything.

Eventually, Sophie opened her mouth. "Prime Minister, we have prepared something in case there is anyone in Ratash who has doubts regarding Keel's achievements in Rohzenheim. We hope this helps."

Two elves stepped forward and held out a tray carrying several scrolls of parchment toward the prime minister.

"Wh-What is this?"

"A record of Sir Keel's achievements since he first stepped foot on Rohzenheim soil."

Man, you have no idea how hard we worked on that.

These scrolls were what Keel had been referring to that morning. The No-life Gamers had prepared them the night before. Ninety percent of it was pure fiction, but it was stamped with the crest that adorned all official Rohzenheim documents.

The prime minister unfurled one of the parchments and skimmed it, then turned to the throne as if seeking help.

Invel cleared his throat softly. "Hmm, that is indeed an impressive number of achievements. I was about to consider House Carnel's matter, but thought it inappropriate to bring up at the expense of our valued guests' time, with them having coming from afar."

Hmm, were you, though? I call bullshit. You were about to end the audience and sweep this under the rug.

"Are Sir Keel's feats sufficient to warrant the restoration of his house?" Sophie asked.

After Invel scanned through the parchment that the prime minister had handed him, he rolled it back up and lifted his face to look at Keel. "Keel, step forward."

"Y-Yes, Your Majesty." Keel stepped forward until he was shoulder to shoulder with Allen, looking extremely nervous.

"The actions of your father, Viscount Carnel, were unforgivable. As the position that bears the weight of the country, the throne had no choice but to sentence him severely. This is something that you understand, yes?"

"Yes, Your Majesty."

"However, our ally Rohzenheim"—Invel took advantage of this opportunity to emphasize that Ratash and Rohzenheim were now allies—"has presented us this list of your achievements. It is undeniable proof of your contributions. As such, I hereby acknowledge House Carnel once again as a servant of the kingdom. However, your fiefdom is only half its previous size, and you are starting off as a baron. You have no complaints, I take it?"

I see, so that's the furthest he's willing to compromise. Whew, Keel's finally back to being a noble! I'm gonna have to thank Viscount Granvelle for all his help. He was the one who got the previous king to write down this promise.

To convey that he was not against this in the slightest, Allen turned to Keel and said, "Good for you, Keel. Your dream's come true."

The other boy nodded deeply. "Thank you. Thank you, everyone."

"Don't forget to ask later which half of the territory you're getting," Allen reminded him.

Hearing this, the king added, "House Carnel has managed the White Dragon Mountains for us through the centuries. As such, I think it would be only right to give you the half with the mountains. Rest assured, the capital of the realm is also included in that area."

Ah, he's probably thinking, "The white dragon's there, but do your best regardless." Oh boy, he has no idea. A certain thought occurred to him, and an evil smirk came over his face.

"Keel, you're gonna have a ton of trouble managing things with the white dragon there," Allen said, "but don't forget to thank His Majesty for his benevolence."

"Your Majesty, I thank you from the bottom of my heart." Keel bowed deeply toward the king, signaling the end of the audience for real this time.

Chapter 3: Homecoming

The Kingdom of Ratash held multiple galas and other social events in celebration of the formal establishment of diplomatic relations with Rohzenheim.

Originally, Allen had no intention of participating, considering how he had just pressed King Invel to fulfill the promise from the previous king. Moreover, he had no interest in such functions in the first place. However, many nobles, including Viscount Granvelle and Count Hamilton, felt indebted to him due to his contributions to the Giamutan war effort and strongly urged him to at least make an appearance so they could properly thank him. In the end, Allen folded and agreed to attend one ball.

He showed up with his party, each of them wearing aptly named "Gorgeous Outfit" equipment they had obtained from Rank A dungeons. Indeed, every so often, inside the treasure chests were not weapons or adventuring tools but fine clothing and other accessories that, while valuable monetarily, possessed negligible durability. At first, the No-life Gamers had considered selling these off, but ultimately decided to keep them in case they might come in handy. The Gamers had also worn these for their audience with the king where Keel got his title back.

After the audience, Keel's name in Allen's grimoire had changed to "Keel von Carnel," confirming that he had indeed regained his status. Depending on his future achievements in service to Ratash, he just might be able to climb higher up the social ladder and restore his family's domain to its original size.

Field Marshal Lukdraal and Elder Filamehl had decided to stay in the Ratashian capital for the time being. There were plans to set up something similar to a consulate in the Nobles Quarter—in Allen's eyes, Ratash was making quite the effort to hurry this process along, as it wanted very badly to be able to show off to the world its newly forged bonds with Rohzenheim—but until it was finished, they were staying in their assigned guest rooms at the royal palace. This was to be the base of operations from which they would be laying the groundwork with various nobles. To start, Allen was asked to get them in contact with Viscount Granvelle and Count Hamilton.

With everything that they had to do in the capital now finished, the No-life Gamers took a magic ship from the royal capital to the city of Granvelle and stayed at the viscount's mansion for the night.

Cecil teared up a little upon reuniting with her mother after not seeing each other for several years. Her father had visited every once in a while while she was at the Academy, and her brother, Thomas, had not been all that far away, as he had gotten a job at the palace. Consequently, she had been missing her mother quite a lot.

* * *

The next day, the No-life Gamers mounted Bird Bs and headed for Rodin Village, the frontier hamlet where Rodin served as its chief.

"It's come into view," Dogora announced to the group.

"It's quite big for only starting development last year," Cecil noted.

"It's still not enough, though," Allen replied. "We're gonna make it even bigger."

The village that spread out below had only been founded a year or so ago. However, it had built up at an incredible rate thanks to Allen's

Summons. For example, Allen's Beast C Summons, giant boars with over 1,500 Attack, had pulled out the stumps of trees the villagers had chopped down, so the village was already farming even though it was only in its second year. As it was now April, everyone was spread out along the tilled rows of soil, hard at work planting seeds.

In the middle of the sprawling fields lay the village proper, which was four times the size of Krena Village and entirely enclosed by a wall and a moat. The villagers had erected the walls themselves, but the moat was the work of the Summons. Built as a defense against monster invasions, it had been dug both deep and wide.

Just like Krena Village, the residences were clustered close to the village entrance. Even though this settlement had started with only a hundred people, it had developed so quickly and grown so much that they had begun accepting even more newcomers that spring. The sound of hammering filled the air as new houses went up all throughout the village.

There was one building that stood taller than the rest in the center of the residential area. This was the village chief's house—in other words, Allen's family's. It was many, many times the size of the one he had lived in back in Krena Village. This one could easily accommodate three whole generations under one roof. It even had space for things like holding meetings related to village management.

The Bird Bs all landed in front of the village chief's house. Unlike the locals who had gotten used to seeing the Summons over the past year, the recently arrived villagers were so surprised their legs almost gave out beneath them.

"Hm, looks like we've made quite the commotion," Allen commented.

Cecil gave him a look. "I *told* you so."

"Well, they're just gonna have to get used to it, 'cuz we're gonna be coming home on these Summons every once in a while from now on. I already told father about this a while ago."

Speak of the devil, Rodin burst out of his front door, growling, "What's all the rucku— Whoa, is that you, Allen?!"

Allen turned around from bringing down his luggage from his mount. "Hi, father. I'm home."

The last time he had seen his father in person was when he became House Granvelle's guest after being a manservant in its service. Just as Cecil had, Allen, too, felt a little emotional after the long absence.

"And is that Krena and Dogora I see there? Whoa, you brought a whole slew of folks with you."

All of the No-life Gamers had come along on this homecoming trip. While Sophie's insistence on meeting his parents had definitely been a reason, more importantly, Allen wanted to bring everyone here to help Keel now that his house was restored and part of the White Dragon Mountains was back under their management.

Watching Rodin ruffle Allen's hair, Volmaar murmured to himself, "What an unusual sight. I can hardly believe it: Lord Allen actually has a father."

Allen raised an eyebrow. "What do you mean by that?"

"Exactly what I said." Volmaar shrugged.

After all the ways that Allen had defied this world's common sense and pulled off incredible feats thought impossible by everyone else, seeing this human side of him now was rather surreal.

All the houses in the village were built on stilts. Rodin beckoned the group into the house and led them up the stairs. Dogora followed him with a bulky sack of meats and vegetables slung over his shoulder as Krena carried a huge cask of fruit wine.

Soon, footsteps could be heard approaching quickly. Two figures burst into view from around the corner and cried out in unison, "Allen!" Allen managed to set down what he was carrying just in time as his younger siblings tackled him with bear hugs.

"Mash! Myulla! You two sure have gotten big!" he gushed while ruffling their hair affectionately.

Mash grunted in response as Myulla said cheerily, "Mm-hm! We're real big now!"

The three of them were horsing around in one delighted clump when their mother, Theresia, came out. "My, oh my! Look who's home all of a sudden. And bringing so many guests too!"

There was no way for Allen to give his parents advance notice of their visit as he no longer had any Summons stationed at this village. He had needed every last card slot when dealing with the Demon Lord Army and its reserves, so he had reverted all the Summons posted here to card form at the time.

"What should we do, honey?" Theresia asked Rodin with a worried look, cupping her cheek in her hand. "We don't have nearly enough food to feed so many people."

Allen gestured to everything his companions were carrying. "Don't worry, mother. We brought plenty with us from the capital."

"Really? You sure are well prepa—" Rodin's eyes widened. "You brought *wine!*" It seemed he cared more about the cask than the food.

"Have Mister Gerda and Miss Mathilda and Dogora's parents moved in yet?" Allen asked. "How about we have them over too?" *Dogora's parents were going to open a blacksmithery here in Rodin Village, right?*

"You bet!" Rodin gave Allen a broad grin and a big thumbs-up.

"Huh?" Dogora pursed his lips while turning his head away. "Nah, we don't need my old man here."

Huh? When we fought the Demonic Deity, you asked me to take care of your old man and everything, though. C'mon, don't be shy.

Rodin barked, "All of you, leave your stuff behind that door. Yeesh, Dogora, you've *really* gotten huge. Don't go tramping around with all that on; you're gonna put a hole in the floor."

The No-life Gamers obediently set everything down in an unused room. This included Dogora's axe and shield, which were so heavy that the flooring had been creaking with every step he took.

Dinner began before long. With the arrival of Krena's and Dogora's families, this had become a rather sizable gathering, but the dining room was more than large enough. There was plenty of room to sit everyone around the dining table. The sight of Rodin giving the opening toast struck home for Allen that, since becoming the village chief, his father had likely had many chances to give speeches in front of groups like this.

Myulla was a lot more curious about the flying squirrel wandering on the tabletop than her father's speech. As soon as everyone began eating, she tried speaking to the creature nibbling at a piece of bread that he was clutching with both hands.

"What's your name?"

"I'm Rohzen. Ha ha."

"Ohhh, it spoke! Allen, is this one of yours too?" In her mind, all creatures that could speak were naturally tied to her brother. Before anyone could stop her, she casually reached out and picked up the God of Spirits, placing him in her lap and stroking his head.

"*Pffffft!*" The sight made Volmaar spit out his food.

"Nope, that one's not mine. He belongs to Sophie over there." Allen indicated toward Sophie.

Cecil's hand stopped in midair as she corrected Allen. "Uh, he doesn't *belong* to anyone."

"Hold on, you're..." Rodin stopped eating as he tried to place Cecil's pale purple hair and willful, slanted red eyes in his mind.

Allen had yet to introduce his companions. Right up until dinner began, Allen's group had been hanging out with Mash, Myulla, and Lily—Krena's younger sister—in the large room where they would be staying that night. Once Krena's and Dogora's parents arrived, the place quickly filled with the commotion of their reunion—with Dogora looking somewhat abashed—which ultimately meant there had been no opportunity for introductions until this moment.

Allen looked up. "Oh right, I gotta introduce everyone. Father, that's Cecil."

Rodin squinted at the girl, still having trouble remembering. "...Have I met her before?"

Cecil inclined her head in greeting without standing up. "Yes, sir. We met when I visited Krena Village."

Clearly misunderstanding something, Theresia said teasingly, "My, what a cute girl you've brought home, Allen. Just what is your relationship with her?"

"She might not act like it," Allen replied matter-of-factly, "but she's Lord Granvelle's daughter."

"And what do you mean by *that*?"

Cecil's hand shot out and grabbed Allen's face in an iron clawhold. Allen yelped in pain as the adults stared with wide eyes.

Rodin exclaimed, "Why is Lord Granvelle's daughter here?!"

In order to avoid worrying his parents, Allen had not told them all that much about his circumstances ever since he left home. Obviously, he could not tell them he was mopping up goblin and orc villages single-handedly when he was with House Granvelle, but even after he enrolled in the Academy, he never mentioned that he was frequenting the dungeons. All he said was that he, Krena, and Dogora had rented a house and were living together. He had not even told them about the other residents.

Cecil glared at Allen as if telling him to introduce everyone properly.

"Ahem." Allen cleared his throat. "Cecil took great care of me when I was a manservant at the Granvelle mansion. We then started attending the Academy together. She's also been living with Krena and Dogora and me."

"You were able to become so close with such an esteemed noble by going to school together?" Rodin recalled how casually Allen had been speaking with Cecil this whole time. He himself had been born a serf and was not very knowledgeable about what was considered normal in the big city, but considering that his son had managed to climb the social ladder from manservant to guest, he figured that maybe it was the amount of time they spent together that allowed Allen to address a noble so casually.

"Wait, so are all your companions here also your housemates?" he asked.

"Yep. These are all my close friends. There's one more, but she's in a really far away place right now. Um, let me introduce everyone aside from Krena and Dogora."

"Please."

"All right. The guy over there with the spiky hair is Keel. He just became the lord of the domain next to ours not long ago. He's a baron."

Keel made an annoyed face. "You're not wrong, but that's a really half-assed introduction, man."

"*Pfft!*" Gerda spat out a mouthful of wine. "A *baron?!* The domain next to ours… That's Carn— OW!"

After having given her husband a good punch in the face, Mathilda said scoldingly, "That's disgusting, hon! What would you've done if you'd gotten wine all over the food?!"

The sight of her mother landing a good one on her father prompted Lily, who had the Pugilist Talent, to excitedly stand up in her seat and start throwing shadow punches.

As he thought about what a waste it was of perfectly good wine he had gone to the trouble of bringing, Allen continued making his introductions. "Next is Sophie. She's the princess of a neighboring country. And the guy next to her is Volmaar, her royal guard." Because the adults here never had the opportunity to learn any of the kingdom's history—much less Demon Lord history!—and had virtually no knowledge of world geography, Allen had decided to go with "neighboring country" instead of naming Rohzenheim.

Sophie stood up. "My name is Sophialohne. Lord Allen's esteemed father and mother, it is an enormous honor to make your acquaintance." She finished off her self-introduction with a warm smile and a deep bow.

Volmaar stood up as well but otherwise only inclined his head slightly.

"She's a princess? Is that true, Allen?" Gerda asked with disbelief.

"Mm-hm. In our second year at the Academy, she came on exchange from her home country," Allen replied before telling of how their homeroom teacher had assigned his group with taking care of Sophie and how she ended up becoming a part of their group and moving in with them.

Gerda whistled softly. "Damn, now that's just…" Suddenly, he noticed Sophie's and Volmaar's ears. Staring a bit too much for comfort, this man who had never stepped foot outside of the Granvelle region murmured, "I guess people from our neighboring country have really long ears."

Sophie smiled wryly as Volmaar huffed a little with displeasure.

"Oh, right." Allen started as something occurred to him. "Krena's become an honorary baron too."

All the parents' heads swiveled to stare at Krena. Hearing her name mentioned, she froze in the middle of taking a big bite out of a leg of meat and looked up with a somewhat goofy "Huh?"

It was customary in Ratash to give children with three-star Talents such as Sword Lord, Archwizard, and Saintess the status of baron when they graduated from the Academy. However, this was only meant as an indication of their ability to serve their country and therefore was not an inheritable title. They were consequently called "honorary barons" as a way to differentiate them from hereditary barons. Of course, should they achieve feats worthy of it, their title could become hereditary; they could even continue to climb the social ladder to become a viscount, a count, and so on. Sword Lord Dverg was one such example—in recognition of his decades of service, he had been granted the status of marquess.

As Krena had not informed Ratash that she had become a Sword King, she ended up graduating from the Academy as a Sword Lord. She was therefore given her noble title when Keel's was reinstated.

Gerda asked his daughter, "Wait, this is all talk about what happens *after* you graduate?"

Krena nodded. "I already graduated. Right, Allen?"

"Yup. Since we fulfilled the graduation requirements, all of us here have," Allen confirmed before taking out Krena's diploma—he was keeping everyone's in Storage—and spreading it out for all the parents to see.

I'm not lying. I'm just not giving the full story, that's all. I can talk about becoming Rohzenheim's grand strategist some other time.

Allen intended on leaving Summons here at Rodin Village again to resume helping out with its development. With this in mind, he would be taking his time giving the more time-consuming explanations at a later date through Spirit Bs.

Rodin studied the diploma with marvel in his eyes. "You've really graduated… I'd forgotten, but I guess it's true that if you were still enrolled, you'd be in class right now and not here."

Hm? Looks like father's learned how to read a bit.

Allen turned to his younger brother. "Speaking of. Mash, you said last year that you were thinking of attending the Academy. How's your studying coming along?"

The boy nodded proudly. "Father and I are studying together, and we're doing great!"

Mash, who was three years younger than Allen, had the Spear User Talent. He was on track to enroll at the Academy in two years. To that end, Viscount Granvelle had sent a tutor to Rodin Village. This tutor *was* teaching Mash, but his primary student was Rodin, who wanted to learn how to read, write, and do basic arithmetic now that he was a village chief.

Of course, there were plenty of village chiefs who were illiterate, perhaps due to being born into serfdom and never having had the opportunity or time to receive a proper education, be it either as a child or an adult. When these chiefs needed to discuss taxes with their feudal lord, confirm the population in their village, and so on, they normally brought along a literate subordinate.

Rodin, however, was determined not to resort to this. Consequently, he had been studying diligently during the winter period after great boar hunting season wrapped up but before it was time to plant new crops in the spring.

Then again, both father and Mash have leveled up quite a bit. Their Intelligence is much higher than most people's now, so they should be able to memorize things pretty quickly.

Having higher Intelligence did not correlate with being more knowledgeable, but it did mean having better memory and comprehension. The difference between Lvl. 1 and Lvl. 20 was drastic, even for someone with Rank E in Intelligence or with no Talent. This rule applied to not only Rodin but also Mash, who had started joining the great boar hunts last year. Rodin had allowed him to come along since the danger of the hunts had gone down dramatically thanks to Allen supplying the village with mithril spears and shields.

This village was currently still in the tax-exempt period granted to all newly founded frontier villages. The lack of taxes meant that obtaining meat here was much easier than in other villages, which led to the residents having robust physiques.

Allen noticed the envious look that his little sister was giving Mash and asked her, "Do you want to go to the Academy too, Myulla?"

"Mm-hm!" The seven-year-old girl nodded enthusiastically. She apparently considered the Academy as somewhere fun to go.

Theresia gently drew Myulla into a hug and stroked her hair. "Aw, I'm sorry, honey, but only those with Talents can go to the Academy." She then glared at Allen a little as if admonishing him for getting Myulla's hopes up.

"You mean…I can't go?" Tears began welling up in her eyes.

"Well, you're in luck," Allen said as he patted his little sister's head gently. "Your big brother just so happens to know *someone* who can give you a Talent."

She looked up at him with bright eyes. "Really?"

Everyone's attention was now on Allen. Feeling his world rocked yet once again, Rodin asked, "Allen, what…? What are you saying?"

Allen ignored his father and told Myulla, "Really really. What Talent do you want? Your big brother recommends becoming a Cleric."

Is it possible to cancel a Talent later on and choose a second time? Allen shot a look at the flying squirrel on Myulla's lap, prompting him to read Allen's mind. The deity then shook his head.

Myulla brought a finger to her cheek and tilted her head. "Hmm… Why is Cleric good?"

Wow, I didn't expect her to already be smart enough to ask that kind of question. I guess girls develop faster in this world too.

Allen straightened his face and replied, "Clerics can heal people. If father or mother ever get hurt, you'll be able to heal them."

The girl's eyes lit up. "Then I'll be a Cleric!"

He pretty much induced her to do it, but Allen now had Myulla's agreement to assume the class he wanted. He told the God of Spirits, "Lord Rohzen, Myulla has said she wants to be a Cleric. Please fulfill her wish."

"Is that how you...? Well, I guess that's how it normally goes when dealing with children. Ha ha."

The God of Spirits set the piece of bread that he had been nibbling on down in Myulla's lap, then floated up into the air and began swinging his hips while looking at the girl intently. Mistakenly thinking this an indication that something fun was starting, she pulled away from Theresia's embrace and hopped up and down in an effort to catch the flying squirrel. The next moment, a drop of light landed on her and her entire body glowed brightly.

"Wh-What's going on?! What's happening?!" Rodin shouted as the rest of the parents, who were witnessing this phenomenon for the first time, also exclaimed with surprise.

When the light subsided, Rodin and Theresia rushed forward to envelop Myulla's small form in a huge hug. Then they began examining her all over. "Are you okay?! What just happened?!" they asked worriedly.

Rohzen declared, "She is now a Cleric. Ha ha."

"Thank you, Lord Rohzen." Allen lowered his head. "Please take care of her again when she maxes out her level."

"I thought you'd say that. Ha ha."

Allen's reward from Rohzen for his part in saving Rohzenheim was to give Myulla, who had been Talentless, a one-star Talent. He was now confirming that the promise to eventually promote all the No-life Gamers to four-star classes also applied to her. Rohzen had clearly read his mind, yet did not refute him.

Allen approached his family. "Father, mother, there's no need to worry. That was the ritual to give Myulla her Talent just now."

Rodin looked back at his son, his eyes wide with disbelief. He barely managed to get out, "I-It sure is a big world out there, huh?"

"Mm-hm," Allen nodded. "I've actually already talked things

through with Lord Granvelle, so Myulla will get to undergo the Appraisal Ceremony again this year."

The Appraisal Ceremony was something that all children who reached five years old, regardless of social status, had to undergo. When Myulla took it two years ago, she had been confirmed Talentless. After Allen told Viscount Granvelle about all that had happened in Rohzenheim, though, the man had agreed to arrange for Myulla to redo it.

"I-I see," Rodin replied in a bit of a daze, his brain struggling to comprehend everything.

"All right. I've introduced everyone, Myulla's got her Talent," Allen murmured under his breath. "Only one thing left to do."

Rodin, however, overheard him. "Hm? What d'you have to do?"

"Well, I already mentioned that Keel became a baron, right? We said we'd celebrate it together. And the realm that Keel's been left in charge of includes the part of the White Dragon Mountains where the white dragon is nesting right now."

"Wait, don't tell me..."

Allen gave his father a huge smile. "Yep! We're gonna go kill it tomorrow."

"Are you crazy?!" Rodin exclaimed.

"Are you serious?!" Theresia asked incredulously at the same time.

"Father, mother, don't worry. I'll be fine. That's what my friends are here for."

The sight of the No-life Gamers nodding confidently left the two adults at a loss for words. Traces of worry could be found on the otherwise expressionless face of Dogora's father.

The people in the frontier villages thought of the tyrannical white dragon of the White Dragon Mountains as a mighty existence to be greatly feared. Allen, however, only thought of it as a security measure to prevent someone else seizing the White Dragon Mountains before the land returned to Keel.

When House Carnel was dissolved, the entire domain of Carnel had been returned to the royal family. This included all the mithril mines within the White Dragon Mountains, which had been rendered inaccessible due to the presence of the white dragon and were thus considered worthless. Allen had worried that killing the dragon too soon would cause the king to delay restoring Keel's house or to return to him his domain minus the part with the mines. This was why he had left the creature alone all this time. For its part, Ratash had never sent forces to deal with the dragon either, perhaps balking from all the casualties that would arise from such an expedition.

Now, however, Keel had been properly reinstated as head of House Carnel, and the part of old Carnel that included the White Dragon Mountains had been officially declared his territory. There was no need to hold back any longer. And if the king ever said, "Oh, the white dragon's gone now, so we'll have to reconsider everything," he would have something far more terrifying than the white dragon to worry about.

With it being so long since Allen and his friends had been home, the dinner went on till late into the night. Afterward, Krena and Dogora stayed at their parents' homes while the rest of the No-life Gamers settled themselves in their spacious designated room in Rodin's house.

Chapter 4: Fighting the White Dragon

The next morning, Allen was making some Blessings of Heaven to leave with his family when Dogora came up to him.

Allen looked up from his work. "Hm? You're up early."

"'S not like I have anything to do."

"Yeah?" *Did he manage to tell his parents that he's become a knight of House Hamilton?*

While they were in the royal capital, the rewards for the No-life Gamers had been decided. Keel had his house and title restored, of course, and Krena was granted the title of honorary baron as she had graduated from the Academy. In addition, Cecil had the taxes lowered for the realm of Granvelle and Dogora was knighted in service of House Hamilton. Although he had fought alongside Krena, as Axe User was only a one-star Talent, his achievements in the Rohzenheim war proved insufficient to merit him a title of his own.

However, his reward was by no means trivial. Normally, commoners who wanted to become a knight had to graduate from the Academy then perform numerous noteworthy feats on the battlefield to build up their reputations before even being considered for the knighthood. Dogora's appointment had led to breaking quite a few regulations. Add to this the fact that the prestige of knights themselves depended on the status of the nobles they served—for example, the royal guards who served the king were considered the most eminent in the country, whereas the knights of a baron were considered the lowest in rank. Given that Dogora was now the knight of a count, it was then obvious that he had indeed been rewarded handsomely.

This particular arrangement had happened largely thanks to Viscount Granvelle; this avoided making Dogora subordinate to a fellow party member as he would have been had either House Granvelle or House Carnel taken him as their knight.

The last Ratashian member of the Gamers—Allen—had turned down any reward for himself. He asserted that Rohzenheim had already more than sufficiently rewarded him.

Which reminds me, has Dogora given his dad the hammer yet?

Back when the party was buying food ingredients and alcohol in the capital, Dogora had also picked up a blacksmithing hammer, calling it a souvenir for his family. It was clearly meant to be a present for his father, a weapons merchant who smithed his own goods.

"Oh, everyone's here already."

By the time Cecil finished getting ready and came down, she found the rest of the party gathered in the dining room. They then ate breakfast together before heading out. Krena's, Dogora's, and Allen's parents saw them off at the village gate.

"Be very, *very* careful," Rodin warned.

Allen nodded. "I will, father. And you look forward to tasting white dragon meat tonight."

Rodin fell silent. Seeing the worry on his parent's faces, Allen wondered if he ought to have just gone ahead without telling them anything.

A short distance away from the village gate, the Gamers mounted Beast Bs and made their way toward the White Dragon Mountains. As they approached, Allen double-checked his holders.

It's about time I adjust my cards, especially since everyone's back up to Lvl. 45 now.

Name: Allen
Age: 14
Class: Summoner
Level: 76
HP: 2,315
MP: 3,660
Attack: 1,284 + 2,000
Endurance: 1,284 + 4,000
Agility: 2,391 + 5,550
Intelligence: 3,670 + 1,550
Luck: 2,391

Skills: Summoning {7}, Creation {7}, Synthesis {7}, Strengthening {7}, Awakening {7}, Expansion {6}, Storage, Sharing, Quick Summoning, Deputize, Deletion, Sword Mastery {3}, Throwing {3}

Equipment
Ring 1: +1,000 Attack
Ring 2: +1,000 Attack
Adamantite Sword: +2,500 Attack
Black Dragon Cape: +3,000 Endurance, Breath Damage Resistance (Mid)

Name: Krena
Age: 14
Class: Sword King
Level: 45
HP: 2,980 + 1,200
MP: 1,269
Attack: 2,980 + 1,200
Endurance: 2,616 + 1,200
Agility: 1,924 + 1,200

Intelligence: 1,279
Luck: 1,286 + 1,200

Skills: Sword King {4}, Slash {4}, Cosmic Smash {4}, Flowing Slash {4}, Stoutness {1}, Sword Mastery {6}
Extra Skill: Limit Break

Equipment
Ring 1: +1,000 Attack
Ring 2: +1,000 Attack
Adamantite Greatsword: +3,500 Attack
Adamantite Armor: +3,000 Endurance

Name: Cecil Granvelle
Age: 14
Class: Archwizardess
Level: 45
HP: 1,614 + 900
MP: 2,628 + 900
Attack: 946
Endurance: 1,037
Agility: 1,654 + 900
Intelligence: 2,955 + 900
Luck: 1,624

Skills: Archwizardry {4}, Fire {4}, Ice {4}, Earth {4}, Sapience {1}, Sparring {3}
Extra Skill: Petit Meteor

Equipment
Ring 1: +1,000 Intelligence
Ring 2: +1,000 Intelligence
Rod of the Wise: +4,000 Intelligence, +10% Magical Damage

Robe of the Wise: +3,000 Endurance, Magical Damage Resistance (Mid)

Name: Dogora
Age: 14
Class: Berserker
Level: 45
HP: 1,805
MP: 1,062
Attack: 2,631 + 600
Endurance: 1,365 + 600
Agility: 1,110 + 600
Intelligence: 813
Luck: 1,184

Skills: Berserker {4}, Full Might {4}, Thunder Strike {4}, Caution to the Wind {4}, Resolve {1}, Axe Mastery {6}, Shield Mastery {2}
Extra Skill: Heart and Soul

Equipment
Ring 1: +1,000 Attack
Ring 2: +1,000 Agility
Adamantite Greataxe: +4,000 Attack
Adamantite Large Shield: +3,000 Endurance
Adamantite Armor: +3,000 Endurance

Name: Keel von Carnel
Age: 14
Class: Saint
Level: 45
HP: 971
MP: 1,865 + 600
Attack: 743

Endurance: 1,036
Agility: 1,185
Intelligence: 1629 + 600
Luck: 1,491 + 600

Skills: Saint {4}, Healing {4}, Poison Coat {1}, Breath Coat {1}, Belief {1}, Sword Mastery {3}
Extra Skill: Drops of God

Equipment
Ring 1: +1,000 HP
Ring 2: +1,000 Intelligence
Rod of the Saint: +1,000 MP, +1,000 Intelligence, +10% Healing
Vestment of the Saint: +2,000 Endurance, Breath Damage Resistance (Mid), Poison Resistance (Mid)

Name: Sophialohne
Age: 48
Blessing: God of Spirits
Class: Spirit Wizardess
Level: 45
HP: 1,154 + 600
MP: 2,043 + 600
Attack: 827
Endurance: 813
Agility: 1,170
Intelligence: 2,212 + 600
Luck: 992

Skills: Grand Spirit {4}, Fire {4}, Water {4}, Wind {4}, Aura {1}
Extra Skill: Grand Spirit Manifestation

Equipment
Ring 1: +1,000 MP

Ring 2: +1,000 Endurance
Rod of the Spirit of Words: +4,000 MP
Raiment of Spirits: +2,000 MP, +3,000 Endurance, Breath Damage Resistance (Mid)

Name: Volmaar
Age: 68
Class: Bow Master
Level: 45
HP: 1,633 + 600
MP: 889
Attack: 1,415 + 600
Endurance: 1,406
Agility: 907 + 600
Intelligence: 599
Luck: 969

Skills: Bow Master {4}, Keen Sight {4}, Drizzle Shot {4}, Aim {4}, Core {1}, Bow Mastery {6}
Extra Skill: Arrow of Light

Equipment
Ring 1: +1,000 MP
Ring 2: +1,000 Attack
Adamantite Greatbow: +3,800 Attack
Garment of the Protector: +3,000 Endurance, +1,000 Agility

While Allen had not been able to promote his class like his companions, the rate at which his stats increased had doubled ever since he reached Lvl. 61. He was currently focusing on raising his class skills to Lvl. 8, as he had a large stock of Rank B magic stones and could therefore freely redistribute his Summons without worrying about rationing his stones. A certain number of card slots were currently occupied by Dragon Bs and Insect As still in Rohzenheim helping mop up the Demon Lord Army's last dregs.

The moment Allen had arrived in Rodin Village, he had sent out several Spirit Bs to wipe out all of the goblin and orc villages in the area, ordering them to prioritize saving any hostages they discovered. To that end, he had made all of the Ellies take a few Blessings of Heaven with them.

The Summons were still going around at that very moment, tirelessly searching out and eliminating targets. Back when Allen had been a manservant for House Granvelle, he had almost completely rid the realm of goblins and orcs. However, new settlements had sprung up again during his time at the Academy. There was no good reason to keep them around and plenty of reasons to get rid of them, including the threat they posed to the villagers and the fact that they ate the great boars the villagers hunted.

Looks like the Spirit Bs still need a bit more time, even though they've gone through quite a lot already. Oh hey, maybe after we finish killing the white dragon, I can have them do some pest control for all of Carnel too.

The thoughts continued whirling furiously in Allen's mind as he and his companions approached the peaks of the White Dragon Mountains. They soon flew over and headed straight for the white dragon's nest, which Allen had already located ahead of time using Bird E's Farsight. Even now, the Summon was hovering hundreds of meters up in the sky, its eyes trained on the dragon.

Allen, who was Sharing with the Bird E, studied the creature, noting its ruby-red eyes, which stood out starkly against pure white scales, and its powerful, muscular body. He wondered whether it could actually fly with how big and heavy it looked.

We've fought dragons before, both in dungeons and the war, but this one's about twice the size of any we've seen so far. Is this normal for wild dragons? Like how wild-caught fish are different from farm-raised? The monsters we faced in Rohzenheim were all roughly the same size as others of their kind. Do monsters created by dungeon masters come in standard sizes? Or do all white dragons grow this large? Or is this one an outlier who got to be this big from living for so long in these mountains?

Allen's mind was running at full speed as he and his party drew closer to the beast.

It isn't running away, hiding, or attacking us. Interesting.

The Bird Bs they were riding flew directly above as if to pass over the white dragon, then circled around as they got closer, landing so that the dragon was sandwiched between the No-life Gamers and the mountain. They did this to ensure that no stray attacks would fly toward the capital or other settlements in Carnel once the fighting began.

When the group was close enough to see the dragon's face with their own eyes, it opened its mouth and said in a low, rumbling voice, "It appears I have some bizarre guests. Who are you?" It apparently found the elephant-sized flying mounts and their riders a mystifying sight.

"It's talking to us," Cecil told Allen, whom she was riding with.

Before Allen could answer, the beast cut in. "Is it so strange for a dragon to speak?"

So it's got incredibly keen eyes and ears. Probably safe to assume that the rest of its senses are just as sharp.

"How about you try introducing yourself?" Allen suggested jokingly.

"Who, me?" Cecil pointed at herself.

"You're the daughter of House Granvelle, after all. Or I guess Keel could do it too."

After discussing with Keel who would be going first, Cecil announced in a loud voice, "I am Cecil Granvelle. We have come to slay you, dragon!"

"And I'm Keel von Carnel," Keel added. "I won't allow you to continue making a mess of my realm."

"So, Granvelle and Carnel have joined forces to kill me! I've been waiting!" Upon hearing Cecil's and Keel's names, the white dragon let out a roar that shook the mountains. It then began charging toward the No-life Gamers with a thunderous gait. At the same time, it began to flap the wings on its back that seemed far too small for its size.

So, it's capable of speech, but the pacifist route isn't an option. Is it overreacting to the word "slay"? Aww, and I wanted to introduce myself too.

Swallowing his disappointment, Allen turned to his party and shouted, "Maintain a safe distance and watch out for any Breath Attacks! Especially those of you in the rear!"

"I've been waiting! I've been waiting for sooo looong!" the dragon growled softly with a toothy grin, rolling the words around in its mouth with a deafening note of yearning as it continued barreling toward the group. The tremors shook the ground and sent flocks of birds bursting from the canopy of the expansive forest that lay at the foot of the mountain. Other monsters made a mad dash for the plains beyond.

Noticing how the dragon was flapping its wings faster and faster, Allen shouted, "Krena! Dogora! It's trying to fly. Stop it!"

"Okay!" Krena replied.

Dogora nodded. "We've got it!"

If the white dragon managed to take to the air, it could begin attacking the Beast Bs and their riders. The vanguard rushed in to prevent that from happening.

It looks like Dogora still isn't very used to using his shield, but he's managing thanks to his Griff.

It was taking the boy all he had to handle both his greataxe and shield, the latter of which was still messing with his balance due to his unfamiliarity with it. He was doing admirably anyway, as his Bird B was doing its best to position itself to make it easier for Dogora to attack and defend. The griffin was capable of flying at its usual speed in spite of its increased load and was intelligent enough to doggedly stay in the dragon's blind spot, making the beast run circles around itself.

"Hmph! Impudent!"

Just as the white dragon started puffing out its chest, the base of its throat swelled up with a bulge that quickly climbed up its neck. Flames then began spilling from gaps between its sharp fangs.

"Cecil, Ice Magic!"

"On it!"

Cecil called forth a shard of ice that ballooned to the size of a Bird B. When she received her class promotion, the four magical elements she was able to wield had been randomly selected again; now she could cast Ice Magic when she could not before.

Man, this promotion just keeps giving and giving.

As a mage raised their level and skill level, they would eventually gain four elemental magical skills. This included those who use spirit magic like Sophie. Back when Cecil and Sophie had been reverted to Lvl. 1, the elements that they started with had been the same as the ones they had before; it was only after they leveled up that it became clear that undergoing a class promotion meant getting to redraw all four elements. There was no way to determine if everything was truly random, but it was clear that gaining access to new elements meant having greater variety in battle strategies.

When Cecil thrust her hands out, the hovering hunk of ice shot toward the white dragon's face. However, the beast unleashed its Breath Attack with a jerk of its chin, blasting its flames at the icicle and evaporating it in the blink of an eye.

I guess at Lvl. 45, her spells are still too weak to stop the white dragon's Breath Attack.

All of the No-life Gamers now possessed Talents one star higher than before. They had started over again from Lvl. 1, having inherited half the previously maxed-out stats of their former classes. Now that they were Lvl. 45 with their new classes, they were actually quite a bit more powerful than they had been before the promotion. As it turned out, though, this was still insufficient to completely negate a Breath Attack—at her current strength, Cecil could only delay it for a second. The next moment, the dragon swung its head, redirecting its attack toward Krena and Dogora.

"Dodge!" Allen barked, prompting the Bird Bs that the other two were riding to abruptly evade.

It was not long before the Breath Attack fizzled out, but the white dragon was already gearing up to unleash another one.

"Volmaar, aim Arrow of Light at its mouth!"

"Understood!"

Immediately following Allen's order, the elf started activating his Extra Skill. If the dragon's Breath Attack was powerful enough to instantaneously vaporize a massive block of ice, what it was capable of doing to

Sophie was too much to bear thinking about. Even had Allen not ordered him to, Volmaar fully intended to use Arrow of Light then and there.

The dragon pulled back its head and arched its neck as the bulge rose to its throat. The instant it opened its mouth, Volmaar's brilliant, shining arrow flew straight in.

"*Gwuah?!*"

The impact of the arrow jerked the dragon's head and made the beast stumble backward a few steps. The Breath Attack died in its throat, with a few rogue wisps of flame leaking from its lips. Taking full advantage of this opening, Krena and Dogora urged their Bird Bs up close and brought their weapons down on their target's pristine white scales. Sparks flew in accompaniment with loud metallic clangs, but the dragon remained unhurt, only losing a few scales.

The monster then spun around by using its backward momentum to swing its powerful tail at great speed. Dogora, who happened to be in the path of its tail sweep, quickly brought up his shield and braced with both hands. He grunted loudly as he and his Bird B both were blown back all the way to Allen's position.

So the white dragon's about as strong as Glaster the archdemon. That puts it near the very top of Rank A. Hmmm, how can we kill it without damaging its body too much?

If the goal was merely to slay the dragon, Allen had plenty of options at his disposal. For example, he had millions of Rank B magic stones at his disposal, so he could simply unleash waves upon waves of powerful Summons. Another option would be to have Cecil use Petit Meteor and just squash the beast. However, there was a reason Allen did not want to resort to such means.

If this is all we can do even with my Summons' buffs, though, then we're getting nowhere.

"Lord Allen, do you want me to call on Lord Rohzen's power?" Sophie asked from behind. Her Extra Skill, Grand Spirit Manifestation, enabled her to call on the God of Spirits to buff the entire party with a thirty percent increase to all their stats. She was suggesting using this to increase Krena's and Dogora's damage output.

Even now, the God of Spirits sat perched on Sophie's shoulder. Except when called on through her skill, Rohzen never participated in the party's fights.

Allen shook his head. "There's no need. Please work on pinning the white dragon down. Judging by its Endurance, Krena's and Dogora's Extra Skills should be able to take care of it."

"Understood, I will stop the white dragon from moving. O grand spirit, please answer my call."

Per Allen's request, Sophie activated a different skill. The next moment, a giant boulder erupted in a fountain of earth and stone from the slope the white dragon had been trampling on. The boulder revealed itself to be a head that was quickly followed by shoulders, a pair of arms, then a torso.

"I am the grand spirit Gnome. Child of elves, in exchange for your MP, I shall now grant you my aid." The massive stone figure reached out with both hands, grabbed the white dragon by its torso, then wrapped itself around the creature's entire body.

"What in the—?! What is this?!" The white dragon wriggled and squirmed in a desperate attempt to free itself from the rock golem's clutches, but to no avail.

"Dora, Mirror, come on out!"

A Dragon B and a Stone B appeared—the former with an enthusiastic "Yes, Master!" and the latter in its usual silence—on either side of the dragon, helping to restrain it.

"What on…?! Why is a dragon siding with the humans?!" the white dragon cried indignantly.

Heh heh, it looks surprised.

When Deputized, Dragon B was just as big as the white dragon. The latter froze for a moment as its mind struggled to comprehend why what it believed to be a member of its kin was assisting the enemy.

I guess being too intelligent can be a problem too. The white dragon's mind is prioritizing trying to understand the situation.

"Dogora, now! Chop off the head with Heart and Soul!"

Dogora's Bird B dashed toward the white dragon. Dogora let go of his shield and grabbed his greataxe with both hands, focusing on it with all his heart and soul.

"RAAAAAAHHHHHH!" Dogora raised a fierce battle cry as he brought his weapon down on the white dragon's neck.

CLAAAAAAANG!

The blade crushed a few scales but failed to cut any deeper. Dogora made a chagrined grimace.

Hm, didn't work. He hasn't gotten that skill to work ever since the fight with Demonic Deity Rehzel.

Dogora had attempted to use Heart and Soul many times when the party was in the dungeons, but not once had he pulled it off. Suspecting that fighting a powerful opponent was key in activating the skill, Allen had asked him to try it against the white dragon, but the result was plain for all to see.

The great beast whipped its head around, its mouth open wide, ready to crush Dogora and his Bird B in one bite.

"Dogora, fall back! Krena, use your Extra Skill!"

"Okay!"

Like always, a heat haze sprang up around Krena's body as she activated Limit Break. The white dragon quickly turned around to target her, but her mount gracefully dodged the terrifying snap of its jaws. The next moment, Krena leaped from her Griff into the air. She then began her descent, free-falling as her sword crackled with even more energy—she was activating another skill. She swung down on the dragon's neck with every shred of strength she possessed.

"*GUH!*"

This time, it was blood, not a Breath Attack, that burst from the white dragon's mouth. Its head and its massive body crashed to the ground—separately—raising a thunderous rumble.

Allen approached the head with his Bird B.

"So this…is how it feels to lose."

"Hm? I suppose so. It's our victory."

"Are you perhaps the human from the foot of the mountains who was always contemplating killing me?"

"What? Uh, maybe? I have always thought of taking you down ever since I was living in a village on the other side, yes." *It knows about me? Or maybe it's sensitive enough to notice anyone who's fixated on or hostile toward it? Those are some impressive detection abilities.*

"I see… I've been waiting for you all this time. It appears I am finally freed of my boredom. O Dragon God, now the restrictions that were binding me…"

The white dragon smiled faintly as its words died in its throat. Soon, the glow of life faded from its red eyes.

<You have defeated 1 white dragon. You have earned 28,000,000 XP.>

Oh, the amount of XP's the same as for an archdemon. Nice, that got everyone to Lvl. 52!

The No-life Gamers earned a massive amount of experience from killing the white dragon.

Chapter 5: Triumphant Return

"We...did it," Cecil murmured.

It seemed like the white dragon was saying something pretty meaningful at the end, but I couldn't hear it properly. Oh well.

"So we did," Allen replied. "Well, time to actually get to work. Everyone, lend a hand, would you please?"

"It's liquid gold, that's what this is," Keel commented, greedily eyeing the white dragon's corpse as Allen passed out large leather sacks that he had purchased back in the capital.

Apparently dragon blood is used in medicines. Welp, since we went to the trouble of killing the white dragon as cleanly as we did, let's make use of everything we can.

Cecil's Petit Meteor, Dragon B's Hellfire of Fury, and Stone B's Reflect and Total Reflect were all very effective in killing monsters, but Allen had opted against these attacks as they would have ended up badly mangling the corpse. The party had struggled a bit more than usual, but it had all been worth it.

Everyone, now with leather bags in hand, rushed over to where blood was gushing out from the white dragon's severed neck and tried to catch every last falling drop. When someone's bag was full, they turned around to empty it into the Storage page of Allen's grimoire. Quite a lot of blood ended up on the ground, but because everyone moved quickly, the total quantity they secured was still quite impressive.

"And now we're bringing this back to town, right? How?" Cecil asked, indicating the massive carcass.

The white dragon's body was about the same size as General Dora's, but the latter weighed significantly less.

"I've got an idea. Doras, come out."

Four Dragon Bs appeared. After being turned into Soldiers by General Dora, they each grabbed one of the headless body's limbs and slowly but surely took to the sky.

As I'd thought, the Summons and monsters are able to fly based on something other than the laws of physics.

Based on his memories from his previous life, Allen was convinced that his Soldier Dragon Bs' wings—despite being fifty percent bigger than normal—were still nowhere near enough to lift the white dragon's corpse, which ought to weigh several dozen tons. In the same way, Bird B had no trouble carrying Dogora even when he was wearing a full set of armor and holding both a greataxe and a large shield. The only logical conclusion was that there was something else at play here.

"That's wild," Keel marveled, looking up. "Kudos to them for lifting something so gigantic."

"There's no time to be impressed. Put this on." Allen retrieved a Gorgeous Outfit (♁) from Storage and handed it over.

"Huh? Why? What's this for?"

"We're gonna head to Carnel City right now and introduce you as the new lord of the realm."

Brooking no further protest, Allen forced Keel to put on the dress clothes. The newly appointed baron only managed a weak "Seriously?" before the rest of his companions joined in to help him get changed, making any resistance impossible.

"You guys are totally enjoying this, aren't you?" Keel grumbled.

"Of course not," Allen replied dismissively. "There now, Baron Carnel. Your outfit suits you wonderfully. All right, off we go to Carnel City!"

Keel found himself wondering if anyone had ever gotten such an insincere compliment before.

* * *

A few hours later, the No-life Gamers approached Carnel City on their Bird Bs, followed by four Soldier Doras carrying the white dragon's body and General Dora with its head. They had made relatively good time, considering the heavy burden they were carrying.

"Allen, what are you going to do about all those knights and soldiers down there?"

It was just as Cecil pointed out: knights and armed soldiers had begun manning the city walls as many citizens below pointed up at the sky and scurried about in a panic.

"I mean, this was bound to cause a bit of a stir. Especially since the white dragon looks basically unharmed."

Perhaps it was difficult to see that the white dragon was headless from the ground. Perhaps because of all the Dragon Bs that were carrying the white dragon's corpse, it appeared that a thunder of dragons was attacking Carnel City. Whatever the reason, the city was in a huge uproar.

"I did inform Count Hamilton that we would be slaying the white dragon today. We should be fine," Allen reassured her.

After their audience with the king, Allen had introduced Count Hamilton and Viscount Granvelle to Field Marshal Lukdraal and Elder Filamehl. Among all the topics that they had discussed that day, Allen was asked what he and his party planned on doing next. It was then he shared that they were going to kill the white dragon and had sought advice on what to do with the body. Count Hamilton had promised he would handle everything.

Sure enough, Count Hamilton could now be seen at the head of the cavalry procession streaming out from the city gates.

"Oh, he's coming out to meet us in person," Cecil noted.

"As expected of a general," Allen replied, ordering all the Bird Bs to land.

The count looked up at the group with an expression of pure awe. "So...that's the white dragon. You've actually killed it."

"Yes, sir. We did our best not to damage its body too much. It should fetch a pretty hefty sum for the realm's operating funds, right?"

"Th-That it would."

The same time Allen had been working on a way to get Keel's title back, he had also been brainstorming ways to relieve Keel's realm from its dire financial straits. Several years ago, the white dragon had moved to the Carnel side of the White Dragon Mountains, therefore making it impossible for the realm to continue its mithril mining operation. Carnel, which had enjoyed a stable, prosperous economy for the past century, slid into destitution in no time at all. No one starved to death, as the output of the farms that produced food remained the same, but the sudden loss of mithril to sell meant Carnel could no longer trade with other realms, and this led to the citizens' quality of life plummeting. Additionally, the former mithril miners had been left without jobs. The public order worsened visibly year by year.

Therefore, the best solution for this realm that had just been returned to Carnel control was clearly to kill the problematic white dragon and resume mithril mining operations. And so the No-life Gamers had done just that.

Unfortunately, Allen had confirmed through Bird Es that the white dragon had destroyed several of the mithril mines to the point that they would need extensive restoration or completely new entrances. Both would take money, and here again killing the white dragon would be an effective solution, as its carcass could be sold off for cash. They would definitely be killing two birds with one stone, so to speak.

"The citizens all look surprised. Did we arrive too early?" Allen asked.

Count Hamilton waved Allen's worries away. "We've already announced to the people that their new lord would be coming today. There's no problem. Let's bring all of you in."

* * *

A short while later, soldiers hurried out of the gates with a large cart for loading the white dragon's head onto. The main body would be left outside the city walls and butchered there, but the head was to be displayed for the citizenry so that they could see for themselves that the white dragon had been slain.

The No-life Gamers were given horses and told to ride into the city alongside the dragon head. The count said that they were to be heralded as heroes who freed both Granvelle and Carnel from the centuries-old threat that had constantly loomed over their heads.

Allen had tried to deflect any commendation for himself, saying, "Keel should receive all the credit," but the count had gripped his shoulder with fingers like iron claws and with a smile, forced the black-haired boy onto a horse.

On Allen's orders, the four Dragon Bs slowly let the dragon corpse they were carrying down onto the ground as General Dora placed the head on the cart. The count had arranged for a sizable cart, but the dragon head still protruded over the sides.

Allen continued giving orders. "All right, Keel, you ride next to Count Hamilton. And Dogora, you'll be right behind them."

"Huh? Why'm I at the head of the party?" Dogora protested. "*You're* the leader, Allen."

"And *you're* a knight of House Hamilton. You're not riding at the head of our party, you're riding behind the count you serve. That's your job as a knight, right?"

"Oh, I see."

Krena watched the exchange between Allen and Dogora brimming with envy. "*Oooh!* You're so lucky, Dogora!"

"Oh, right." Allen turned to the count. "Count Hamilton, would it be all right if we took some of the dragon meat that's being butchered right now? We want to bring some home to our families. In my case, I also want to bring some to some people at the Granvelle house who looked after me."

"Hm? Oh, of course. Is that really all you want?"

"Yes, sir. Please use the rest to develop the realm."

"I see. Just as Viscount Granvelle said, you really aren't an ambitious man." The man pulled a bit of a troubled face.

This expedition to kill the white dragon was not just any old side quest to eliminate a monster threat. This was *the* white dragon who, after making its nest among the mithril mines, had brought operations previously yielding massive wealth to a grinding halt. And yet, the ones who had successfully slain it were asking not for status, fame, or money—just a mere portion of meat. This was frankly terrifying for the count insomuch as it ran completely counter to how he believed people ticked.

With everyone situated, they started out, and soon the procession passed through the city gates and entered Carnel City.

"Hey Cecil, we're back. They just let us waltz in here."

"What, are you *trying* to make me remember that traumatic incident?"

Back when Cecil was a little girl, she had been kidnapped by a hit man hired by the then-Viscount Carnel—Keel's father. She now glared at Allen, recalling how he had been holding her when he leaped out of a flying magic ship nearly a hundred meters up.

The main avenue leading to the city center was packed with residents. They pushed and jostled each other, all craning their necks to get a glimpse of those who had slain the white dragon. The crowd numbers were so great, soldiers had to form barriers to clear an open path for the procession.

The air was filled with excited chatter from the citizens.

"Is that person our new lord?"

"Hmph. He's still just a child."

"You dare say that again in a louder voice? Look at that dragon head behind them. Our new lord is our champion."

Hmm, I don't hear that many comments speaking badly of Keel's father. I guess his rule must not have been all that harsh. Regardless of what he did, it doesn't look like the people hate him much.

And now, Keel, their new lord, had shown up wearing splendid clothing as one of the champions who had taken down the white dragon. Allen spotted some in the crowd with tears streaming down their faces as the dragon head passed by before them. When the dragon came to this realm, it had destroyed many mines and caused a large number of casualties. Those reminded of their losses were now tasting sweet revenge as well as gratitude toward those who had brought them vengeance.

Allen's group finally parted from the dragon head when they reached the center of the city. Apparently the head was going to remain on display there for quite some time, under surveillance by a knight guard, to serve as a spectacle for the citizens.

Soon, the procession came up on the Carnel mansion, which turned out to be even larger than the Granvelle one. The group dismounted and walked inside to find a large number of people waiting to welcome Keel with applause. Some of them were wearing outfits that Allen recognized from the royal palace.

Oh, those are palace officials.

It had only been a few days since Keel was reinstated as lord of Carnel. After Viscount Carnel was arrested and tried for his crimes, the realm had been confiscated by the royal family. Consequently, the palace had installed officials to take over realm management. They were still here because they had yet to hand over their duties to Keel's administration.

Suddenly, a young girl's voice cut through the noise of the crowd. "Keel! I'm so glad you're safe!"

Keel's head whirled around. "Nina!"

People parted to make way for a ten-year-old girl who was slowly approaching Keel with her face scrunched up half in laughter and half in tears. Keel walked forward just as slowly and spread his arms wide, enveloping the girl in a bear hug when she finally reached him.

The way they went to each other seems so well-mannered. What a stark difference from Mash and Myulla with me, ha ha.

Allen could not help but compare what he was seeing with how he had reunited with his own younger siblings the other day, which made him think of the differences in the two families' upbringing.

"What a wonderful day it is, Baron Carnel."

"Huh? Uh, yes, I suppose it is."

Keel looked up to see who had addressed him and found one of the officials in the room approaching while rubbing his hands.

"Please accept my heartfelt congratulations for your recent conferment. I am a royal envoy—"

"This is hardly the setting for such talk, is it?" Count Hamilton coolly stepped between the official and the pair of siblings.

"O-Of course, Count Hamilton. My apologies."

So, Count Hamilton has no qualms standing up to a royal envoy. That's upper nobility for you.

Due to his title, not only was Count Hamilton considered one of the upper nobles, but he also held significant influence within the political group known as the Alliance faction, a smaller body mainly composed of Talentless nobles within the Academy faction. All this together gave him the authority to stand up to even royal envoys here on orders from the king.

As instructed by the count, servants led the group to the mansion's conference room. Count Hamilton, the No-life Gamers, Nina, and the top servants of the house would be sitting in on the meeting between the royal envoy and Keel.

"Once again, allow me to congratulate you on being conferred the status of baron and on the successful restoration of your realm."

"The restoration has only just begun, but thank you."

Keel's goal had been to create a place for his sister and servants to call home, as they had lost a place to belong after House Carnel was dismantled. As such, he had not been all that bothered at having been given the lowest possible noble title or that he was now lord of only half of the land that his father had overseen. In fact, having only half the land suited him just right, given that he was only fourteen years old and had not received any education whatsoever in noble matters or realm management. He was aware that he still had a lot to learn.

The envoy changed the subject. "Baron Keel, I have heard that you intend on leaving a magistrate to administer the realm in your place. Is this so?"

Of course he would. Since he's gonna be traveling with us.

"Yes, I will," Keel replied.

There was no rule that Ratashian nobles must always be present in their realm. While they were away, they could appoint a magistrate, someone who would manage the domain in their place. Count Hamilton already knew that Keel would be relying on this system in order to continue traveling with the No-life Gamers. Allen had originally planned on asking Viscount Granvelle to find someone for this post, but Count Hamilton, with his wealth of connections, had taken it upon himself to do so.

Sure enough, the count nodded and said, "I have already reached out to someone about that. He will be arriving soon."

"You have been too good to me, my lord." Keel lowered his head. "I thank you from the bottom of my heart."

Oh hey, so Keel can *speak politely too.*

"Now, the white dragon." Here, the envoy changed the subject yet again. "Bringing back its head is certainly one way to make an impression upon assuming office. I am sure His Majesty will be greatly pleased to hear the news."

"I hope so," Keel nodded.

Silence filled the room as the envoy studied Keel without saying anything.

The hell you lookin' at, huh?

"In regards to this... Would you be favorable to presenting the white dragon to the royal family?"

Yep, there it is. I knew he'd ask that.

Allen and his companions had talked it out beforehand and agreed to dedicate the entire dragon, magic stone and all, to rebuilding House Carnel, aside from a small portion of the meat that they would be eating. They had no plans to give anything to the royal family.

"Are you asking House Carnel to hand over the dragon?" Count Hamilton cut in, unable to stay silent. "What is the meaning of this?"

"Oh, no, far be it from me to so rudely ask for the entire beast. However, is it not the duty of nobles to give back to the royal family who grant them their titles and the land they manage? I would not go so far as to suggest presenting everything, but conversely, to present nothing at all is…"

"Count Hamilton."

"Yes, Allen?"

"My understanding of the concept of profit is what's left over after costs are subtracted from income. In this case, there is a need to restore the mines destroyed by the white dragon, dig new shafts, and recruit miners. Only after all these expenses are paid would the leftover be considered profit. Please correct me if I am wrong."

"You are entirely correct."

The white dragon had dealt so much damage to the realm of Carnel that even if its entire body was sold, the price still would not fully cover what it would cost to get everything back up and running. The count also agreed with this estimate.

Keel spoke up. "It is as my friend just said. My duty is to develop this land that the crown has entrusted me with and to enable my people to work for the kingdom's sake. To make that happen, I'm afraid I do not have anything tangible, such as any parts of the dragon carcass, to present to His Majesty." He added that he also planned on giving condolence money to those who lost family members to the dragon.

The royal envoy gasped at the fact that the newly instated baron had just refused a request to offer something to the royal family.

Then again, there's no need to come across as overly confrontational against the royal family either.

"However," Allen said, "in light of his recent coronation, we understand His Majesty's wish to assert his authority. Now that the white dragon is dead, it can definitely be helpful as a showcase of his dignity."

"Riiiiight." The envoy looked at the black-haired boy with narrowed eyes, suspicious of why he suddenly seemed cooperative.

"To that end, after the dragon head is left on display at the city square for the next few days, would the crown be interested in *buying* it?"

"Buying…?"

"Don't let this leave this room, but as long as we get some money, we'd be more than happy to play along and pretend to present it."

"But that's..."

"We will be looking forward to a favorable response."

Seeing the conspiratorial grin on Allen's face, the other No-life Gamers sat back and sipped at their tea, watching him get up to his usual antics.

Oh right, we have to do that too. "By the way, we'll be heading to the local Adventurer's Guild right after this."

"Hm? Do you have business there?" the count asked.

"Well, we did just complete the quest for killing the white dragon that the royal family had posted years ago, so we have to collect the bounty. It was a thousand gold, if I remember correctly."

"Wha—?!" The envoy was struck dumbfounded.

I did tell Viscount Granvelle to take down the request in his realm.

Decades before, House Granvelle had also put up a request at the Adventurer's Guild for killing the white dragon. The bounty they posted was a thousand gold, which was a massive sum for the family considering their financial situation, but they thought it part of their duty as the nobles entrusted with administering to the realm.

The white dragon had then moved to Carnel, and the realm was brought back under the palace's management. The royal family had then posted a similar request at the Adventurer's Guild in Carnel City, setting the same bounty of a thousand gold.

When informing Viscount Granvelle of his plans to take down the white dragon, Allen had reminded him to take down the request on the Granvelle side if it was still up. He had zero intention of demanding payment from someone who had done so much for him, after all. Conversely, he had no qualms whatsoever wrangling money from the royal family.

Fearing that anything else he said would make things worse, the royal envoy fell silent. Seeing that the conversation was over, Nina asked with an earnest gaze, "How long will you be staying, Keel? I want to hear stories of your time away!"

"Uh..." This time, it was Keel's turn to fall silent as he struggled for words.

Count Hamilton answered on his behalf. "Well, before we came here, I was told that it would take a few days to issue the traveling permits for your party. How about staying here until the process is finished?"

Nina blinked. "Traveling permits?"

"Yeah," Keel nodded. "We're actually heading to Baukis next."

"I…see." Nina lowered her eyes.

Myulla also looked sad when I told her I was leaving. I guess this *is the same in all families.*

And so, after finishing their talk with the royal envoy, the No-life Gamers decided to stay in Carnel City for a few days, during which they also dropped by Rodin Village and the Granvelle mansion to deliver white dragon meat. After that, they set out for Baukis.

Chapter 6: Traveling to Baukis

The No-life Gamers were headed for the largest landing pad at the Ratashian capital magic ship port, where their flight to Baukis awaited them. Viscount Granvelle and Thomas had gone to see them off.

The viscount clasped Allen's hand in his. "Take care of my daughter."

"Of course, sir. And thank you for everything you're doing for Myulla."

After the God of Spirits granted Myulla the Cleric Talent, Viscount Granvelle had requested the Church send someone to Rodin Village who could teach her how to use her newfound powers. And by "the Church," everyone in this world understood that to mean the Church of Elmea. Of the many deities of this world, the God of Creation undoubtedly had the most followers.

Rodin Village was steadily building all the facilities it needed, and a church was already in the plans for that year, with the Church dispatching a clergyman once the building was completed. In a sense, all that was happening was moving up the construction schedule.

The great boar hunts in autumn had gotten far less risky with the addition of Allen's Summons, but once Myulla mastered Healing Magic, they would become even safer. Plus, Healing Magic could be cast from a distance, so she ought to be able to level up easily.

Cecil was the last to bid farewell to her family. Once she was finally done with her goodbyes, the whole party boarded the magic ship.

There were many types of magic ships, differing in size and speed. This time, the No-life Gamers were taking a large one meant for international travel that flew at normal cruising speed. The group had reserved two comfortably sized rooms for the boys and girls to sleep separately.

Everyone was familiar with riding magic ships by now, as they had done it many times before. They dropped by their rooms to set down their luggage, then gathered in the guys' room to discuss their plan going forward. The group was like a bunch of students on an overnight field trip; in fact, this had been the mood around them ever since they left the Academy.

"By the way, what was that thousand gold for?" Cecil asked. She was referring to the amount that Allen had pressed upon his father as village development funds when they left. The village was still in its tax-exempt period, so Cecil could not imagine what the village would need that would be so expensive.

"It costs money to bring expert tradesmen to the village. For example, to build flood control works."

A normal village would reach a point where it no longer needed much by way of development. Krena Village was one such example. However, Rodin Village was set to become a hub for handling monsters, and that would be a whole different story. It would need to hire experts in many fields, such as architecture, civil engineering, and flood management. The way Allen saw it, as soon as long-term development plans were drawn up, the funds would practically evaporate.

"You left quite a lot of money too, didn't you, Keel?" Dogora asked with a yawn from where he lay on his bed. It was not uncommon for him to fall asleep during these meetings.

Seeing Krena nodding off in her seat, Allen considered laying her down in his bed.

"It's fine. I'm the feudal lord, after all," Keel scoffed. He had entrusted a thousand gold of his own with Count Hamilton, asking the man to pay for anything that his sister or servants might need with it. This was the reward he had received from the queen of Rohzenheim, who had given all the Gamers—aside from Allen—a monetary reward.

"The Rank S dungeon is filled with Rank A monsters, so we'll probably be picking up a whole bunch of valuable equipment that we can just sell off." Allen was not that hung up on money; in his optimistic view, he could always earn more.

"I suppose that's true," Cecil said as she nodded. "On an unrelated note, I wonder how Meruru's doing."

"Using official Rohzenheim channels," Sophie replied, "I have reached out to Meruru's Academy to formally request for her graduation, as well as to Baukis for permission for her to accompany us. I am sure it will not be long before we receive an answer made in good faith."

It was the party's unanimous opinion that they absolutely needed Meruru to clear the Rank S dungeon in Baukis. She was a strong, reliable companion, true, but besides that, she also was the only one who knew much of anything about Baukis or dwarves in general. Everyone was hoping that she would give them the lowdown during their time together in the dungeon.

This was why they had submitted a request that her Academy let her graduate early like they had, with the assumption that she had also accomplished plenty of feats in the Baukisian effort to repel the Demon Lord Army. Citing the same reason, they had also asked Baukis to permit her to accompany them to the Tower of Tribulation. The last they heard from Rohzenheim had been through a magic tool in Ratash, but at the time, no reply from Baukis had come yet.

For what felt like the hundredth time, Allen asked, "They haven't responded yet, right?"

"They have not." Sophie shook her head before continuing in a reassuring tone, "However, Baukis has never turned us down out of hand for anything else before. There should be no cause to worry."

The No-life Gamers soon wrapped up their party meeting, and Allen carried Krena—now fast asleep—over to the girls' room.

* * *

Several days later found the magic ship still in the middle of its uneventful journey. During this time, the party had eaten meals together and spent the rest of their time however they pleased, with Allen dedicating all of his time alone to making Blessings of Heaven to expend his MP and earn skill XP. He was doing the same today in the private dining room the party had reserved next to the cafeteria while he waited for his friends and food to arrive.

The No-life Gamers always reserved a private room for their meals specifically for Sophie's sake. Outside of Rohzenheim, elves were really only ever seen on battlefields or at the Academies, so their long ears tended to catch a lot of attention. Sophie herself also had especially pleasant features, which only made her stand out even more. She wore a hooded cloak that hid her face most of the time, but for situations when she had no choice but to remove her hood—such as when she was eating—alternative measures had to be taken.

Cecil soon came in. "You're here again, Allen? Weren't you making those during lunch too?"

Allen shrugged. "I'm replenishing my stock now 'cause I left pretty much everything I had in Ratash." *Since there's no guarantee we'll make it back alive.*

When handing Rodin the money, Allen had also left him with a large number of Blessings for emergencies. Of course, this had hardly been the first time Allen had done that. And by now, Cecil thought nothing more than *Oh wow, he's really stepped up his pace making those ever since he got his MP Recovery Ring*

One by one, the other Gamers showed up for dinner. The last one in today was Krena, who arrived right after the food had been brought in.

"Yay, *food!*"

She was at the door cheering when an unfamiliar woman approached from behind her and called into the room. "Excuse me. Is Lord Allen here?"

Allen looked up. "Yes, that's me. How may I help you?"

"I am an envoy from Giamut. If I may have a bit of your time, please?"

"Huh? Uh, sure."

The Gamers watched vigilantly as a woman who appeared to be in her early twenties walked in. As an extra precaution, Allen sent a Spirit B into the nearest wall, just in case.

Hold on, I recognize her. She spoke to me at the palace in Ratash.

Allen recalled that, at the time, she had been wearing an outfit similar to the formfitting suit she had on now. She had introduced herself as a Giamutan diplomat and asked to speak with him then too. Unfortunately, Allen had been surrounded by dozens of other nobles at the time and therefore never had the chance to meet with her.

Did she follow us onto the ship?

Deciding to at least hear her out, Allen invited her in to take a seat. And because she had not eaten yet, Allen ordered food for her as well.

"Thank you for your generosity." The woman was adopting a humble manner, but she had not let her eyes stray from Allen's face even once.

When all the food had been served, Allen said, "Let's eat."

"Okay!" Krena replied eagerly.

After the diplomat bobbed her head in acknowledgment, the meal began. As always, the party had ordered family-style, because while Krena and Dogora had massive appetites, Sophie and Volmaar did not eat all that much, with the rest of the group all over the spectrum in between. As such, the most effective thing to do was to order large portions of various dishes and have everyone just take however much they wanted.

The two elves only touched farm-raised meat on rare occasions and never ate monster meat. For example, they did not partake during the Rodin Village white dragon meat celebratory cookout.

"So, what is it that you wanted to talk about?" Allen asked as he slurped a spoonful of soup.

"I have been ordered by His Imperial Majesty to escort you to meet with him. This magic ship will be arriving in the capital soon. Since you'll already be in the city, would you please accompany me?"

Yeah, I figured it'd be something like this. I see, so that's why she waited until now to approach us.

In truth, they were not on a direct flight from Ratash to Baukis. These two countries did not have any official diplomatic relations; therefore, travel had to be routed through the capital of Giamut. The magic ship would be landing there tomorrow. The envoy had apparently been biding her time until this moment.

"I'm sorry, but we have plans," Allen said.

"Plans more important than answering a direct summons from the emperor of Giamut himself?" the lady returned, maintaining firm eye contact.

"In the first place, I can't think of anything we've done that would merit earning an audience with the ruler of the greatest nation on the entire continent. We don't deserve it."

"And you will not change your answer?"

"My apologies. However..."

"Yes?"

"Am I correct in understanding that we can always find *you* at the Ratashian palace? If we are ever in need of aid, we will be in touch."

Wouldn't hurt to keep an open channel with the person who represents the entire Central Continent in the Five Continent Alliance. Maybe there are dungeons that can only be accessed from within the empire's borders. Or maybe legendary weapons.

The woman studied Allen for a while in silence, then replied, "Of course. Both you and Lord Helmios have proven to be tough nuts to crack."

"Oh, it is too much of an honor to be mentioned in the same sentence as the very man who will save the world."

The envoy had nothing more to say. Their conversation ended with Allen turning down an invitation straight from the emperor of Giamut.

* * *

Allen's group disembarked the magic ship at the Giamutan capital where they stayed the night, then boarded their connecting flight for Baukis the next day. This second magic ship was packed with passengers, evidence of the heavy travel between Baukis and Giamut. Almost all of the passengers were dwarves, who were generally shorter than fourteen-year-old Allen, despite clearly being adults with large, scruffy beards and stocky, muscular builds.

"They never seem to tire of that, do they?" Cecil sighed.

The No-life Gamers were having lunch in a private room next to the cafeteria as usual when the noise outside suddenly swelled to a crescendo. The dwarves on board kept their faces permanently buried in their tankards from sunup to sundown, and since the Gamer's room was not soundproofed, all the drunken ruckus outside was perfectly audible. Their commotion grew so loud that Allen could not hear what Cecil was saying, even though she was sitting next to him.

"The dwarves do love their alcohol, after all," Sophie replied with a wry smile.

"Speaking of, Meruru loved to drink too," Allen pointed out.

In this world, the general drinking age was twelve years old. However, Allen firmly maintained from his previous life that "real gamers don't drink" and therefore had always refrained. He did not want his concentration and sense of judgment to become muddled. This was the reason there had been no alcohol in the No-life Gamers' base at the Academy during their first year.

During their second year, however, the dwarf Meruru joined the party and started living with them. Allen noticed that whenever she walked past liquor stores, she would unconsciously stop and stare longingly. This was the origin of how the base finally started stocking liquor—in barrels, of course, given the ridiculous amount that Meruru drank. And once it became available, Keel and his servants—the eldest few—partook every once in a while as well.

Memories of Meruru flitted through Allen's mind as he got up from his seat to look out the window. The desolate land flowing past below indicated that the magic ship had already crossed the ocean between the Central Continent and the Northwest Continent. More specifically, it had entered Baukis airspace and was heading straight for the capital. It was just as Meruru had said—most of Baukis's land was barren, painting a stark contrast from the lush greenery of Rohzenheim.

I suppose that's why they put so much effort into developing magic tools. Wait, hold on...

A Bird E that Allen had left stationed back at the White Dragon Mountain Range had made an incredible discovery.

Krena looked up, her cheeks bulging with food. "Whuh hap'pnf, Alfn?"

"Everyone, listen up," Allen said to the whole group. "The white dragon's been reborn."

Krena swallowed her mouthful, then tilted her head with a puzzled look. "What do you mean?"

The plan was for Carnel and Granvelle to resume mithril mining now that the white dragon was gone. Allen had left Summons behind to help with this effort by eliminating all hostile monsters in the area. Just now, one of those Summons had been flying over a large recess halfway up a peak on the Granvelle side of the mountain range where it had discovered a juvenile white dragon.

The white dragon definitely just respawned. Is there always supposed to be a white dragon in the White Dragon Mountains? Is that a principle of this world?

Allen recalled from his previous life that in some RPGs, some enemy bosses in certain areas or dungeons would reappear again and again, no matter how many times they were killed. This phenomenon, commonly called "respawning," also occurred in this world. For example, the bosses at the deepest levels of the dungeons in Academy City could be fought once per day. In other words, even if these bosses died one day, they would reappear the next day—either having been resurrected or replaced by a copy, Allen did not know which.

Ten days had passed since the No-life Gamers slew the white dragon. The fact that a new white dragon had appeared in the same area pointed to this being yet another instance of respawning.

"What're you going to do, Allen?" Cecil asked, peering at his face. "Do you plan on killing this one too?"

Allen shook his head. "Nah. We'll raise this one."

"Huh? Raise it...like a *pet*?"

"Pretty much. If a new dragon's just gonna respawn anyway, there's no point killing it again. Rather, this could be a good chance to learn something about the Demon Lord's power."

Though I'm sure there are also things I could analyze by killing the white dragon over and over too.

"The Demon Lord? What's this got to do with the Demon Lord? Allen, explain it to us properly."

As always, Allen's train of thought had left his friends behind. To avoid getting strangled by Cecil, he hurriedly proceeded to elaborate.

It was said that the Demon Lord had made all monsters stronger by one rank, so Allen was planning on observing the white dragon's growth to figure out if it had ranked up from the start or if it would suddenly turn more powerful and belligerent after a certain period of time.

The white dragon that the party fought had clearly been self-aware. Was that another effect of the Demon Lord's power? Or did the Demon Lord's power only make monsters stronger? Allen wanted to find out.

One other thing that Allen wanted to check was the white dragon's memory. Did it retain memories from before it was killed? If so, this creature might be a key to understanding a lot more about this world.

Krena let out an impressed "Whoa," although it was not clear how much she actually understood.

"We're heading to a Rank S dungeon now, right, but that's just one waypoint on our journey toward our ultimate goal: defeating the Demon Lord. We learned in Rohzenheim that we need to get stronger because we're barely as strong as his subordinates. We're gonna really have to put in the work and do everything we can to beat him."

Everyone recalled how ineffective their attacks had been against Demonic Deity Rehzel and nodded silently in response.

Allen instructed one of the Dragon Bs he had stationed out in the mountains to head to the white dragon's location, making sure to have it pick up a great boar to feed to the whelp along the way. He was banking on the youngling more easily accepting a fellow dragon as a parent.

"Let's name it Haku. When we fought it, it told us to name ourselves but never gave us its own name." It was not clear whether the white dragon even had a name in the first place.

"You're already giving it a name? How do you know if it's even possible to tame a dragon anyway?" Cecil was not having it.

"That's also part of the experiment."

Allen shot a look at the flying squirrel that was currently perched on the table and devouring a steamed potato. As always, the God of Spirits looked unconcerned with whatever was going on. Still, Allen could swear Rohzen knew something relevant. Not that he would ever share, of course, so Allen had every intention of figuring everything out himself.

"Hey, guys! You can see the city now," Dogora called out from where he was keeping a lookout, prompting the rest of the party to also rush to the windows.

Far below the ship lay a gigantic city that stood out conspicuously against the otherwise barren landscape, its urban sprawl tightly packed with buildings of varying sizes. The architecture had a distinct look involving shiny, reflective walls and lots of rounded corners. This was Dongbao, capital of Baukis. At the very heart of the city sat a shining, golden-roofed palace that towered over all its surroundings.

So this is the capital of the nation said to possess the world's mightiest military. I see a lot of pretty tall buildings. And they're clearly far more technologically advanced than the rest of the world. Which has its charm, true, but I did also like Fortenia with all its nature throughout its streets.

"Wooooow! So coooool!" As usual, Krena had her face plastered against the window.

"Once we arrive, let's look for Meruru first thing," Allen suggested.

"That sounds wonderful," Sophie agreed, nodding.

Soon after, the magic ship landed, and the No-life Gamers disembarked with the throngs of dwarves. It was almost nighttime, so they actually decided to put off their search for Meruru until the next day and instead find a place to stay the night. They headed for a nearby magic train station, listening to the announcements coming over the loudspeakers grow louder and louder as they approached. They boarded a train at the station; when their train reached an area downtown that looked sufficient, they got off.

I know I shouldn't be surprised, but… Wow, it really is just dwarves everywhere you look.

Visiting a foreign country for the first time always came with a strange sense of excitement. Perhaps it was the opportunity to expand one's horizons and explore a new city within a new country that made traveling such a compelling experience.

The No-life Gamers eventually set their eyes on a relatively expensive-looking building and strode inside. They approached the counter, and after receiving confirmation that this was indeed a hotel, booked two rooms. No one ever insisted on a single room for themselves, so the party normally only took two when checking into places.

"Your rooms are on the third floor. Please take the magic elevator."

"Magic elevator?" Krena parroted back.

"It's probably a device that goes up and down," Allen explained.

Krena looked even more confused. "Up and down?!"

The staff member behind the counter gestured toward what looked like a kind of alcove in the wall at the far end of the lobby. When the party approached, they found it to be a small room just spacious enough for ten people to stand inside. They all walked inside.

"What even is this? Is something going to happen?" Cecil asked, looking around.

"There's probably a panel or something to operate…" Allen peered around the room and discovered two button-like gems glowing blue that were buried in the wall. Each was triangle-shaped, with the bases facing each other and the apexes pointing up and down, respectively. "This must be it."

So we can't choose the floor. This probably stops on each floor, then.

Allen pressed the up button on behalf of the group.

Bwum.

The entrance seemed to suddenly collapse, quickly becoming replaced by a featureless wall. The room the Gamers were standing inside was rising up.

"Uh, a-are you sure this is safe?" Dogora was feeling somehow apprehensive from the novel experience.

"It's fine. Interesting, I don't feel the acceleration of going up at all."

The slight sensation of being pressed against the floor that Allen recalled from riding elevators in his prior life was absent here, strangely enough. The only feedback that he had received was the button lighting up.

Eventually, an entrance seemed to come down from above, stopping when the floor outside was exactly level with the floor of the elevator. Allen took a quick peek outside and found a giant "2" on the ground, indicating that this was the second floor. So he stepped back into the room and pressed the up button one more time.

Just like before, the room started rising and stopped when it was level with another entrance. There was a large "3" on the floor outside.

Dogora stared at the number and murmured, "So, we were going up in this thing?"

"That's right," Allen nodded. "Travelers tend to have a lot of luggage, so having a magic tool like this probably makes things easier."

Without further ado, the No-life Gamers retired to their rooms for the night.

* * *

The next morning, as the party was slowly gathering in the lobby, a group of dwarves walked up to them. One stepped forward to approach Sophie, then bowed respectfully.

"I hope you are having a wonderful morning. We are terribly sorry to bother you out of the blue, but would you happen to be Princess Sophialohne of Rohzenheim?"

"Um, y-yes I am."

Oh? We've got someone else coming up to us now. They're here for Sophie this time, looks like.

"It is an honor to make your acquaintance. My name is Nukakai, and I am this country's foreign minister. If you are not in a hurry, may I have a bit of your time? We have already made arrangements for a private venue. Perhaps you would be interested in having breakfast together?"

Whoa, they sent a minister right off the bat? Well, I guess that makes sense. Sophie is *the princess next in line for the throne, after all. I should probably be more surprised at the fact that the government already knows that we're in Baukis and that this is where we're staying. But now that I think about it, they probably already knew from the magic ship manifest, didn't they?*

Ratash had sent Baukis information regarding the No-life Gamers' trip, including the date of their arrival. As it happened, the Gamers had plenty to discuss with the Baukisian government too, so this opportunity had appeared at the perfect time.

"We appreciate the offer," Sophie told the minister. "However, please wait a moment. We have one more companion who is still coming down."

"Thank you very much for accepting our invitation despite the short notice. We shall make the necessary preparations." The minister gave the men behind him a look, and a few nodded in acknowledgment before heading off.

The last person down today was Keel. Allen was always the first of the boys to rise, as he greatly valued living efficiently and therefore kept strict sleeping and eating schedules. However, he always made sure not to disturb the others when he went through his morning routine.

Before long, Keel also made his way down, and the minister led the entire party to a spacious dining area inside the hotel. The room was especially opulent, with walls inlaid with gold and gems.

Seems like the dwarves have a bit of a nouveau riche disposition. I wonder if it's the same in Giamut.

The foreign minister took a seat across from Sophie. "Would you like a drink?" It was clear to all that when the minister said "a drink," he was referring to alcohol.

Did he seriously offer her booze this early in the morning?

"I'm fine, thank you."

Sophie's stopped drinking as of late. And she didn't eat any of the dragon meat either. I feel like the variety of her diet is shrinking.

Sophie no longer touched alcohol because Allen did not; Allen did not because his memories of his past life made him wary of becoming drunk, the consequences of which included making mistakes in-game and falling asleep at his computer. He was wearing an MP Recovery Ring that restored one percent of his MP bar every second at the moment, and since he used that MP to raise his skill levels, he could not afford to waste even a second. For him, accidentally passing out would mean suddenly losing several hours' worth of MP down the drain.

Sophie not eating monster meat was not anything new, though. Allen had learned at the Academy one difference between the two races was that while humans and elves both ate meat from wild animals, the latter did not eat monster meat. It was theorized that this was the reason the Demon Lord Army's forces sent to the Central Continent were mainly composed of only monsters humans could not eat, whereas those sent to Rohzenheim had a decent number of species that were edible for humans. It made sense, as the Demon Lord Army would not want to end up sending rations to their enemies. As such, the great boar meat secured by Ratash's frontier villages remained very valuable rations for the front lines of Giamut.

Allen watched the hotel staff carry out the soup course as childhood memories of hunting great boars flashed through his mind.

Seriously? A full-course meal this early in the morning? I guess we're gonna be here a while, then. Oh well, their foreign minister did go to the trouble of coming all the way here. Let's think of this as an opportunity to tell him what we want.

"Once again, I am Nukakai, the foreign minister of Baukis. Thank you for making time for breakfast."

"Thank you for coming to us. I am Sophialohne, and these are my companions." Sophie gestured toward the rest of the Gamers, who bobbed their heads in greeting.

Allen kept quiet about being Rohzenheim's grand strategist. It was something that could be easily found out with only a little digging, but he generally disliked flaunting his position and status. He wanted to avoid being involved with things as best he could.

"Before all else, please allow me to convey our collective gratitude for the valuable elven elixirs your country supplied us. They were an immense help in the war effort against the Demon Lord Army. Thank you very much."

Nukakai briefly explained that thanks to the large number of "elven elixirs" they had received, the Baukisian casualties were at a record low despite the Demon Lord Army sending twice their usual numbers. Nukakai was now officially acknowledging this and thanking Rohzenheim for its aid on behalf of Baukis.

However, the truth was that Rohzenheim had not sent any elven elixirs to Baukis. The only thing that came to mind was the items Allen had given to Meruru. However, that was something that he had done as a friend and not in any official capacity.

To confirm how Baukis was understanding the situation, Allen spoke up. "I don't believe the items were supplied directly to Baukis, though."

"Indeed, it was the student named Meruru who brought them to us. We made effective use of them based on the counsel she offered."

In other words, Nukakai was insisting that they had not forcibly seized the recovery items from Meruru. Moreover, they had mistaken those items for elven elixirs because Meruru had been schoolfellows and housemates with the princess of the elves herself.

The fact of the matter was that Meruru had not been given elven elixirs but Seeds of Magic, which required only five Rank D magic stones to make and recovered 1,000 MP for allies within a fifty-meter radius. These were far inferior to the Blessings of Heaven—the item that Rohzenheim was officially calling "elven elixirs"—supplied to Giamut; those required five Rank B magic stones and restored both HP and MP to full for allies within a hundred meters, and were even so potent they could regrow lost limbs.

Allen had given Meruru Seeds of Magic because he figured a source of MP recovery would be useful for Baukis's golem pilots. The Demon Lord Army had attacked Rohzenheim, Giamut, and Baukis simultaneously, sending double the usual number of forces to the latter two. To protect itself, Baukis had conscripted all of its students to the front lines as well as its soldiers. Meruru, who had been on exchange at the time, had received orders to return home; she complied, though not before

Allen entrusted her with a whole bunch of Seeds of Magic for her to use while fighting. He had heard that golem users needed MP not only to use skills but also to move their golems.

"I see." Allen nodded. "We are glad to hear of the many lives that were saved. Now, shall we talk about the future?" He was trying to move the conversation along, figuring there was little point in pursuing how the Seeds of Magic were used.

"Indeed." Minister Nukakai lifted his teacup and took a sip before continuing. Because Sophie had turned down the offer of a drink, Nukakai decided he would not be drinking either. "Princess Sophialohne, we have received word that you plan on attempting the Rank S dungeon in the Temple of Yanpany. Is this true?"

Sophie nodded. "Yes, I will be going with my companions here. Is this what we need to gain access?" She took out the party's Rank S dungeon invitation card.

The dungeons in Academy City began at Rank C, with parties later being able to enter successively higher-ranked dungeons once they met certain requirements. Allen's group had smoothly made their way up the ladder and eventually cleared their fifth Rank A dungeon, at which point the Executive Dungeon System appeared and gave them their invitation.

"Indeed, possession of that invitation card serves as proof of Lord Dygragni's acknowledgment that your party are worthy challengers of the dungeon."

Oh? They're not gonna stop us?

The Rank S dungeon was located within the Temple of Yanpany, a place where the dwarves of Baukis worshiped Dungeon Master Dygragni. Even though the No-life Gamers had received their invitation card from a dungeon in Ratash, the dwarves believed that issuance of these invitation cards was by Dygragni's will.

"Thank you for the confirmation," Sophie said, inclining her head.

"However, although we normally celebrate any and all who wish to challenge the Rank S dungeon, when it comes to someone of your station, we feel it our obligation to ask you to reconsider your plans."

"And why is that?"

"Your Highness, half of all challengers die within a year. The Rank S dungeon is an extremely dangerous place."

Little wonder no one's cleared it before.

The Gamers exchanged nervous glances. Only those who had successfully cleared five Rank A dungeons were allowed into the Rank S dungeon. The fact that half of these tried-and-tested warriors were dying in less than a year spoke volumes about just how perilous the place truly was.

"We are fully aware of the risks" Sophie replied. "However, we also believe that there is no circumventing our entering the Rank S dungeon in our quest to take on the Demon Lord Army."

"Fair enough. There are indeed many things that can only be obtained within the Tower of Tribulation. It is clear to me that you have no intention of changing your mind. As such, I will now explain how our country will handle the matter of your entering the dungeon."

Nukakai explained that Baukis issued permits for entering the Rank S dungeon that were separate from the invitation cards. These permits were effective for a year and had to be renewed within a month of expiring. If Sophie's permit was not renewed after a year and there was no record of her ever leaving the country—such as via magic ship—in the following six months, Baukis would announce her death to the rest of the world. The country had to resort to such measures because it was often difficult to confirm the deaths of those who died within the dungeon's walls.

Sophie listened to all this seriously. The gravity of the Baukisian foreign minister coming in person to tell her in no uncertain terms that this was a dangerous undertaking was not lost on her. The risk of the party wiping in the Rank S dungeon was far higher than any other place the Gamers had visited thus far.

I suppose if one of us survived and made it back to give their account of which of us died, then they wouldn't have to wait half a year.

"And that is it for the explanation. If you have any specific questions regarding the dungeon itself, please ask one of the clergy in service to Lord Dygragni," Nukakai said, wrapping things up.

"Thank you very much," Sophie replied. "Incidentally, would you happen to know what's become of our friend? I believe we sent word conveying our wish for her to join us."

"We...did receive the request, yes."

In sharp contrast from mere moments ago, Nukakai now seemed to have difficulty expressing his thoughts.

"Minister, has something happened to Meruru?" Sophie pressed.

The Gamers had received word that Baukis had beaten back the Demon Lord Army, but they still had no idea what had happened to Meruru specifically.

"Oh, no, Meruru is fine. In fact, she did so well on the battlefield that her Academy has agreed to allow her to graduate early. It's simply that, well...His Imperial Majesty is worried for her safety."

Meruru's Talos General Talent was so rare that it appeared in one out of ten million people. The Baukisian emperor was reluctant to risk losing someone with such a valuable Talent.

"So you mean to say it will be difficult for Meruru to come with us?"

"N-No, the possibility still exists. The Empire of Baukis simply wants to be compensated appropriately."

Oh? Was all that talk about how dangerous the Rank S dungeon is just a lead-up to this?

The breakfast negotiations with Foreign Minister Nukakai were clearly not going to be over any time soon.

* * *

Quite some time had passed since breakfast began—the main course was long past and dessert was rapidly approaching. Even after wolfing down cuts of meat anyone else would find too large for breakfast, Dogora and Krena still had not had enough. Was it because they were in puberty? Did they just have large appetites? Either way, they asked the servers for more bread. When the breadbasket arrived, however, it was the God of Spirits who got to it first. He scampered over to grab an unclaimed roll, drawing curious looks from the dwarven servers.

"So you mean to say there are conditions for allowing Meruru to join us in the dungeon?" Sophie looked straight into Nukakai's eyes as she questioned him.

"That is so, yes." The dwarf nodded firmly, but refused to elaborate further.

It's not like I don't get where they're coming from. We are literally asking to take their one-in-ten-million Talent someplace where the chance of dying is equal to a coin toss.

In all likelihood, Nukakai was not lying about the statistics. Any other country would set conditions if asked to send their valuable Sword Lord, Saintess, Archwizard, or other three-star Talent somewhere similar.

Recalling how much appreciation the foreign minister had just expressed for the Seeds of Magic that Allen had given Meruru, Sophie asked coolly, "Would the elven elixirs that were passed to Meruru suffice to fulfill those conditions?"

"It is true that the elixirs saved innumerable lives of our brethren. His Imperial Majesty was so moved that he is considering returning the favor."

"In what way?"

"We have heard that your country is currently occupied with rebuilding many cities destroyed by the invading Demon Lord Army. Baukis would like to offer the magic tools needed in that effort entirely free of charge. We will not be able to extend our support to cover any ensuing maintenance costs, which I'm sure you understand."

The foreign minister was referring to things such as illumination magic tools used as streetlamps or contraptions for purifying drainage. He was also specifically offering the state-of-the-art models—the ones used in Baukis that had yet to be installed in any other country. However, all magic tools required continuous maintenance, and Baukis would naturally be charging for replacement parts as well as dispatching and stationing experts in relevant fields.

These dwarves are merchants through and through. It's just as we learned at the Academy.

Allen had been taught that Baukis was a country that specialized in magic tool development and that it was trying to control the world economically by exporting their technology. To this end, they would offer valuable magic tools to countries that had no hopes of developing such tools themselves as a way to secure routes of export. This was why sixty percent of the magic tools in Ratash were Baukisian imports. Giamut was doing its best to make do with what it was developing domestically, but it was far from stamping out Baukisian products both on its open market and in its citizens' consciousness.

Despite being fully aware of Baukis's intentions, Sophie replied, "I see. I am sure Her Majesty would be more than happy to hear this."

Rohzenheim's dependence on magic tools was significantly less than that of the Central Continent. After all, they could call on the spirits' powers to light their streets and purify their water. In the first place, as a race that loved harmony with nature, the elves had an instinctive aversion to using magic tools. This was why there was no magic train line in the country.

That said, there was no denying that the magic ships had played a crucial role in evacuating civilians and bringing the fight to the enemy forces during the war. What was more, if Sophie simply said, "We don't need what you're offering," the dialogue would have ended then and there.

"If there are any particular magic tools that come to mind, please feel free to let us know."

"That aside, Minister, Meruru is someone we befriended while attending classes with her. Paying money to have her accompany us seems somewhat inappropriate, don't you think? This leaves us at a bit of an impasse."

Sophie cupped her cheek with her hand and frowned thoughtfully.

It was said that elves were a race that disliked violence but were skilled political negotiators. Their diplomatic abilities were one reason Rohzenheim was a superpower within the Five Continent Alliance despite having a population far smaller than that of Baukis or Giamut.

The way Sophie naturally began negotiating with Foreign Minister Nukakai revealed that she, too, had what it took to be a great politician.

"O-Of course not. We would not be as boorish as to ask for money.

It has reached our ears, though, that your country has figured out a way to mass-produce your elven elixirs. All we want is for you to export some to us."

"What we have achieved is not exactly mass production, but a way to make elixirs that are far more potent than before. During the war, we distributed a significant number to various allied nations and used up a lot ourselves, so I'm afraid we do not have much left in stock."

"Oh, we would be more than satisfied with whatever quantity you can manage to export."

"Then it sounds like I should do what I can to seize this opportunity to foster friendly relations between our nations."

"Now I can breathe easy, knowing I get to keep my head! To be honest with you, His Imperial Majesty did warn me to resolve myself should I fail to secure a promise for more elven elixirs. Goodness gracious, what a predicament!"

"Oh, I'm sure you exaggerate. Incidentally, where would Meruru happen to be at the moment?"

The minister shot a look at the clock on the wall, which indicated it was almost nine o'clock.

"She should be arriving at this hotel very soon."

"Thank you, Minister. Kindly convey my gratitude to His Imperial Majesty for me."

"Of course. I'm sure you will become quite occupied when you begin taking on the Tower of Tribulation, but if you ever have the opportunity to visit the palace, please don't hesitate to ask for me, Nukakai."

Because Sophie had implied that she had no intention of seeing the Baukisian emperor for now, Foreign Minister Nukakai responded accordingly. After that, Allen got some time to ask the minister a few questions about Baukis. When he was finished, the dwarves made their exit, leaving the Gamers to continue waiting for Meruru.

Once they were all alone, Cecil made a displeased groan. "Are all dwarves like that?"

"I have heard that Baukis is a country that prioritizes national benefit above all else," Sophie replied. "He was actually going easy on me."

Fifty years ago, Baukis was not an empire but merely one among the many other dwarven kingdoms on the continent. However, it possessed magic tool technology that the other countries did not, and when war broke out against the Demon Lord Army, it managed to use this unique technology and the power of its golems to beat back the monsters. By offering its technological prowess to the other dwarven kingdoms, Baukis gradually expanded its influence over the entire continent, eventually swallowing many other nations under the just cause of "protecting the dwarven race" to form the Empire of Baukis of today. The Gamers had learned this history in their classes at the Academy. What they had just witnessed had verified the contents of those lessons beyond a doubt in their minds.

"Well, this *is* a country that clawed its way to power by using the Demon Lord. I'm sure they don't want to return to their days as a mere kingdom." *While everyone else is suffering from all the Demon Lord Army incursions, I think Baukis is the only one that's managed to successfully use the crisis to its benefit and develop itself.*

"You should probably be careful about saying stuff like that where people can hear you," Cecil hissed.

That moment, there were knocks on the door to the dining area.

"Come on in!" Allen called out as the whole party turned around. Framed in the doorway was the nostalgic face of someone who had been living with them at the Academy until just a few months ago.

"*MERURUUU!*"

Krena rushed over and wrapped the dwarven girl in a big hug on behalf of the whole group. Everyone else quickly crowded around with big smiles on their faces to celebrate their reunion.

When everyone's emotions had calmed down a bit, each side caught the other up on what had happened in Rohzenheim and Baukis.

"It was so strong! My golem's arm flew off like, *whoosh*! And it was like, *booooom!*"

The other Gamers gave their full attention as the diminutive Meruru excitedly swung her arms and legs, telling of how she had fought

while riding a golem. From what they could glean, her golem had proved capable of tearing through the hordes of monsters with ease.

We finally have Meruru back, but it would be annoying if Baukis did anything to get in the way of her coming with us to the Tower of Tribulation. I should come up with some countermeasures when we're going through the dungeon.

There was no way that Baukis was going to let go of someone with a one-in-ten-million Talent so easily. Allen knew he would have to come up with something to allow her to stay with the group.

"If only there was a way for her to borrow a golem to bring into the Rank S dungeon," Allen sighed.

Cecil sighed in commiseration. "Nukakai did say that it was not possible."

Just now, Allen had asked the foreign minister whether they could borrow a golem for Meruru to pilot, but he had been turned down on the spot. However, when pressed, the man did reveal that there was a way to obtain a personal golem.

"The lowest floor of the dungeon drops the slates that you need, right, Meruru?"

"Mm-hm! Once I have all the parts, I can build my own golem!"

Meruru confirmed that she had indeed summoned the golem she used when she fought the Demon Lord Army using such slates. This meant the minister had in all likelihood been telling the truth.

What is this "slate" thing? Oh man, I'm getting excited just thinking about it.

It was unclear why or how these slates related to the golems that supposedly could reach a hundred meters in height. For any more details about this and other aspects of the Rank S dungeon, the group would have to actually head to the Temple of Yanpany. And so, without further ado, the No-life Gamers set off once again, their roster fully restored after what felt like ages.

Chapter 7: Rank S Dungeon

So far on their journey, Allen's group had been approached by representatives of two different emperors requesting their appearance: the Giamutan envoy on the magic ship and Baukisian Foreign Minister Nukakai at the hotel.

The thing was, just because an emperor was interested in meeting someone did not necessarily mean the audience would happen immediately. For example, it took ten days for the king of Ratash to arrange everything for Sophie's audience. With these two emperors, it would not at all be surprising if the Gamers would have to wait over a month to meet with them. And of course, Allen thought anything short of immediate access like what he had to the elven queen's audience hall was wasted time that could be put to much better use.

With Meruru back in the group, the No-life Gamers mounted their Bird Bs and flew northeast for the Temple of Yanpany. As always, they intended to use Allen's Summons to travel around the country as well as to fight inside the Rank S dungeon.

Allen had given Nukakai a brief introduction of his Summons earlier. The minister had apparently known close to nothing about Allen's being a Summoner, and his reaction was nothing more than "Oh, yes, I believe I've heard mention of this." He asked Allen to refrain from calling out his Summons inside any settlements, but said there should be no issue doing so out in the open.

This general lack of alarm was very likely tied to the fact that Baukis had golems in its command. Baukisians were very aware that their country had the strongest military in the world, and they all harbored a deeply rooted belief that it was simply impossible for anyone to be more powerful than a golem.

As a change of pace, Allen's co-passenger today was Meruru, not Cecil.

"So you've become a noble as well?" he asked her.

"Yep! I showed 'em who's boss!" Meruru beamed as she recounted tales of the events following her departure from the Ratashian Academy.

Back in Ratash, Meruru had always seemed somewhat insecure and unsure of herself. Now, however, she could talk about herself while grinning from ear to ear. The war had clearly been a good experience for her, serving as an opportunity to build up both her military achievements and self-esteem.

In recognition of her efforts, Meruru had been made an honorary baron, the same rank as Krena. Apparently making those with three-star Talents—such as Sword Lords and Saintesses—honorary nobles when they graduated from the Academy was common practice in this world. However, in Meruru's case, she had been given her status due to her military exploits, as she had yet to graduate at the time. There was no worldwide agreement behind this particular practice, but all nations did it anyway to ensure that valuable personnel did not get siphoned away by foreign powers.

That's my confirmation that Meruru's class really is three stars. However, since she gave some of the Seeds of Magic away, she hasn't quite maxed out her skill levels yet. Her overall level has reached Lvl. 60, though, which is great.

Despite her countless dungeon runs as a part of the No-life Gamers in Ratash, she never earned a single point of skill XP. This was because all of her skills were related to piloting golems, and there were no golems to use in Ratash. It was only after she returned to Baukis and fought the

Demon Lord Army as a pilot—with her Baukis-issued golem—that she started raising her skill levels. However, because she gave away so many Seeds of Magic, she ended up using her skills less frequently than Allen had expected. Her skills were still only Lvl. 4.

Name: Meruru
Age: 14
Class: Talos General
Level: 60
HP: 1,677 + 900
MP: 2,420 + 900
Attack: 782 + 900
Endurance: 1,318 + 900
Agility: 782
Intelligence: 2,420
Luck: 1,503

Skills: Talos General {4}, Rocket Punch {4}, Drill Punch {4}, Laser Sword {4}, Alloy {1}, Spear Mastery {3}, Shield Mastery {3}
Extra Skill: Union (Right Arm)

Skill Levels
Rocket Punch: 4
Drill Punch: 4
Laser Sword: 4

Skill Experience
Rocket Punch: 430/10,000
Drill Punch: 550/10,000
Laser Sword: 280/10,000

Meruru's Status looked very similar to Krena's back when she was still a Sword Lord; Meruru now had +900 buffs to four stats.

All her stats have gone up significantly. But…I see, her battle strength still very much relies on her having a golem. Ooooh, I see "Drill Punch" listed here. I can't wait to see it in action!

Meruru's skills all dealt damage with the assumption that she had access to a golem. So, once the Gamers found all the necessary golem parts inside the Tower of Tribulation, she would be able to use those skills all she wanted. With that, Allen wrote up a list of things he wanted to find within the Rank S dungeon:

- The slates that serve as parts for Meruru's golem
- Orichalcum weapons and armor
- Accessories that provide buffs higher than +1,000
- Useful magic tools

The No-life Gamers had obtained many desirable items from Rank A dungeons that were otherwise impossible to obtain from Auctions, and intel had it that they could expect more of the same from the Rank S dungeon. Given this, Allen was hoping to upgrade his entire party's gear in one go. Moreover, Helmios had told the Gamers they could expect to find other kinds of items that would prove indispensable on future adventures as well.

"So you got to meet Hero Helmios in Rohzenheim?" Meruru asked.

"We sure did. He was the same as ever. Speaking of, he said he'd be coming to Yanpany once Giamut is done celebrating the end of the war."

Helmios had himself been promoted from Hero to Hero King, the process of which had reverted him back to Lvl. 1. He was planning on giving the Rank S dungeon another go with his own party as a way to level himself back up.

"Whoa, so the esteemed Hero is coming." Awe tinged Meruru's eyes. "You sound like you've gotten real close with him."

"Hm? I'm not at all, though."

The party landed for a lunch break, then resumed flying northeast. A few hours later, a shape came into view on the horizon that completely broke their sense of distance, like a landscape painting with poorly drawn perspective. This silhouette gradually turned into a mountain-like structure with a base area wider than Dongbao that stood so tall it pierced the clouds.

"That's the dungeon?" Allen asked.

Meruru peered out from behind his back. "Mm-hm, should be."

"Um…it's *really* big."

"Aha ha, ya can't even see the top!"

I did sorta expect it to be a tower, since the dungeon's name is literally the Tower of Tribulation. That said, it couldn't look any more different from the dungeons back at Academy City.

The Academy City dungeons looked like small apartment buildings on the outside but were actually massive spaces accessed via portals. The way the portals worked was quite complicated, as they sent parties to uniquely generated, isolated dimensions, but the exterior of the buildings looked entirely normal. In contrast, the Tower of Tribulation was so tall that clouds obscured it a certain distance up, making it impossible to gauge the structure's exact height.

"Hm? Where's the Temple of Yanpany? I only see the Tower of Tribulation."

Contrary to his expectations, Allen failed to see anything resembling a temple near the tower, which stood on its lonesome. He now wondered just where exactly it was the dwarves conducted their worship of Dungeon Master Dygragni.

"The Temple of Yanpany is on the first floor of the Tower of Tribulation!" Meruru replied in a confident voice. She had firmly believed that she would eventually get to challenge the Rank S dungeon with her friends, and so had done her best to gather information from comrades and superiors during her time on the battlefield.

"Seriously? Both the temple and the dungeon are in that giant tower?"

Allen then asked Meruru to share everything she knew. Apparently, this tower that bridged the endless wasteland below with the sky above was more than ten times the size of the World Tree in Rohzenheim. The sight of the Tower took the Gamers' breath away as they wondered how on earth such a structure came to be.

The only one who reacted differently was the God of Spirits. From his usual position on Sophie's shoulder, he gazed at the huge tower with an intense expression.

* * *

Eventually, the No-life Gamers drew close enough to make out a line of people stretched in front of the Tower of Tribulation. Recalling Nukakai's warning, the party landed their Bird Bs some distance away to avoid causing a panic and headed over to join the queue on foot.

The size of the tower indicated that it likely physically housed the Rank S dungeon inside, unlike how the dungeons in Academy City had been separate dimensions. The Bird E that Allen had sent ahead to observe the exterior of the structure confirmed that there were no windows and that there were doors located at regular intervals on the ground floor of the tower.

So there isn't only one entrance.

Out of curiosity, Allen had Bird E continue flying up. However, no matter how much time passed, the top of the tower never came into sight.

Well, this is *a world with magic ships. I guess Dygragni isn't stupid enough to let people cheese the tower by getting in from the top.*

At a certain distance from the tower, the line of people split up into smaller streams heading for the various entrances. Allen and his group picked one at random and fell into step. When Allen noticed the man who was standing before them in line, however, a "Huh?" involuntarily escaped his lips.

The man was taller than every one of the Gamers and was not wearing anything above the waist aside from the greatsword on his back. As Allen looked up, he noticed the thick fur covering the man's skin and, eventually, the doglike ears crowning his head.

The beastkin turned around in response to Allen's voice and, upon noticing his gaze, bared his teeth in a less-than-friendly manner and glared. "The fuck you lookin' at, huh?!"

"Sorry, sir. It was nothing."

"Hmph." After giving Allen a slow once-over from head to toe, the man snorted and turned back.

As it turned out, the line in front was filled with not only dwarves but also a decent number of humans and beastkin.

At the Academy, Allen had learned the difference between "human" and "person." Namely, "human" was the race, and "people" was a term that also included elves and beastkin. Naturally, that meant Krena and Allen were also "people," and so if a distinction were to be made, they would be called "humans." This was a concept that had arisen out of the need to refer to all races with one term when the Five Continent Alliance was assembled.

There are quite a lot of beastkin here. Did they come over from the continent to the south? Wow, this world's animal people are all so furry.

To the south of the Empire of Baukis lay the Garlesian Continent, which was split up among numerous beastkin countries. The beastkin in line had very likely originated from there. Allen wondered if they were here hoping to get rich quick.

The line steadily crept forward until the No-life Gamers finally reached the front. Their mixed-race party garnered a few weird looks from the guards, but once they showed their adventurer cards, they were let in without a fuss.

When they stepped through the doorway, Krena's eyes lit up. "It's a whole city!"

The inside of the tower was so brightly lit that one would never guess that it had no windows. There were buildings packed tightly together, creating a townscape that was undoubtedly a metropolis.

"This is incredible… You're right, this really is a whole city inside a dungeon," Allen agreed.

It was clear that the walls of the city matched the external shape of the tower. The illumination inside was somewhat distinct from actual sunlight, and it became immediately obvious where this light was coming from.

"Look! It's glowing!" Krena pointed toward the heart of the city, her excitement rising another notch.

One building towered over the rest of the cityscape, topped by something radiating bright light.

"Is that the Temple of Yanpany?" Allen led his companions toward the building, recalling what he had just heard about this Rank S dungeon and the temple, all as he took in the sights all around.

"Yep, it sure is!" Meruru confirmed.

"And it's…in the middle of the city, of course."

A Bird E appeared above Allen's head and flew up to get a bird's-eye view of the area. Barely half a day earlier, someone very important had told him not to use his Summons inside a city, but Allen decided he must have simply heard wrong.

It's very spacious in here, but it looks like there is an actual ceiling. That said, this is a massive city. So, if the first floor is this city, does that mean the actual dungeon starts on the second floor? Okay, Bird E is coming up on the temple.

The clearance of this floor was so high that Hawkins had more than enough space to leisurely circle the air way up above everyone. The layout of the city was circular, with the structure that was most likely the Temple of Yanpany located in the center and the buildings in concentric circles radiating outward. From high above, this looked quite similar to tree rings.

According to Meruru, the Temple of Yanpany had existed since the days when Baukis was still a kingdom thousands of years ago. This countryside temple was dedicated to Dygragni, the being who controlled the dungeons and oversaw everything related to magic tools. The more the priests prayed, the larger the temple grew until this dungeon appeared all around it. That was how the temple and the dungeon were related, and people claimed that it was Dygragni who had made all this happen.

So this is what's illuminating this whole city.

Atop the temple was an illumination magic tool. Back when he was a manservant, Allen had seen something similar installed in the Granvelle mansion. This one, however, was powerful enough to light up a city that dwarfed even Baukis's capital.

"What're we gonna do now, Allen?" Cecil asked.

"Huh?" Roused from his thoughts, Allen turned toward her. "Well, we arrived earlier than I expected. How about we go to the temple and see what they can tell us about the dungeon?"

Everyone nodded. They already knew that Allen was not the kind of person to spend time aimlessly wandering around the city.

"Man, there's even a magic train here," Keel commented.

Dogora looked over to see what Keel was talking about. "Damn, you're right. Is this place seriously a dungeon?"

Upon overhearing this exchange, Allen had Bird E look for a train station. It quickly found one close to their current location and confirmed that the tracks did run to the center of the city, passing close to the temple. The group made their way to the station and boarded a train.

As they rode the train, Allen gazed out the window at the people going to and fro outside. "Why were there so many adventurers outside just now, by the way? Isn't everyone here to explore the dungeon inside the Tower?"

"Um, I remember hearing that there are a bunch of other dungeons all around the Tower of Tribulation," Meruru explained. "So, a lot of adventurers staying in this city are probably heading for those dungeons instead."

The Tower was surrounded by countless dungeons ranging from Rank C to A. As such, a significant percentage of the adventurers in the Tower were actually there for those dungeons instead. This city was almost a whole world unto itself, with a unique community revolving around dungeons—especially the Rank S one in particular.

These thoughts were still rattling around inside Allen's mind as the magic train reached the station before the temple. The party got off and hoofed it the rest of the way. The glimpses that they caught in the gaps between the buildings gave them the impression that the temple itself looked very much like a magic tool, a stark contrast to the wooden temple in Rohzenheim where the elves worshipped Rohzen.

"That's one tall-ass building," Dogora observed with a bit of a sigh as he stared up.

"It sure is," Allen agreed as he looked up with him. "And the magic tool at the top is very likely what's illuminating this city."

The Temple of Yanpany turned out to be a pencil-shaped structure that was around the same height as the tallest radio tower in Japan. At its very top, just as Bird E had spied, was a giant, brightly shining magic tool. The area surrounding the temple was filled with the whir and hum of some power source at work.

Many adventurers were busily going into and exiting the temple in a vigorous flow. The No-life Gamers joined them to walk inside.

"Wha—?! You there, you squirts! This ain't a place for you kids to be!"

Suddenly, Allen's group found their path blocked by a temple guard at the door.

"Huh?"

"Only those with the right to enter the Rank S dungeon are allowed to pass. Go home! Shoo, shoo!"

Wait, are you serious?

Apparently the guard had jumped to conclusions based on how young the Gamers looked. Despite his surprise, though, Allen still had the presence of mind to produce his invitation card.

"OH! My deepest apologies. You're so young, and already..." Now it was the guard's turn to be surprised, but he yielded the way without any more fuss.

When they were inside the temple, Cecil huffed a little. "How rude, judging us by our looks!"

Allen made a noncommittal sound. "So he did."

"Why're you acting so blasé about it now? You were surprised too!"

"I mean, it *is* the guards' job to keep an eye out and stop people that they think don't belong from getting in. Most adventurers who look our age wouldn't have a license, right? If he just let all of them through, they'd probably die the first day they stepped foot in the Rank S dungeon."

Even though Cecil was getting in his face about it, Allen actually did not have any issue with the way the guard had handled the exchange just now.

Guards are supposed to stand at doorways. Oh man, I still remember how much trouble it was waiting for the guards to change shifts whenever sneaking in at night.

"Huh? I-I mean, you're right, but… You looked surprised too."

"Of course I was. Just now the guard confirmed that only those with a Rank S dungeon invitation card are allowed inside. And look how many adventurers there are here. The world sure is huge!"

Only now did Cecil take a good look around. The temple was packed with dwarves, humans, and beastkin alike. Back during their days at the Academy, their homeroom teacher had told them that Ratash no longer had any citizens powerful enough to enter the Rank S dungeon. And yet here there were so many, every last one powerful enough to have earned their right to be here.

"Would that perhaps be the reception desk?" Sophie gestured toward a row of counters.

Allen nodded. "Seems like it. Let's go see what they can tell us."

The No-life Gamers approached a counter being manned by a dwarf wearing priestlike robes.

"Oh my, such young adventurers. How may I help you today?"

I love how dwarves don't have any sort of height complex.

"We're about to give the Rank S dungeon a try, so we want to know more about it. Is this the right line?"

"Of course." The priest suddenly noticed Meruru. "Oh? You have a dwarf among you."

"Mm!" The dwarven girl beamed cheerfully.

"Are you perhaps a golem pilot?"

Good guess. Then again, she's not holding a weapon or wearing any armor.

Meruru was not currently holding the spear and shield she had used during her time at the Ratashian Academy.

"Yep!" Meruru confirmed.

"Do you have a magic disc?"

"Nope, I don't. I was told to return the one I used when I was in the navy."

What's a magic disc?

"I see. Would you like to rent one of ours?"

"Mm! Yes, please!"

The receptionist left his post for a bit, then came back holding what looked like a round black slab.

"Here it is. Please provide your adventurer card for registration purposes."

What's going on? I feel like I'm watching someone borrow a library book.

Unable to hold it in any longer, Allen interrupted Meruru's conversation with the priest. "Excuse me. Um, what is a magic disc?"

The receptionist looked up. "Huh? Ah, this is a magic tool necessary for calling out a golem."

"Yep, that's right!"

"A magic tool for calling out a golem, you say." Allen took a good look at the pitch-black slab with a metallic sheen on the counter. It was circular in shape, with one side being entirely smooth and the other having ten depressions. A strap or chain was attached to it as if it were a pocket watch.

Is something supposed to go into these grooves?

Meruru accepted the slab and happily hung it from her neck. Many of the other dwarves in the room were wearing similar pitch-black discs around their necks as well.

I can't help but think that they look like a bunch of elementary kids who're showing up for summer break morning radio exercises at the local park with their stamp cards hanging around their necks.

"I'm supposed to slot in slates that form golem parts into these grooves, right?" Meruru asked for confirmation's sake.

The priest nodded. "Correct. You'll be able to find such slates on Floor 2 and higher in this dungeon. The bosses in the surrounding Rank A dungeons also drop them on rare occasions."

And there are grades to the golems too, if I remember correctly.

According to what Allen had heard, golems were ranked on a grading system that indicated their relative power, with a pilot's Talent determining which rank they could control.

* * *

Golem Pilots' Talents vs. Golem Ranks

- Talos Pawn: can control up to Bronze Grade Golems
- Talos Soldier: can control up to Iron Grade Golems
- Talos General: can control up to Mithril Grade Golems

"I've heard that golems are in grades such as Bronze, Iron, and Mithril Grade," Allen said. "Can the parts be used for all grades, or are they all distinct? We're asking because Meruru here has the Talos General Talent, so…"

"T-Talos General?! Are you sure?!" The receptionist's eyes flew wide open as he grabbed his counter with both hands and pulled himself forward to study Meruru closely from head to toe.

I see, so this is how valuable someone with a one-in-ten-million Talent is. I've heard that the more powerful golems can single-handedly kill a dragon.

The dwarves in line behind the No-life Gamers also started buzzing excitedly.

"Did you hear? That girl's a Talos General!"

"Seriously?!"

Meruru turned around and replied brightly, "Mm-hm! Sure am!"

When he regained his composure, the priest cleared his throat and said, "The slates that a golem needs are indeed specific to its grade."

"So we'd need bronze slates, mithril slates, and so on?"

"Yes. If you slot in a part that isn't the same grade as the others, it will not work. To call forth a golem, you at least need a head, a left arm, a right arm, a torso, and a lower body. That makes a total of five parts."

There were slates that could grant golems additional abilities, and it was up to the golem pilot to pick and choose according to their preferred fighting style. It was pretty much the luck of the draw, and Allen resigned himself to the fact that they would probably end up drawing parts that they already had.

"What should we do if, say, we get multiple iron torso slates?"

"Some choose to keep spares in case their golem is damaged. If you determine that you do not need it, though, you can sell those parts to us here."

Needless to say, the majority of adventurers entering this dungeon were not golem pilots, and the Temple of Yanpany bought all the slates that they had no use for. The pricing differed depending on part and grade, but most went for more than a hundred gold apiece.

As expected of loot from a Rank S dungeon.

The priest further explained that golem parts were the only thing that the temple handled. All other drops, such as magic stones obtained by killing monsters or equipment found inside treasure chests, had to be sold at the Adventurer's Guild close by the temple.

He went on to recommend that the Gamers check out the Adventurer's Guild should they want even more information. He then reminded them once again of the high death rate in the dungeon and warned them to not overextend themselves.

Everyone who walked into this temple had cleared five Rank A dungeons. Presumably, this meant they had the ability and presence of mind to research a dungeon before stepping foot in it.

"Thank you for the explanation. There's still something that I want to know. Would you mind?"

"Please, ask me anything."

"Is it possible to find magic discs inside the dungeon?"

"It is not. Lord Dygragni makes them himself and bestows them to this temple through us, his priests. You will not find them as drops within the dungeon."

So this is the sole source of the magic discs.

"I see. Now, you just helped Meruru rent this magic disc. Is it possible to purchase one outright?"

Of course, Allen intended on having Meruru continue journeying with them in the future. And since she was a golem pilot, she needed a golem of her own. This was a problem that needed to be resolved.

"Um, I'm terribly sorry. Magic discs are considered Baukis's national property. They are generally not for sale."

"'Generally'? As in, there are exceptions?"

"We *can* technically let you have one for ten thousand gold."

Yeesh, talk about overcharging. That's enough money to buy a magic ship. But I see, this is how Baukis has more than ten thousand golems that it can mobilize all at once.

Allen took away several things from his conversation with the priest. First, this temple was under Baukis's management. Second, one of its main roles was to lend magic discs to golem pilots and collect golem parts from the dungeon. After all, even pilots sold them to the temple whenever they picked up parts that they already had. The reason that magic discs were generally only on a lending basis was so the country could demand their return in times of need, such as wartime. To buy one of these discs, one had to fork over ten thousand gold, an amount that could purchase a decent magic ship. There was little point in Allen equating this price with the value of money in his previous life, but he could not help doing so. He understood one gold to be worth around a hundred thousand yen; the receptionist was basically saying that it would cost one billion yen to buy a magic disc.

"Ten thousand gold? Understood. Please give me a moment to take it out."

"What?" The receptionist blinked.

Allen positioned his grimoire above the counter, opened it to the Storage page, and flipped it over. The next moment, pouches filled with a hundred gold coins each—Allen kept his money this way for ease of trading—fell out in a quickly growing pile.

"This should be ten thousand gold. Please confirm it."

Cecil sighed. "Yep, Allen's being Allen again." She had known this would happen from the start.

The receptionist asked for a moment and gathered a few colleagues to count the money together. After they confirmed the amount, he added information to Meruru's adventurer card showing that she had purchased her magic disc and now had full ownership of it. The whole process took slightly under an hour.

"Th-Thank you..." Meruru was choking up a little with emotion. Even though she was familiar with Allen's personality from their time together in Academy City, she still could not help feeling astonished and moved by his bold action.

"Don't worry about it. We would've had to do it sooner or later anyway. Now, it's gotten dark outside, so let's put off visiting the Adventurer's Guild until tomorrow."

"That sounds good," Cecil agreed. "Let's find a place."

And so the No-life Gamers checked into a hotel close to the temple and spent the night.

* * *

The next day, after hitting up the Adventurer's Guild, the party made their way to the Real Estate Guild and went through the process to rent a house near the temple. While hotels were great in that they provided meals and cleaning service, the party wanted a place where they would not have to worry about keeping away from prying eyes when doing things such as creating Blessings of Heaven. As soon as they received their keys, they headed to their new base.

According to the receptionist at the Real Estate Guild, most rentals in this city did not come furnished. This was due to the large variety of races living there who all had different body sizes and therefore needed different furniture. Sure enough, when the Gamers walked into their new place, they found it entirely empty. Because the dining room did not even have a table, they had no choice but to spread sheets out on the floor and sit on them in a circle.

Halfway into the meal, Allen suddenly said, "I have something to talk about. Feel free to keep eating while you listen."

"Huh?" Krena looked his way as she took a big bite from a piece of bread.

"So, we've finally got everything in order and are ready to begin clearing the Rank S dungeon."

The usage of the term "clear" was intentional. For everyone else in this city, it was common sense that the Tower of Tribulation was to be *challenged*, not *cleared*. If half of the people who challenged the dungeon died in their first year, the number of sacrifices necessary to beat it would be astronomical. Allen had used the word "challenge" when talking to the king of Ratash and Foreign Minister Nukakai to avoid making waves. However, he now told his companions that reaching the very end of this Rank S dungeon and defeating the last boss that lay in wait had been his intention from the very start.

"Yep!" Krena's grin conveyed that she would not have it any other way.

"With that in mind, there's something that I want to ask you all."

The serious look on Allen's face caught Dogora and Keel off guard, as they had assumed this was a normal discussion regarding their formation or strategy tomorrow. They did their best to focus.

Cecil had a similar reaction. "Is something the matter?"

"I'm pretty sure that even after we clear this dungeon, we'll still have a tough time fighting Demonic Deities."

"*Huh?!* What do you mean?! Explain!"

"Sorry, I might have phrased that badly. I'm not saying we definitely *can't* win. Hmm…let me use Rehzel as an example." The way Allen saw it, their chances of beating Rehzel before his transformation—if Helmios had not been around—was around ten percent. "In short, Rehzel was so powerful that we had almost no chance against him. I know it's said that monsters get a lot stronger when you jump a rank, but that was miles above a mere Rank A."

Not once had Rehzel called himself Rank S, but his strength was significantly superior to normal demons, who were Rank A. So, even if the No-life Gamers managed to completely deck themselves out with equipment from the Rank S dungeon, Allen did not think they had a guaranteed shot against someone like Rehzel.

Dogora frowned. "Huh? How would you know? We haven't even gotten in yet."

"Well, Hero Helmios had a five-star Talent and *was* wearing a full set of gear that he had gathered from this dungeon. Of course, he didn't clear it, but even if he did, it probably wouldn't have made much of a difference."

"Oh right, that's true."

"All of you carried over half of your stats from before your class promotion, but that's still nowhere near enough for us to comfortably beat a Demonic Deity."

By my estimation, if everyone in the party maxes out their levels and skill levels and is wearing orichalcum from head to toe, then we might have a fifty percent chance of winning. Maybe a little below that.

"Even so, we still have to go through this dungeon, right?" Cecil asked.

"Of course. The way I see it, our adventure's only just begun."

"Adventure?" Krena tilted her head, now munching on a fresh piece of bread.

"Yep! An adventure. This is an adventure for killing the Demon Lord. Getting caught up in the war during our student years was just a side thing. This Rank S dungeon is the first real step of our party's adventure."

Krena paused eating. "I see. So this dungeon is still only the beginning for us."

"That's right. We're going to clear this Rank S dungeon and claim every last drop of power it can give us. However, even once we do, we're still far from done."

"We've gotta level up as fast as we can, then!" Krena clenched both her fists, brimming with enthusiasm. The memory of how the fight against Rehzel had gone now served as fuel for Krena to constantly push herself to improve.

Looks like the girl who was only fooling around with a sword at first is slowly growing up. Now she's found a proper reason to swing that sword of hers.

"One thing that'll be different if we ever encounter a Demonic Deity again is that we have Meruru with us now. We still have no idea just how powerful a golem is, but that's something we can see for ourselves inside."

Meruru puffed out her chest. "Tam-Tam is suuuper powerful! It's gonna knock your socks off!"

"Who's Tam-Tam?" *I don't know anyone by that name.*

"Tam-Tam is my golem! I set that as the name when they issued me one during the war!"

"I see. Well, names are important. Tam-Tam. Okay, I'll remember it."

"Yep!"

Hmm, she's got good naming sense, just like me.

"You said the golem you used was Iron Grade, right?"

"Mm-hm! They didn't have a spare Mithril Grade."

As a Talos General, Meruru had the ability to pilot Mithril Grade golems. The fact that she was not issued one likely meant Baukis had more Talos Generals than Mithril Grade golems. Although her Talent was said to be one in ten million, the dwarven nation had a population of two hundred million; it would not be surprising if there were other Talos Generals besides Meruru. It was either that, or because the majority of Baukis's golem army was Bronze Grade and Iron Grade, they simply did not have enough parts to field all that many Mithril Grade golems.

"We'll prioritize finding parts for Meruru's golem. When that's done, we'll focus on maxing out everyone's levels and skill levels as soon as possible. The bottleneck will probably be the skill levels, so use your skills as often as possible, everyone."

By Allen's estimates, it would take more than three months to max all the levels for everyone in the party. Based on that, he was planning on sticking around this dungeon for a year.

"Fingers crossed the Demon Lord Army doesn't attack again during that time."

"I'm pretty sure that won't happen, Cecil. Not after it lost so many troops. In fact, they probably won't show up again for the rest of the year."

"Ah, that makes sense."

The Demon Lord Army forces that attacked Giamut and Baukis had been beaten back, meaning that some portion of it had simply retreated. Those that were sent to Rohzenheim, however, had been almost entirely wiped out, including both the original three million plus the four million sent as reinforcements.

"One more thing—Dogora, you've gotta learn how to use your Extra Skill."

Dogora's Extra Skill, Heart and Soul, was currently the most powerful attack in this party's arsenal. Even back when he was only a one-star class, this skill had enabled him to destroy one of Rehzel's hearts when the rest of the party had struggled to even lay a scratch on the demon. On top of his class promotion, once Dogora found a better weapon, the damage that he would be able to dish out ought to be significantly higher than before. He just might become capable of killing a Demonic Deity in one strike.

Dogora stared at his hands, opening and closing them a few times before finally replying with a simple "Will do."

"As for you, Keel, we're going to get you more equipment that raises your Intelligence stat."

"Sounds good, thank you. I don't want Drops of God to fail again like the first time I used it on Dogora."

Keel's Extra Skill, Drops of God, resurrected the dead. It was Allen's theory that the success rate of this skill was dependent on Keel's Intelligence. As such, the way to maximize the reliability of this skill was, besides maxing the skill level, to wear equipment that gave the highest possible Intelligence buffs.

"Sophie—one day, you'll become capable of manifesting spirits under your control. Please keep working on your ability to communicate with them in preparation for that day."

"Understood, Lord Allen."

The next time Sophie underwent a class promotion, she would become a three-star Spirit User, which would give her the ability to call forth spirits into the visible world. However, according to Spirit User Gatoluuga, the most powerful combatant in Rohzenheim, the spirits were fickle and thus very difficult to handle. The relationship between Spirit User and spirit was not one of absolute obedience, unlike that between Summoner and Summon. In fact, spirits were more powerful than Spirit Users, so it was more accurate to say that it was Spirit Users who were begging spirits for their aid.

Seeing that the conversation was about to wrap up, Cecil pointed at herself and asked, "What about me?"

"You don't have to do anything special for now. Something may or may not come up later. Either way, just focus on raising your level and skill levels as quickly as possible. We'll prioritize Keel when we see Intelligence-boosting gear, but once he's got everything, you'll be our next focus."

"Okay, that's fine by me."

"Last comes me. I very much want to reach Summoning Lvl. 8 by the end of this year. After all, there's no telling when war might break out again."

The Summons at Lvl. 7 had been incapable of hurting Rehzel. And after the Demonic Deity transformed, he simply pretended they were not even there.

"Allen, there's something that I've been wondering for a while: why're you always so hung up on the Demonic Deities?" Cecil asked.

"Oh, did I not mention this before? I get the impression that killing Demonic Deities is part of my goal."

"What do you mean?"

"When I kill a Demonic Deity, I level up right then and there, no matter how much more XP I need. Based on this, I'm thinking that Elmea *wants* me to kill more of them."

After Rehzel died, Allen had received a level up notification that did not mention the specific amount of XP that he had gained. He had only killed one Demonic Deity so far, but was quite sure that any successive ones would also level him up, regardless of XP amount.

"Did you just casually refer to the God of Creation by name?" Cecil stared at Allen in disbelief. Similarly, the rest of his companions also stared at him in shock for a brief moment.

Allen, ignoring them, continued, "Conversely, it's almost impossible for me to level up any further the normal way. That leaves me no choice but to prioritize earning skill XP."

At his current level, he needed so much XP to level up that it would take forever simply killing monsters. Killing Demonic Deities was practically his only way to level up any further. In order to make it easier to kill the next one that he encountered, he was now focusing on raising his class skill levels.

"So that's why you asked the Adventurer's Guild for magic stones again this morning."

"Yep. I heard that this city processes nearly as many magic stones as Dongbao. I'm gonna buy as many stones as I can, even if it raises their price on the market a little."

When the No-life Gamers had visited the Adventurer's Guild this morning, Allen had asked the staff how many Rank D magic stones he could request for at a time. The staff had replied that there was no upper limit, so Allen took out seven thousand gold, only for the staff to immediately backtrack and ask him to keep it to a thousand at a time. This was how Allen ended up making a request for a hundred thousand Rank D magic stones for a thousand gold this morning. The Guild had promised to have the order ready in five days.

"Um..."

"Allen, a moment."

Keel was about to say something, but Cecil talked over him, so he drew back and let her talk. The rest of the Gamers also looked like they wanted to say something but sensed that Cecil was probably going to say it for them, so they stayed quiet.

"Yeah, wassup?"

"We're all one party, right? I think it's about time we stopped splitting what we earn from the dungeons."

"What do you mean?" he asked. Allen had maintained the even split of loot this whole time because it was common sense for him to do so. It was the right thing to do both when dungeon crawling and monster hunting.

"We all understand that you need a ton of magic stones, and we know how much money that costs. So, let's use everything we earn in the dungeons to buy those magic stones."

Cecil went on to say that everyone in their party wanted different things, and it just so happened that the thing Allen wanted could be resolved with money.

"I like Cecil's idea!" Krena chimed in.

Allen looked at his friends' faces, and they all nodded back in turn. Seeing that, he bowed deeply and said, "Thank you very much, everyone. That would be a huge help."

After this touching display of friendship, the meeting ended, and the No-life Gamers dispersed to prepare for their very first foray into the Rank S dungeon tomorrow.

Chapter 8: Admiral Garara and His Crew

"All right, let's head out," Allen announced before turning to his friend—the one with an impressive appetite characteristic of pubescent boys. "C'mon, Dogora, you full yet?"

Dogora cast a glance at his plate, then nodded. "Yep."

After they had finished eating breakfast in a dining room devoid of both table and chairs, the No-life Gamers left their new home base. They were renting a prime property that was close to the Temple of Yanpany and large enough to house more than thirty people. The house that the party rented in Academy City had certainly been quite nice too, but this one here cost three times as much, with rent being thirty gold a month. According to the Real Estate Guild, the only listings that met Allen's three requirements—close to the temple, the Adventurer's Guild, and any shops necessary to everyday life—were large ones around the size of this property. When Allen saw the place for himself, he realized its size reflected just how large the parties coming to Yanpany to challenge the Rank S dungeon were.

Ten minutes of walking later, the Gamers reached the temple. It was packed with adventurers, so they lined up with the rest until it was their turn. They showed their invitation card to the same guard from yesterday, who let them through this time without comment.

The last time the Gamers were here, they had asked where the entrance to the Rank S dungeon was in this temple building. To alleviate the crowding, there were several rooms that served as points to send the numerous adventurers through to challenge the Rank S dungeon. Each and every room was spacious enough to comfortably hold far more people than just the No-life Gamers party.

The dungeon looks as crowded as ever. Well, the next floor is mainly just Rank B monsters, so even a party of all one-star classes with good equipment can still handle it no problem.

Allen had been told that there was currently no one in Ratash capable of stepping foot inside the Rank S dungeon; here, however, there were huge crowds of adventurers, with some sporting long ears that identified them as elves and others with short, stocky builds who were clearly dwarves. What's more, they were all wearing high-quality equipment made of either hihiirokane or adamantite.

Even someone with a one-star Talent, once partied up with some others with two- or three-star Talents, would have no trouble clearing five Rank A dungeons. If a country were to get serious about clearing its dungeons, this would likely be the party composition it would have its adventurers aim for.

Then again, if the party steps on a teleportation trap and gets scattered, they'd very likely wipe. So they'd definitely need a Scout to help them avoid those kinds of traps.

Because more than ten adventurers were heading into the Rank S teleportation room at a time, the line was moving at a swift pace. It was not long before it was the No-life Gamers' turn. They walked inside to find a familiar cube floating around eye level.

Huh, the same cubes? Do they control the dungeons on every continent?

"Greetings, No-life Gamers. I am Floor Operating System S108. Do you wish to travel to the next floor?"

It's even got the same robotic voice.

They were currently still on the first floor of the Tower of Tribulation.

"Yes, please," Allen replied on behalf of the group.

A split second later, the Gamers found themselves standing before an expansive grassy plain that stretched far as the eye could see. They were not alone, though; they could spot many groups of adventurers who had likely arrived ahead of them here and there in their vicinity.

"What the hell? Are we really inside a dungeon right now?!" Dogora exclaimed.

It's just as we heard at the Adventurer's Guild—everyone's on the same server. There were multiple entrances, but everyone gets sent to the same space regardless.

In the Academy City dungeons, parties were sent to their own instances whenever moving between floors. Allen called these instances "servers" in his head. In the Tower of Tribulation, however, it was clear that all the adventurers traveling from Floor 1 to 2 ended up on the same server.

"All right, guys, give me a minute to assess our situation." Allen sent out a Bird E and had it use Hawk Eye.

So this is an open plaza... And the other adventurers are being sent to empty spots around here.

The plaza was about a kilometer in radius, and the adventurer parties arriving after the Gamers were popping up in random locations here and there. Some of the parties who had arrived earlier had picnic sheets spread out on the ground and were eating or resting. Beyond the plaza was the vast grassland, on the other side of which lay a forest.

It's so spacious here. And not surprisingly, I can't see the ceiling. I'm gonna need some more time to confirm exactly how big this floor is. Hawkins, use Farsight.

By activating Bird E's Awakened Ability, which gave it the ability to perceive all visual information in sight within a hundred-kilometer radius, Allen confirmed that they were in a seemingly endless green space expanding out from their current location.

"Are you serious?! This floor looks even wider than the first floor! In fact, it's wider than the tower itself!"

Allen blurted out his thoughts in surprise, caught off guard by just how much bigger this space was compared to outside. Not only were there grasslands here; the plains were also framed by a luxuriant forest of towering trees.

No, that's not right. It's true that this is a massive area, but I see space being warped in places. The same power that prevented Hawkins from reaching the top of the dungeon tower is probably at work here. This is the Rank S dungeon, huh? Interesting.

"I heard you talking to yourself. Did you figure something out?"

"Oh, Cecil. You bet I did. Let's call everyone over."

Allen gathered his companions, who had spread out while he was occupied with his analysis. He then shared with them what he had just confirmed about the layout of the floor. When they had stopped by the Adventurer's Guild before to put in an order for magic stones, they had asked the staff member for information about Floor 2, and most of the intel they received turned out to be correct. Besides getting a handle on the situation, however, there was one more thing that Allen wanted to confirm.

"So, that there is what we're looking for, right?" Keel pointed at a cube floating in midair. Just that moment, a group of adventurers who had walked up to it just before disappeared.

"Probably," Allen agreed. He then led his party over to it.

Sensing the group's approach, the cube said, "Greetings, No-life Gamers. I am Floor Operating System S201. Do you wish to travel to the next floor? Or do you wish to return to Floor 1?"

Cecil frowned. "What's this? We can already go to the next floor?"

This is also just as we heard. In this dungeon, the cubes that take you to the next floor are pretty close by.

Allen recalled Hero Helmios telling him that the cubes for escaping were highly accessible in this dungeon and that therefore, getting out of the dungeon was extremely easy. S201 had indicated that it was capable of sending adventurers both ahead to the next floor and back to a previous floor. This was going to have a major effect on how long it would take to clear this dungeon.

As I'd thought, there must not be all that many floors here. It was

Floor 4 where Helmios gathered the gear that he equipped his party with, if I remember right.

"I'm kinda getting the feeling it wouldn't take us all that long to clear this dungeon!" Dogora chuckled.

Rank A dungeons were quite large inside and had complicated paths. Getting through just one floor took a significant amount of time. Based on what the group currently knew, the Rank S dungeon's layout seemed much, much simpler.

"Nah, I'm sure things aren't that easy." Allen shook his head. "But for now...Floor Operation System, please take us to the next floor."

"Floor 3 it is. Please present three bronze medals."

"We don't have any."

"Then, please gather three bronze medals."

Allen's conversation with the cube was cut short by the sudden approach of a group of around twenty dwarves.

"Yer late! Ye want me to leave ye behind?!"

"I-I'm sorry, Admiral! It's my head; you made me drink too much last night."

"Oho, so it's *my* fault, is it, Pepeku? And don't call me Admiral in th' dungeon!"

"Oh gods... Admiral, could you not make such a fuss?"

"Shut yer trap!"

At the head of the group was a middle-aged dwarf wearing a pirate hat and another dwarf earnestly apologizing to him. The former's voice carried so well that all the other adventurers in the vicinity looked over as well.

Meruru's eyes widened. She pointed and blurted out, "Admiral Garara?!"

"Huh?" The man in the pirate hat looked over. "Well, if it ain't Meruru! What're ye doin' in a place like this? And..."

As it turned out, Meruru and this dwarf knew each other. His eyes took on a doubtful glint, however, when he saw her among humans and elves, and he started walking over.

He's much more a pirate than an admiral, if you ask me. Both in appearance and attitude.

"These are my companions!" Meruru told Garara with a cheerful smile.

"What're ye sayin'? Ye know how valuable yer talent be, don't ye? Meruru, there's still space in me crew. Wanna join us?"

Apparently he was having trouble understanding why Meruru was in a party with humans. Despite Allen's group standing right there, Garara invited her to his party as if it were the most natural thing to do.

So, he's an "admiral." They use a different military ranking system in Baukis, right?

Apart from language, many things were the same all throughout this world, including currency and units of measurement such as for weight, length, capacity, and time. The differences between the original systems were not all that drastic to begin with, but there had been a conscious effort over the past few decades—ever since the Demon Lord began attacking—to standardize everything. Having the same units of measurement eliminated unnecessary confusion when sending supplies to the front lines, while having the same currency made negotiations and trading much simpler. The Five Continent Alliance had spearheaded this endeavor in order to streamline the war effort.

One standardization that Baukis resisted, however, was changing the names of their military ranks. They argued that they had no need for military aid in the fight against the Demon Lord, and so kept their historic titles of admiral, captain, commander, and so on.

If I remember right, admiral is equivalent to grand marshal, right? What's the top dog of the Baukisian navy doing here? Ah, does he love dungeon crawling like me?

Interrupting Allen's unrelated thoughts, Meruru responded clearly, "I 'preciate the offer, Admiral, but I'm gonna clear the dungeon with my friends here!"

Admiral Garara's companions—or more correctly, his subordinates—gave Meruru dumbstruck looks.

"What nonsense have ye lot been fillin' Meruru's head with?!"

Garara roared indignantly at Allen's group. "Did ye deceive her just t'make her join ye in challengin' this here dungeon?!"

Allen stepped forward. "We didn't trick her. And we're serious about clearing this dungeon." *What even is this conversation?*

"Did ye just talk back'ta me?! Ye got guts, boy, I'll give ye that. Ye wanna do this the hard way?"

In response to Garara's provocation, Dogora reached for the hilt of the greataxe on his back. Seeing this, the dwarves standing behind Garara wordlessly touched the magic discs hanging around their necks.

Fwum.

The magic discs shone with holographic geometric symbols that almost looked like characters.

Oh? Something's showing on the slates slotted into their magic discs.

The dwarves' reaction indicated that they had identified Dogora as an enemy. One who was standing farther back even barked, "Do you louts even know who we are?!"

"Don't know, don't care," Dogora growled. "Meruru is *our* companion. And we don't sell out our companions." He lowered his center of gravity, ready to lunge forward at a moment's notice.

I see Dogora's as hot-blooded as ever. Hmm, what should I do? It'd be a problem if getting into a fight here somehow affects our dungeoneering going forward.

Allen was racking his brains on how to resolve the situation when Garara sighed loudly. "Don't be risin' ta some brat's provocation, ye lot." He waved his raised hand, indicating that the exchange was over.

Uh, you're the one who provoked us first.

Seeing the dwarves let go of their magic discs, Allen ordered Dogora to let go of his weapon. The other boy studied the situation, then grunted in acknowledgment and slowly complied.

"So, ye th' party leader?" Garara asked Allen, likely having figured it out from the boy's words and attitude.

"Yes, I am."

"Well, if Meruru says she wants t' stay wi' ye, then she can do as she pleases. That said..."

"Yes?"

"If ye dare use Meruru as a shield and run away, I will find ye no matter which country ye hide in and make sure to end yer life. Ye hear me?"

Leaving the threat hanging in the air, Admiral Garara walked past the No-life Gamers and headed for the floating cube. The other dwarves followed behind.

"Gods, I told you not to kick up a fuss, Admiral."

"And I told ye t' shut it! Get th' medals out already. Why d' I hav'ta clear the blasted dungeon right after that godsforsaken war? Curse that greedy pig of an emper—"

The admiral's very audible grumbling was cut short by his subordinates lunging over and clapping their hands over his mouth in a fluster.

"Hurry! The medals!"

"What're ye lot doin'?! L-Leggo of me! I'll kill ye!"

They're carrying him like he's on a palanquin.

"Gods, Admiral, can you not say that kinda thing in public?"

"How many times have I told ye not t' call me Admir—"

The air suddenly went quiet as the entire group of dwarves disappeared in the blink of an eye. They had apparently been sent to the next floor.

I'm not sure what just happened, but never mind that. I'm more interested in those medals we just saw. Hmm, so that's what they look like. They were pretty big.

Allen had paid extra attention when one of the dwarves took out medals that they then gave to the cube. The medals had been about as large as the magic disc hanging from Meruru's neck.

"And that's how they're used, I see… Now, about being a shield… I guess it really has to be a shield."

"What are you mumbling to yourself, Allen?! More importantly, what was with those people just now?!"

With the dwarves gone, Cecil unleashed all the anger she had kept bottled up. As the rest of the Gamers joined in to express their anger,

Allen suddenly shouted out loud, "So Meruru was meant to be our tank after all!"

The girl in question looked bewildered. "Um, what's a 'tank'?"

"A *tank*, Meruru! Oh, I bet you've got potential to be a very good one after all!" Allen said before proceeding to explain.

Until now, the No-life Gamers had a big problem as a party: they did not have one member dedicated to defense. Instead, most of them had Talents that made them more suitable for staying in the middle or to the rear of the formation. Keel the Saint, Cecil the Archwizardess, and Sophie the Spirit Wizardess all had to stick to the back line. As a Bow Master, Volmaar's position was not all that far off from theirs either. And last but not least came Allen, a Summoner, who had to stay in the middle so as to provide support to both those in front of and behind him.

Dogora and Krena fought together as the vanguard, but they were better suited for dealing damage than blocking it. However, considering the powerful enemies that the party would be facing going forward—be it the monsters in the Rank S dungeon, the Demon Lord Army, or even Demonic Deities—the need for a dedicated tank would only grow.

This was why Allen had asked Dogora to wield a large adamantite shield, and the two frontline attackers had put in a lot of effort practicing how to protect the five people at their backs. And thinking back on it now, the reason Allen had given Meruru a spear and a shield back at Academy City was to increase the party's defense, even just by a little bit.

Against a truly powerful foe, such as a Demonic Deity, Krena and Dogora would have a hellacious time protecting everyone. Allen could help them out with the numerous Summons at his command, but even so, it would likely prove difficult to ensure everyone's safety.

When Garara warned him not to "use Meruru as a shield and run away," a certain thought had occurred to Allen. In short, if the party managed to gather all the parts to build a mithril golem in this dungeon, then the golem could be the one to take all of the enemy's hits when the party ever encountered another Demonic Deity. That way, the rest of the party members could be free to focus on dealing damage.

Allen perfectly understood just how much better everyone could perform their roles if they had a reliable tank: Cecil, Sophie, and Volmaar could focus on going all out with their most powerful attacks, while Keel could focus on healing anyone who needed it. The arrangement was not only for the sake of those in the back—it would free Dogora from having to carry a shield and allow him to throw himself completely into his attacks. This was obvious, but enemies only went down after taking damage. As such, the more attacks that the Gamers could pull off, the faster they would win, and therefore the higher their survivability. Lowering the time they needed to finish each fight meant increasing their efficiency.

"Um, Allen..." Cecil was so overwhelmed by how passionately Allen described the usefulness of a tank that she was left at a loss for words. She even found herself wondering if she was wrong to be angry at the earlier exchange.

"Now, then... Apparently Bronze Grade slates can be found on this floor, but I feel like we should probably start with Iron Grade at the very least. So for now, we'll just be focusing on gathering bronze medals. Is that okay with you, Meruru?"

"Yep!"

"All right, our top priority right now is to reach the next floor."

One of the things that the Gamers had learned back at the Adventurer's Guild was where each grade of slate could be found.

Golem Slate Drop List

- Bronze Grade slates: Floor 2
- Iron Grade slates: Floor 3
- Mithril Grade slates: Floor 4

Their ultimate goal was Mithril Grade slates, but Helmios had warned Allen about how powerful the monsters were on the fourth floor. Allen had talked it out with his friends before entering the dungeon and reached a consensus that they needed to complete an Iron Grade golem before heading to Floor 4.

"All right! Off we go to find three bronze medals, then head straight to the next floor!" Allen cried out and pumped his arm, brimming with motivation.

"Sounds good!" Krena replied with equal enthusiasm.

Now, what was it Helmios said about the medals?

After working together to take down Rehzel in Rohzenheim, Allen had squeezed all the information he could get out of Helmios about the Rank S dungeon. Thanks to this, the Gamers already knew that they needed medals to gain access to higher floors, and furthermore, that the number and type of medals required also differed for each floor.

"There are three ways of obtaining medals, right?" Allen asked half to confirm with himself.

Cecil nodded. "That's right."

Unlike Rank C to A dungeons, which only had a final boss at the final level, each floor in the Tower of Tribulation had multiple especially mighty monsters that the adventurers referred to as floor bosses. Defeating one of these bosses was a guaranteed way to obtain a medal.

Which Floor Bosses Drop Which Medals

- Floor bosses on Floor 2: Bronze medal
- Floor bosses on Floor 3: Iron medal
- Floor bosses on Floor 4: Mithril medal

The second way to obtain medals was from treasure chests. In addition to the weapons, equipment, and stat-boosting accessories one would normally expect, treasure chests in this dungeon also had a fifty percent chance of including a medal. The types of medals obtainable corresponded with the types bosses dropped based on floor number. There were a variety of ways to discover such treasure chests.

Last but not least, it was always possible to trade or purchase medals from other adventurers. The market price for a bronze medal was a hundred gold, and the Guild helped facilitate many such trades, given that bronze medals could be found on Floor 2, the lowest floor of the dungeon proper.

Allen had more than enough money to buy three bronze medals.

However, he had chosen to hold off for today, as he wanted to first see how long it would take to find them to handle it personally as opposed to going through the whole process of a trade.

"Griffs, come on out."

Not caring that he was in the middle of a large gathering of adventurers, Allen Summoned out everyone's Bird Bs. Nukakai had said that Summoning inside cities was a big no-no but had given permission to do so inside dungeons.

"Wha—?!"

All the surrounding adventurers were bowled over by the Summons' sudden appearance, with some even reaching for their weapons. However, no one attacked right away, either having sensed that the Summons were not hostile or holding back to see how others were reacting.

The No-life Gamers planned on remaining in this dungeon for the next year. It would be impossible to keep hiding the Summons from the rest of the adventurers, and attempting to do so might come across as even more suspicious. With this in mind, Allen decided to do it in broad view today, hoping that the other dungeon crawlers would grow accustomed to the sight. If anyone did attack, Allen planned on using Stone C's Ability, Substitute, which had proved effective enough to withstand a serious strike from the Hero.

Looks like no one's actually attacking, though.

Since no one was stopping them, the No-life Gamers mounted the Bird Bs and flew off.

All right, Hawkins. Use Farsight again.

The visual information gathered by the freshly Summoned Bird E rushed into Allen's head. He had heard before that, aside from the floor bosses, Rank B monsters primarily occupied this floor. As no one in his party had Analyze, there was no way to check the ranks of the monsters below based on their appearances alone.

Darn, I should've asked Helmios for descriptions of each floor's floor bosses too.

In the absence of any other clues, Allen decided to focus on monsters that were exceptionally large or were moving about on their own.

Hmm, there are quite a few species here that I've never seen before. Oh, hey! Is that one Rank A?

Upon spotting a sizable lizard-like creature he had never seen before, Allen shouted, "I think I've found a Rank A monster! It's that way!"

The group of Bird Bs swooped down, but just before they got close enough, a different group of adventurers began attacking the lizard. According to Farsight, they were doing so while staying just out of range of the creature's attacks, making it follow them a distance away to where another group—likely their companions—were lying in wait in a half circle formation.

The person who fired the first shot was probably their scout. Wow, beastkin sure move fast. Is that their top speed?

Allen gave up attacking this particular monster and had the Bird Bs stop in midair.

"What happened?" Meruru, who was riding with Allen today, peered over his shoulder.

"Some other adventurers got to it first. Let's find another one."

So we're going to be competing for the monsters. This sure brings me back. I had to do the same thing in the first MMO I ever played.

The common sense from Allen's previous life was that monsters belonged to whoever attacked first. This was an ironclad rule that was never to be broken. Anyone who did would be expelled from the hunting grounds and no one would party with them anymore. If they did it multiple times, their name would be blasted on the game forums, and they would be known by the entire player base all the way to the end of the game's service as someone who breached the most basic of online gaming dos and don'ts.

Although this was not an MMO, Allen still considered it basic manners to not attack a monster that someone else was already fighting unless the monster changed targets and came after him instead.

Once more, Allen had a Bird E use its Awakened Skill to look for a floor boss, making sure this time to confirm that it was not already someone else's target.

"Oh hey, this time I see a giant bird, and there's no one nearby. Maybe that's a floor boss too."

There were no other monsters within the range of Farsight that looked similar to the unbelievably large bird. Based on this, Allen suspected that there was only one of each kind of floor boss at any given moment.

Unfortunately, halfway to the bird, Allen had to stop the Griffs again.

"Why're we stopping *this* time?!" Cecil's cross voice could be heard from her Bird B at the rear.

"Sorry," Allen apologized. "The target disappeared."

By using Farsight again, Allen found the bird much farther away than before. There was no sign of the creature having used a teleport skill, which led him to the conclusion that floor bosses randomly respawned in a different location in the dungeon after a certain period of time.

"Huh? What does that mean?!"

Allen gathered his companions and shared his observations and hypotheses.

Sophie pulled a troubled face. "If a floor boss were to suddenly appear next to a group of adventurers, wouldn't it be very dangerous for them?"

This floor was extremely vast, so the chances of a floor boss reappearing right on top of a group of adventurers were quite unlikely. However, if they were already in the middle of fighting another floor boss or resting, the worst-case scenario just might involve the entire group getting massacred.

"It certainly wouldn't be pretty," Allen agreed. "According to Helmios, these floor bosses are anywhere between Rank A and Rank S."

This feature was likely at least partly responsible for why half of all adventurers who entered this dungeon died in their first year.

"What're we going to do?" Cecil asked. "We're not finding anything to fight."

"Tsk, tsk, what are you saying?" Allen wagged his finger. "Our hunt has only just begun. We'll still keep going, of course."

Now then, are there any other unique-looking mon— Oh, found one.

Looks like a red rhino beetle? Stag beetle? Either way, looks like it's gonna make contact with a party soon. We're not gonna lose this time!

Allen had spotted a creature that looked like a cross between rhino and stag beetles and was red all over. It was flying in lazy circles some ways up directly in the path of a group of adventurers who did not seem to have noticed it yet. According to Allen's rules, that meant the monster was still up for grabs.

"There's one close by, but it's gonna get taken soon. Let's hurry!"

"Wait, what?!" Cecil let out a shriek as the Bird B that she was riding accelerated all of a sudden. Despite this, Allen refused to slow down; he was not going to strike out for the third time in a row.

Dammit! At this rate, the adventurers are gonna beat us to it!

"Griffs, use Jet!"

"*Kieee!*"

The Bird Bs accelerated even faster, rushing toward the red beetle at breakneck speed. Unfortunately, once they were almost there, the monster changed its flight pattern and started heading for the adventurers of its own accord.

No! I refuse to give up! Or so I'd say, but distancewise, we're probably gonna lo— Huh?

Just as Allen thought he was going to let his prey slip away again, the group's Scout shouted something and the adventurers all promptly turned tail and ran away helter-skelter.

From the rear, Cecil shouted to be heard over the wind rushing past. "Allen, something doesn't seem right!!!"

The No-life Gamers had gotten close enough to see the red beetle in much greater detail. It had a large horn on its head, large jaws jutting out from underneath small eyes, and a long, wriggling tongue protruding from a mouth lined with jagged teeth.

"I can tell! We're charging in!" Allen shouted back.

All of the members of the party being chased were beastkin. Despite having lost all semblance of a formation, they were managing to stay ahead, albeit barely, seemingly thanks to their superior physical prowess.

Is that monster that strong? I see one of them's got an adamantite greatsword. This isn't some scrubby party with cheap equipment.

Suddenly, one of the beastkin, a catkin, tripped and fell flat on her face.

The red beetle immediately flew straight for her, making a hair-raising noise that sounded like "*Kishaa! Kishaa!*"

"Sara!" A wolfkin noticed the catkin falling and, despite hesitating for a split second, rushed back to help her. However, the monster was closer to her than he was.

"Uru, no! Run away!"

The moment the catkin screamed back at her companion was exactly when the No-life Gamers arrived on scene.

Allen barked, "Krena, Dogora, take the vanguard!"

Krena and Dogora acknowledged his command and, using the momentum from Jet, rushed past the wolfkin and smashed the beetle's face with their weapons.

"Wha— Who're you guys?!" the wolfkin asked, but there was no time to answer him. The monster bounced twice on the ground from the impact, making its disgusting "*Kishaa!*" noise, but it quickly regained its balance and spread its wings to hover in midair.

"Allen, it's super tough!" Krena reported.

"We did almost no damage to it," Dogora agreed. "What's its deal?!"

Even though we took it completely by surprise, we didn't manage to hurt it at all.

"Okay, seriously, who *are* you guys?!" the wolfkin shouted again.

"Um, it looked like you were in trouble, so we decided to jump in to help you out," Allen replied. "We'll handle this monster, so you all run."

Which is a lie, of course. We came because we want to kill this floor boss. If you fight with us, we'll have to figure out how to split the spoils, so please, get out of here.

"Do you even know what you're doing?! That's BB!"

"BB?" *Is it famous?*

"Its full name is Blood Blast Beetle. It's Rank S. You guys were really gonna fight it without knowing all that?"

So it really is a Rank S monster.

Each floor in this Rank S dungeon had several floor bosses, but there was one that was guaranteed to be Rank S. On Floor Two, that was BB here. Currently, BB was facing Allen's group, hovering motionlessly in the air.

During this time, the scattered beastkin had returned and assumed a protective formation around the fallen catkin as she treated her own wounded foot and got back up. She was likely this party's healer.

Having determined that BB was an enemy that required complete focus to face, Allen said to the wolfkin, "I'm sorry, but we want to concentrate on this fight. Would you mind leaving this to us?"

The wolfkin studied Allen's face, then nodded. "Okay. If we both make it out of here and live to see another day, I'll repay you somehow."

"Thanks. I'll make sure to come calling," Allen replied, figuring that framing this encounter as a transaction rather than charity would make it easier for the beastkin to leave.

"All right, we're getting outta here!" The wolfkin was about to turn around, but stopped. "By the way, what's your name?"

"Allen."

"See ya around, Allen. Name's Uru. By the way, if you didn't know, magic doesn't work on BB."

The catkin tugged on the wolfkin's sleeve. "Uru, come on."

Uru nodded. "You guys, we're outta here!" He turned around and ran off at top speed, his companions following close behind.

Oh damn, that is useful advice. On top of being ridiculously tough, it's immune to magic? Hmm, looks like its weapons are mainly the horn and jaws. Doesn't look like it has a poison stinger. Does it know how to use magic?

Allen wasted no time in observing the enemy closely and formulating ways to defeat it.

Everyone besides Meruru still has yet to raise their class skill to Lvl. 6, but in terms of pure stats, they should be a bit stronger now than when we fought Rehzel.

All the Gamers had skills that gave them stat buffs when their class skill reached Lvl. 3 and Lvl. 6. Although the fight with the white dragon had helped them level up a lot—except Allen and Meruru, of course—their class skills were not quite there yet. Even so, they were already a bit stronger now than when they fought the Demonic Deity in Rohzenheim.

"Krena, Dogora, those jaws look nasty. Keep your distance when attacking!"

"Okay!"

"Got it!"

As the two vanguards warily approached the monster, it lowered its head and charged forward as if to skewer them with its horn. The two dodged it flawlessly, even landing attacks as the boss sped past. Since they were both wielding two-handed weapons, they could attack while maintaining enough of a distance that they could get out of the way of any sudden attacks.

"Cecil, shoot a few fire spells at it!"

"Huh? But that guy said that magic doesn't work against it!"

"He did, but we should probably test it out instead of just taking him at his word."

"Very well. You've got it!"

Without further ado, Cecil shot a large fireball at BB. Having heard what Allen said to Cecil, Dogora and Krena dived to the sides with perfect timing; they did not even have to look back, as they had trained how to keep tabs on what was going on in the back lines. Thanks to them, BB could not see the spell until the last second and therefore shot straight into what ended up being a huge explosion.

"*Kashuu! Kashuu!*"

However, when BB reemerged from the flames, it remained entirely undamaged.

Hmm, bug-type monsters are supposed to be weak to fire. This confirms that it does *have extremely high magical resistance. Guess we'll have to stick with non-magical attacks.*

Since he now knew that Uru's advice was indeed true, Allen moved on to the next strategy. This was the same strategy that he had used ever since his Academy days. And thanks to participating in the war in Rohzenheim, the party now had much better teamwork.

"Krena and Dogora, be ready to use your Extra Skills at a moment's notice."

"Sure!"

"Got it!"

"Sophie, use the Blessing of the God of Spirits! Volmaar, use your Extra Skill to destroy one of BB's eyes!"

"Of course, Lord Allen."

"Understood."

"Cecil, stop BB from moving by barraging it with spells. Match my timing!"

"Very well!"

First, Sophie activated Blessing of the God of Spirits using all her MP, prompting Rohzen to do his hip-swinging dance. Shining bubbles fell on the No-life Gamers like rain, raising all their stats by thirty percent.

BB just happened to be retreating at that time. Seeing this, Allen seized the opportunity by Summoning several Stone Es and making them blow themselves up. As BB got slammed against the ground, a Dragon B appeared and bathed it with Hellfire of Fury.

How's that timing for you?!

"*Gagh...*"

The next moment, BB shot out of the flames and stabbed the Dora with its horn, reducing it to bubbles of light.

"Take this!"

Aiming for the moment when the Dragon B was disappearing, Cecil unleashed a giant icicle that slammed into BB. However, once again, the monster only bounced on the ground a few times but otherwise looked none the worse for wear. It quickly regained its balance and resumed hovering in midair.

"Mmph!"

Volmaar used his Extra Skill, Arrow of Light, but it was deflected by one of the beetle's large jaws.

"*Kishaa! Kishaa!*"

BB opened its jaws and mouth wide, revealing its fangs and tongue and making disgusting sounds. It then abruptly charged forward.

How about this?

A Stone B suddenly appeared in BB's way, holding out its large round shield. At the moment of impact, the Summon used Total Reflect, a counter move that dealt three times the damage received.

"Oh! We finally damaged it!"

The beetle's bloodred carapace now bore visible cracks that leaked purple fluid. Immediately, a heat haze sprang up around Krena's body as she activated Limit Break to follow up with more attacks that made the cracks grow steadily larger and larger.

"Good work, Krena! Now we're finally getting somewhere. Go for broke!"

"Yep!"

Krena was about to press her attack when BB suddenly grabbed Dogora with its massive jaws. Dogora struggled as hard as he could, but BB held him fast, shield and all. The beetle closed its jaws, trying to split the boy in half.

"Uh-oh! Krena, destroy one of the jaws to free Dogora!"

"Okay!"

Using Limit Break and one of her Sword King skills, Krena focused her attacks on one of BB's mandibles. Just in time, the jaw snapped, allowing Dogora to slip free. Apparently the attack that had worked against Rehzel after his transformation was also effective against BB.

"Dogora, you okay?!"

"Mm, all good."

Seeing Dogora bleeding from both arms, Keel rushed forward to cast Healing Magic.

Things would've been bad if Dogora hadn't been holding that large shield.

BB's carapace was now cracked all over and one of its jaws was completely bent out of shape. Thanks to Dogora holding on, however, Krena had been able to get in several good hits.

"Almost there, everyone! We're taking it down!" Allen shouted.

For some reason, BB headed for Stone B all of a sudden and, ignoring the fact that one of its jaws was bent, clamped them around the Summon. The next moment, its body started flashing.

"Wait, is it— It's using Energy Drain?!"

Allen caught on to what BB was doing almost immediately. He quickly reverted the Summon to card form, but it was too late. BB's giant jaw had already returned to normal and most of the cracks on its carapace were gone.

Aww, after all the effort we put into whittling down its health... So this monster can't use Healing Magic, but it does have a way to heal itself.

"What're we gonna do now, Allen?!" Cecil asked.

Allen nodded. "All right, looks like we don't have a choice. Everyone!"

"Yes?" Krena lifted her greatsword, eagerly awaiting Allen's command.

As everyone focused on Allen, waiting to see what strategy he would come up with in the face of this despair-inducing development, he announced in a loud voice, "We're running away!"

"Huh? O-Oh, very well." It took Cecil a moment to comprehend what Allen just said, but she quickly conceded right after.

Someone's gonna get hurt if we continue forcing ourselves to fight this monster.

And so, the No-life Gamers hopped onto their Bird Bs and flew away.

Chapter 9: Gathering Medals

When Allen saw that Blood Blast Beetle (BB) possessed a means to heal itself, he realized the chances of the No-life Gamers defeating it here and today were extremely slim, considering how hard it had been for them just to hurt it. Back when he played online games in his previous life, he had defeated many self-healing bosses like this through careful positioning and strategizing. However, he recalled that a single slipup in positioning often cost him greatly, and in cases where he had no way of interrupting the boss's healing ability, the price of victory often included numerous casualties.

The longer it took to make a judgment call on whether to stay or leave, the more danger his companions would be exposed to and the more recovery items they would end up wasting. This was why Allen had immediately called for a retreat. He considered quick decision-making to be an important duty of a party leader.

BB had high Endurance and was extremely fast, but the Bird Bs the No-life Gamers were riding had Jet, an Awakened Ability that boosted their already impressive speed by severalfold. The giant beetle chased them for some time, but once they were far away enough, the monster gave up the pursuit, allowing them all to heave a collective sigh of relief.

As everyone caught their breath, Allen called out another Bird E and had it act as a decoy by leading BB somewhere far away from other adventurers. Even after the No-life Gamers resumed searching out and killing floor bosses, he continued to study the red beetle through the eyes of that Summon, as he was particularly curious about how far away it could detect its targets from and how long before it would teleport after not making contact with anyone. Thanks to the infamy of this boss among the adventurers, no one actively sought it out, and therefore Allen had no worries of his observations being interrupted.

An hour after losing the No-life Gamers, Hawkins caught sight of BB disappearing.

As expected of a Rank S dungeon, throwing something like that *at us right off the bat.*

For the next half a day, the No-life Gamers dedicated themselves to killing the other floor bosses. Each one dropped a magic stone and a large bronze medal. The group now had three medals in their possession.

They had thought they would have come across treasure chests while wandering around, but for some reason, this had not been the case. Even Bird E, whose Awakened Ability enabled it to scout up to a hundred kilometers away in a split second, did not find anything. Of course, Farsight could not see through obstacles, so there was still the possibility that all the chests were obscured somewhere.

This place almost feels like a newly released zone in a game, what with how hard it was to get to fight the floor bosses and the distinct lack of treasure chests. I don't think we'll ever come back to Floor 2 to farm medals again.

Many of the online games Allen had played in his previous life would release new maps or areas every once in a while. Whenever this happened, the game's player base would balloon, sometimes to the point where there would be more players than mobs. This phenomenon seemed to be exactly what Allen was observing on Floor 2 here in the Tower of Tribulation.

"All right, let's leave this absolutely lousy floor behind and move on to the next," Allen said in a huff.

"You still goin' on about that?" Dogora asked Allen with a smirk.

"Of course. It's been a while since I had such a terrible experience."

"What d'ya mean by 'it's been a while'? This is your first time here."

Allen's group made their way to the cube that led to Floor 3, their hard-earned medals in hand.

"Greetings, No-life Gamers. I am Floor Operating System S201. Do you wish to travel to the next floor? Or do you wish to return to Floor 1?"

"Take us to Floor 3, please."

"Floor 3 it is. Please present three bronze medals."

"Here you go." Allen held out three bronze medals bearing depictions of a chicken, a lizard, and a third monster. As it turned out, the medals bore cutesy engravings of the floor bosses that dropped them.

"Three bronze medals received. Proceeding to send you to Floor 3."

The next moment, the ground beneath Allen's feet changed from dirt to sand.

Oh? This is Floor 3? Hmm, I don't see any prominent features nearby. Wait, the ground here is sand. Does that mean this floor is a desert? Is the visibility on this floor good like on the last one?

"There seem to be a lot of dwarves on this floor," Allen observed out loud. "Gimme a second to get a grasp of the land."

"Please and thank you." Due to Allen's influence, Cecil had also come to prioritize information gathering. She and the rest of the No-life Gamers checked out their surroundings as Allen sent a Bird E into the sky.

From the air, Allen confirmed that they had been teleported to an open plaza about a kilometer across, similar to the one on Floor 2. Beyond the plaza was an expansive desert of sand interrupted here and there by rock outcroppings large enough to be small mountains.

Multiple figures could be seen wandering about on the sand. They looked vaguely humanoid, but their heads were not held up by necks but appeared buried in the top of their torsos. Arms nearly long enough to graze the ground sprouted from their shoulders, and something crystalline was embedded in their abdomens.

Wait, those are golems! And there are quite a lot of them. They look a bit different from what I'd imagined, but that's nothing new. So, all of those crystals contain a dwarf that's piloting it, right?

The golems in this world had almost none of the mechanical vibe that came to mind when Allen heard "golem." At the end of the day, these were not so much robots as they were puppets. Their bodies gave off a metallic sheen and did not look all that angular. And although Allen had heard they were a hundred meters in height, almost all of the golems here were only about ten meters tall.

I can see how this floor is totally suited for golem pilots.

Floor 2 had a large forest and expansive grasslands, both of which were perfect environments for beastkin with their exceptional physical prowess that enabled them to move fast and maneuver deftly. Perhaps they even possessed abilities that helped them find treasure chests where Allen's group had failed.

Which reminds me, we've yet to meet Uru and his group again.

Uru had promised to pay Allen back, but Allen was not particularly interested in chasing this debt. There was nothing he wanted from adventurers who mainly stuck to Floor 2, and he highly doubted they knew any information that would be useful for clearing the dungeon. If he were to demand bronze medals from them, with these medals going for a hundred gold each on the market, there was no telling how many they would be willing to part with. In all honesty, Allen thought it unlikely he would ever meet them again, mainly because he was not interested enough in his reward to go look for them.

Allen was in the middle of these thoughts when he suddenly realized something. "Ohhh, so this is what Admiral Garara was referring to."

"What's happened, Allen?"

"Oh, hey, Cecil. Turns out this desert is actually really advantageous for dwarves."

Once his full party was gathered around him, Allen pointed toward what he had been looking at: a battle between a golem and a scorpion-like monster. While the golem was defending against the monster's attacks with its thick armor, the rest of the pilot's companions had encircled the scorpion and were attacking it from every angle.

"Apparently this desert has monsters that hide in the sand to ambush people. So it's the golem's job to take that first attack and protect the rest of the party." *Thanks to being so tough, golems are great for triggering surprise attacks.*

Whenever the scorpion tried to attack the surrounding adventurers instead, the golem used its bulky body and long arms to interfere. There was even a beastkin shooting arrows from atop the golem's shoulder. Its height both protected him from attacks and provided a great vantage point. It was truly killing two birds with one stone.

The admiral knew this is how things are on Floor 3.

"Meruru, we're gonna do our best and find you at least five slates."

"Thankees!"

I won't say this out loud since Meruru's here, but so many things in Baukis are huge rip-offs. Like, seriously, three thousand gold for an Iron Grade slate? Are you kidding me?!

A golem pilot had to slot slates into their magic disc in order to summon their golem. Each magic disc had ten depressions, but filling just five of them with slates representing the head, torso, left arm, right arm, and the legs was the bare minimum to complete a golem. These slates were, as a general rule, obtainable only inside the dungeon. The temple did sell them, but at a thousand gold for a Bronze Grade slate and three thousand gold for an Iron Grade slate, this was nothing short of price gouging. To buy a bare-bones set of Iron Grade slates would require fifteen thousand gold. Add on the fact that adventurers could sell any slates they did not need to the temple, who would purchase all Bronze Grade slates for a hundred gold and all Iron Grade for three hundred. This meant that regardless of the part or grade, the temple sold slates for ten times higher than they paid for them.

"Oh, look! There's a golem speeding through the sand." Allen now pointed toward a golem in the form of a ship with some adventures aboard that was swiftly parting the sands.

Meruru's eyes sparkled with both surprise and excitement. "So *cool!*"

So that's the effect of one of the movement slates.

Allen had heard about a few special slates from Meruru beforehand.

Types of Golem Slates

- The five basic slates that are absolutely necessary to summon a golem: head, torso, left arm, right arm, and legs.
- There are movement slates that transform golems into forms suitable for land, overwater, underwater, and air travel.
- There are special slates that give golems unique properties, such as being able to attack or defend while mid-motion or transformation.

There was a particular special slate Meruru had mentioned that particularly captured Allen's imagination.

No matter what it takes, we've definitely gotta find the slate that turns her golem into a friggin' house!

Supposedly, a golem house was perfect for spending the night and was as tough as a fortress.

"Things are starting to get exciting now! Let's go check how many medals we need to reach the next floor and then get to it!" Allen strode off with a skip in his step.

Hm, should we focus on gathering the five basic slates and then head right for the next floor? I wonder which floor would be the most efficient for everyone to level on. Oh, right, we gotta collect magic stones too. There's so much to do, I can't help getting excited! Is Dygragni a god?! Oh, right, he's not quite a god yet.

The Gamers still had many more class promotions to go, so they had to do their best to level up while gathering golem slates. And in order to continue putting in requests for Rank D magic stones at the Adventurer's Guild, they also had to earn at least one thousand gold every five days. Just thinking about the sheer number of things that had to be done made

Allen positively giddy. It seemed this Tower of Tribulation had quite a bit of replay value.

Allen gave thanks to Dygragni inside his heart as he led his friends in search for the cube. They found it very quickly as, just like on Floor 2, it was within the same plaza they had arrived in. Before checking out Floor 3, however, Allen wanted to confirm the conditions to reach Floor 4.

"Greetings, No-life Gamers. I am Floor Operating System S301. Do you wish to travel to the next floor? Or do you wish to return to Floor 1?"

"Huh?" *Wait a sec, are you serious?*

"What's wrong?" Krena looked at Allen, catching on to the surprise in his voice.

"Hold on. Let me confirm something."

"'Kay."

Allen turned back to the floating cube. "Excuse me. Can we not return to Floor 2?"

"My apologies. I can only send you to the next floor or Floor 1."

"You can't be— This means we're gonna need a ton of medals!" *What the heck? Is this Rank S dungeon a medal game?!*

The other Gamers finally caught on to what Allen was so surprised about. Every time they climbed a floor, they needed to give medals to the cube. If they returned to Floor 1, however, they would need to prepare the same number of medals again to make it back to the last floor they had reached.

"Well, for now, please tell us what we need to go to the next floor."

"Floor 4 it is. Please present four bronze medals and four iron medals."

Damn, we don't have a single medal on us right now. So we're gonna need bronze medals again for Floor 4?

"What is with that requirement?!" Cecil protested, recalling how the party had spent half an entire day gathering medals just the day before. "Does that mean we're going to need more and more medals?!"

The others in the party were dumbfounded at the realization that the higher the floor, the greater the quantity *and* quality of medals they would need. Here, too, Allen discovered why the Rank S dungeon was so difficult to clear.

Allen nodded thoughtfully. "It sounds like it. We are going to have to consider staying overnight in the dungeon, then."

"So it seems," Sophie agreed, putting a hand on her cheek with a frown.

The party had gone to the trouble of renting a house close to the dungeon, but apparently going home to sleep would cost them an unnecessary number of medals. They now looked at the other adventurers resting in the plaza with newfound comprehension, realizing they were probably there precisely because of this feature of the dungeon. There were probably many parties who were camping out for multiple nights at a time.

"Well, let's get started gathering medals while familiarizing ourselves with this floor."

Everyone hopped onto Bird Bs and took off into the sky under the astonished gazes of the other adventurers.

Hmm, there are quite a few adventurers all over the desert, but it's not overly crowded. That's good at least. Problem is, the only monsters I see are those already fighting with adventurers. Are the rest hiding under the sand? How can we find— Oh?

Through Bird E's eyes, Allen spotted a group of a few dozen people approaching a hill-sized craggy peak.

What are they looking at? Oh! There's a cave on the side of the mountain! Is something inside?

The adventurers began getting into formation in front of the large cave entrance. Two golems stepped forward, both with bowmen wearing light armor perched on their shoulders, as the rest stayed back a step. Allen could tell, even through his Summon's eyes, how keyed up they were for the upcoming fight.

Two beastkin who were likely scouts slowly entered the hole. When they ran back out, they were being chased by a stream of scorpion monsters. Just as Allen was wondering how so many scorpions could fit inside a mountain of this size, a particularly massive one came out and the fighting began. Thanks to being in proper formation, however, the adventurers managed to maintain the upper hand.

I see, so there are monsters hiding in the rocky caves as well as under the sand. Hold on, is it the same on Floor 2? I do remember seeing super huge trees every few kilometers.

On a whim, Allen ordered the Bird E he had left on Floor 2 to head toward the closest giant tree. Sure enough, there was a large hollow in the trunk. The Summon flew to another tree and found a hollow inside it too. Apparently this was a feature that all these trees shared.

Ahh, so that's where the treasure chests probably are. And monsters too, maybe? But the hollows are smaller than the caves, so maybe they only hold treasure chests. Either way, this is a major discovery!

"What's wrong?" Meruru asked, finding it strange how Allen seemed to have frozen after making the Bird Bs hover in midair.

"I think I've just figured out how to beat this floor."

Always ready with praise, Krena exclaimed, "Really?! That's amazing!"

"Let's head for that rocky mountain over there and test out my theory."

Allen led his party to a mountain with no adventurers nearby. Sure enough, it had a huge cave.

"Let's land here. Okay, guys, be careful. There might be monsters inside."

The group got into position, with Krena and Dogora at the head. When everyone was ready, Allen sent a Spirit B inside. "Huh? There's nothing in here."

"Aw, so these caves can be empty too?" Cecil sounded a bit disappointed.

Contrary to the party's expectations, Ellie soon reached the far end of the cave without finding anything. It really was just an empty cave.

"Guess there can be duds," Allen shrugged. "Well, let's try another mountain."

One round of Farsight alone caught sight of more than a hundred mountains in the desert. So, the No-life Gamers formed up in front of another mountain and sent a Spirit B inside. But alas, she did not find anything in this one either.

Another miss. Hmm, now that I know what they're doing, I realize there are a lot of adventurers aiming for these mountains like we are.

In fact, there were two main ways the other adventurers were handling this floor. One was to explore these mountains. The other was to wander around, hunting the monsters hiding under the sand. Allen determined the second way to be very inefficient for his party, as they did not have a golem with them, so he led the others to their third mountain.

This time, when Ellie reached the end, a magic circle made of geometrical shapes arranged like a language suddenly appeared, and scorpion-like monsters surged out from it with hair-raising cries of "*Kishaaa!*"

"Incoming!" Allen shouted, prompting his companions to brace themselves for battle.

The monsters charged out of the cave, and so the No-life Gamers dealt with them as previously planned, maintaining formation.

"Rah!" Krena brought her sword down upon the head of the first one, dashing it against the sand and making it burst with a splatter of bodily fluids.

<You have defeated 1 rock scorpion. You have earned 24,000 XP.>

Based on the amount of XP given, Allen announced, "It's a Rank B monster. Total riffraff." For the No-life Gamers, who had already killed millions of monsters during their time in Rohzenheim, Rank B monsters were not even a threat.

"Very well. Shall we clean them all up, then?"

"Yes please, Cecil. Go ham."

The scorpions went down one by one in quick succession. When the giant one thrust its massive pincers forward, Dogora blocked them with his shield with a grunt. He lowered his center of gravity and tried to stand firm, but he ended up being pushed back, drawing ruts in the sand with his feet.

"That one's probably Rank A. Hang in there, Dogora! Everyone else, hurry and finish off these trash mobs."

Rank A monsters were significantly more powerful than Rank Bs. In this situation, finishing off the weaker monsters first meant everyone could focus their attacks on the big one and would lead to the party taking less damage overall.

"Guys, seriously! Please hurry!" Dogora groaned as he struggled to pin down an opponent ten times his size.

At that moment, another scorpion the same size as the one Dogora was dealing with appeared from the cave.

"Krena, there's another one! Wait, huh?!"

"*KISHAAAAAAA!*"

Another scorpion even larger than those came out next, hissing ferociously. The tally now came to two large scorpions and one massive one.

"This one's probably a floor boss. Even so, guys, try not to use your Extra Skills if you can help it! Oh, but Dogora, feel free to use yours anytime."

"Yeah, yeah! Gee, thanks!"

The group had talked it out ahead of time and agreed that, because they were going through a Rank S dungeon, they would try to keep their Extra Skills available as much as possible. Extra Skills all had a cooldown time of a full day, and the party still had plenty of fights coming up later that day, possibly even ones with Rank S monsters. Dogora did not seem to appreciate Allen's last line, though.

As Krena rushed over to deal with the second large scorpion, Allen sent a Rock B out to the floor boss. It was taking Krena and Dogora all they had merely to keep their opponents occupied; they lacked the strength to end things alone without the usage of their Extra Skills.

Cecil, who had been systematically going through the various elements in her repertoire, announced to the group, "These scorpions are weak to Ice Magic." Just at that moment, a scorpion that had taken an icicle in its back curled up in blatant agony.

Oh? They have an element they're weak to? That's definitely helpful to know.

"Gotcha," Allen replied. "Focus on taking down the one that Krena's dealing with first, if you would. Sophie, can you try using water elemental Spirit Magic? Just to see if they're weak to water too."

"As you wish, Lord Allen."

When facing three opponents at least Rank A in strength, it made sense to strategically eliminate them one by one. Allen helped Dogora hold out as Sophie, Cecil, and Volmaar whittled down the health of Krena's scorpion.

Should I secure more Summon slots to deal with situations like this?

Allen could call out seventy Summons max. Of this number, he could really only use ten at the moment. He kept thirty Fish Bs, which buffed his MP, in his grimoire for the sake of earning skill XP. Another twenty slots were taken up by the Insect As and Dragon As still in Rohzenheim that were mopping up remnants of the Demon Lord Army. Around ten slots were split between the Spirit Bs that facilitated long-distance information sharing and the Beast Bs that were busy helping with Rodin Village's development. The Bird Es he was scouting with and the Bird Bs the party were traveling on counted toward the few remaining slots.

No, me holding back now leads to greater efficiency in the future. Don't give in to temptation, me.

Allen had made the conscious choice to not bring out as many Summons, hoping that this would become a growth opportunity for his companions. The No-life Gamers had cleared numerous dungeons during their time in Academy City and gotten much better at fighting while participating in the war in Rohzenheim. Their teamwork was far smoother now than ever before. However, there were no one-size-fits-all solutions on battlefields, and even a manner of fighting thought to be the most suitable imaginable could end up becoming useless after a class promotion. It was a learned skill being able to adapt a strategy that best suited the situation and the specs of those fighting.

In between casting Healing Magic, Keel told Allen, "It's getting tough keeping everyone's HP topped up by myself."

"I'm sure it's not easy being the healer," Allen replied, "but try thinking of this as practice."

During the war, the Gamers had used Blessings of Heaven like they were limitless resources, but they were now trying their best not to use any at all. Instead, it was Seeds of Magic—which restored 1,000 MP for all party members within fifty meters—that they were spamming, since Allen would be obtaining a large number of Rank D magic stones. Allen activated some himself periodically to ensure that Keel could keep casting his Healing Magic nonstop.

Before long, the two Rank A scorpions died.

<You have defeated 1 death scorpion. You have earned 200,000 XP.>

I lost two Mirrors during that, but they managed to leave quite a bit of damage on the boss.

"Good job taking down the two Rank As, guys! I've weakened the last one for you, so let's finish it off!"

Everyone focused their attacks on the massive scorpion who had appeared last. Allen had ordered his Stone Bs to use Total Reflect each time the scorpion launched a particularly powerful blow. It was not all that intelligent and never wised up to the fact that it should not be using big attacks, so this had happened three times. As a result, the monster's body bore cracks all over, and it was spurting bodily fluids.

"Uh, Allen, this big one isn't Rank S, is it?" Cecil asked worriedly.

"Nah, it's just upper Rank A," Allen asserted. He had known this even before the fighting began.

Seeing how sure Allen was, Cecil decided to take him at his word. "Well, it does look quite weakened. It's definitely no match for the red insect from yesterday."

The giant scorpion writhed as Krena and Dogora prioritized attacking where its armor was already cracked. At the same time, Sophie, Cecil, and Volmaar maintained a barrage from a distance, interfering with the monster's attempts to use its large pincers and massive barbed tail on the two vanguards.

Eventually, the floor boss collapsed on the patch of sand soaked with its own goo and stopped moving.

<You have defeated 1 death scorpion king. You have earned 4,000,000 XP.>

When the boss faded into glowing bubbles, it left behind a Rank A magic stone and an iron medal bearing a scorpion engraving. Just like the dungeons in Academy City, monsters in dungeons did not drop materials. Anyone who wanted to obtain materials from monsters would have to find them outside of a dungeon.

"The medal proves that really was a floor boss." Allen nodded in satisfaction.

"Oh?! Nice. Would never say no to two hundred gold coins!" Keel replied, rushing forward from the back to get a closer look.

Allen picked up the medal and said slowly, "So, this alone is worth two hundred gold, huh. Little wonder everyone tries to get into this dungeon."

If I converted all the medals we need to go to Floor 4 from Floor 3 to a monetary amount, it would be 1,200 gold coins total.

"I feel like my sense of money is getting skewed just by being here," Cecil sighed. "But then again, maybe it's already beyond saving after all the time I've spent with Allen."

"Are we gonna enter the cave?" Krena asked.

Allen shook his head. "There's nothing left in there." He had already sent Spirit B inside one more time after the scorpions stopped coming out.

"'Kay, then let's go to the next one!"

Even though she had just finished a fight, Krena was already raring to go. She gripped her greatsword tightly and pumped her other fist.

"We're going that way next." Always thinking ahead even during battle, Allen had already sent another Spirit B off to confirm their next target.

And so the No-life Gamers set off for another rocky mountain in search of more magic stones and medals.

Chapter 10: Memories of the Past

Three days had passed since the No-life Gamers first stepped foot inside the Rank S dungeon. Before leaving their house for the dungeon that morning, Allen had informed everyone that they would be staying inside for four days and three nights.

Monsters did not spawn in the open plaza where the adventurers arrived from different floors; due to this, many parties set up camp there, and the No-life Gamers had observed them to learn what they themselves would need to prepare. Of course, some parties lived inside golems that transformed into houses, so those had not been of much help to refer to. Yet.

The party swiftly worked their way through Floor 2 to reach Floor 3. Now that Allen knew that the rocky mountains were floor boss spawn points, he repeated the previous day's strategy of sending Summons to scout them out. Today, he also dispatched the Fish Bs that he had been keeping for their MP buffs along with the usual Spirit Bs. By having them swim through the sand toward the mountains, he learned that there were a large number of monsters lurking under the sand.

The Fish Bs, which looked like massive prehistoric sea turtles called Archelons, had high enough Endurance that they could simply ignore Rank B monsters. When it came to Rank As, however, they could not avoid taking a bit of damage—so Allen had ordered them to avoid all monsters wherever possible, and to keep an eye out for rocky mountains while taking care not to get themselves killed. Whenever their HP went down, Allen re-Summoned them close enough to Keel to heal them before sending them out again. This was the method that spent the least number of magic stones.

And so the Gamers spent the entire morning tearing through rocky mountains in their search for floor bosses. They found two treasure chests in the process, bringing their total loot pool to three iron medals and a sword and helmet made of hihiirokane. Throughout all this, they steadily collected Rank A and B magic stones from all the monsters they killed. The treasure chests were supposed to also hold golem slates, but unfortunately, the group had not yet been blessed with even one.

At the moment, they were resting and having lunch.

"Looks like this is a good place for leveling," Allen noted.

"It is," Cecil agreed. "Will we be staying here until we're ready for our next class promotion?"

"Probably a good idea. A month on this floor will probably be enough to max out everyone's levels. All right, break's over. Let's get back to looking for monsters and slates."

In a despondent voice, Meruru said, "I'm sorry you're all going to so much trouble just for me..."

Oh? She seems down all of a sudden.

Allen was having Meruru hold a large shield and stand guard in front of Cecil and Sophie in battle for now until the party gathered all the necessary slates. She did this with full confidence at first, but when she saw how much stronger everyone had become compared to when they were in Academy City, she started feeling guilty that she still could not use a golem. And when the group failed to find even a single slate in the morning, it made her even more uneasy.

"Nah, don't worry about it," Allen reassured her. "It's not like it's gonna take us months to gather all the slates."

We did find two chests in half a day. It's probably only a matter of time.

"But..."

"I know for a fact that you're full of potential that we're just not tapping into right now. We just have to look at other parties with golems to know how useful they are as tanks."

Everyone else voiced their agreement, having seen for themselves how other parties fought alongside golems.

Eventually, Meruru was appeased. "Thanks everybody."

"Still, Allen, you really do keep going on about 'tank' this, 'tank' that," Cecil commented. "Why're you so particular about it?"

"Hm? I'm not really, though," Allen replied reflexively. "I just, uh, know a little about how it works, that's all."

Sophie spoke up as well. "Now that you mention it, Cecil, I've thought so too."

Sensing everyone's eyes on him, Allen folded. "Well...it's not like I'm trying to hide it, but... Yeah, I used to be a tank in my previous life."

"So that's why you're so knowledgeable about being one." Cecil recalled how enthusiastically Allen had talked about the importance of this particular role. She had only ever seen him as a Summoner, so she somehow thought being a tank was similar to being a Summoner.

I didn't exactly choose to be a tank because I wanted to be one, but let's not talk about that.

"Pretty much," Allen replied. "So yeah, Meruru—I chose to be a Summoner, and what I've come to realize is that you never really know what a class is about until you actually try it. They all become fun eventually. And the longer you stick with it, the more you develop a sense of attachment to it."

The Summoner class in this world turned out to be quite different from what Allen expected, but he was wholeheartedly enjoying it now.

"Basically, what I wanna say is...don't let how things are right *now* get you down."

"I see."

"Wow, sounds really convincing coming from someone who's gone through it themselves." Cecil nodded appreciatively.

In his previous life as Kenichi, Allen had chosen a tank class back when he started his very first online game. At the time, he was not even aware of the concept of a tank. He chose the class simply because it looked strong, and aside from the facts that it had lower Attack but higher Endurance than other frontline classes and that it came with class skills to protect party members, he had thought nothing more of it. It was only after a whole year of playing that he learned that using these skills and serving as a party's shield was called "being a tank." He continued to serve this integral party role until the game's end of service, believing he had done the position justice. That was the first and last game where he mained as a tank.

And clearly, that position is needed here in this world too.

Kenichi's memories of the very first video game he fell in love with had greatly shaped his values and the rest of his life as a gamer. His desire to treasure those memories was a big reason why he had come to this world in search of a fulfilling experience in the first place.

"That said, Lord Allen, this 'tank' that you are talking about is more of a role, yes? Your class was called something else, was it not?"

Uh-oh.

"It...was."

"Hold on... Allen?" Cecil narrowed her eyes. The shifty way Allen answered Sophie just now had given her an overwhelming sense that something was off. She was sure beyond a doubt that he was hiding something.

"Hold on for...what?"

"Out with it. What was your class?" Cecil put down her spoon and leaned over.

Krena joined in. "What were you, Allen?"

"I...was an adventurer, of course." *I was on a grand adventure. What else could it have been?*

Allen's attempt to dodge the question earned him Cecil's divine punishment as she grabbed his face with her fingers in an iron vise.

"Eep! Why?! That hurts! Seriously!" *This is so unfair!*

"Are you going to answer or not?"

"Um, I wore armor...and I switched between using a spear and a sword. I also had a shield."

My nostalgic memories as Kenpy are coming back to meeeee...

The name that Kenichi assigned his tank character was "Kenpy." He was a student at the time and was struggling to come up with a cool name and ended up going with a version of his own name that he thought was cool. After playing under that name for a long time, however, he grew attached to it.

"Woooow! Is that a cool name?" Krena asked, pressing the matter.

"Oh, yes. It's very cool." Allen desperately wanted his friends to drop the topic, but they clearly did not share his sentiment.

Sophie cut in again. "You only told us what your equipment was, not what your class was."

C'mon, Sophie, I thought you of all people would be on my side!

The sight of Allen in Cecil's clutches had only compelled Sophie to comment, "I'm sure that's uncomfortable." Not a trace of her usual kindness was to be seen. Clearly, no one here was Allen's ally. Even though Cecil's iron grip was squeezing with the most force she could muster, everyone was just watching on with grins on their faces.

"Hold on, that actually hurts for real!" Allen was on the verge of tears.

"Well, speak."

"Y-Yes, m'lady! I used to be a Holy Knight!"

I chose it because I thought the class name and the equipment both seemed cool.

Krena shot to her feet. "Knight?! You used to be a *knight*, Allen?! That's incredible!"

"Wait, a knight?!" Dogora shouted in surprise. "Why didn't you tell us?!"

See?! I didn't want to say it because I knew Krena and Dogora would react like this! Now I have a misunderstanding to clear up.

Allen knew full well how much Krena and Dogora looked up to knights after growing up with them. This is why, during their time in the Academy, he had not mentioned Holy Knight when talking about any experience he had playing a large variety of classes.

"D-Don't misunderstand. That was just my class. Sure, I was called a knight, but my status was still just a commoner."

I was just a salaryman. Just your average corporate warrior.

"LIKE HELL YOU WERE!" Dogora roared with the most indignation he had ever expressed in all fourteen years of his life.

"Hold on, a cube! We've got a cube!" Allen shouted suddenly. One of the Summons that he had left searching while the party rested had found a floating cube inside a cave.

It's just as Helmios told me yesterday.

Last night, Allen had asked the Hero through the Spirit B he had left in Helmios's house in the Giamut capital about BB and other things related to the Tower of Tribulation that he did not yet know. Even though Helmios started with the caveat that he was not too knowledgeable about Floors 2 and 3 because his own party mainly stayed on Floor 4, he still ended up providing a lot of very useful information. One thing that he talked about was the hidden cubes in the dungeon.

Allen currently had Summons stationed in numerous locations all around the world besides Helmios's house: In Rohzenheim, this was in Tiamo, the city where the queen of the elves and the elven Elders were located. In Ratash, this was in the elven embassy in the capital. Of course, he also had the Granvelle mansion and Rodin Village covered. The main reason for leaving his Summons all over was to make it easy to exchange information and to get advance notice of any sudden movements by the Demon Lord Army, but in Rodin Village, the Summons also actively helped with the village's development and protected the villagers from monsters.

The safety and prosperity of his family were two of Allen's top priorities.

Additionally, there was always a Dragon B in the White Dragon Mountains that worked to keep the realms of Granvelle and Carnel free of monsters by feeding them to Haku, the newly reborn white dragon.

The whelp ate everything Dora brought back with a voracious appetite, growing larger and larger each day.

Without further ado, Allen shot to his feet and started clearing things away.

Dogora looked up in puzzlement. "Uh, what'd you say?"

"We found a cube in a cave in one of the rocky mountains," Allen replied, playing up the excitement in his voice. "Everyone, you're done resting, right? Let's go!"

"H-Hold on! We're not done talking!" Dogora shouted. "You gotta tell us more about your time as a knight! Starting with why you've kept mum about it!"

Pretending not to hear him, Allen brought out the Bird Bs and pushed everyone to get going as a way to dodge his companion's barrage of questions.

* * *

The No-life Gamers were zooming through the sky above the desert on their Bird Bs.

"You definitely have to tell all the details about you being a Holy Knight later on!" Cecil called out from a Bird B positioned behind Allen's. "And stop ignoring us!"

Allen, however, maintained his silence, hoping against hope that this storm would eventually pass.

Now then, a hidden cube! We sure are lucky, finding one the very next day after learning about them.

The party reached the mountain they were heading for and walked into the cave. Deep inside, they found a cube that looked similar to the one in the open plaza.

"Whew, we got here in time. Guys, I'm gonna try talking to it, so be on your guard. There's a chance it might teleport us somewhere."

Volmaar unshouldered his bow and clutched it tightly in front of his chest. "Mm, understood."

"All right, here goes." Allen warily addressed the cube. "Um, hello?"

"Greetings, No-life Gamers. I am Dungeon Reward Exchange System S302. Would you like to exchange medals and slates?"

So we got an exchange one and not a trap one.

"Exchange, is it? Excuse me, would you mind if we ask a few questions first?"

"Go ahead."

In response to Allen's questions, the cube explained that it served to exchange medals for slates. It could trade both ways at a ratio of three medals to one slate, but it could only be used once and it only handled iron medals and Iron Grade slates. For the medal-to-slate trade, it would be giving out a basic slate—one for a golem head, torso, left arm, right arm, or legs—chosen at random.

Aw, so this one won't give special slates.

Yesterday, Allen had learned from Helmios that each floor had many different hidden cubes. Just like floor bosses, they teleported after a certain time, reappearing in caves on Floor 3 and tree hollows on Floor 2, among other locations. There were many types, such as ones that exchanged medals and slates, ones that gave out medals or slates for free, and ones that teleported parties to places separate from the normal dungeon floors such as bonus stages—and death stages.

Some of the cubes' medals-to-slates exchange gave not just basic slates but also movement ones and special ones that, for example, made a golem much larger or strengthened its armor. In some cases, the cube would demand more than ten medals for a slate.

The troublesome thing with these cubes was that some of them would immediately teleport the entire party when someone talked to them, with there being a chance that the party would find themselves surrounded by a large number of monsters in what was aptly called a "death stage." If all the monsters were Rank A, the adventurer party would very likely be massacred. This was one more reason why the death rate was so high in this dungeon. Therefore, it was common sense among the adventurers here that those who were not strong enough should never talk to these cubes.

Allen took out three medals from Storage without hesitation. "I'd like to exchange these, please."

I totally can't wait to see Meruru's golem!

Even though it had taken the party half a day of running around to gather these three medals, no one said anything. Ever since their Academy days, they fully understood that Allen was always doing what was best for the party and for them.

"Confirmed. Here you go."

The medals in Allen's hand disappeared and were replaced by a basic slate. The slate had a protrusion the same size as one of the holes in Meruru's magic disc. On the opposite side of the protrusion was a depiction of a golem head.

"So this is a head slate. Now we have the first one. Four to go." Allen handed the slate to Meruru. "Sorry if you end up getting dupes of the head."

Though for stuff like this, you almost always end up getting dupes over and over when you're waiting for the very last piece.

"Th-Thank you." Meruru accepted the slate as tears welled up in her eyes.

"Try putting it in."

"O-Okay." When she slid the slate into the slot, Meruru's face lit up with delight. "Whoa..."

"Come to think of it, Allen's always been like this," Cecil said thoughtfully. "I guess it makes sense that he used to be a Holy Knight—I'm sure it's because he has a big heart. Ahhh, so when he did *that* then, it was because he was a Holy Knight..." Apparently Cecil was applying Allen's being a former Holy Knight to past events in this world and connecting dots in her head.

Understanding dawned on Keel's face as well. "I see, that explains why he seems so used to talking to royalty and nobility."

Seeing everyone else nodding in agreement, Allen thought, *Uh-oh, the misunderstanding is getting worse.* By this point, it was really hard for him to explain that he only chose the class because he thought it sounded cool. He turned to the floating cube just in time to see it fade away starting from its edges.

Oh, it simply disappears when its job is done. All right, moving on.

"Let's head to the next rocky mountain, everyone. This one's got a treasure chest! We've gotta nab it before it's gone."

At any given moment, Allen always had multiple Summons out and about, checking the caves of rocky mountains. This enabled them to know exactly where to go, giving them a significant advantage over other adventurer parties and greatly shortening their time exploring.

"I knew you were special, Lord Allen." Sophie, the party's cheerleader so to speak, clasped both hands before her chest and appeared deeply moved.

I wish you'd help resolve this misunderstanding instead, honestly.

The No-life Gamers remounted their Bird Bs. After traveling for a while, one of the visions that Allen was Sharing with a Summon abruptly changed.

"Huh? Wait, is this the sky? Is Genbu in the air right now?"

"What's wrong, Allen?" Meruru asked as Allen made all the Bird Bs stop.

"Wait, again?!" Cecil protested from behind.

"No, it's something else. Something's got Genbu. I saw something long, red for a split second. I think it's Scarlet. Let's go check it out."

"Wait, Scarlet is the Rank S boss for this floor, right?" Cecil asked incredulously. "Are you sure it's safe?"

It was only yesterday that the No-life Gamers had fled from BB, another Rank S monster.

"If we can't handle it, we can just run away again. For now, let's go see what it's like. C'mon guys, it's close!"

It's not like there's a hard rule that says we can't beat Rank S monsters.

Everyone looked nervous as they set a course for what seemed likely to be a coming fight with a Rank S monster. Not too long after, they spotted a towering form that made for quite the eye-catching landmark.

Damn, Genbu's line of sight is almost a hundred meters in the air.

Fish B was rather heavy, even among Allen's Summons. Despite that, its ten-meters-long form was now being lifted that high up by the steely jaws of a creature protruding from the sand.

"Allen, everyone's running away!"

The adventurers below all had their backs to the giant creature as they employed various methods to flee as quickly as possible. Not a single one of them showed any intention of fighting the monster.

"Yep, they're definitely running away from that thing."

The monster that the No-life Gamers were approaching looked like a worm that measured hundreds of meters in length. All the visible parts of its body were scarlet, and sharp thorns protruded from its body segments.

"Oh, Genbu got done in," Allen commented as a shower of glowing bubbles burst in the monster's mouth and faded away. "Hmm, so that's Scarlet Sandworm, the strongest monster on this floor. It's huge. Good, good! Now this is exciting!" His chest thumped with excitement at the sight of the most massive monster he had ever beheld.

We'll have to watch out for the thorns on Scarlet's body, of course, but is its only method of attack its fanged mouth?

"A-Allen, what're you saying? This is way too much for us to handle!" Meruru's voice was filled with fear as she stared up at the overwhelming mass of the Rank S monster.

"No enemy is ever too much for us to handle!" Allen replied.

The group flew in closer until they could see Scarlet's body in greater detail. The top end was all one big mouth, the inside of which was densely packed with disordered rows of teeth. This was what it had used to hold Genbu so tightly just now.

"Getting caught in that mouth is clearly bad news, guys. We're gonna be using Jet now, so hold tight! Krena and Dogora, fly in circles around it while attacking its body. Stay away from the mouth; we'll be the ones to attack it!"

"Got it! Let's go, Griff!" Krena gave her mount a few gentle pats on the head.

After acknowledging the command with a sharp "*Kiehhhh!*" the Bird B accelerated. It flew around and around Scarlet as Krena unleashed her most powerful attacks on the sandworm.

"All right, that leaves the head for us. Cecil, I'll be counting on you to figure out its weak element again. I'll let you know when to use your Extra Skill."

Allen had always stressed that timing was crucial for making the most of Extra Skills.

For now, let's bring everyone back.

Allen called back all of the Summons that were out investigating rocky mountains. Even if they had gone far away, since Allen was Sharing with them, he could Unsummon them at will. Scarlet's size indicated that it likely had a huge HP pool, so Allen was hoping to have his entire party attack it all at once to whittle down its health within a short period of time.

"Allen, it recovers right away!" Krena reported back.

"It really does!" Dogora confirmed. "What's with this guy?! Our attacks aren't working at all!"

The boss monster's body was healing itself almost as soon as Krena's blade passed through. The same was happening with Dogora's axe.

"Got it!" Allen replied. "Looks like your attacks are at least hurting it, so keep at it. And I'm gonna keep saying this again and again, but don't let Scarlet catch you!"

This is strange—it's almost like this boss monster doesn't have any Endurance at all. Is its regenerative ability there to make up for it?

Krena's and Dogora's attacks revealed that Scarlet had unbelievably low Endurance for a Rank S monster, but its healing powers were so effective that all wounds it suffered seemed to simply disappear in the blink of an eye. Even when showered in attacks by the entire No-life Gamers party, all of whom were close to max level, the boss didn't seem to care or and be weakening at all.

"I find it hard to believe, Allen, but I don't think Scarlet has any elemental resistances at all!"

So it doesn't just have low physical resistance but magical as well?

"Thanks for letting me know, Cecil. In all likelihood, it doesn't have resistances to any type of damage. Its Endurance is also super low. It's the kind of monster that relies on its massive HP pool and very high recovery powers. You don't get these often!"

"Instead of being impressed, how about having a strategy?!"

"I have one. Krena, use Limit Break! Everyone aside from Cecil and Sophie, match Krena's timing and use your Extra Skills too!"

"Okay!" Krena activated Limit Break, then had her mount use Jet to bring her close so she could begin slashing away at the boss, carving away even more blood and flesh than before and drawing out more of the monster's healing fluids.

The rest of the No-life Gamers promptly joined the fray. Allen also went all out, invoking Spirit Bs and Dragon Bs and having them use their Awakened Abilities before quickly changing them out, not caring how many magic stones he burned through.

Okay, good—looks like the pace we're dealing damage to it has finally surpassed how fast Scarlet can heal itself. We're almost there.

In this previous life, Allen had fought plenty of enemies that could heal themselves. He had learned that the only way to defeat them was to damage them faster than they could regenerate.

"Cecil, use Petit Meteor. Crush its head!"

"Very well. As you wish!"

When the moment seemed right, Allen gave Cecil the green light. A heat haze sprung up around her body as she activated her Extra Skill.

"Krena, Dogora, get away! Petit Meteor incoming!" Allen barked out a warning.

"Okay!" Krena shouted back.

Dogora also grunted, though half out of frustration at once again failing to activate his own Extra Skill.

"Here I go! Petit Meteooor!"

The moment the two vanguards fell back, a burning red boulder around ten meters across appeared in the sky. For some reason, even though this was the inside of a dungeon, the meteor was able to come down without destroying the ceiling. Scarlet had reared itself up like a cobra, allowing the meteor to score a clean hit on its head. The clash of the two gargantuan masses generated a shock wave as meteor fragments and bubbling bodily fluids scattered everywhere. The now headless monster carcass collapsed with a deafening boom, raising a huge cloud of dust and sand.

"We did it!" Cecil cheered.

However, no message appeared in the log on Allen's grimoire.

Damn, so it didn't die instantly. That means it might heal itself back up.

"No, not yet. It isn't entirely dead," Allen corrected. "Sophie, please use Blessing of the God of Spirits."

"Understood. Lord Rohzen, please lend us your strength."

"Ha ha, sure thing."

On top of buffing the party's stats, the Blessing of the God of Spirits also had the effect of refreshing the cooldown timers of everyone's Extra Skills.

To the No-life Gamers' dismay, Scarlet's body spasmed a few times, then the wounds that had covered it suddenly all healed as more bodily fluids spurted everywhere. Scarlet even managed to grow a brand-new head. The sight filled Cecil, who had until now had immense confidence in her Extra Skill after the role it played in the fight with Rehzel, with despair.

"Don't worry, guys. The fight isn't over!" Allen called out reassuringly. "We've just returned to square one, that's all."

Thus the fight against the giant, grotesque-looking worm resumed.

About half an hour later, however, Allen admitted, "I'm afraid we just don't have the firepower to take Scarlet down."

"It...seems like it," Cecil reluctantly agreed.

Unlike BB, they could hurt Scarlet. However, it always healed itself faster than the No-life Gamers could damage it. Even after the entire party—everyone except Dogora, of course—activated their Extra Skills again, they failed to fully wipe out the monster's HP. They had continued fighting in the faint hope that the boss's recovery speed might eventually flag, but it never happened. Even now, it stood before them looking unscathed.

"In order to kill Scarlet, we need to get stronger. I think that's enough for this attempt."

"Very well. Pity." Cecil stopped attacking with a regretful face, and the entire party retreated.

Scarlet's movement speed was not all that impressive. Once the No-life Gamers got far enough away, it gave up pursuing them and dived headfirst into the sand.

The No-life Gamers' first encounter with the Rank S floor boss of Floor 3, Scarlet Sandworm, thus ended with their retreat.

Chapter 11: Joining Up with the Hero's Party

Keel shifted uncomfortably under Allen's gaze. "C-C'mon, don't glare at me, man. This is good, right? Now we've got all the slates."

"Who's glaring? I'm not glaring," Allen replied.

"Good for you, Meruru," Cecil said. "Now you can call forth your golem."

"R-Right." Meruru nodded awkwardly as the hidden cube next to the party faded away.

The No-life Gamers were currently in one of the rocky mountain caves on Floor 3. During the roughly twenty days that had passed since their fight with Scarlet, they had been hard at work scouring the caves for monsters, treasure chests, and hidden cubes in search of golem slates. Although they had managed to find slates for the head, torso, left arm, and legs earlier on, the right arm slate had continued to elude them until now. No matter how many treasure chests they opened, no matter how often they traded with hidden cubes, they only ever got parts they already had.

Allen, who had been the one opening all the chests and talking to all the cubes so far, had started to fret about never pulling the right arm slate. Seeing this, Keel had come forward and said he wanted to give it a try. And the result of him talking to the hidden cube they had just found was the current situation.

God frickin' dammit!!! This always happens! It always takes absolute ages whenever I'm the one trying to gather a full set of something.

Even in his previous life, whenever Allen did anything that required luck, such as gathering a full set of armor or upgrading a weapon to max, it always took ages for the conditions to finally line up for him. Apparently that curse of his was still alive and well in this world.

In an attempt to buoy Allen's gloomy mood, Sophie changed the subject. "What should we do now? We finally have all the slates, but we can't very well keep Lord Helmios waiting..."

It was almost the time when the party had agreed to meet up with Helmios. The festivities in Giamut celebrating his victory over the Demon Lord Army had finished, so he would finally be coming to Yanpany.

Wow, it's already been two months since we last met in person.

"I suppose you're right," Allen said grudgingly. "It *is* almost time for lunch. Let's call it a day for now, and we can check out Meruru's golem the next time we enter the dungeon. Is that okay with you, Meruru?"

"Sure, okay! Thanks a bunch, everybody!" Meruru could barely control how happy she was about gathering all the slates she needed in only twenty days. After accepting the last one from Keel and fitting it into her magic disc, she hugged it tightly and burst into tears.

"Wha— No, no, no, don't cry!" Keel said in a fluster, trying to assuage her.

Geometric shapes floated up from the magic disc in Meruru's embrace, seemingly responding to her heightened emotions.

Oh! So it lights up when you put in all the slates.

"Aw, Meruru, you okay? Are you hungry? I'm also— *Myuuuh!*"

Krena was about to ruin Meruru's touching moment by making it about her appetite, so Allen punished her by kneading her cheeks before he led the party out of the cave and to the open plaza. From there they returned to Floor 1.

It had been a while since the No-life Gamers last saw Floor 1. Of course, it was not as if they had stayed on Floor 3 the entire time since

they fought Scarlet twenty days prior. Because the size of the Storage page in Allen's grimoire was limited, the party ended up with a little more gear to carry after every treasure chest they opened. As such, they had to periodically sell off any hihiirokane and mithril equipment that they were lugging along. Furthermore, Allen had to register a new request at the Adventurer's Guild every five days to purchase another hundred thousand Rank D magic stones for a thousand gold. After that, he also needed time to convert all those magic stones into Seeds of Magic.

Consequently, the party had agreed to stay in the dungeon for three and a half days out of every five days. That meant camping inside for three nights and keeping the remaining day and a half for rest outside. Allen sorted through their luggage during this off time and did his trading with the Adventurer's Guild. The rest of the party spent their time however they wanted, including helping harvest the Seeds of Magic from the small indoor farm Allen had set up in his room, heading out into town, just chilling out in their rooms, and so on.

Every time they returned to Floor 1, Meruru would insist on drinking that night, so it had become custom for them to hit up a nearby restaurant. Perhaps it was due to having walked around in a desert for three days straight, but Meruru gulped down alcohol like it was water every time; the rest of the Gamers were convinced by now that dwarves would die if they did not have alcohol.

Just in case, Allen did keep bottles of alcohol in his Storage. However, Meruru was expected to act as a member of the Gamers during her time in the dungeon, and that included abstaining. In Allen's mind, real gamers should know to always stay sober so they could immediately react to the situation, no matter what happened.

"Phew, we're finally back." Cecil stretched. When she noticed the direction Allen was walking in, however, she asked in a puzzled voice, "Hold on, Allen, aren't we meeting up with Helmios at the Adventurer's Guild?"

Allen held up an adamantite bow that was too big to fit in Storage. "We picked up a lot of stuff from treasure chests this time, so I was thinking of dropping it off back home first."

After walking for ten minutes, the No-life Gamers approached their home and were greeted by a very unexpected sight.

"Hey there! Are you guys just now getting back from the dungeon? You're a bit late."

"Huh? Uh…what's going on here?"

We were supposed to meet Helmios at the Adventurer's Guild later in the afternoon today. I thought it'd be a good idea to meet up, since we'd both be frequenting the dungeon from now on… But what's that got to do with the Hero moving a whole bunch of luggage into our base?!

There standing in front of the No-life Gamers' base with a friendly smile on his face was none other than Hero Helmios. Behind him, dwarven movers were busily going in and out of the base. There were even a few adventurers with familiar faces among them helping out and giving instructions. Allen recognized these as Helmios's party members.

One woman who had been directing all the movers noticed Allen's group and came over. Seeing the dumbfounded expressions on their faces, she asked, "Wait a minute, Helmios, did you not ask permission for this?"

"Aha ha, I thought it'd make for a fun surprise," the Hero answered, not looking sorry in the least.

When Allen's brain had rebooted after blue-screening, he asked, "Um…are you going to live here too, Mr. Helmios?"

"Yep! Well, it's not so much *me* as it is *my party*, Sacred. What do you say?"

The adventurers in the back started gathering around Helmios. Allen's eyes fell on the woman with an exposed midriff who looked to be a Scout or a Thief. There was little doubt she was the one who had opened the door to the base.

I see. And here I was, thinking we had locked up properly. Wait, Mr. Dverg's here too.

The Hero had around ten companions. Aside from Sword Lord Dverg and Sword Lord Sylvia, the female thief and the rest were clearly all powerful in their own right. They now watched the exchange between Helmios and Allen with guilty looks in their eyes. Their expressions

indicated that this was not the first time they had been roped into playing along with Helmios's bad ideas.

Looks like I don't have a choice... You know what? I'll just charge him more for rent, then.

Instead of asking them to leave, Allen replied, "I see. How about we talk it over while the movers do their work?" Just like Krena, he was also feeling hungry.

Helmios smiled. "Sure thing. I'll introduce you to a place—I highly recommend it. Let's bring everyone along!" He turned to his party and told them to get ready for a night out.

Similarly, Allen explained the situation to his party and led them into the underground storage room to put down their latest loot.

Leaving the movers with servants most likely working for Helmios, the two parties followed Helmios out to a major avenue.

"Here we are. This is the place."

Seeing where Helmios was pointing, Meruru clutched both fists to her chest and cheered, "WHOAAAA! YAY!" She was almost more excited than when she got the last slate for her golem.

The establishment Helmios had brought them to was famous for its delicious alcohol, and the sounds of dwarves merrymaking could always be heard spilling out through its doors. The No-life Gamers passed by it often, as it was close to their base, and every time, Meruru would freeze and get drawn inside as if being pulled by a powerful magnetic force.

"Ah, I see." *Turns out it was a place we already frequent.*

Allen followed Helmios inside while doing the adult thing and making a face that could be interpreted both as this being his first time here *and* him already being familiar with the place.

"Welcome!" the store owner shouted in a lively voice.

Like always, it's packed full with dwarves. And the fact that they're drinking here means they're all powerful enough to make a living off of the Rank S dungeon.

As this tavern was close to the Temple of Yanpany, most of its customers were adventurers farming the Rank S dungeon. These were the elite of the elite who brought back not just hundreds but thousands of gold coins every time they ventured back out safely. Conversely, adventurers frequenting the Rank C to A dungeons surrounding the Tower of Tribulation mainly stayed in the outer edges and rarely came this close to the city center.

Allen's group was much bigger than usual today, so it was hard to find seats. While an employee hurried off to secure a table, Allen looked around the tavern. This was when he noticed a dwarf wearing a pirate hat standing on top of a table and performing a cobra twist on someone who was likely his subordinate.

Ah, Admiral Garara's here again.

Apparently the admiral and his party of around twenty were taking the day off and had come here to drink as well.

"Wait, isn't that the black-headed guy?"

"Looks like it."

Hm? What's going on?

Moving only his eyes, Allen spotted a pair of beastkin at a table close to the entrance.

"Let's go tell Prince Zeu."

"Mm, let's."

After whispering among themselves, the two paid for their meal and left the pub. Soon after that, the employee from earlier returned and led Allen's group to a table. Only after they sat down did Helmios finally notice Garara's party.

"Huh? If it isn't Admiral Garara!" he exclaimed.

"Who said that?" Hearing his name, Garara turned around and his eyes lit up. "Well I'll be! It do be th' esteemed champeen o' th' Central Continent hi'self! Men, I be fixin' to give me regards." He jumped down from his table and came over, a wooden tankard in hand and a few subordinates in tow.

"You two are acquainted?" Allen asked Helmios.

"Yep." Helmios nodded. "He comes to this dungeon often too, so we share information sometimes. We also see each other at the Five Continent Alliance summits."

"I see." *So they have opportunities to see each other outside the context of being adventurers.*

Allen shot Meruru a look and found her busy rattling off a list of orders to a dwarven waitress. She did not seem to have noticed the admiral's approach.

Awww, even though the first time we saw him, she was all like, "He's my senior officer! He took real good care of me in the navy!"

Sitting on the table was Rohzen, who had descended from his perch on Sophie's shoulder and was glaring at the menu parchment with his arms crossed, muttering, "Maybe this?" and "No, maybe *this*?" under his breath.

You're still going to choose fukaman in the end like you always do, aren't you? We've already got a ton of freshly baked ones in Storage.

Fukaman was a delicious, chewy steamed bun very popular in Baukis. Rohzen had gotten so hooked on them lately that he even made Allen put a whole batch inside Storage.

When Garara reached Allen's table, he downed the contents of his tankard in one swig and addressed Helmios. "Th' champeen o' th' Central Continent has already returned t' tha dungeon? Ye sure be workin' hard!"

Allen was reminded of an episode in his previous life when he had been nursing a glass of oolong tea at a drinking party and thinking about the computer game waiting for him at home when the middle-aged man sitting next to him suddenly began talking his ear off and went on and on.

"I can say the same for you, Admiral Garara. Are you already hitting the dungeon?"

"Aye, ye bet! Th' war's already o'er an' all. I been told it be 'bout time I cleared th' damn thing."

"I see." The smile on Helmios's face gave way to a serious expression when he heard Garara say the word "clear," but it was back to his usual grin in no time. He cast a glance at the admiral's table. "That explains your group. So Baukis is getting serious about *clearing* the dungeon."

"Pretty much. Looks like th' beastkin are too, so I been warned not t' let them get th' better o' us. Try bein' in me shoes, servin' that greedy emperor o' our— What be y— *Mmfgh!*"

A few dwarves sitting at the admiral's table dashed over with incredible speed, covered his mouth, pinned his arms behind his back, and carried him back.

"Mr. Helmios, how can you tell that Baukis is getting serious?" Allen asked.

"Hm? Oh. Everyone at that table over there is a Talos General. Except for Admiral Garara, that is."

Seriously? So Baukis has gathered all of its strongest assets and is going all in, then. Guess they really are getting serious.

During the past twenty days, Allen had asked Meruru about Garara's Talent. All twenty dwarves at Garara's table were Talos Generals, a Talent said to be one in ten million. And leading them all was Garara, the most powerful golem pilot of Baukis and the country's one and only Talos King.

"Awww, that sounds fun. Brings me back," Allen murmured as memories of his previous life flashed by.

"Oh? Besides Holy Knight, did you also use to be a golem pilot?! Wait—why?! *Mmmfgh!*"

In an attempt to stop Cecil from saying anything else unnecessary, Allen swiftly clapped a hand over her mouth and smiled politely. "Sorry, please ignore what she said. Oh, look, our food has come. Let's eat!"

Back when Allen was Kenichi, he basically focused solely on leveling his characters efficiently and min-maxed all their stats. However, that did not mean he never tried other play styles. For example, he had experience playing as a mage character and joining a gathering of only mages to go run a dungeon; they were all basically glass cannons with paper armor trying their best to wipe out the enemies before the enemies got to them. In short, they had formed an utterly unbalanced group on purpose. The term for this was "memebuilding."

When Allen heard that Garara's party was composed of only golem pilots, he thought it sounded as extreme as memebuilding. Of course, golems could both tank and dish out damage, so this was probably a pretty effective party setup, actually.

"I was just thinking that a party of nothing but golem pilots sounds interesting," Allen mused before changing the subject. "By the way, what is the composition of your party like, Mr. Helmios?"

"Hmm… This time, our priority isn't really to clear the dungeon but to level up and gather equipment. So, we'll be sticking to Floor 4. Your party is aiming for the clear, right, Allen?"

"That is what we're here for, yes. I guess that means we'll be sharing a base but won't actually meet each other all that much inside the dungeon."

"Yep, seems like it."

Even though Helmios's group had made themselves at home with no prior notice, Allen had no intention of chasing them out. The place was large enough to house around thirty people anyway, so he was thinking he might as well let them stay and make them pay a portion of the rent based on the number of people they had. Naturally, he would also count the servants who had stayed behind to help the movers.

In the first place, management of the base was something that was gradually becoming an issue for Allen and his friends. They wanted to focus their attention on the dungeon, but that meant there was no one to take care of the base. And whenever they came out after spending back-to-back-to-back days in the dungeon, they wanted to rest, not do chores.

Well, I don't see any problem with letting them stay with us, as long as we don't talk about my previous life or my class's abilities. Hmm, so Helmios isn't gonna try clearing the dungeon despite how stacked his current party is. Should I try probing a bit more?

"With how strong all your party members seem, I automatically assumed you had come here to clear it."

"No, no, no. This dungeon is hard enough even for a party like mine. Oh, I'd forgotten. Let me introduce everyone."

According to Helmios's introduction, Sacred was a party of ten, with everyone aside from Helmios having three-star classes:

- Hero Helmios
- Sword Lord Sylvia
- Sword Lord Dverg
- Holy Knight × 1
- Saintess × 2
- Archwizardess × 2
- Bow Lord × 1
- Phantom Thief × 1

They're all women except for Mr. Dverg. I think there were a few men among the servants, but that's it. And they only have one Holy Knight. Do people in this world also know the "only one tank per party" rule?

Allen introduced all the members of the No-life Gamers as he reminisced about his time as a Holy Knight.

In the majority of online games, there was a limit for each class when forming parties. In the case of the MMO that Kenichi used to play, it was generally accepted that a party only had at most one Holy Knight. This was because although the class was great as a tank that could cast buffs, it had lower damage output than other classes and its buffs were not stackable. As such, there was no benefit to having two or more of them in the same party.

After Allen finished introducing his friends, Dverg, who had stayed silent all this while, opened his mouth. "Krena is now a Sword King? So, the rumor about changing classes really is true?"

Allen nodded. "Yes, it is."

"Dverg—" Helmios was about to warn his companion, but Dverg ignored him.

Instead, the man stood up and bowed deeply toward the squirrel stuffing his cheeks with fukaman. "Lord Rohzen, O God of the Spirits."

"Hm? What is it?"

"I came to beseech you to grant me a class promotion too."

"Hm." Rohzen raised a paw to his chin and crossed his legs, adopting a thinking expression.

I knew it. Anyone who hears that it's possible to get stronger through class promotions is going to want one of their own. Makes sense.

"I heard that it should be possible if I pay the price."

"And what is it that you are willing to pay me, Dverg? Ha ha."

"I only need one year more on this earth. You can have everything else. Would that suffice?"

Dverg's earnest tone threw everyone else besides Allen and Helmios into disarray.

"Hold on!" Cecil exclaimed. "Allen, aren't you going to stop him?!"

However, Allen held up a hand, asking her to wait. He wanted to give Dverg the time to have this conversation with the God of Spirits.

"Sword Lord Dverg."

"Yes, my lord."

"Lord Elmea, the God of Creation, told me about how you gave up everything to fight the demons and Demonic Deities. He is deeply impressed with your way of life."

"Thank you, my lord. Does that mean…?"

"I'm not finished."

"My apologies."

"When I promised to give Allen's party class promotions, I did so at my own discretion. As a result, things are a bit…*chaotic* in the Heavenly Realm at the moment. The deities are quite big on equality, you see. So, wait a while."

"You want me to wait, my lord?"

"That's right. Let's just say that the Heavenly Realm is working on something related to class promotions. I hope you're satisfied with that answer. That's why I'm here. Since it *is* something that I started. Ha ha."

"I understand. I shall be patient."

"Ha ha."

Dverg sat back down and lifted his tankard to his mouth. He kept his eyes closed as his shoulders quivered a few times. Perhaps the knowledge that he might finally gain more power had struck something deep inside him. On the other hand, Rohzen had gone back to stuffing his face with fukaman.

I see, so there's a reason why Rohzen's accompanying Sophie. Knowing him, he probably won't tell us what it is, of course.

Allen looked at Meruru and found her basically pouring alcohol down her throat. Worrying that that was going a bit too far, he was about to admonish her when the door to the tavern banged open.

"This the place?"

"Y-Yes, Your Highness. This is the place."

A lion beastkin towering nearly two meters high strode in, followed by other beastkin. His mane swayed a little as he swiftly made his way to the center of the establishment.

Wait, I recognize the wolf guy behind the lion dude. Isn't he the one we saved from BB on Floor 2? His name's Uru, if I remember correctly.

"So, who here is Allen?"

"That one, Your Highness."

Upon being asked, Uru immediately pointed at Allen.

"Him?"

The lion beastkin turned, looked into Allen's eyes, and immediately started walking over.

Allen maintained their eye contact. *What? You wanna fight? Wanna go outside?*

When the lion beastkin reached Allen's table, Helmios looked up and greeted him. "Greetings, Beast Prince Zeu of Albahal, the Country of Beastkin. It's been a while."

The lion beastkin looked down at Helmios. "Hm? The champion of the Central Continent? I had heard they sent you to the front lines. Is the war over?"

Oh wow, so this is the prince of the Beastkin nation?

"The Alliance was victorious in the war, yes. Is His Majesty the Beast King in good health?"

Despite the Beast Prince's haughty attitude, Helmios maintained the smile on his face.

"Hah! He won't die even if he's killed. He hasn't changed a lick since the time he made you kneel before the emperor of Giamut."

Huh? The Beast King made Helmios kneel?

"I am glad to hear it."

Zeu gave Helmios one last look, snorted, then turned to Allen. "So, you're the one who saved my brethren? I see, so you are a companion of the champion of the Central Continent."

Allen nodded. "If you're referring to twenty days ago, then yes, that was me."

"I heard BB attacked you instead. Well done getting away from it."

Purposely choosing not to indicate how hard or easy it was, Allen simply said, "Thank you, sir. So, how may I help you?"

"I've come to pay you back for saving my brethren. What do you wish for?"

Oh? Because I saved some adventurers, a prince has now come to reward me?

Allen recalled seeing a pair of beastkin in this restaurant whispering among themselves when he walked in earlier. Despite being haughty and violent, perhaps the royalty of the Country of Beastkin had a strong sense of duty.

"Well..." Allen gave it serious thought.

"Speak."

"I'm sorry, I can't think of anything on the spot. Can I bank it as a favor?"

Uru's eyes widened indignantly. "Wha— How dare you speak to His Majesty that way?!"

"Interesting. You want a favor from me?"

"To be entirely honest, I didn't even know there's a member of royalty in town. Since you're offering me a reward, I hope I can ask you for help when I really need it in the future. My party is aiming to clear the dungeon, so it might come in handy."

"You're clearing the dungeon? So Giamut is finally moving to clear the Tower of Tribulation?" Zeu turned to Helmios with much sharper eyes than before.

The Hero shook his head in denial. "Nope, his party has nothing to do with mine."

"Hmph. No matter. Allen, come find me when something comes to mind. Simply ask any passing beastkin and they'll lead you to me. Helmios, another time."

"Of course, Beast Prince," the Hero replied. "Conversely, should you ever need anything, feel free to ask us. We're in the same boat, after all."

What does them being in the same boat mean?

"Hmph." Beast Prince Zeu snorted one last time before exiting the restaurant. The other beastkin in the room also got up and followed him out. Allen thought they were leaving with him, but it turned out they were merely seeing him off.

Ignoring the ruckus outside, Cecil looked at Allen with narrowed eyes. "You really never get nervous talking to royalty, no matter the country."

"I mean, it's not like I have to offer my allegiance to royalty from some other country, right?"

"You don't have to offer your allegiance, but at least offer respect," Keel retorted. The memory of the party's audience with the king of Ratash flashed through his mind, prompting him to add, "Though it didn't exactly look like you offered allegiance to the king of your own country either."

As soon as Zeu was gone, Krena and Dogora resumed gobbling down their food. Helmios's companions looked on with wide eyes, murmuring about how the No-life Gamers were just as they had heard. Allen also resumed his meal while wondering to himself just what Helmios had said about them.

"So, what was that about making you kneel? It almost sounds like you lost to the Beast King."

"It was the year before I had that match with you. During the Five Continent Alliance summit, the conversation somehow led to me having to fight him."

"What? You fought a king?"

"Yep. And he pretty much wiped the floor with me too. Oh, you have no idea how embarrassing it was." Helmios guffawed while recounting the story of how he had lost.

Apparently the Giamutan emperor had claimed that, because of

Helmios's continuous victories against the Demon Lord Army, he should be called "champion of the world." Of course, a country extolling its champion was the same as glorifying itself, so all countries did it. This time, however, two major powers objected: Baukis and Albahal. They both insisted that Helmios was only "champion of the Central Continent" at most.

"Because we have Admiral Garara in Baukis," the Baukisian emperor had argued.

"Because we have mineself," the Beast King had rebutted.

Unable to back down, the Giamutan emperor replied, "If you doubt that Helmios has the strength to be called 'champion of the world,' then you can test him yourself." This was how Helmios ended up having to fight the Beast King in front of all the leaders of the Five Continent Alliance nations.

"You lost that badly?"

"Like you wouldn't believe!" Helmios laughed. "It was essentially a one-sided beating. And after that, I even got scolded by my emperor for not being strong enough. So unreasonable, right?"

"I'm sorry to hear it," Allen replied while thinking about why Helmios lost.

This doesn't make sense. Royalty should only have a one-star Talent at best. How did the Hero lose? Hold on. Is the rule that royalty only get one-star Talents applicable only to humans?

Allen thought he had both gotten closer to and further from a principle of this world at the same time. It was a very strange feeling.

"So in short, the Beast King's strength is specialized for fighting against people."

"You can say that. I mean, I don't say this as an excuse, but he was so fast my eyes honestly couldn't keep up."

So, his greatest strength is his speed. Being faster than the Hero is no joke.

"What does this all mean, Allen?" Cecil asked.

"In all likelihood, the Beast King's Status is exceptionally well suited for hand-to-hand combat, with an emphasis on speed," Allen replied. "In contrast, Mr. Helmios's Status is probably pretty even across the board. He lost because he couldn't land his attacks on the Beast King."

No matter the world, it's common sense that the Hero is a balanced fighter who's a jack-of-all-trades. Hmm, the fact that even Baukis protested means Admiral Garara is likely at least as strong as Helmios. That probably takes his golem into account, but even so, there's a definite reason he's known as the strongest in Baukis.

"Yep, that's pretty much it." Helmios nodded.

Everyone else at the table was focused on Allen as he thoughtfully listened to Helmios's account. All of them knew what Allen had done during the war in Rohzenheim several months ago. Some looked at Allen with wary eyes, feeling threatened by the fact that he had achieved so much despite being a whole generation younger than the Hero.

"What is the meaning of the last thing you said to Beast King Zeu? You offered him your help, but it sounded like you were referring to something bigger."

"Oh, that. Hmm…"

Seeing Helmios's hesitation, Allen added, "If you can't tell me, I won't press it, of course."

Is it tied to Giamutan politics?

"No, that's not… Well, you've been a huge help to me, and seeing how many Ratashians there are in your party, I should probably tell you this. Problem is, I'm not very good at drawing the line between what I'm supposed to say and what I'm supposed to keep secret."

Sword Lord Sylvia cut in. "You should probably tell Allen. I'm sure he'll help out."

I haven't promised anything, though. How can she sound so sure?

"Well, all right then." Helmios sighed. "If the current Beast King is dethroned, there is talk that the Country of Beastkin would invade the Central Continent."

Allen choked on his food. "Wait, what?! Mr. Helmios, what're you saying?! What about the Five Continent Alliance?!"

"As things stand, it's probably Beast Crown Prince Beku who'd succeed the throne. If he does, Albahal will definitely withdraw from the

Alliance. And they'll probably attack at the same time the Demon Lord Army does."

"Wh-Why?! Why would they do that?!" Cecil's voice caught in her throat. When she looked at Helmios and his companions, however, she found all of them with a straight face.

The gears were turning furiously in Allen's head as he asked, "They never mentioned this in our classes at the Academy, but has Albahal ever attacked the Central Continent before?"

"Not since the Demon Lord Army appeared," Helmios replied, "but yes, a few times since Albahal became independent more than a thousand years ago."

Long ago, the beastkin had suffered severe persecution at the hands of Giamut. The grudge from back then had not faded a shade, even after a millennium. The beastkin were ready to attack at the drop of a hat should their king call for it.

Understanding dawned on Allen's face. "That's why you mentioned us being Ratashian."

"Huh?" Cecil, who did not quite get it yet, frowned. "How's that relevant?"

Helmios nodded. "That's right. If the Country of Beastkin attacks in earnest, they'll probably eat up the entire southern third of the Central Continent. Especially if they attacked at the same time as the Demon Lord Army."

Ohhhh, so that's why Giamut has allowed small countries like Ratash to continue existing right next door.

Allen finally got the answer for something that he had been wondering about for years.

"What did you understand, Allen?! Tell me!"

"In all likelihood, for the past thousand years, Giamut has been keeping Ratash as a wall to protect its own citizens in case of an invasion by Albahal."

The Empire of Giamut occupied the northern two-thirds of the Central Continent. The remaining one-third in the south was composed of a bunch of small countries that the beastkin would have to go through first to reach Giamut, one of which was Ratash. During the time the beastkin were occupied with these countries, Giamut would mobilize its own forces to protect its own border.

"So, Mr. Helmios, are you saying that this can be avoided if Beast Prince Zeu is the one who takes the throne next?"

"Yep. That's why Giamut wants it to be him. There are voices calling for it to be the War Princess too, but either way, the point is that things should be fine as long as it isn't Beast Crown Prince Beku."

He did come to thank me for saving his brethren even though I'm human.

"Who's the War Princess?"

"Word is that the youngest child of the current Beast King, the Beast Princess, has an outstanding personality and is gifted in battle. I've never met her before, though. Speaking of which, I haven't heard anything about her recently."

Apparently even the Hero could not tread far into Albahalan affairs so easily.

In short, this world isn't made up of countries all at peace, holding hands as friends and all that. Though I guess it shouldn't be a surprise, what with the history between the elves and dark elves.

Allen thought back to Demonic Deity Rehzel, who had been a dark elf. As it turned out, this world under threat by a Demon Lord was quite a lot more chaotic than he had known.

Chapter 12: Golem, Come Forth!

Allen had just learned about the bad blood between the Country of Beastkin and the Central Continent and of how the millions-strong population of beastkin had actually attacked multiple times in the past. They might have currently been part of the Five Continent Alliance, but they remained a lurking threat to the Central Continent. Allen suspected this was why, of the two southern continents, the Demon Lord Army had never attacked the one where the beastkin lived. Naturally, Allen had come to prefer that Beast Prince Zeu, who seemed open to being on friendly terms with the Central Continent, become the next Beast King. Allen very much wanted to talk things out with him, given the opportunity, and find a path toward resolution.

The way Allen saw it, there was plenty that could be done before the worst-case scenario came to pass. However, if Albahal really became dead set on attacking the southern Central Continent, then Allen was ready to become a Demon Lord himself—whatever he had to in order to protect the village and country where his family lived, even if it meant wiping out every last beastkin in existence. When the words "no matter how much blood is spilled" left his lips, the members of Sacred—who were well aware that his party had killed most of the ten million monsters in the Demon Lord Army—gasped in shock.

Helmios, however, merely chuckled. "Well, let's make sure it doesn't come to that, then."

The rest of the dinner with Helmios's group went by without any further mishaps. On their way back home afterward, Helmios asked Allen how frequently the No-life Gamers were going into the dungeon. Apparently he wanted to match his party's schedule to theirs.

The new home base had three floors, so it was decided that, just like it had been at Academy City, that the second floor would be the guys' floor and the third floor would be for the ladies. However, because Helmios's party bordered on being an outright harem, the third floor did not have enough rooms for everyone. Consequently, some of the girls had to stay on the second floor.

As he had said before, Helmios's party would be mainly sticking to Floor 4. Their focus would be on raising Helmios's levels and skills while keeping an eye out for valuable weapons and armors.

* * *

"All right, it's finally time! Meruru, show us your golem!"

"O-Okay."

The No-life Gamers were currently in the plaza on Floor 3. This was a safe area where monsters would not spawn, making it perfect for Meruru to experiment with her new golem.

She held her magic disc in front of her with both hands, making its surface shine with geometric shapes.

"Whoa, your magic disc's gone all crazy!" Keel instinctively clutched his staff, startled at the sight. "I-Is that supposed to happen?"

When the glow reached a climax, Meruru took a deep breath and shouted, "Tam-Tam, come forth!"

In response, a giant magic circle appeared above the sand before her, and a massive metallic form measuring ten meters high leaped out headfirst. The rest of the Gamers stared up at the towering form with wide eyes, sighing with wonder.

"This is incredible," Cecil said breathlessly. "How do you move it?"

"I get in it!" Meruru replied.

Dwarven golems did not move by themselves. Instead, pilots had to board them and control them from inside.

When Meruru held her magic disc up to her golem, a ray of light projected from the crystal in the golem's chest toward Meruru and her disc. The beam lifted them up and sucked them into the crystal.

Dogora whistled softly. "Woooow... How does that even wo—Damn, it moved!"

The golem proceeded to walk and jog around, throwing punches. Once it finished going through all the fundamental motions for fighting monsters, Meruru reemerged.

"That was sooo *cooooool!*" Krena gushed, prompting Meruru to chuckle and scratch the back of her head bashfully.

"I see, so that's what a golem can do." Allen examined Meruru's magic disc, looking it over closely. He flipped it over from the side with ten impressions and found displayed on the disc's smooth back surface the golem's specs.

Name: Tam-Tam
Pilot: Meruru
Rank: Iron Grade
HP: 1,500 + 900
MP: 1,500 + 900
Attack: 1,500 + 900
Endurance: 1,500 + 900
Agility: 1,500
Intelligence: 1,500
Luck: 1,500

Tam-Tam's Status did not show up in Allen's Grimoire even though it could be seen on the back of Meruru's magic disc. This fact, when considered along with how Helmios could see the numerical values of the No-life Gamers' Statuses, proved that there were definitely skills and items in this world that enabled users to see Statuses in actual numbers.

The buffs are probably from Meruru's Alloy skill. Hm, so the golem's affected by its pilot's skills. And if Alloy's currently giving the golem +900 in everything, that'll probably become +1,800 when it reaches Lvl. 2.

"Wanna try putting in an enhancement slate too?"

"I thought you'd never ask!"

While they were trying to gather basic slates, the group also picked up three additional slates the same size as the basic ones that were part of the enhancement category. After the five basic slate slots, Meruru's magic disc still had five slots available, so it was possible to go all out and fill them with enhancement slates—but there were other special slates, such as Gigantify, that were sized differently. Meruru would have to take all this into account when thinking about how to best utilize all ten slots on her disc.

Slate Sizes

- Basic slate: 1
- Enhancement slate: 1
- Gigantify slate: 2
- Supergigantify slate: 3
- Movement slate: 3
- Special slate (other): 5

The three enhancement slates the Gamers had on hand improved HP, Attack, and Agility. When Meruru slid them into her magic disc, the respective stats all jumped up by +2,000. Apparently all enhancement slates for iron golems buffed for the same amount, regardless of the stat.

I guess if we want to make Meruru's golem more tanky, we should keep an eye out for HP and Endurance enhancement slates. Luckily there's at least a little bit of wiggle room to experiment. I'm just happy that Meruru can finally resume leveling her skills up again.

"All right, Meruru. Wanna try taking your golem into a real fight?"

"You bet!"

The party mounted their Bird Bs and headed to the nearest rocky mountain with an active cave. Everyone readied themselves before the cave entrance as a Spirit B went inside and drew out a flood of scorpion monsters.

Meruru stepped up, drawing in front of Krena and Dogora.

"MEGATON PUUUNCH!" she shouted, using the name that Allen had taught her as she activated her Flying Arm skill. Her golem held out its balled fists that then promptly shot out with such speed and force that they squashed the scorpions to a pulp.

I see, so the fists are still connected to the body with cables. I guess "Megaton Punch" was the right call after all.

The skill's actual name was "Flying Arm," so Allen had been torn between renaming it "Megaton Punch" or "Rocket Punch." Of course, "Iron Punch" had been eliminated from the get-go; that name would quickly become obsolete since the party had every intention of improving Meruru's golem to Mithril Grade on the next floor. As it turned out, the arms did not fully detach, so "Megaton Punch" had proven correct in the end.

When the monsters were all wiped out, the party took a moment to catch their breath.

"You did great, Meruru," Cecil praised her. "Your golem is going to be quite helpful when it remains just as powerful as ever after we lose our levels with our next class promotion."

Roughly a month from then, all of the No-life Gamers—except Allen and Meruru—would be maxing out their skill levels and going through another class promotion. That meant they were about to have their stats slashed, but so long as Meruru's golem was with them, they figured they ought to be able to manage even on this floor, despite it having Rank A monsters.

Meruru nodded. "Thanks for the vote of confidence, you guys. But I really don't think my golem's strong enough to take on Rank A monsters all by itself..."

Right, her golem's Attack is 4,400, which isn't quite enough to get through the tough hides or shells of some Rank A monsters.

"That may be true at the moment, but we've only just started collecting slates," Allen pointed out. "If you can handle the Rank Bs, then we'll leave those to you. Krena and Dogora will take care of the Rank As for now."

Krena grinned and puffed out her chest. "Yep! Leave it to us, Meruru!"

In this way, Meruru obtained her golem and the No-life Gamers resumed their efforts at clearing this Rank S dungeon.

* * *

A month had passed since Meruru made her golem. During this time, the party picked up more slates, including additional enhancement ones and Gigantify, helping Tam-Tam grow even stronger.

The No-life Gamers were currently gathered in the parlor on the first floor back at the base they were sharing with the Hero's party, Sacred. The house itself was large enough for thirty people to live in, but it was still pretty crowded trying to fit everyone from both parties—around twenty people—into a single room.

As part of the arrangements the two parties made for living together, Allen's group was now paying ten gold a month for rent and Helmios's group was paying twenty gold. Sacred also had servants who had brought in a lot of furniture and decorations, giving the previously barren dwelling some much-needed life. Now, they had a large dinner table to eat at and a luxurious sofa that would not look out of place in a noble's mansion.

Allen was currently sitting on this sofa, sandwiched by Cecil and Rosetta, the Sacred member with the Phantom Thief Talent who always wore outfits exposing her midriff. She seemed to have taken a liking to him, given how often she talked to and teased him.

"Mr. Helmios, aren't you taking your party into the dungeon today?"

Allen asked. "And Ms. Rosetta, there's no need to scrunch up next to me. There's an open seat right over there."

Hmph! Who gave you permission to touch me, woman?

"C'mon, don't be like that," Helmios replied, sounding hurt. "We're friends, aren't we?"

"Yeah, c'mon, Allen," Rosetta echoed, smirking while placing a hand on the teenager's shoulder. "That's not how you should talk to your elders."

Apparently the fact that Allen never got flustered no matter what she did made it that much more fun for her to mess with him. This time, though, was enough to make him sigh.

Cecil wordlessly smacked Rosetta's hand off his shoulder, prompting an amused "Oh?" from the woman. She then started pressing her thigh against Allen's instead, pointedly ignoring the daggers shooting out of Cecil's eyes. Rosetta's continued smirking indicated that perhaps she was having fun teasing Cecil too.

According to the briefings of how each member joined Helmios's party, Rosetta had been leading a group of burglars operating in the Giamutan capital but was apprehended by Helmios. She was almost put to death, but was ultimately spared execution on the condition that she joined his party. These days, she would sometimes declare that she was trying to steal his heart whenever she was feeling good after a drink or two.

When Allen heard this story, his opinion of Helmios improved a little, impressed by how he managed to secure a rare three-star Talent for his party. And just like Rosetta, all eight of the women in Helmios's party were around twenty years old and had their own story for how they joined.

Allen was thinking, *What a freaking harem protagonist*, when the flying squirrel on Sophie's shoulder floated into the air and looked down on him.

"Let's get started, shall we? Ha ha."

Today was finally the day of the No-life Gamers' second class promotion. They were taking the day off from dungeon diving because after this, they planned on discussing possible changes to their battle formation. Rohzen had been waiting quite a while for someone to call for the promotion process to begin, but since no one did, he had to interrupt their conversation instead.

"I see that everyone in the party has maxed out both their levels and skill levels, ha ha."

"Yes, my Lord," Allen replied. "So, please promote all of them."

"You got it. I'm going to go through this, chop-chop. Ha ha."

As the Spirit God began doing his hip-shaking dance, tears welled up in Dverg's eyes.

"They really are getting new classes..."

The rest of Sacred were also watching on with wide eyes. A few more Gamers were offered class choices this time, so Allen picked the ones that would form the most effective party. Before long, the entire process was complete.

Name: Krena
Age: 14
Class: Sword Emperor
Level: 1
HP: 1,790
MP: 770
Attack: 1,790
Endurance: 1,608
Agility: 1,150
Intelligence: 775
Luck: 1,095

Skills: Sword Emperor {1}, Slash {1}, Sword Mastery {6}
Extra Skill: Limit Break
XP: 0/10

Skill Levels
Sword Emperor: 1
Slash: 1

<u>Skill Experience</u>
Slash: 0/10

Name: Cecil Granvelle
Age: 14
Class: Wizardess King
Level: 1
HP: 995
MP: 1,614
Attack: 578
Endurance: 624
Agility: 1,022
Intelligence: 1,778
Luck: 1,007

Skills: Wizardess King {1}, Fire {1}, Sparring {4}
Extra Skill: Petit Meteor
XP: 0/10

<u>Skill Levels</u>
Wizardess King: 1
Fire Magic: 1

<u>Skill Experience</u>
Fire Magic: 0/10

Name: Dogora
Age: 14
Class: Rampager
Level: 1
HP: 1,098
MP: 651
Attack: 1,615
Endurance: 817

Agility: 683
Intelligence: 504
Luck: 727

Skills: Rampager {1}, Full Might {1}, Axe Mastery {6}, Shield Mastery {3}
Extra Skill: Heart and Soul
XP: 0/10

<u>Skill Levels</u>
Rampager: 1
Full Might: 1

<u>Skill Experience</u>
Full Might: 0/10

Name: Keel von Carnel
Age: 14
Class: Greater Saint
Level: 1
HP: 583
MP: 1,120
Attack: 447
Endurance: 623
Agility: 712
Intelligence: 979
Luck: 895

Skills: Greater Saint {1}, Healing {1}, Sword Mastery {3}
Extra Skill: Drops of God
XP: 0/10

<u>Skill Levels</u>
Greater Saint: 1
Healing: 1

<u>Skill Experience</u>
Healing: 0/10

Name: Sophialohne
Age: 49
Blessing: Spirit God
Class: Spirit User
Level: 1
HP: 712
MP: 1,231
Attack: 504
Endurance: 489
Agility: 713
Intelligence: 1,406
Luck: 594

Skills: Juvenile Spirit User {1}, Fire {1}
Extra Skill: Grand Spirit Manifestation
XP: 0/10

<u>Skill Levels</u>
Juvenile Spirit Manifestation: 1
Fire: 1

<u>Skill Experience</u>
Fire: 0/10

Name: Volmaar
Age: 68
Class: Bow Lord
Level: 1
HP: 982
MP: 535
Attack: 850

Endurance: 846
Agility: 543
Intelligence: 360
Luck: 582

Skills: Bow Lord {1}, Keen Sight {1}, Bow Mastery {6}
Extra Skill: Arrow of Light
XP: 0/10

<u>Skill Levels</u>
Bow Lord: 1
Keen Sight: 1

<u>Skill Experience</u>
Keen Sight: 0/10

The No-life Gamers' Class Progression Trees

- Krena: Sword Lord → Sword King → Sword Emperor
- Cecil: Wizardess → Archwizardess → Wizardess King
- Dogora: Axe User → Berserker → Rampager
- Keel: Cleric → Saint → Greater Saint
- Sophie: Spirit Mage → Spirit Wizard → Spirit User
- Volmaar: Archer → Bow Master → Bow Lord

"The gods sure chose a weird naming convention for your class," Allen said sardonically to Cecil before turning to Dogora and adopting an even snarkier tone. "But damn, Dogora—'Rampager' sounds really cool. I thought your Extra Skill would disappear from *this* class promotion, but no dice, I see. Maybe next time?"

In a way, our party is in Hell Mode because you can't use your Extra Skill, man.

Dogora was unable to come up with a comeback. He was sure that his Extra Skill had the potential to completely change the momentum of a fight. He had asked Helmios for advice about any unique requirements or situations that might enable him to master this skill. Unfortunately, Helmios did not have a quick and easy answer either.

"Thank you for showing us something incredible," Helmios said to Allen before turning to his companions. "All of you were watching, right? Now you know that humanity has hope."

Allen, who had gone back to recording the results of his party's class promotions, shrugged in reply. "It's not like this is something to hide."

If what Rohzen had said about the Heavenly Realm making preparations so that everyone could promote their classes was true, then there really was no point keeping what happened today secret.

That said, Allen was still hiding the process of him making Blessings of Heaven and Seeds of Magic. When asked what he did locked up in his room on his off days, he only ever said he was "resting."

"I'll still be keeping you to your word, though," Allen reminded Helmios.

"I know, I know," the Hero replied wryly. "I was gonna introduce you to him even if you hadn't let us sit in on it."

When Helmios had asked Allen to let Sacred observe when the No-life Gamers underwent their class promotions, Allen had agreed in exchange for Helmios introducing him to a blacksmith who could refine and forge orichalcum.

Orichalcum, called "metal of the gods" by some, could be found on Floor 4 of the Rank S dungeon. However, according to Helmios, it did not appear in the form of weapons or armor, but as metal ore. And in order to forge the metal of the gods, one had to borrow the divine power of Freyja, the Goddess of Fire. This was why Allen had asked to be introduced to the best blacksmith in all of Baukis—a supposedly cantankerous old dwarf.

"Oh, and Sophie, use this the next time we go to the dungeon." Allen handed her an adamantite bow. He had planned on giving it to her after her class promotion and had thus kept it at the base instead of selling it.

"Th-Thank you, Lord Allen. I'll d-do my best to use it well."

Seeing how nervous Sophie was, Volmaar asked, "Sir Allen, should she not first focus on mastering the usage of her spirits?"

However, Allen was of a different mind. "We don't have much time. Let's have her try it out first. If it doesn't work out, *then* we'll have her focus solely on the spirits."

Now that Sophie was a Spirit User, her fighting style was to involve manifesting the spirits she was contracted with. However, she had seen Gatoluuga, the Spirit User in Rohzenheim, fighting with a bow during the war.

Through Spirit B, Allen had asked Gatoluuga if using a bow would clash with the abilities of a Spirit User. The man had replied that there should be no issue as long as the Spirit User was in tune with their spirits.

Consequently, Allen had tasked Sophie with two challenges: to learn how to use the bow and to learn how to communicate with her spirits. An adamantite bow was supposed to be powerful enough to kill Rank B monsters in one shot and, with the help of Attack rings, still ought to be effective against Rank A monsters. Allen had been insistent when convincing her to learn archery, reiterating that it was all to raise the party's damage output.

"First, let's go back to Rohzenheim to find the spirits you want to contract with."

"Yes, Lord Allen." Sophie nodded with resolve.

Spirit Users could not simply manifest spirits on their own. Consequently, Sophie now needed to form contracts with spirits. Luckily, she had already met a few she had taken a liking to the last time she was in Rohzenheim.

"When we come back to Yanpany, we'll stick around on Floor Three and level for a month, then finally give Floor 4 a go," Allen declared.

"So those are the No-life Gamers, huh," Rosetta murmured, looking on. She felt like she finally understood what Allen had told her a while back about the meaning of his party's name.

* * *

Their class promotions reverted everyone, aside from Allen and Meruru, back to Lvl. 1. They then traveled to Rohzenheim to help Sophie contract with spirits. Afterward, they returned to the Rank S dungeon to spend one more month on Floor 3. That was enough to get them to Lvl. 50, after which they moved up to Floor 4 as planned.

They had decided to buy the medals that they needed to travel to higher floors from the temple on Floor 1. One reason was because Allen had used up most of the medals they found trading with hidden cubes, but the other, more important reason was they had the financial leeway to do so. Every time they returned from Floor 3, they sold off all their duplicate slates and hihiirokane equipment, which often came to a total of more than ten thousand gold.

In fact, they now had so much money that Allen had begun putting in requests for Rank D magic stones as well. Since he was putting up his max limit of a thousand gold each time he made a request, his stock was increasing at a steady rate. He did not order any Rank B magic stones, though, as the party already had plenty after farming them in the dungeon.

The No-life Gamers were currently back at base, having breakfast before heading back into the dungeon later.

"No, stop that. We're eating now. Please, settle down." Sophie set down her spoon and reached down to the creature that was rubbing against her leg, lifted it up to her lap, and began trying to calm it.

"*Au au.*"

The creature was her contracted juvenile fire spirit. It looked similar to a Japanese giant salamander and was red all over, with a flame-tipped tail that burned fiercely. This flame could not actually catch furniture and clothes on fire—it was really only just for aesthetics.

"You seem to have gotten used to it," Allen commented.

"Y-You think so?" Sophie blushed a little.

Krena lifted a piece of meat to her mouth. "Maybe Salamander's hungry too?"

"No, no, the spirits don't need food. Whenever they need energy, I give them my MP."

Our dear Spirit God over there eats food like normal, though.

When Sophie started tickling the creature and rubbing its stomach, it flopped its legs about and squealed happily as its beady eyes sparkled with delight.

According to Gatoluuga, spirits had wills of their own, meaning they were not guaranteed to always follow their contracted Spirit User's instructions during battle. In order to make it more likely that they obey, Spirit Users were to keep them materialized for as long as possible and bond with them.

The process was supposed to take a long time, but the party was on a tight schedule. Therefore, Allen had instructed Sophie to keep her spirits materialized for as close to twenty-four seven as possible, even during meals and while sleeping, all the way until she ran out of MP.

Salamander was apparently not intelligent enough to understand Sophie's words. At the moment, it mainly only repeated actions that one might expect from a small pet, such as rubbing its face against her, pacing in circles around her, crying out, and so on.

It's interesting how the logic behind Summoning, calling forth golems, and spirit materialization are all completely different.

During his fourteen years as a Summoner, Allen had never stopped analyzing his class. Now that he had both a golem pilot and a Spirit User as party members, he had started analyzing their classes too, and in doing so, he had discovered many places where they differed from Summoning.

Every time he himself created a new Summon, he had to expend MP and magic stones. For example, a Dragon B required more than 3,000 MP and twenty-nine Rank B magic stones. In contrast, a golem pilot only needed a magic disc and slates to call forth golems, and could do so repeatedly with no limit. Instead, it cost MP to keep the golem out.

Materializing a spirit did not require MP or magic stones. Similarly to golems, keeping a spirit out also cost MP. In Meruru's case, if she fought while using skills, 3,000 MP would not last her even an hour. The situation was similar for Spirit Users; it would cost Sophie about the same amount of MP were she to fight while keeping a spirit out.

Now I understand better why Minister Nukakai—and Baukis in general—want Seeds of Magic so badly.

The dwarven nation's military capability hinged on the total number of available golem pilots they had enlisted. And now they knew about the Seeds of Magic, which recovered MP much more effectively than any other recovery item so far.

And this is precisely why Mr. Gatoluuga also wields a bow.

Gatoluuga had explained that his bow was for when he ran out of MP and could no longer materialize his spirits. When he and his spirits were perfectly in sync, he could also give them instructions while using it, asking them to set his arrowheads on fire, boost the speed of his arrows, guide his arrows toward his target, and so on.

Meanwhile, under Volmaar's tutelage, Sophie was getting better and better at archery.

"There's a reason for everything," Allen murmured.

Cecil started. "Huh? What's that out of the blue?"

The members of Sacred also looked at Allen quizzically.

"Oh, sorry, it's nothing." Allen shook his head slightly. "I was just talking to myself. Something just clicked in my mind."

"There you go again," Cecil sighed.

"You really never stop thinking and analyzing, do you?" Helmios marveled.

After living together with Allen for a whole month, Helmios now knew how much Allen loved analyzing things and that he often involved his companions with his experiments. Most of the time, though, exactly what Allen was getting at went completely over Helmios's head.

"Well, there's a lot I still don't know," Allen replied.

"Oh wow, things *you* don't know? Like what?"

"Hmm… For example, what is Lord Rohzen's element?"

"Wha— S-Sir Allen, that's a bit..." Volmaar tried to indicate that this questioning was over the line.

However, Allen turned to him instead and asked, "Do you know, Volmaar? You've been with him for decades now, right?"

The fact that Volmaar was in Sophie's direct service meant that he must have spent decades living under the same roof as Rohzen back when the flying squirrel spirit was still a mere Spirit King.

"That's, well..."

It was clear that Volmaar did not know, so Allen turned to Sophie, who answered apologetically, "I-I'm sorry, we don't really probe..."

Finally, Allen turned to the Spirit God himself. "All right, Spirit God Rohzen, what kind of spirit are you? I can't really tell what element you are."

"Wha-?! Sir Allen!" Volmaar could not believe that Allen had failed to get the hint based on his and Sophie's reactions.

"*Om nom.*" Rohzen swallowed the fukaman in his mouth. "I'm actually a wood spirit. The World Tree did birth me, after all. Ha ha."

"I see. So that's why your skill is a buff skill." *I've always associated the wood element with passive abilities and buffs.*

"Pretty much. Though I'd prefer it if you didn't prod too much further. Ha ha."

Sophie watched this exchange in dumbfounded astonishment.

"You sure are an inquisitive person, Allen," Helmios chuckled.

"Inquisitive? Mr. Helmios, it's not that I'm inquisitive."

"Then what is it?"

By now, almost everyone at the table had stopped eating and was focused on Allen.

"You can't strategize effectively if you don't understand how things work. That's why this world has been at the Demon Lord's mercy for decades."

"Oh?" Dverg lifted an eyebrow. "Care to elaborate?"

Allen continued. "Finding answers to the 'why' questions is the key to understanding your current situation. That's how you know what to prepare against."

The Sword Lord closed his eyes pensively. "I see," he said, internalizing what Allen said.

"What's something else you don't know?" Cecil asked.

"Why are the deities enabling class promotions now when they had never done so before?"

Cecil tilted her head. "Sorry, I don't get what you're asking."

"The more I think about this, the more it doesn't make sense. If the deities simply handed out class promotions, there would be no need to fear the Demon Lord. So why didn't they do this earlier? When he first showed up, even."

And I highly doubt the idea never occurred to them before I brought it up.

Being promoted from a one-star class to a two-star class was a very significant boost in stats. Promoting ten thousand troops would greatly raise the possibility of defeating the Demon Lord Army.

As such, it seemed very strange to Allen that the deities were scrambling to introduce the class promotion system only now. His memories from his past life whispered to him that the process would very likely be gated by some sort of quest, but still, he felt things were not adding up.

Noticing Allen's look, Rohzen shrugged. "Now that's a thought, right? How strange. Ha ha."

So he won't tell. Maybe he actually doesn't know. Or he can't say. In any case, our priority right now is for Sophie to build a rapport with her spirits.

Allen's mind continued racing as he looked at the juvenile fire spirit clinging to Sophie.

Chapter 13: The Power of a Spirit

Today, the No-life Gamers were going to step foot on Floor 4 for the first time. As they approached the Temple of Yanpany, the guard wordlessly looked at Sophie and the red salamander that she was cradling.

"Oh, come now, please settle down," Sophie cooed.

"*Au, au.*"

Every once in a while, it would move its hands about and fuss a little.

It really is like a baby. And the guard is still staring.

The first time Sophie tried to enter with Salamander in her arms, the guard had stopped her, asking what it was and whether she was trying to bring a monster into the temple. This was the same guard who had stopped them the first time here due to how young they looked. He was doing his job properly by being careful about whom he let inside the temple.

Even when Sophie explained that it was a spirit, he continued eyeing her suspiciously and refused to budge.

Seeing this, Volmaar stepped up and brought his face so close to the guard's it seemed they might kiss, growling, "Are we to take this as an indication of the Empire of Baukis's rejection of the spirits?" As the personal attendant of Sophie, the princess whom all the elves expected to succeed the throne, his standing was quite high in Rohzenheim.

And yet the guard still stood firm.

That day, upon being informed of what had happened, the queen of Rohzenheim sent Baukis a letter through official channels asking for proper treatment of the spirits. Furthermore, she said she would raise the issue of treatment of spirits at the next Five Continent Alliance summit.

Thanks to this, the guard did not give the No-life Gamers any more trouble about Salamander. Since all this was for the purpose of eventually fighting the Demon Lord, Allen was not above relying on a little political browbeating.

After paying the Floor Operating System the needed medals, the party arrived on Floor 4.

"Is this it?" Allen knelt down. "Interesting, the ground really does have the texture of a leaf."

"It even feels kinda soft," Cecil said with a few firm stomps.

The ground on Floor 4 was green with lines that looked like leaf veins. The Gamers took a few steps and found it somewhat springy under their feet. However, it showed no signs of tearing no matter how much force they exerted, indicating that even if it was a leaf, it was a very thick one.

All this matches up with what Helmios said. Okay, Hawkins, come on out. Give me a view from the sky.

As Helmios's party, Sacred, operated mainly on Floor 4, he had had a lot of information to share with Allen. Now Allen sent out a Bird E to confirm some of the intel for himself.

From up high, Allen could see that his party was currently standing on top of a massive lotus pad. The wider view offered by Farsight revealed that this floor was like an expansive sea with lotus pads dotting its surface. Adventurers and monsters could be found doing whatever on top of these pads.

That confirms that Floor 4 really is an ocean biome.

Allen announced to the party, "It's just as Mr. Helmios described. Though it doesn't make much difference to us if it's sand or water, since we'll be riding our Griffs regardless."

"That's true, I suppose." Cecil nodded. "Should we also check to see if that cube will say what Mr. Helmios told us?" Because Allen kept calling the dungeon operation systems "cubes," the rest of his party had also taken to referring to them as such.

"Of course. Let's go."

The Gamers approached the nearby cube to ask for the conditions for progressing to the next floor.

"Greetings, No-life Gamers. I am Floor Operating System S401. Do you wish to travel to the next floor? Or do you wish to return to Floor 1?"

"Next floor, please."

"Floor Five it is. Please present five bronze medal variations, five iron medal variations, and five mithril medal variations."

So this is what Helmios was talking about.

Up until now, the dungeon cubes had never shown any sort of discernment regarding the engravings on the backs of the medals when receiving them. However, proceeding to Floor 5 would require five medals with unique depictions. It was just as Helmios had said.

"So we can't just bring five of the same kind of medals?" Allen asked to clarify one other detail.

"That is so. The requirement for traveling to Floor 5 is to bring five medals with different depictions on them."

"And how many floor bosses are there on the second to fourth floors?"

"There are five on each floor."

Cecil crossed her arms and sighed. "Mr. Helmios was right. We'll have to kill the Rank S bosses in order to reach Floor 5."

The five floor bosses on each floor that the cube mentioned included BB on Floor 2 and Scarlet on Floor 3. This requirement was the reason Helmios had given up trying to reach Floor 5. His party just might, if they were to go all out, manage to kill one of the Rank S floor bosses. However, doing so would require skirting very, very close to incurring casualties.

"All right, well, we've confirmed the conditions for reaching the next floor. It's time to see what Floor 4 is like for ourselves."

Allen needed more information about this floor in order to decide whether to stay here or return to Floor 3. And so out came the Bird Bs, taking the entire group high above the lotus pads.

"Looks like the dwarves are able to make it on this floor just fine," Cecil commented. "Golems really are incredible."

"Well, the dwarves *have* always managed to repel the Demon Lord Army out on the open sea," Allen pointed out.

Down below, golems in the form of boats—a sight that the Gamers had grown familiar with on Floor 3—were parting the water as effortlessly as they had parted the sand dunes. The sight of a whole fleet of these facing the Demon Lord Army forces each year was probably a scene to behold indeed.

Currently, Meruru was flying on her own Bird B ahead of the rest of the party. For a while after she first rejoined the party, she had ridden with Allen and held a large shield in order to protect those in the back. However, now that she had her Iron Grade golem, she was riding solo, just like Krena and Dogora. Her golem was massive enough to act as a shield just standing up front, so she was working in tandem with the vanguard to add more variety to their battle tactics.

To no one's surprise, Cecil had simply said, "Well, if Meruru's not sitting here," before reclaiming her place behind Allen as if it were only natural. While the back line consisted of her, Keel, Sophie, and Volmaar, it was not ideal for her to ride with Keel, as the party would lose both its mage and healer if anything happened to their mount, and there was no way Sophie and Volmaar would ride separately. Staying with Allen in the middle of the formation also gave Cecil the most freedom in terms of coordinating her attacks with other party members.

The Bird E scouting ahead spotted three monsters that looked like a cross between newts and dragons resting on top of a floating leaf.

"There are monsters this way!" Allen shouted loud enough for his whole party to hear.

Helmios also said that this floor has a lot of aquatic monsters, and that nearly everything on this floor is Rank A.

As the three members of the vanguard made a beeline for the monsters, Meruru held aloft her magic disc and shouted, "Tam-Tam, come forth!" Her golem promptly leaped out of the giant magic circle that had appeared above the lotus pad up ahead and sucked her inside when she got close enough on her mount.

Of course, the monsters were not just lying around. They noticed the golem when it appeared and immediately pounced at it. The twenty-meter-tall figure in turn reached out its long arm to hold down one of the monsters.

Name: Tam-Tam
Pilot: Meruru
Rank: Iron Grade
HP: 3,000 + 1,800
MP: 3,000 + 1,800
Attack: 3,000 + 5,800
Endurance: 3,000 + 3,800
Agility: 3,000
Intelligence: 3,000
Luck: 3,000

The Gamers had found a Gigantify slate back on Floor 3. This slate took up two slots but doubled both the golem's stats and size. In addition, because Meruru had maxed out her skill levels, her golem now had the Endurance to hold even Rank A monsters at bay. Although Krena's and Dogora's Attack was still higher when they wielded their weapons, Tam-Tam had way more Endurance than anyone else in the party and was therefore filling its role as tank very well. Unfortunately, there were downsides, as maintaining a Gigantified golem cost double the amount of MP.

While Meruru's golem kept the monsters occupied, Krena and Dogora moved in. Cecil and Volmaar assisted them with long-range attacks, taking the monsters out one after another.

"Hell yeah, you're the last one!" Dogora charged toward the remaining monster.

Suddenly, Sophie cried out, her voice filled with alarm. "Huh?! No, please, w—" She lost consciousness midsentence, collapsing against the neck of the Bird B she was riding.

"P-Princess Sophialohneeee!" Volmaar reached forward to grab his charge so she would not fall off.

What just— Ah!

"Dogora, dodge it! Incoming from behind you!" Allen also shouted in a fluster.

However, it was too late. A giant ball of flames shot forward from the back of the party's formation, heading straight for the monster that Dogora was about to attack.

"Huh— *YEEEOWCH*!"

This was, of course, Salamander. It rushed ahead, dragging along the superheated air around it, and instantly reduced Dogora's Bird B to bubbles of light. The boy leaped off in a hurry, but unfortunately was not fast enough to avoid getting his rear end burned. The spirit grazed Tam-Tam's arm before it reduced the final monster to nothing but cinders. It went on to burn a hole in the lotus pad and vaporize the water underneath, causing a large burst of steam to shoot up through the hole.

When Sophie regained consciousness, she immediately began apologizing profusely, tears at the corner of her eyes. "I'm so sorry, everyone! I went and did it again."

Allen's group peered down at the expanding hole in the lotus pad and the violently churning water it revealed. Through the billow clouds of steam, they caught brief glances here and there of what truly looked like hell.

* * *

Thankfully, Dogora had managed to get out of the way of the attack from Salamander, the juvenile fire spirit; his behind, however, ended up completely roasted. Upon landing on the giant leaf, he writhed around in agony, clutching his butt.

"H-Hey man, you okay?" Keel leaped down onto the leaf and rushed over to cast Healing Magic on Dogora's bared buttocks.

"The hell do you think?!" Dogora retorted. "How many times has this been?! And why is it me every time?!"

"Here ya go, extra underwear. This is the last pair; if they get ruined too, we'll have to go buy more." Allen took out a pair of boxers and handed it over.

Sophie also landed on the leaf and bowed profusely. "I'm so sorry! I'm so sorry!"

"Huh? Oh, nah, it's fine." Dogora turned away with a red face, bent over.

Sophie said, "B-But..." and was about to continue, but Dogora insisted, "Seriously, it's fine!" while desperately raising and lowering his boxers to hide the lower half of his body.

During this time, Allen checked up on Sophie's Status in his Grimoire. *Her MP's gone to zero, and she lost half her HP. Absolutely nuts.*

"Keel, make sure to heal Sophie too, please."

Keel nodded. Once he finished with Dogora, he then tended to Sophie.

"Au, au!"

Salamander appeared from the surface of the water that, though no longer bubbling, was still giving off steam. After evaporating the excess water off its skin, it glided through the air and into Sophie's embrace. Unable to comprehend from her obvious body language that she was dejected and on the verge of tears, it looked up at her with its beady eyes and wagged its tail vigorously as if begging to be praised.

With the scene of chaos from just now still fresh in her mind, Sophie had to summon all her patience to manage the words, "Th-Thank you, Salamander."

How many times does this make? I think Dogora's butt might be nearing its limit. But wow, when Salamander takes Sophie's HP too, the power of its attack is incredible.

Allen began analyzing what had just happened while watching

Dogora, who had gone off a distance to change, from the corner of his eye.

The spirits of this world expended their contracted Spirit User's MP to use their abilities. In other words, the power they wielded depended on how much MP they used. This was similar in principle to Cecil's Extra Skill. What was different, however, was that it was up to the spirit to decide how much MP it would use.

This time, Salamander had managed its impressive attack because it had taken all of Sophie's MP and even half her HP. Anyone who underestimated a juvenile spirit could very well get burned—or worse.

"Sophie, I've said this many times, but being impatient doesn't help," Rohzen chided in a gentle voice. "Spirits listen closely to their User's voices. Salamander picked up on the unease in your tone."

"U-Understood, Lord Rohzen."

There we go again, our dear Spirit God's preferential advice-giving!

Even though Spirit God Rohzen never answered any of Allen's questions, he had started proactively offering Sophie advice after she became a Spirit User.

Ever since the start of the fight, Sophie had been trying to give Salamander orders; however, it had remained glued to her side, seemingly unresponsive. When she started getting impatient, she unconsciously put too much force in her voice, and the spirit responded accordingly.

"If things remain this way, maybe we should put off Sophie's next class promotion for a while," Allen mused out loud.

"That's actually a good idea," Rohzen agreed. "Remember, this was all caused by a juvenile spirit—an adult spirit could kill Dogora here. Ha ha."

"Now that would be a problem." *Hmm, so the next tier up is called adult spirit.*

All spirits were born as nascent spirits. They then gradually evolved into adult spirits, grand spirits, spirit kings, and spirit gods. Although the elves called him "the" God of Spirits, Rohzen was actually just one spirit god among countless others.

The next time Sophie would promote her class, she would gain the ability to materialize adult spirits. However, if she was having this much trouble handling juvenile spirits, things might become even more dire were she to deal with adult spirits. This was a worry that Rohzen and Allen shared.

Gatoluuga had said that it took him a long time before he reached the point where he could communicate with his spirits without issue. If their priorities were solely to raise Sophie's skills and promote her class, then the consequences would not matter. For each MP her spirits used, she gained her an equal amount of XP, so letting her spirits do whatever they pleased would be in line with their goals. However, it *was* a problem so long as her spirits continued rampaging because the consequences were very much real. Given all this, everyone was in agreement that her class promotion should be put on the back burner for now.

"You know what? Here, Sophie, have Helmios's ring. Being able to keep your spirits materialized all day should help somewhat." Allen handed Sophie the MP Recovery Ring that he had received from the Hero.

"Th-Thank you, Lord Allen. Are you sure about this?"

Well, he didn't specify how long I could keep it, so I don't actually plan on ever giving it back.

Helmios had given up trying to reach Floor 5. So, because he figured he would not need his MP Recovery Ring for the near future, he had traded it with Allen for a hundred Blessings of Heaven. With that many of them, his party would be able to handle any traps they fell to, and Allen had told him that he could always go through Rohzenheim to ask for more should his stock ever run low.

As a result, Sophie got to wear matching rings with Allen. This put her in extremely good spirits, but that was a story for another time. At the same time, Cecil's mood turned extremely sour, but this too was another story for another time.

"You okay, Meruru?" Allen asked, worried about the damage that Tam-Tam had taken when Salamander grazed its arm just now.

"Mm-hm! I can repair this by myself," Meruru replied.

Name: Meruru
Age: 14
Class: Talos General
Level: 60
HP: 1,677 + 1,800
MP: 2,420 + 1,800
Attack: 782 + 1,800
Endurance: 1,318 + 1,800
Agility: 782
Intelligence: 2,420
Luck: 1,503

Skills: Talos General {6}, Flying Arm {6}, Drill Punch {6}, Laser Sword {6}, Repair {6}, Alloy {2}, Spear Mastery {3}, Shield Mastery {3}
Extra Skill: Combine (Right Arm)

Skill Levels
Rocket Punch: 6
Drill Punch: 6
Laser Sword: 6
Repair: 6

When Meruru maxed out her class skill, the last skill she received was Repair. There were two ways to repair damaged golems. One was to replace the slate for that part; golem parts were manifested based on the slates, so if, say, the right arm was destroyed, the pilot could put in a new right arm slate and their golem's arm would be as good as new. Of course, if they put the old right arm slate back in, the arm that appeared would go back to being the broken one. The second way was the Repair skill. This skill enabled golem pilots to repair their golems by expending MP. However, this process also took time. The only way to instantly repair a part was to swap out the slate.

This time, the Gamers were in no hurry, so Meruru could make do using her skill.

"Hold on, I see a treasure chest!" Dogora, who had moved toward the center of the leaf to change, announced to the party.

"You serious?!" With that, Keel immediately took off.

Allen sighed with apprehension. *I keep telling you, it can be a monster. Please stop opening them yourself.*

Whenever Keel saw a treasure chest, he simply could not bear *not* opening it. However, there were monsters in these dungeons that took on the appearance of treasure chests. In fact, the Gamers had encountered them before—specifically, these were Rank A monsters called abyss boxes. Dogora must have been thinking the same thing as Allen, as he promptly opened the chest himself.

"What does this do?" Dogora picked up the ring inside the chest and brought it back to where Allen and the rest were.

Allen put the ring on and opened his grimoire to check his Status. "Nice, we got a good one right off the bat. This gives +3,000 Intelligence."

Hooray for rings! Very good luck for our very first day. This is a good floor. The Rank S boss here is apparently really dangerous, but I still think this floor is better than Floor 3, at least in terms of loot and XP.

So far, the Gamers had only ever found rings that gave +1,000 buffs. This was their first time obtaining one the next tier up. And since two rings could be equipped on each hand, there was a lot of room for upgrades.

"All right. As discussed before, this ring is going to K—"

"No way am I taking it." Keel made a big "X" with his arms and, using just his eyes, indicated toward the person behind Allen.

Catching onto what Keel was so afraid of, Allen cleared his throat. "*Ahem.* This ring is going to Cecil." He turned around and found Cecil standing right there.

"Aww, are you sure? Thank you!" She grinned brightly as she accepted the ring.

Well, considering our current situation, I suppose it makes more sense giving it to Cecil first to raise her damage output. Hopefully, we'll eventually find enough rings for everyone. And while we look for those, we'll also have to keep an eye out for orichalcum on this floor.

And so the No-life Gamers began their foray into Floor 4 while keeping the plethora of goals they had to achieve in the backs of their minds.

Chapter 14: Searching for Orichalcum

"C'mon, lemme tag in already," Dogora called out impatiently. "I'm the one who asked him."

"Aww… Okay!" With visible effort, Krena brought herself to relent and stepped back.

Sword Lord Dverg watched their exchange without saying anything, holding a mithril practice greatsword.

They were standing in the yard of the house that Sacred and the No-life Gamers were renting. As expected of a property large enough to house thirty people, the yard was rather spacious. Even after Helmios's servants finished hanging up the twenty adventurers' laundry, there was more than enough space to practice.

Allen's group would stay inside the dungeon for three and a half days before they came out for one and a half days to rest. Dogora used the free time he had to practice swings in the yard. When Krena saw him doing this, she joined him, and the two started having matches every once in a while. This made Allen wonder if his party really needed a rest period, but Keel and Meruru were insistent upon it. Allen himself needed time to create Seeds of Magic, and as a result, they kept their current schedule.

When Dogora headed out to the yard on one of their days off, he found Dverg there, already practicing. Making the most of the opportunity, Dogora asked to practice with him. Dverg agreed without missing a beat. After that, Dogora, Krena, and Dverg took to training together in the yard. When Allen learned of this, he went to thank Dverg, but the man simply replied that it was "not a problem." Allen wondered just what it was that Dverg saw through his remaining good eye.

Today, as always, the three of them were training hard in the yard with their respective weapons in hand. Allen gazed at them from a table off in the corner, surreptitiously adding "Musclehead Trio" to their profiles in his head.

"Lord Helmios, Lord Allen, Princess Sophie, I've brought you tea."

One of Helmios's servants brought over a tray of teacups to Allen's table and began setting them out. Helmios, the one who had asked for the tea, and Sophie were sitting there with Allen.

"Thank you." Sophie smiled at the servant, who in turn lowered her head courteously and retreated.

Helmios lifted his cup and took a sip, then asked, "So, how're you guys finding Floor 4?"

"We're done leveling, so we're focusing on raising everyone's skills now," Allen replied. "Speaking of, there's something I wanted to ask you."

"Hm? What's that?"

The No-life Gamers had already been at Floor 4 for a month now. Their efforts at gathering equipment and items were going smoothly, but they had yet to get their hands on a very important something in particular. Allen was about to ask about it when suddenly...

"Kelpie! No, don't do that. Please, settle down!"

"*Kee, kee.*"

The small, light blue dolphin with a white belly in Sophie's arms started thrashing about as it tried to drink from her cup. This was the juvenile water spirit that she had contracted with. She was keeping Kelpie out now, partly because she had already gotten relatively used to handling Salamander and partly because messing up with Salamander meant Dogora burning his buns. As she generally could only keep one spirit out at a given moment, she had swapped them out.

The name "Kelpie" brought an aquatic horse creature to Allen's mind, but the kelpies of this world looked different from the monsters in the games that he knew so well. This was fine and all, but every time Allen heard the name "Kelpie," it also reminded him of "Kenpy," the nickname that he had assigned his character in his very first MMO. He would never share this with the others, but regardless, chills still danced down his back whenever Sophie called out to her spirit.

"So, what was it that you wanted to ask about?"

"Well, we can't find any orichalcum." *Like, at all. Were you lying?*

Sure, the No-life Gamers had only been on Floor 4 for a month, but they had covered a lot more ground than other adventurers as they were always flying on Bird Bs. Thanks to this, they had already opened what Allen thought was a much higher number of treasure chests than average. However, the party had yet to get their hands on any orichalcum weapons and armor, one of their goals from the start.

"Ohhh. We found ours at the bottom of the ocean."

"At the bottom? There are treasure chests down there too?"

Allen had sent some Fish Bs down into the sea in case there was anything of note, but they had only found monsters and no chests.

"Ah, that's..."

According to Helmios's explanation, treasure could be found in places other than treasure chests on Floor 4. His party had found orichalcum ore inside large clams at the bottom of the sea.

Seriously? We have to look out for things other than chests? And deep in the sea too, no less.

"That's incredible. How'd you find out? I doubt it was by coincidence."

Rosetta walked into the yard, grinning proudly. "Oh? You're interested? I was the one who found it! Aren't I great?"

"Do you have a skill to detect treasure?" Allen asked her.

"I do, actually. How'd you know? Want me to tell you all about it some time?"

"I'm good, thank you."

It wouldn't help us, in any case. Hmm, but that does sound like a skill that a phantom thief would have. It probably lets her know the location of valuable things within a certain radius.

A while later, Allen headed out to the Adventurer's Guild. As he walked, he brainstormed ways to explore the seafloor. He went alone, as this trip was only for his usual magic stone trading. Despite the massive number of magic stones that he had bought so far, the market price had not budged, going to show just how many adventurers there were and how vast the supply was. Little wonder, considering that this was the city that produced the most magic stones in the country that was trying to control the entire world with magic tools.

When night fell later, the No-life Gamers hit up their usual restaurant for dinner. There were days when some of the party could not attend—they were allowed to spend their day off however they wanted, after all. Tonight, however, they were all present.

When Allen walked into the restaurant, he panned his eyes around the dining room.

Hmm, Admiral Garara isn't here today. Oh, but Mr. Uru is.

The wolfkin man whom Allen's group had saved from BB was eating with Sara, a catkin from his party. He looked up and happened to meet Allen's gaze, prompting the boy to walk over.

"Mr. Uru, it has been a while. How's your meal?"

"It's good, it's good. Your party's eating here today?"

"Yes, sir. Meruru loves this place. Would you like to join us?"

A while back, Uru had approached Allen to apologize about suddenly bringing Beast Prince Zeu to see him out of the blue. Ever since, the two had taken to exchanging information whenever they met in town. Sometimes they even ate together, like tonight.

Allen was proactively communicating with Uru to get updates on Albahal's movements as well as on Beast King Zeu's progress on clearing the dungeon. Uru was a run-of-the-mill adventurer and therefore did not know much about his country's politics or the power struggles between members of the Albahalan royal family; however, he did have useful information related to Beast Prince Zeu.

"So, His Highness is still on Floor 2," Allen murmured.

"Well, Beast Crown Prince Beku is making damn sure that he's not sending our best adventurers. Oh, don't go spreading this around, okay?"

Allen was still talking with Uru while his companions put in their orders.

"Mr. Uru! C'mon, you know I won't. So, Beast Prince Zeu is still going to need some time?"

"Basically, yep. How about you? You gonna be on Floor 4 for long?"

Perhaps Uru was also trying to keep tabs on Allen's progress. Or maybe Beast Prince Zeu had ordered him to get updates on Helmios's entire group.

"Well, I think we'll be there for about six months. Speaking of, you also have six months left here, right? Hang in there."

"Yeah, we do. Still another half a year until we go home!"

Uru had previously explained that Beast Crown Prince Beku had mandated that all beastkin with Talents spend one year at Yanpany for the sake of their country's prosperity. They were issued hihiirokane and adamantite equipment and told they could keep half of the money they found. However, one must not forget this was a place where half of those going in died within a year. Those who tried to shirk this duty would be charged with treason, so many beastkin were here reluctantly, not because they wanted to.

When he realized what the situation was like, Beast Prince Zeu had gathered all the beastkin into an organization and did what he could to make it safer for them to enter the dungeon. Allen could hear the gratitude in Uru's voice when he spoke of Beast Prince Zeu. Of course, Zeu was not purely helping his countrymen out of the goodness of his heart. The current Beast King had declared that he would yield his throne to whichever of his children cleared the Rank S dungeon first. This was what prompted Zeu to come to Yanpany, but he could not overlook the harsh conditions that he found his people facing and therefore ended up taking action.

Uru lamented about the fact that because the clearing of the dungeon was tied to the succession of the throne, Beast Crown Prince Beku was preventing the best fighters of Albahal from coming to Yanpany.

When I speak to Mr. Uru, I get the feeling that he doesn't completely hate all humans. Though maybe that's just because I saved his life once.

Allen had heard that the beastkin resented and hated the Central Continent and the humans who lived there for the persecution that they had received in the past. However, he did not feel this hostility from Uru.

When he was at the Academy, he was taught that beastkin, just like elves and dwarves, were equally "people." The Academy treated all the other races as equals to humans and its curriculum did not particularly discriminate against them.

"I've always wondered, why are *you* here at this death trap, Allen? It's not like your king gave you an order, right?"

"Of course not. I'm here because I want the reward for clearing the dungeon."

"You serious? Is that even a thing?"

"Apparently Mr. Helmios heard it directly from Dygragni, so I'm pretty sure it is."

Back during his Academy days, the Hero had supposedly asked the priests tending to Dygragni here for an opportunity to speak with the Dungeon Master in person. His request was granted, and Dygragni had told him that, just like all other dungeons, the Rank S dungeon also held a reward for those who cleared it.

It was this reward that Allen was after. He had high expectations for it, in light of the fact that this dungeon had lumps of orichalcum just sitting around waiting to be picked up.

"Damn, you really mean it. Even Admiral Garara hasn't made it to Floor 5, y'know?"

"So I've heard. However"—Allen grinned with total confidence—"there's no dungeon that my party has ever failed to clear."

* * *

The No-life Gamers arrived at Floor 4 of the Rank S dungeon.

"Now, then. Today's goal is to find us some orichalcum!" Allen declared.

"And we're supposed to look inside the clams that Lord Helmios described, yes?" Cecil asked for confirmation's sake.

Allen nodded, then the entire party mounted their Bird Bs and took to the sky. Because they had done this so many times now, the other adventurers were no longer surprised whenever it happened, now thinking nothing more of it beyond "Strange abilities some people have."

The plan was to get Krena and Dogora some orichalcum weapons first. As they were major damage dealers, upgrading their weapons should make it easier for the party to kill whatever they encountered, floor bosses included. So the party was going to focus on gathering orichalcum until everyone had upgraded weapons, then return to hunting the monsters and treasure chests on top of the lotus pads.

Without ado, Allen Summoned fifty Fish Bs in the water and sent the Archelons scattering in all directions.

Do your best, Genbus. If you find a big clam, destroy it and check inside for orichalcum.

During his time here in Yanpany, Allen had learned a few things about the dungeon. First, according to Uru, this dungeon was expanding by the day. This included Floor 1, meaning that the city on Floor 1 was also growing. This was the reason that all the buildings were arranged in concentric rings centered around the Temple of Yanpany. Second, this dungeon was not static. The leaf that Salamander had burned through the other time had either healed or been replaced. The Gamers therefore had no qualms about breaking clams, knowing that they would be back to normal the next day.

"Now that I know, I see so many places that I want to check out," Allen murmured.

"Are you going to?" Cecil was sitting behind Allen, sharing the same Bird B as him.

"Nah, we'll concentrate on looking for clams with orichalcum today."

The water was so clear that it was possible to see the seafloor from the surface, but it actually went all the way down to around a hundred meters. According to Helmios, it was the Tridacna clams—more commonly known as just "giant clams"—that held treasure. Besides these clams, however, the seafloor was also dotted with what looked like crab holes and sunken ships. These points of interest likely held items too, but Allen hardened his heart and resolved to only look for the clams.

Half a day passed, during which time the Fish Bs destroyed hundreds, if not thousands, of giant clams. However, not one of them revealed the golden glow of the metal of the gods. Even now, the Summons were out searching, swimming swiftly past all the monsters in the water.

I guess orichalcum isn't common enough to be found in a day or two. Maybe I should change up how I do things.

"We're not having much luck. You think I should ask Ms. Rosetta for help?" Allen asked.

Cecil, however, did not answer. She was clearly quite unenthusiastic about being in the older woman's favor.

Allen suddenly sat up. "Hold on."

"What happened?"

"Just found a super big clam."

One of the Fish Bs that Allen was Shared with had discovered a clam several meters across and tried biting down on it. Fish B's bite was powerful enough to pulverize any random rock lying around or kill Rank B monsters in one snap. Consequently, the attack had made short work of all the other clams so far. This one, however, did not break.

Oh? Is this it? Everyone, gather up.

Determining that this unique and seemingly indestructible clam was a winner, Allen called back all the Fish Bs as he and his party made their way over.

"Down there?" Cecil asked when the party stopped right above where the indestructible clam lay.

Allen nodded. "Yep. Hmm, how should we handle this? Ellies, can you bring it up?"

"Your will is our command."

The clam had remained impervious against the concentrated attacks of several Fish Bs who arrived earlier, so Allen decided to bring the whole thing up. Just as he sent several Spirit Bs into the water, however, the Bird E that had been circling above spotted a large school approaching.

"Hold on, we've got incoming. Wait, they're really fast!"

Behind Allen, Cecil gripped her staff as the rest of the party promptly readied themselves for battle.

Hmm? What's that crimson one?

Realization dawned on Allen when he noticed the large crimson form swimming in the center of the group of blue monsters.

"It's Crimson! It's this floor's Rank S boss!"

This bloodred monster was Crimson Kaiser Sea Serpent, the greatest threat here on Floor 4. The ten blue forms that swam alongside it as if guarding it were Rank A monsters called kaiser sea serpents.

The school of crimson and blue sea serpents surrounded the Spirit Bs trying to lift the giant clam and the Fish Bs that had gathered to destroy it, then attacked all at once. The monsters swam deftly through the water with spectacular coordination, reducing all the Summons to bubbles of light in no time flat. There was no greater demonstration that underwater was home ground for the sea serpents.

Hmm, Helmios said his party ran away at Mach speed whenever this guy showed up. But let's see how well we can do.

The Hero had never defeated Crimson before. Allen was completely on his own when it came to figuring out a way to kill this boss.

"Our enemies are in the water. Let's first whittle down their numbers. Cecil, Fire Magic probably isn't very helpful here, so go with Ice Magic."

"You got it."

That moment, a few of the kaiser sea serpents leaped out of the water in an attempt to swallow the party. Krena and Dogora brought their weapons down on the monsters' faces with all their strength. The Gamers proceeded to focus on taking them out one at a time, understanding that strength lay in numbers. Thanks to having maxed out their levels after going through two class promotions, the party had the strength to steadily reduce the number of opponents.

However, Crimson was not just sitting around waiting. It roared in a voice that was audible even up in the air, sending waves rippling out in all directions.

"*Kiaaaas!*"

Oh? Is this what I think it is?

Just as Allen's group took their distance by climbing higher, the same number of kaiser sea serpents they had just killed appeared seemingly out of nowhere.

"This boss can call for backup!" Allen shouted in warning.

"Now we're back to square one—" Cecil suddenly screamed, "Watch out!"

Jets of water abruptly shot out of the water like spears, aimed directly at the Gamers' Bird Bs. Apparently, the sea serpents could use Water Magic to launch long-distance attacks. The water jets reached hundreds of meters high but could only go straight and therefore could be easily dodged. However, because all the kaiser sea serpents were shooting off jets at the same time, it was difficult for the party to get close enough to make their own attacks.

Dammit. Should we retreat now and sneak back later to grab the clam?

The party's current goal was not to kill the kaiser sea serpents, so they had no reason to continue this seemingly endless fight. It made sense to leave the area for now, wait until the floor boss was gone, and then come back to retrieve the giant clam.

"Ah!"

"Princess!"

One of the water spears had made a clean hit on the flank of Sophie and Volmaar's Bird B, throwing it off-balance. It managed to recover, but Sophie's leg had gotten hurt.

Keel promptly cast Healing Magic on her. "You okay?!"

"Yes, I am. Thank you." Sophie turned to look at Volmaar, who nodded at her. "Volmaar is fine as well."

The juvenile spirit in her arms looked up at her face and cried softly, its eyes filled with unease. Sophie repeated, "I'm all right," and tried to stroke it, but it shook off her head by shaking its head and cried loudly in Crimson's direction.

"*KEE, KEE!*"

"Kelpie, I really am—"

That was all Sophie could say before all the MP left her body, taking her consciousness with it. Volmaar's voice alone reverberated in her head as everything faded to black. Clearly, Kelpie had taken her HP too.

Okay, this is bad. If attacks are reaching our back lines too, that's a sure sign we need to get away.

Just as Allen was about to give the order to retreat, Volmaar cried, "Wha—?! Princess Sophialohne!"

As Sophie collapsed against the neck of her Bird B, Kelpie went out of control in a very visible way. It jumped out of her limp arms and hovered above the sea. The next instant, water rose up as if responding to the spirit's call.

"What the…? You gotta be fucking with me, right? How the hell does Kelpie do that?!" Dogora shouted in shock.

The water was now rising like an open umbrella. Crimson's scream vibrated the air as it was forcibly dragged up.

"It's gonna get us too! Everyone, back up!" Allen shouted.

The next moment, a giant ball of water rose up into the sky. Its clear, jellylike surface revealed all eleven sea serpents, including Crimson, trapped within.

Damn, the seafloor's supposed to be a hundred meters down and it's completely exposed.

By some strange power, the surrounding sea was being held at bay. Consequently, there was now a giant, gaping hole in the sea, with the exposed seafloor entirely bare.

"Ha ha, so even you can feel surprised, Allen," Rohzen chortled.

Allen turned around, his eyes wide. "Juvenile spirits can be this powerful?!"

"Doesn't matter if they're juvenile," Rohzen explained, grinning. "All spirits are familiars of the gods. Kelpie is undoubtedly a familiar of the Goddess of Water, Aqua, one of the four Elemental Deities. When it's given all of its contractor's MP and half of her HP, something like this is a piece of cake. Ha ha."

I see. Water is *a powerful element too. Whoa, the sphere's gonna be destroyed soon.*

The sea serpents had been slamming against the water ball from the inside this whole time. As a result, cracks were beginning to appear on its surface. There was no time to do any more observation or analysis.

"Ellies, grab the clam now!"

"Yes, master!"

Three Spirit Bs dived into the empty hole and lifted the massive clam. As soon as they came up, Allen's group began to retreat, making sure to protect the Spirit Bs. The moment they were a certain distance away from the water ball, they heard a resounding crash that indicated the ball had either been destroyed or dispelled by Kelpie. All the monsters who had been held up in the air slammed against the seafloor, along with tons of water.

The No-life Gamers left the area behind as fast as they could, not so much as sparing a glance backward. A lot had happened, but they had successfully obtained a massive clam. Once they had gotten far enough away, they stopped on top of a random lotus pad with their prize. They waited awhile, confirming that there were no sea serpents pursuing them.

Keel pressed his face close to the wavy mouth of the clam in an effort to peer inside, but it was shut tight. "Let's open it up."

"Lemme at it." Dogora jabbed both his hands into the gap and started pulling both sides apart with all his strength. "Hnnng!" The shell that had withstood the Fish Bs' attacks now slowly but surely parted, revealing a peek of what the party had been desperately seeking.

"Whooaaaaa!" The rest of the No-life Gamers, including Allen, exclaimed in unison.

"RAAAAAAH!" Dogora roared as he opened the clam wider, the veins on both his arms bulging from the strain. Soon, a heavy, rugged lump of ore that faintly glowed with a golden color came fully into view.

The boy sat down heavily, sweating all over, as everyone came over to pat him on the back. During this time, Allen peered into the clam and thought about what could be made from the amount of orichalcum inside.

Our priorities for orichalcum equipment are weapons and armor for Krena and Dogora first, then a large shield for Dogora. This much orichalcum is only enough to make one of those items. In that case, I already know what I should choose.

Both Krena's and Dogora's weapons were huge. Conversely, the lump of orichalcum was only around the size of an adult man's torso. It was only enough for one weapon or piece of armor.

"This will be Krena's greatsword," Allen announced.

"What?! You sure? Yay! Orichalcum sword!" Krena grabbed the lump with both hands and held it up to the sky, happiness radiating from every inch of her body.

Whenever this party picked up a piece of equipment or item that multiple members needed, Allen was the one to make the call on what was most effective for the party and therefore who would get the item. This had been the arrangement ever since their Academy days, and all of the party completely accepted it. Given this, Dogora did not complain when Allen declared it was Krena who would be getting an orichalcum weapon first.

Over the next three days, the No-life Gamers flew here and there, destroying every clam they found, but failed to find a second orichalcum ore. Per their usual schedule, they left the dungeon and returned to base.

Helmios's eyes widened when he saw what Krena was hugging. "Huh? Is that an orichalcum ore? You guys already found one?"

"Yes, we did," Allen replied.

"Mr. Helmios, I wanna make this a sword, please!" Krena's eyes positively sparkled.

"O-Okay. I'll take you guys to the blacksmith tomorrow."

The next day, the party left the Tower of Tribulation for the first time in quite a while and flew over the barren wastelands of Baukisian countryside.

"Master Habarak lives quite far away. At this speed, I think it'll take two days."

Helmios had ridden a Bird B during the Rohzenheim war and therefore had a general idea how fast they were. He was now accompanying the No-life Gamers to introduce them to a blacksmith who could handle orichalcum, as promised.

After two more days of flying, Allen looked down and commented, "The landscape has changed."

They were now over a rugged land with far more mountains and large boulders all over. Many of the mountains were volcanoes, judging by the billowing smoke rising into the air.

"Yep," Helmios nodded. "We're already in what used to be the Kingdom of Melka, also known as the Country of Fire."

I see. So this had been a separate country that got swallowed up by Baukis.

At the Academy, Allen had learned that Baukis had unified the entire continent under the justification of resisting the Demon Lord Army's invasion. The No-life Gamers were now very far away from Baukis's original borders.

Helmios checked the sun's position. "At this rate, we should be arriving within the day."

Sure enough, a town gradually came into view. According to Helmios, there were maybe only three blacksmiths in this world capable of handling orichalcum. However, nothing about this town indicated that it was home to someone so legendary. The only thing special about it was its prominent chimneys.

"This is the town where Master Habarak lives," the Hero declared.

Allen nodded in acknowledgment. "Let's land a distance away."

Just before sunset, Allen's group approached the town gate. When they produced their adventurer cards, the guards let them in without a fuss. They then proceeded through the streets under Helmios's guidance.

Everyone they passed was a dwarf. The stores that lined the way displayed not only weapons and armor but also goods such as earthen dishware, grills, farm tools, and metal fixtures. This was a town that did not have much that adventurers would be interested in.

Eventually, Helmios pointed at a building ahead that, in Allen's eyes, looked no different from the surrounding ones. Smoke was coming out of the chimney, indicating that a forge was lit inside. "There, that's Master Habarak's workshop."

"Ohhh!" Krena cried happily. She had been hugging her orichalcum ever since she entered the town.

Helmios knocked on the door.

A calm voice asked, "Yes? Who is it?" and the door opened a crack. A young dwarf's face peeked through.

"My name is Helmios. I've come with business for Master Habarak. However, it's late, so we hope to come visit tomorrow. Would that be possible?"

"Helmios? As in Hero Helmios?" The half of the dwarven man's face that was visible looked up at the Hero.

I totally feel like we're being treated like door-to-door salesmen.

"Ah, yes. I've come to ask Master Habarak to forge an orichalcum weapon."

"I'm sorry, but please leave."

"Huh? Can you help check with Master Habarak please? When I saw him last, he invited me to come again at any time."

"Uh, it's more that he's in very bad spirits. I'm sorry."

However, Helmios was not ready to back down so easily, especially when this was for the sake of Allen's group. He insisted, "This is very important, though. Could you please ask him somehow?"

"O-Okay, I'll try. I doubt he'll change his mind, though." The young man withdrew into the house and closed the door.

"Looks like he's at home, at least," Allen noted.

"Y-Yeah..." Krena's voice was faint. Her spirits had been doused by the shock of being rejected.

A short while later, the young man came back.

"What did Master Habarak say?" Helmios asked.

The dwarf shook his head apologetically. "Unfortunately..."

"B-But..." Krena timidly walked forward. "W-We brought the orichalcum with us. Can't you make this into a sword for me?"

"Um…as I said, it's not possible."

"Please! I beg you!" Krena lowered her head and held out her ore.

"Krena, that's enough." Allen shook his head slightly. "You're bothering him."

Only after being admonished by Allen did Krena finally pull back. "Okay. I'm sorry…"

That moment, a voice roared from inside the house, "SHADDUP OUT THERE ALREADY!"

The young man turned around in a fluster. "I'm very sorry, Master! I'm trying to turn them away r—"

Before he could finish, the door banged open with such force it almost fell off its hinges. A middle-aged dwarf with cloth wrapped around his head sized the Gamers up. "And who da hell are ye lot?"

Helmios stepped forward with a friendly smile. "Master Habarak! I'm so glad to see you again."

"Huh? So it's you, Helmios."

This guy is the legendary blacksmith we're looking for?

"Yes, sir. I'm visiting today to ask you to make an orichalcum weapon."

The young man clapped both his hands over his face.

"Did you say…*orichalcum*?" Habarak growled.

"Yes, please!" Krena eagerly held out her lump of metal.

The veins on Habarak's forehead bulged so prominently they seemed on the verge of popping. "You… Where did you find that?!"

Seeing the change in the dwarf's attitude, Allen answered on Krena's behalf. "In the dungeon, sir."

"Dungeon? So you lot are adventurers?"

"Yes, s—"

Habarak's hands shot out and grabbed Allen by the collar. The dwarf was shorter, but his arms were thicker than Allen's legs. He had no problem lifting the boy up.

"Master Habarak, what is the matter?!" Helmios exclaimed in alarm. "What did he do that displeased you?" He grabbed the blacksmith's arms in an attempt to free Allen.

Ignoring Helmios, Habarak glared at Allen with bloodshot eyes and roared, "It's all because you lot keep going on about Dygragni this, Dygragni that! Who even is he?! Lady Freyja is so furious, she's not letting me forge orichalcum anymore!"

The Gamers took a step forward, but Allen lifted a hand to stop them. Still being held up by his collar, he asked calmly, "Can you tell us more?"

"I-It's all you adventurers' fault! Blast it all!" The dwarf shoved Allen away, then crumpled to his knees, grinding his hands and head into the ground.

"U-Um…" Allen stood up and tried to question Habarak further.

However, the blacksmith merely pounded the ground with his fists, his hunched back shaking. "Lady Freyja, I'm so sorry. Please don't be angry. I'm so sorry. I'm so sor—" His heart-wrenching apologies flowed nonstop, filling the air and rising to the darkening twilight sky.

A different story was about to unfold on the No-life Gamers' path toward clearing the Tower of Tribulation.

Side Story 1: Treason

The king of Ratash frowned with thought, deepening the wrinkles on his forehead and making himself look even older than he already was. At over seventy years old, he was bedridden most of the time and had to receive all visitors in his chambers. The reason for his furrowed brow was his guest of the day.

Sitting up in bed, the king said, "Granvelle…you've truly made a mess of things."

"I'm terribly sorry, Your Majesty."

His guest, Baron Granvelle, bowed so low his head almost touched the carpeted floor from his seat. A lower noble being allowed into the king's chambers was practically unprecedented, but something had happened that made it unavoidable.

Everything had begun when the minister of justice at the time announced he would be resigning and the king recommended a particular noble to take up the seat. As this noble was from the Academy Faction, one of the two main political parties in the Ratashian government, the endorsement had startled the opposing Kingdom Faction. The Kingdom Faction made political moves to prevent someone from the Academy Faction being installed, and Viscount Carnel conspired with them to carry out his own plot to kidnap Baron Granvelle's daughter, Cecil. The incident was ultimately resolved thanks to Cecil's manservant, Allen, saving her. In the end, not only had Viscount Carnel failed to coerce Baron Granvelle into doing what he wanted, but he now found himself facing enormous blowback.

Baron Granvelle had used the mining rights to a new mithril mine Allen discovered to motivate the royal family and numerous nobles in the court to investigate the kidnapping incident, identify all involved parties, and establish safeguards so that it would never happen again.

Viscount Carnel, the one held responsible for the kidnapping, had been the type who threw his weight around using money—the Carnel family had grown rich thanks to the mithril mines in their realm—and therefore had earned a bad reputation. Many disgruntled nobles were more than happy to aid Baron Granvelle's cause, not least of whom were those in tight financial states from royal decrees to send supplies and manpower to aid the war effort against the Demon Lord. As a result, voices condemning Viscount Carnel went up all around the royal palace, their numbers increasing by the day. The viscount was eventually summoned to court for a hearing, but he ignored it and cooped himself up in his mansion instead.

The current state of affairs greatly saddened the king, who wished the situation had been taken care of when it was but a spark or that the baron had come to consult him in person. That way, things would not have snowballed into such a huge commotion.

From his position at the king's bedside, the prime minister counseled the monarch. "Your Majesty, this is an opportunity to demonstrate the royal family's power. What Viscount Carnel did was unforgivable; if we do not punish him severely, it will set a bad precedent for the other nobles."

"You have a point," the king said slowly. "Hmm, but 'severely'..."

"Our investigations have revealed that the viscount had invested a significant amount of money in the crown prince. If you do not act, it may well cost you your dignity."

When the prime minister mentioned the crown prince, a dejected look came over the king's face. As he was old now and rarely sat on the throne, his influence was understandably weakening. He was not sure he even had enough power to keep the crown prince, whom everyone expected to be the next king, in check.

The crown prince was being held up as the figurehead of the Kingdom Faction, which prioritized Ratash above the Five Continent Alliance. And currently, nobles seemed to be leaning more and more toward this side. In light of this, as well as the fact that Viscount Carnel had been a significant financial backer of the crown prince, how the king chose to deal with the viscount could very well dictate the kingdom's future.

The king fell into thought. Before he could say anything, however, there was a knock at his door.

"Announcing Sword Lord Dverg and Captain Reinbach of the Royal Guard!" called one of the guards outside.

"Let them in," the prime minister replied.

The Sword Lord and royal guard captain came in and took their seats on either side of Baron Granvelle, which induced a drop of sweat that trickled down the baron's temple. Dverg was a champion who had fought the Demon Lord Army for decades when many soldiers died their first year; Captain Reinbach was the highest authority of the knights who personally served the king. Baron Granvelle was painfully aware that he was now literally sandwiched between Ratash's top two fighters.

"Thank you for coming, Dverg," the king said.

"I only happened to be in the castle," Dverg replied as he closed his remaining eye, implying that he would not have answered the summons had he been on the battlefield. One might not guess it by how he spoke, but the lowborn warrior's current attitude inside the castle was actually a significant improvement over the years.

"Is that so." The king was already plenty familiar with Dverg and therefore did not take issue with his attitude.

"I also wanted to offer Your Majesty my wholehearted thanks for recommending me for Hero Helmios's party."

"Ah yes, I did do that. The Demon Lord is an existence that threatens the entire world. Our country naturally ought to do its part and support the Five Continent Alliance."

Hero Helmios and his party of around ten served in the fight against the Demon Lord as a strike force that infiltrated deep behind enemy lines to kill the demons and greater demons that served as commanders and officers. As a result, they faced much greater danger than those manning the fortresses. Even those with three-star Talents such as Sword Lord and Saintess could easily die during a mission. However, this strike force was indispensable to the Five Continent Alliance's strategy. Consequently, replacements were enlisted from not only Giamut but also other signatory countries whenever a member died.

Even though Dverg was nearly seventy years old, the king of Ratash had officially recommended him for Helmios's party, Sacred, a while ago.

"Dverg, I asked for you today because I have something to ask of you," the king said with a troubled face. "We have a problem here at home—"

"I'm very sorry, but I don't have time." Without even hearing the king out, Dverg bluntly turned him down.

Alarm flashed across the prime minister's face for a brief moment. In recognition of Dverg's achievements, he had been made a noble long ago and gradually promoted all the way to his current status of marquess; however, he was still spending all his days fighting the Demon Lord Army and had not once carried out any of his noble duties. Of course, he had a reason for so stubbornly dedicating his entire life to the cause.

"You're still looking?" the king asked in an understanding tone.

Dverg touched the eye patch he was wearing and nodded. "Yes."

"I see. Very well. In that case, Reinbach."

The captain, who had been waiting, promptly answered, "Yes, Your Majesty!"

"Can you do it?"

Baron Granvelle shivered a little. Both the king and Reinbach had expected Dverg to decline; that was why the latter had come. Baron Granvelle was keenly feeling the weight of the commotion he had set off.

"I am the shield of the kingdom. I shall bring you Carnel's head on a silver platter."

In sharp contrast to Dverg, Captain Reinbach of the royal knights was fiercely loyal to the crown. His reply was so ardent that Baron Granvelle unconsciously raised his head.

"Y-Your Majesty?!" the baron exclaimed.

The prime minister glared at him. "Silence. We are beyond the point of no return. Carnel ought to be well aware of just how severe the sin of taking His Majesty's name in vain is."

The baron lowered his head back down, quivering.

"Granvelle," the king said in a heavy voice, "know this: so long as I draw breath, I will never forgive such a travesty."

"O-Of course, Your Majesty," the baron replied before imagining what the king would say next. His prediction proved correct.

"I, Izunowad von Ratash the Third, find Viscount Carnel guilty of the crime of treason for the matter at hand. Reinbach, I order you to take him into custody."

"At once, Your Majesty!"

After giving a spirited reply, Reinbach approached one of the knights who had been guarding the king's bedchamber from the inside. The knight barked, "Regiment One of the Royal Guards is ready to move out any time!"

"Mm. Then Regiment One is to gather at the landing pad posthaste. I will follow soon."

The knight nodded, then swiftly left the room.

"Your Majesty, please await my return. With a high-speed magic ship, I should be back by tomorrow afternoon." Reinbach bowed to the king, then headed for the door.

Before he stepped out, however, the king stopped him. The wrinkles on his head furrowed even deeper as he forced out the words, "I'm sorry, Reinbach, but bring Carnel to me alive. In spite of it all, he has weathered these trying times with us and played a part in forging our nation's future."

The mithril from Carnel's realm had been in demand by not just Ratash but the entire Five Continent Alliance, thus serving as a steady method for Ratash to earn foreign income. It was not an exaggeration to say that Carnel's mithril had been a linchpin in maintaining the kingdom's stability. Though what the viscount had done was unforgivable, the king still wanted to show him some clemency—whatever he could do, that was, for someone who was to be purged for treason.

* * *

Viscount Carnel faced his butler in a dark room with curtains fully drawn on the top floor of his mansion.

"My lord, perhaps you really should consider heading to the royal palace..." The butler was once again voicing advice that he had given many times by now.

"*Fool!* What would be the point after all this time?!" Viscount Carnel shouted before peering outside through the gap between the curtains.

Several rolls of parchment lay at Carnel's feet, all of them bearing the royal seal. These were summons from the royal court.

Viscount Carnel had conspired with a royal envoy to use the king's name to trick Baron Granvelle into signing a contract. It did not take a genius to realize that, now that his entire plot was exposed, he was in for an extremely heavy sentence. Continuously ignoring royal summons was not helping matters either. Just the thought of the accumulative weight of his sins made him tremble in terror.

That said, there was a reason he was staying put inside his realm. This reason came in the form of a letter that he had clutched in his hands.

His butler tried to reason with him. "However, my lo—"

"Enough! His Highness the crown prince said that he would bail me out when the time comes!"

The letter in his hands had been delivered by someone who identified themselves as an envoy from the crown prince. The only thing written was "Stay at home." This gave the viscount hope, hope that he could not get go of—the crown prince had not abandoned him. So long as he continued ignoring the royal summons, he would be saved.

Knock, knock.

The knocks at the door sounded unnaturally loud in this room shrouded almost purely in shadow. The viscount whirled around to face the door.

"Wh-What is it?!"

The door opened, and a servant practically tumbled inside.

"I'm very sorry, my lord. An unscheduled magic ship is heading for the city! It will be arriving soon!"

"Wha—?! Are you sure?!"

The servant held out a tubelike object. "Please use this, my lord."

It was a magic tool that functioned like a spyglass. The viscount snatched it from the servant and stuck it through a small gap in the curtains where a bit of the setting sun was still shining through. When he looked to the sky, he confirmed there was indeed a giant magic ship heading for the city. A certain something on the side of the ship made him unconsciously pull back.

"That crest, it's the royal f-f-family's…"

Indeed, the magic ship was bearing the royal crest of the Kingdom of Ratash.

Comprehension dawned in the butler's eyes. "C-Could it be that everything is over?" he asked. After all, the number of people who could dispatch a royal magic ship was extremely limited.

"Wh-What are you implying? His Highness the crown prince will—" Viscount Carnel's voice trailed off. He could not bring himself to continue.

As long as he kept believing, things would work out.

As long as he kept believing, it was true.

Even though the viscount knew he was merely deluding himself, he had no choice but to believe in the lie he was given. If he finished his thought out loud, he felt he would be forced to face reality. *Why did the crown prince not write his name on this letter? Am I being used to buy time so he can erase all evidence implicating himself?* All the bad thoughts that the viscount had been suppressing so far flooded his head as he looked at the magic ship through the spyglass again, his eyes now begging to spot some salvation.

The ship eventually hovered right over the open plaza in the center of Carnel City. After the ship adjusted its positioning, its lower hatch slowly opened.

The moment his servant asked, “What is happening, my lord?” the viscount witnessed numerous figures appearing in the open hatch. The setting sun reflected off their suits of armor, identifying them as knights.

“What is th— He’s coming down?!”

CRAAAAASH.

One knight holding a shield nearly as tall as himself had jumped out of the magic ship and plummeted more than a hundred meters, all while wearing armor that weighed over a hundred kilograms. He landed on a water feature in the middle of the plaza and pulverized it with a resounding boom. Water burst out in a stream that soared higher than all the surrounding buildings. The people who happened to be in the plaza froze with shock for a moment, then ran away in a panic. The other knights in the magic ship looked down at the now empty plaza, then also jumped down one by one.

CRAAAAASH.

CRAAAAASH.

CRAAAAASH.

By the time the full regiment of one thousand knights had landed, every last stone in the plaza’s pavement had been shattered. These knights were all members of the royal guard, an elite chivalric order with strict requirements. Knights could only apply to join the royal guard if they had at least a two-star Talent and after serving at a fortress on the Giamutan front for ten years minimum. In other words, everyone present was at least as strong as Captain Zenof.

The knight with a large shield—Captain Reinbach—shouted to his men, “Remember that we, the greatest knight order in the Kingdom of Ratash, are here to exercise His Majesty’s royal authority! Knights of the royal guard, go and seize Viscount Carnel for his crimes of treason against the crown!”

The rest of the knights shouted through their helmets, “SIR, YES, SIR!” and began marching down the streets.

Viscount Carnel, having watched everything unfold through

his spyglass, screamed at his servant, "HURRY! Tell them to shut the gates! NOW!"

The man rushed out in a hurry. Soon, the viscount's knights closed the mansion's solid iron gates and bolted them shut. After watching them secure everything from his window, the viscount heaved a sigh of relief that they had managed before the royal guard's arrival. He then began racking his brains for what to do next.

Unfortunately, time was not a luxury that he had.

BOOOOOOM!

A dozen or so royal guards charged through the viscount's mansion's gates, blowing them away, bolt and all. Carnel threw open his window and shrieked at his own knights deployed in the yard.

"What are you doing?! Don't think, just shoot them!"

"H-However, my lord..."

"SHOOT THEM NOW!!!"

Unable to disobey a direct order, Carnel's knights loosed their bows at the dozens of royal guards closing in on them.

Clink. Clink. Clink.

All of their arrows bounced harmlessly off their opponents' armor despite the fact that they were using mithril arrowheads. The royal guards ambled into the compound as if they were on a leisurely stroll.

One of the viscount's knights pointed up at the window to the viscount's room. "He's in there, sir."

"Mm." Captain Reinbach looked up and nodded to confirm. He then coolly proceeded through the gap in the viscount's knights' formation that his subordinates had opened up.

"W-We should escape, my lord," the butler urged.

"Huh? O-Oh, right." Viscount Carnel came back to his senses and stepped back from the window. He was about to leave the room when several figures appeared in the doorway, blocking his way.

"We kindly ask that you remain here."

"What?! When did you—?!"

These turned out to be scouts belonging to the royal guards who had infiltrated the mansion through some other way. The viscount was unconsciously backing away when the window behind him smashed open. The royal knights somehow began pouring in, despite this being the fifth floor.

"Viscount Carnel, you are under arrest for treason. Come with us without resisting, and we will not hurt you."

Left with no choice but to surrender, the viscount raised both hands and knelt on the ground.

"Hm, looks like we'll be able to wrap everything up before sunset," Captain Reinbach murmured as he came into the room, walking past the viscount being hauled off and looking through the now-drafty window at the painted sky.

At last, Viscount Carnel was apprehended, and the House Granvelle Affair finally came to an end.

Side Story 2: Rosetta the Phantom Thief

Among the members of Hero Helmios's party was a woman with the Phantom Thief Talent, Rosetta. This is the story of how she and Helmios met.

Long ago, Rosetta had been the leader of Rosetta's Ring, a close-knit crew of around ten burglars who went around stealing from nobles and major merchants.

On this particular night, they had once again infiltrated a noble's mansion and were stripping it of anything valuable they came across.

"Rosetta, we got everything in the magic bag!"

A young man named Abel called out to his leader with a voice full of satisfaction as he tightened the neck of the bag in his hand. This bag was a magic tool with a storage capacity hundreds of times larger than normal bags its size that could hold anything able to fit through its mouth.

Rosetta nodded. "Got it. All right, everyone, we're outta here!"

"Roger!"

With that, the gang left the treasure room and made their way down a hallway that was lined with carpet so expensive a commoner could work their whole life without ever seeing anything comparable, much less walking on one. They then went through a section adjoining a garden, making their way to the back door they had infiltrated from, when a portly man wearing sleepwear suddenly appeared around the corner. The man, who was none other than the owner of the house on his way back from the toilet, rubbed his bleary eyes and peered at Rosetta's group.

"Huh? Who're you—" His eyes widened with realization, then he shouted, "R-Robbers! Men, we're being robbed!"

"Shit! Through the windows!" Rosetta shouted.

CRAAASH!

Rosetta's Ring smashed the windows and leaped down into the mansion's garden. They made a mad dash for the mansion gates in the dark of night, their feet flying over the manicured lawn as the shouts of servants went up throughout the compound. An alarm sounded, and magic tools came to life in the windows, illuminating the garden.

Thankfully, Rosetta's group reached the gates first. Or so they thought.

"Impudent robber scum! You're not getting away!"

A knight was waiting for them, weapon in hand. Having no mercy for criminals, he promptly swung his sword at Abel, who had been the one running at the very front.

"AHHHHH!!!"

Suddenly finding himself under attack, Abel froze up and instinctively brought his arms up protectively. However, he was wearing no protective gear; the knight's sword was going to slice through his arms too.

"*ABEL!!!*"

That instant, a heat haze sprang up around Rosetta.

"Huh? My sword...?!"

The knight thought his sword had cut through one of the robbers, but instead, he felt himself lose his balance and start to fall. He thrust both hands out to prop himself up in the nick of time. For some reason, Rosetta now had his sword. When he looked up in a daze, the robbers were already through the gates.

"Phew. Thanks for saving me back there, Rosetta."

"Hm? Oh. Of course. I mean, you're the one holding all the loot! C'mon, hand it over."

"Seriously?" Abel smiled wryly as Rosetta snatched the magic bag from his hands.

"I can't get over it; this bag is *super* useful! It's just perfect for what we do."

The gang had obtained this magic bag when robbing another rich man's house.

"By the way, Rosetta, what do you think about moving on to another town? There really aren't any joints left for us to hit up here."

"You're right..." Rosetta broke into a cheeky grin. "How about we head to the imperial capital next?"

"Ohhh! Are we finally doing it?!"

After Rosetta's Ring hopped around some of the major cities within Giamut, word about them had spread, putting all nearby settlements on guard. Naturally, that made it hard for them to find new targets. This was why they had taken to choosing smaller towns like this particular one, but they were nearing their limits under such restrictions. Their only remaining option was to head for the imperial capital, where the most goods and wealth gathered in this nation.

Seeing the confident look on Rosetta's face, Abel whooped. "Hell yeah! In that case, let's celebrate our last night here!"

"You're on fire tonight, Abel!"

Rosetta gave Abel a good ribbing, to which he shrugged, and the rest of the gang burst out laughing together.

Their whole group was made up of children who did not belong anywhere else. More specifically, Rosetta, Abel—who was three years younger than her—and the rest of the crew had grown up together in an orphanage. Giamut was overflowing with orphans after decades of fending off the Demon Lord Army's advances. For as far back as she could remember, Rosetta's home had been an orphanage run by a church, her parents were nuns, and Abel and the other kids were her siblings.

Then, everything changed when she turned five.

It was revealed at her Appraisal Ceremony that she possessed the one-in-ten-million Phantom Thief Talent. After that, the nuns made Rosetta study in preparation for attending the Academy. They told her it was a place only those with Talents could attend and that she must not waste this rare gift that the deities had bestowed upon her.

Rosetta had asked what would happen to the other children without Talents. She was told there were plenty of work opportunities in the north, positions where the others would get food, clothes, and shelter. Believing this, she threw herself into her studies and successfully managed to enroll in the Academy.

The adults at the Academy had praised her for her rare Talent and gave her special training on how to effectively harness its abilities. She absorbed everything like a sponge, picking up numerous useful skills. The more she developed her Talent, the more the adults fawned over her, and their praise was exhilarating.

In her second year, Rosetta then learned the truth about what was *really* happening in the world.

The place with "plenty of work opportunities" in the north for Talentless children the nuns had mentioned was a bloody battlefield where the empire was fighting an endless war against the Demon Lord Army. Many people were sent there each year—if not to fight, then to build fortifications, transport supplies, or carry out any number of countless tasks needed to support the war effort; more than half of them died to monster attacks.

Rosetta ended up sneaking out of the Academy just before her graduation, returning to the orphanage in time to see Abel and other familiar faces getting carted off in a steel cage at the back of a horse-drawn carriage. She promptly used her newly learned skills to free them. Of course, she did not bring them back to the orphanage.

In order to live independently from the adults, she formed a gang of thieves with her friends. At first, she did all the stealing alone and had the rest help secure escape routes for her. However, once she trained them, they each started taking a more active role in heists until the entire group became a full-blown larceny ring. They also picked up more and more homeless orphans in the cities they hit, steadily expanding the size and scale of their operations.

When Rosetta reached adulthood, she led the group to the imperial capital, where they operated for several years.

One night, Rosetta's Ring infiltrated a noble's mansion with such lax security that it aroused their suspicions for a moment. However, because they had never once been caught since the formation of their gang, they were confident they could slip away even if the place was trapped. Just as feared, however, the moment they stepped into a particular room in their search for valuables, an alarm rang out.

"I knew it! Okay, we're outta h— Shit, the window!"

Before the gang reached the window in the room, a steel shutter came down, cutting off their route of escape. They were now literally backed into a corner as the owner of the mansion appeared in the doorway, flanked by knights.

"Heh heh heh, so these are the cat burglars who've been tearing the city apart as of late. Rosetta's Ring, was it? You scum are never seeing the light of day again."

The noble proudly flaunted the magic tool in his hand, explaining that it was a recent purchase from Baukis that notified him as soon as intruders entered the grounds.

"Capture them alive! They've all got bounties on their heads! I'll be presenting them to His Imperial Majesty as tribute!"

As the knights closed in, Rosetta considered using her skills to get away but remembered that Abel and the rest were all Talentless. She could not bring herself to abandon them and escape by herself, and so the entirety of Rosetta's Ring was captured and locked up.

* * *

The next day, Hero Helmios happened to be having a meal with the emperor of Giamut. The current emperor believed in properly rewarding capable young people with achievements; for example, Helmios had been born a commoner, but because he had developed his abilities as a Hero and used them for the sake of the empire, he was granted the truly enviable privilege of not only being a duke but also having the right to personally dine with the emperor.

Suddenly, a member of the imperial guard came in. "Reporting, Your Imperial Majesty."

"Speak."

"Viscount Unuleus has reported that he has captured all of Rosetta's Ring."

"Hm. Is that so." The emperor swirled his glass of wine. "Go on."

"All of them are alive. The viscount is asking for further orders."

"Sounds like the magic tools I passed out to the nobles have come in handy. Hm, let me see..."

Public order in Giamut had been on the decline due to prolonged war with the Demon Lord Army. There were far too many refugees with nowhere else to go forming criminal groups and targeting the homes of prominent people such as nobles. To deal with this situation, the emperor had ordered magic tools useful for crime prevention and sold them to nobles and major merchants at a significant markup.

He now considered what he should do with Rosetta's Ring as Helmios watched on in silence, expecting some cruel and unusual form of execution.

To the Hero's surprise, the emperor said, "First, we'll say that it was Helmios who apprehended them."

Helmios's eyes widened in surprise. "Huh? Me?"

"After all, the more achievements you have, the better it is for me."

Viscount Unuleus might have been the one to capture the gang, using the emperor's magic tool and whatnot; however, the emperor preferred that Helmios have all the credit, since a boost to Helmios's reputation meant an increase in his own influence as the Hero's backer.

Thus, several days later, an official proclamation went out that Rosetta's Ring was to be executed publicly and that all citizens were encouraged to attend.

* * *

The night before Rosetta's Ring was to be executed, Helmios found himself standing within a templelike structure with rows of massive pillars and flagstone flooring. There was a faint mist in the air, and light shone from somewhere. A man was framed within that light in a way that made it impossible to clearly see his face, clothes, or any other aspects of his appearance. However, Helmios recalled having felt his presence before.

"Where…is this? Who are you?"

"My apologies for calling you out so suddenly. I would have reached out through what you call an oracle, but there was no time."

Helmios immediately caught on. He tried to kneel but found his body refusing to listen to him, almost as if he were half-asleep.

"L-Lord Elmea. Your Holiness."

The God of Creation waved a hand dismissively. "You don't need to do that. So, there's something I must ask of you."

"Anything, my Lord."

"Tomorrow, a woman named Rosetta is to be executed—I want you to save her."

"Are you referring to the thief?"

Helmios recalled that the emperor had indeed announced that Rosetta's Ring would be executed the next day. All of the members were to be tied up and left to be eaten alive by goblins. Helmios had suggested sending them to the northern battlefront and releasing them if they survived a certain period of service, but the emperor had refused to listen.

"The very one. I have bestowed her with the power to grasp the future. That includes your future too."

Helmios was just about to ask Elmea to elaborate when his vision shifted and he was back in his room. He sat bolt upright in bed, but found himself alone in the dark.

"The power to grasp the future, huh?"

The Hero peered through the darkness at his own hands.

* * *

The next morning, Helmios descended a flight of stairs as a few men followed after him in a fluster.

"U-Um, Lord Helmios, why are you...?"

"I just need to talk with her real quick."

Eventually, the Hero stopped before the cell holding Rosetta. He looked between the bars into the eyes of all the prisoners within, one by one, before eventually stopping on her.

"You. You're Rosetta?"

"Wh-Who wants to know?"

The other prisoners looked over curiously.

"I've come to free you."

"Huh? ...Really?! Yay!"

Despite having been in custody for a few days, there was still cheer in Rosetta's voice.

"However, there's a condition: you have to join my party."

Hearing this, Abel shouted from the neighboring cell, "Huh?! The hell does that even mean?! Rosetta! Don't listen to this guy!"

However, Rosetta merely asked in a cool voice, "You're Hero Helmios, aren't you?"

Everyone who lived in the imperial capital knew who Helmios was; he was that much of a champion to the people. Of course, Rosetta had also seen his face before from a long distance away.

"That's right, I am. And my party doesn't have a scout at the moment."

More accurately, his entire party—excluding himself, of course—had been massacred by Greater Demonic Deity Kyubel. But he was not lying.

"So you're asking me to fight the Demon Lord Army?"

Rosetta could not immediately say yes or no. One reason she had run away from the very institution for raising elite troops to face the Demon Lord Amy, was that she did not want to join the war. But there was also another reason.

Helmios caught her meaning and nodded in understanding. "Ah,

I see. If you agree to become my party member, then you won't be the only one I'll be saving."

His words had touched on Rosetta's second reason, the one that meant she could not turn down his offer.

"In that case..."

As Abel continued shouting at her to refuse, Rosetta parted her lips to give her answer.

* * *

At noon, the residents of the imperial capital of Giamut had filled the seats of the coliseum, waiting for the execution of Rosetta's Ring to start. The circular stage at the lowest tier of the coliseum was usually where warriors dueled and knights trained. Today, however, the prostrate forms of the thieves whose syndicate had shaken the whole country were on display, their hands and feet bound.

"Dammit! Untie me!" Abel shouted. Despite being trussed up, he still tried to kick the guard who had thrown them onto the stage like mere baggage. The guard easily dodged the swipe, retaliating with a kick to Abel's stomach with all his strength.

"Hmph!"

"*Oof!*" Abel gasped for breath as all the air left his lungs.

"Abel!" Rosetta cried in alarm.

"Worry about yourself. You're all gonna be eaten by goblins anyways," the guard spat at her, looking down at the pair as if they were hot garbage.

When all of Rosetta's Ring were onstage, the executioner began reading out their charges into a voice-amplifying magic tool. The audience listened to the reverberating words and filled the air with jeers and verbal abuse of their own. Eventually, the executioner finished and rolled up his scroll. The bars sealing the doorways that lined the bottom tier of the stands were raised, and goblins crawled out from the darkness beyond. They made a beeline for the struggling bandits.

"*Gyah, gyah!*"

One goblin strutted over to Rosetta licking its lips, clearly in high spirits. It reached out to grab her head, only for its head to suddenly fly off with a *psheeew!* sound as blood fountained onto the ground.

The audience watched in shock as Helmios, who had wordlessly descended to the stage, went around taking out the dozens of goblins. Even the nobles and the emperor were dumbfounded.

The executioner hurried over. "L-Lord Helmios, what is the meaning of this?"

"I have to talk with Rosetta over there." Helmios's usual smile was nowhere to be seen. In a low, intense voice that bordered on a growl, he told the executioner to step back.

"Y-Yes, my lord."

Helmios then approached Rosetta. As everyone in the coliseum watched with bated breath, he used the orichalcum sword that had killed all the goblins with to cut her ropes.

"Oh, what a miracle!" Rosetta got on her knees and held both hands up to Helmios in a way that seemed almost a charade. "A-Are you here to save me, my lord?!"

"I am."

"You would forgive one such as myself who has committed acts so unworthy of forgiveness?! You are too kind, my lord!"

"I'm now looking for companions who would fight the Demon Lord Army with me."

"I would gladly join your cause!"

The audience did not understand what was happening but stayed quiet, letting things unfold.

The Hero turned back toward the executioner. "Can I see that?" he asked, gesturing toward the microphonic magic tool.

"Huh? Uh, of course. Here you go, my lord." The man handed it over, looking bewildered.

Helmios accepted the mic, then turned to face the audience. "I, Hero Helmios, came here today to invite Rosetta to my party and give her a second chance to use her abilities for the greater good. She has agreed, so I'm calling off her execution."

The emperor, the executioner, and the nobles could not believe their ears. However, after a beat, applause went up here and there from the spectator seats. The fact that Helmios was forgiving a sinner and accepting her into a party that would be fighting for their homeland had moved the hearts of some people.

As planned, the rest of Rosetta's Ring, whom Helmios had also freed, began clapping as well. This prompted even more clapping from the audience, creating a chain reaction that eventually ended with thunderous applause and cheers that shook the coliseum's very walls.

The emperor was about to stand up but realized that this outcome would still garner him influence. Since it was the same either way, he sat back down, satisfied.

"So, why *are* you making me join your party? What's the real reason?" Rosetta asked while still smiling toward the audience.

"As I said this morning, I saw in a dream that you are someone who will grasp my future for me."

"What does that even mean? Forget the future; I want to grasp your heart now."

A faint smile came over Helmios's face. "Now that's a problem. I hope you'll go easy on me."

Instead of answering, Rosetta merely grinned.

And so, under the eyes of a whole coliseum of people, Rosetta became a member of Helmios's party.

Side Story 3: Meruru's Golem

After parting with Allen's group at the Academy, Meruru headed for the capital of the Empire of Baukis. There, she regrouped with a large number of Talented students who had been studying at Academies in Baukis or on exchange overseas.

In the war against the Demon Lord Army, Baukis was currently facing twice the enemy's usual numbers. Although the Demon Lord Army had never once managed to land on Baukis's shore, the Baukisian navy knew better than to let its guard down.

Meruru was then instructed to board a magic ship with her classmates from before she went on exchange. They were joining up with the Baukisian navy, which was currently sailing north on the open ocean; it was headed toward the coordinates where they would be facing the Demon Lord Army, which was sailing from the Forgotten Continent to the far north.

When their magic ship drew close, one ship dwarfed the rest of the naval fleet, arresting their attention. This was the flagship of the Baukisian navy that also operated as its headquarters. Meruru and her fellow students disembarked onto the deck of the massive ship, where their stats and Talents were checked. They were then made to line up along the deck.

Admiral Garara arrived with subordinates in tow to question each of the students about their readings. However, when it was Meruru's turn, the admiral's expression changed.

"Huh? Ye never called forth a golem before?" he asked incredulously.

"U-Uh, yes, sir. I only got to observe when I was in my first year."

The other students looked equally bewildered for a moment until they remembered that Meruru was still a second-year student. At the Academy, students were only permitted to ride golems and practice using them for battle in their third year—pretty much right before graduation, at that. After all, actually calling forth a golem and piloting it were not all that difficult.

"Guess there be no helpin' it. There's still a few days 'til we reach base. I'll teach ye."

"Huh?"

"Meruru. Ye 'ave the Talos General Talent. Ye'll be a leader one day. Think o' this war as a learnin' opportunity."

And so it was decided that Meruru would be getting a crash course on golem piloting right here on this ship.

Pepeku, one of the admiral's men, interrupted while making a troubled face. "Sorry, Admiral, but we're almost at Lamchatka Strait."

There was still a lot to confirm and work out before the navy was to make contact with the Demon Lord Army.

Garara sighed. Unlike Pepeku, he thought there was still enough time, as there were still a few days until the actual fighting would begin. "Aren't we nearly done talkin' strategy? Pepeku, ye help out, then. An' be serious when talkin' with the lass 'ere."

The northbound fleet eventually reached Lamchatka Strait, the point where the Central Continent and the Baukisian Continent were closest. The water there was shallow, and sheer cliffs loomed over both sides of the strait. The navy could fight here without worry of the Demon Lord Army surrounding them.

However, the continental plate fell off just south of the strait, making the ocean there incredibly deep. If the Demon Lord Army managed to break through their lines, the Baukisians would be forced to fight not only by air, sea, and land, but deep underwater as well.

Furthermore, Dongbao—the capital of Baukis—was located close to the northern edge of the continent and right next to a canal. If the Lamchatka Strait were breached, the imperial capital could easily come under attack. Knowing this, Baukis had built a massive fortress at the strait, Base Lamchatka, which was constantly manned by a hundred thousand troops.

"I'll be workin' yer arses off. Brace yerselves!"

"Aye, aye, Admiral!"

As Meruru's ship continued making its way to Base Lamchatka, Admiral Garara was personally instructing the specially selected students with especially promising futures. The Empire of Baukis had gathered thousands of Talented students for this clash with the Demon Lord Army, and these ten were the cream of the crop. Meruru was here because she possessed a one-in-ten-million Talent; the others were all the top scorers at their respective Academies. One of the aims of this elite squad was to provide them field experience and instruction from the most distinguished teacher available.

"Ye 'ear me, ye lot?! We haven't got time. Especially ye, Meruru, since ye ain't got experience ridin' a golem. So, I'm gonna beat it into yer flesh bags! Pepeku—ye be in charge o' helpin' Meruru with'r golem!"

The students looked nervous but managed to reply, "Aye, aye, Admiral!" in unison.

Admiral Garara was the chief commander of the entire Baukisian navy. Not only did he have an impressive title, but he was also the national champion credited with foiling every single one of the Demon Lord Army's attempts to land on Baukis's shore.

Being able to receive personal instruction from him was the greatest motivator for these elite students. And off to the side, Pepeku and Meruru were about to begin their own one-on-one lesson.

"First, make sure that all the slates I handed you are firmly fitted into your magic disc," Pepeku said.

Meruru obediently checked the disc hanging around her neck. "Yes, sir. They're all in."

When she received the magic disc earlier, she had already confirmed that it had all the necessary slates slotted in. However, thorough checks were a crucial part of being a golem pilot. For example, not realizing a slate was loose could prove fatal in the thick of battle, and even worse, could lead to allies dying too.

"Next, register a name for your golem into your disc."

"What kind of name should it be, sir?"

"It can be anything you want. Just make sure to steer clear of any names of the gods or Baukisian emperors."

It was impossible to change the name of one's golem afterward. With this in mind, golem pilots chose their golems' names very carefully. The names of deities and past emperors were off-limits, so many went with the names of powerful monsters, other famous historic champions, or world-renowned treasures. The one that Meruru chose, however, was a bit different.

"I'm going with Tam-Tam, then!"

"'Tam-Tam'? As in, the tam-tam tree? That's a first."

The tam-tam was a rare species of tree that could survive even in Baukis's dry and arid climate, producing large and sweet fruit. Choosing "tam-tam" as a name was the equivalent of choosing "melon" or "watermelon" in Allen's past world. Needless to say, almost no other golem pilots named their golems anything like it, so Pepeku's comment just naturally came out.

"I can't name it that?"

"Oh, no, you totally can. It's a good name."

The tam-tam fruit meant a lot to Meruru, who was born and raised in the port city of Heratana, close to Dongbao. Her father provided maintenance for the ships that came in. One day, he had gone to the market to buy a tam-tam sapling, then came home and planted it in the family's yard.

This type of tree grew very slowly and required a lot of care. What was more, the fruit from their tree ended up not being all that sweet and was more watery than the produce on sale at the market.

Meruru grasped her magic disc while recalling how dearly her father cared for the tree—despite her brothers complaining about how mediocre the fruit tasted.

With a bright flash, the name "Tam-Tam" registered to Meruru's magic disc.

"Now, lift your hands and shout, 'Come forth, Tam-Tam!' You don't have to make a cool pose this first time. Focus only on summoning your golem."

"Yes, sir. Come forth, Tam-Tam!"

A magic circle appeared before Meruru, and from it arose a ten-meter-tall golem.

"I'm sure you already know this, but while your golem is out, you'll gradually lose MP, even if you're not doing anything."

Meruru could actually feel the sensation of MP leaving her body. She nodded.

"Yes, sir!"

"'Kay, let's have you try and ride this thing, then. I'll teach you how to pilot it and use your skills. Hold up a hand toward your golem's crystal."

"Yes, sir! Yah! Wait, wh-whoa!"

When Meruru thrust her hand out toward the large crystal embedded within her golem's chest, it glowed and shot a beam of light in her direction. The next thing she knew, she was floating in midair and being sucked toward the golem. She was so surprised she started flailing about. Once inside the crystal, she floated about as if she were underwater but had no problems breathing.

"How's it feel? Try moving your hands and legs *slowly*. The magic disc should respond."

"Okay! M-Move! Whoa, my view!"

When Meruru willed one hand to move, the magic disc hanging around her neck flickered and the sea and sky abruptly filled her vision. Through the power of the magic disc, she was now seeing what Tam-Tam was seeing. When she moved her right hand, the magic disc relayed her intention, and her golem also moved its right hand. She looked at the arm that had just moved, her heart overflowing with emotion. After this, she learned a few simple movements as well as how to use her skills, then got to work practicing them. Pepeku had a calm voice and was good at teaching. He had a good sense for when to give her time to rest and broke up the humdrum of the lesson with interesting tidbits every now and then. When he told Meruru that his golem served as one of the parts that combined with Admiral Garara's golem whenever he did large-scale transformations, stars practically shot out of her eyes.

"Thank you very much, sir!" she said appreciatively after their lesson.

"You're a fast learner, Meruru. We'll get to using your Extra Skill tomorrow. You're a right arm, right? I'll think about how to set things up."

"Thank you, sir!"

"Hoy, Pepeku! Meruru! Wrap it up for t'day!" Admiral Garara shouted to them, then turned back to the students he was teaching. "You lot come too! It's time t' drink!"

"Aye, aye, Admiral!" the students replied, bowing respectfully. Apparently Garara had completely won them over while Pepeku was teaching Meruru. When she saw this, she realized the truth in something Pepeku had just told her before.

Golem pilots had the ability to combine their golems to form even bigger golems. To make this happen, a group needed to be made up of pilots who each handled a different part—like how Meruru's Extra Skill was "Union (Right Arm)." Each part had its own role to fulfill, and golem pilots would purposely pick up skills that enhanced their role in a combined golem. For example, Pepeku taught Meruru that, since she was a right arm, she should learn more attack skills.

The Role and Relevant Skills of Each Golem Part

- Head: Overall command of the whole golem. Needs finisher skills.

- Torso: Coordination between all other parts. Needs buff skills.
- Left arm: Defense. Needs blocking and recovery skills.
- Right arm: Attack. Needs attack skills.
- Legs: Movement. Needs speed-boosting skills and skills that alter the golem's form.

Furthermore, Pepeku had taught Meruru that a golem pilot's personality also influenced their role within the combined golem.

Pepeku's Golem Part-Based Personality Analysis

- Head: Charismatic and has good leadership qualities
- Torso: Good at cooperating with and mediating between people
- Left arm: Reactive
- Right arm: Proactive
- Legs: Either hasty or likes to do things at their own pace

Whereas Meruru had the Right Arm Extra Skill, Pepeku had Torso, and Admiral Garara had the Head. Pepeku had been all too happy to explain that golem pilots with different personalities and specialties working together and combining their powers was one reason they were so powerful.

Pepeku had ended this talk about personalities and golem parts by saying that it was Admiral Garara who had come up with this theory. Meruru now looked in the admiral's direction and saw him with one of the students in a headlock as he led everyone to the drinking party. She giggled with the realization of how spot-on his theory was.

* * *

Three days after Meruru's group boarded Admiral Garara's ship, the navy reached Lamchatka Strait. The Empire of Baukis had plenty of military bases spread out all over the continent, some of which were also out in the ocean, but this one was the largest by far due to how crucial it was. Half of the total military strength of Baukis—one of the major powers of the Five Continent Alliance—was stationed here at Base Lamchatka.

Admiral Garara gathered all of the sailors and students, including the elite squad that Meruru was a part of, on the deck of his ship, then barked, "Ne'er forget that Baukis'll be finished if th' enemy breaks through! E'ryone, t' yer stations!"

More than ten thousand dwarves shouted at the top of their lungs, "Aye, aye, Admiral!"

"Chosen Corp, yer with me at th' very front! Brace yerselves!"

"Aye, aye, Admiral!"

The dwarven race gave birth to many golem pilots, blacksmiths, and magic tool users, but of Baukis's total population of two hundred million, only ten percent were born with a Talent. The golem pilots put their lives on the line to protect the futures of the remaining 180,000,000.

Meruru now felt the weight of the responsibility of standing at the front lines with Admiral Garara and the expectations placed on her as a Talos General through and through. She responded to the admiral's cry with as much zest as the rest of the Chosen Corp.

The dwarves burst into action as they carried out the plan hashed out over the past three days. Some made their way to the ocean fortress, while others prepared their ships for combat. Admiral Garara had based the strategy this time on the recovery items that Allen had given Meruru back when she parted with the No-life Gamers at the Ratashian Academy. After the effects of the items had been confirmed, Meruru had given the admiral full rein to use them however he saw fit.

Several golems were deployed to the north of Base Lamchatka in three lines, positioned so as to not let a single monster through. They did not have to wait long before the one-million-strong Demon Lord Army force showed up and began their assault.

This was the first day of what eventually became a whole month of pitched battle.

The war ultimately ended with Baukis's victory. With help and advice from Admiral Garara and Pepeku, Meruru had desperately fought to protect her homeland. They suffered some casualties, but those numbers were incredibly low considering the size of the enemy force. There was a reason for this: the recovery items from Allen had made a massive difference.

The navy had structured their three lines of defense so that they could switch positions whenever a fighter ran low on MP from taking attacks, but the recovery items made it so easy to recover MP that there was almost no need to switch out. Their defensive lines held fast against the Demon Lord Army, which lacked the firepower to make any decisive push.

Thanks to this, the supply ships positioned between the lines never came under attack either. The Baukisian defense proved so much more effective than before that the Demon Lord Army had started getting impatient. Normally, a general would escape once he realized his army had no hope of winning, but this particular commander seemed very distressed by the unexpected resistance and showed up in person. The general was a Demonic Deity, and he had Rank S monsters at his command as well.

When the Demonic Deity appeared, however, Admiral Garara used his combined golem to obliterate him and his Rank S monsters, sending them to a literal watery grave.

* * *

After the Demon Lord Army was defeated, the sailors still in their service period remained, but Meruru and the rest of the students were summoned to Dongbao. There, the emperor recognized Meruru by showering her with money and making her an honorary baron.

The country was not simply giving her preferable treatment for having a valuable Talent. She was also being evaluated for providing Allen's recovery items and for her performance fighting with Admiral Garara on the front lines. Baukis was a country that valued money above all else, but it was very liberal when rewarding those with exemplary achievements or worthy abilities.

The other members of the Chosen Corp were also rewarded in various ways, such as with a knighthood or promise of future employment in a prominent position in the Baukisian navy after graduation.

As was customary, a flashy parade was then held on the main avenue of Dongbao to announce to the people the empire's victory. Meruru and the rest of the war heroes rode on top of golems transformed to march on land as the hundreds of thousands—nay, millions of dwarves lining the road showered them with thunderous applause.

"No way, I see my dad!"

From her position near the front of the procession, Meruru spotted her father, who had also been aboard her ship during the campaign as a mechanic, in the crowd. He was with the rest of her family in the stands reserved for the families of those recognized for their distinguished service. When Meruru flailed her arm around at them, they waved back, bringing tears to her eyes.

At the end of the parade, there was an announcement that the tax on alcohol would be suspended for the next ten days. This led to so much merrymaking in the capital that nearly all its liquor stores were cleared out.

Meruru herself was invited to a celebration held in one of the lavishly decorated palace's banquet halls. Her family was also invited to attend, so she arrived, her parents and four older brothers in tow, with everyone wearing crisply ironed outfits.

"Then a super giant monster showed up, and Admiral Garara ordered me to be his right arm! So I went *boom boom boom*!"

Meruru now recounted her exploits to her family with excitement and pride at the party. They all listened with interest while also a little overwhelmed by the extravagant dishes covering the tables around them.

"Damn, that's quite the story," her father said. "So that's why they gave you such a big reward."

"Mm-hm!"

In the end, Meruru had given all the money she had received to her parents. They refused profusely, saying that they could not accept such a large amount, but she insisted that this was her way of thanking them for raising her. After a lot of heated back-and-forth, her parents eventually folded.

"So, what're you gonna do now? Return to Ratash?"

"Um…I think so."

"I see. So we won't see you again for another year."

"I-I think so."

Because Baukisian students going on exchange received a stipend on top of their tuition being subsidized, Meruru had chosen to go on exchange to lower the financial burden of her parents, who were paying her way through school. At this moment, Meruru had no idea that Allen was going to arrange for all the No-life Gamers to graduate after only two years of school, and therefore she still thought she would be returning to Ratash soon.

What she did already know, however, were Allen's plans for after graduation. She was torn whether to tell her father now.

"Mm? Wassup?" One of Meruru's brothers noticed that she had fallen into thought.

"Oh, it's nothing."

Meruru was still mulling when a rough voice called for her from a distance away.

"Ahoooooy! Meruruuuuuuu!"

Admiral Garara was standing on top of the tables laden with food and making his way toward Meruru, dragging Pepeku along in a cobra twist headlock. The nobles could not believe their eyes, but no one tried to stop him. This was pretty much how the admiral always acted whenever he got drunk; he had done the same even on the group's way back to Dongbao.

"Sorry, I have to talk with him." Meruru excused herself to her family before heading over. "What is it, Admiral?"

"Ye'll like this! Word just came in—Rohzenheim beat back their own bunch'a Demon Lord Army forces. And they did it *after* losin' their capital! It be a miracle! I sure wanna know how they pulled it off!"

"Are you serious, Admiral?!"

"I ain't no liar. Word is, 'twas an overwhelmin' victory. Th' elves ain't half bad!"

Although Rohzenheim had yet to declare their war was fully over, they had informed all the other nations that they had succeeded in recapturing their capital. Admiral Garara had remembered that Meruru had elven friends like Sophie, and so he came over to give her the update on their front.

"Th-Thank you, Admiral!"

Meruru recalled the sight of a million monsters at Lamchatka Strait. Hearing that the elves had beaten back twice that number, she could not hide her surprise.

"Hm, ye look like yer thinkin' about somethin'. Here, I'll lend ya Pepeku!" The admiral roughly tousled Meruru's hair, as if telling her to get whatever it was off her chest so she could fully enjoy the party.

Finally freed from his drunken superior, Pepeku turned to Meruru and asked her kindly, "What's the matter? Do you want to talk about it?"

"O-Okay. Actually, I'm not sure if I should tell my family what I'll be doing after graduation."

"Are you not going to work at the imperial court?"

"I'm actually thinking of going to the Rank S dungeon with the friends I made in Ratash."

"What?! ...Ah, you did mention your group managed to clear all the necessary Rank A dungeons during your time at the Academy. Is that them?"

Pepeku had already asked Meruru about her time in Ratash and was surprised to learn that she had joined a party that had helped her clear five Rank A dungeons within a single year.

Meruru nodded. "Yep. And I haven't been able to bring myself to tell my parents yet."

"Well...I think it's entirely up to you whether to tell them or not."

"Huh?!" The girl's eyes widened with bewilderment.

"It's my turn to be honest with you. I actually joined Stinger without telling my parents either."

"Really?"

Stinger was the party that Admiral Garara led back when he was an adventurer. They were famous for clearing all the dungeons in Baukis in the blink of an eye and for showing up to save settlements under monster attack, no matter the rank of the threat. And because Pepeku's home village was close to a Rank A dungeon, the party had stayed in town for a while.

"At the time, I already knew that I had the Talos General Talent, just like you. So I thought they might accept me in their party."

"Did they?"

"I got a punch to the face instead. The admiral was like, 'What's a brat jumping into danger for?!'"

"Aww, he said no."

"He said, 'Doesn't matter how great yer Talent be. Ye're just a brat, and ye joinin' will worry yer parents.' But I didn't give up. I enrolled at an Academy and did everything I could to get stronger. And after I graduated, I went to the admiral and asked to join his party again. Turns out he still remembered me."

"No way!"

"He went, 'Looks like ye won't take no fer an answer,' and finally accepted me."

Pepeku looked positively pleased when he finished telling his story.

"And you're saying that you didn't tell your parents you got in right away?" Meruru understood that Pepeku recounting his story was his way of answering her question.

"That's right. Because they would've worried. In the end, I only told them when Garara became the admiral of the Baukisian navy."

The Empire of Baukis could not simply leave Garara to his own devices—not when he was the one and only Talos King in their country. With the intensity of the Demon Lord Army's assault increasing every year, Garara was eventually persuaded by the ministers to accept the promotion to admiral. It was only then that Pepeku revealed to his parents that he was in Garara's party. In the end, his parents had already figured it out by the time he told them, though. In short, Pepeku was making the point that if his parents could deduce that he was in Stinger, he was sure Meruru's parents and brothers also could make out what she was worrying about.

"I see..." she murmured. With the weight now off her shoulders, Meruru started pestering Pepeku for tales of his adventurers as a member of Stinger.

"Our Extra Skills are only useful when there are five of us, so we always had to work together to beat our enemies. For example..." The alcohol was starting to get to Pepeku, making it hard to understand what he was saying.

"And? And?!"

"Whenever we met a strong enemy, Admiral always charged in first..." Halfway through telling Admiral Garara's story with as much pride as if it were his own, Pepeku slumped over, dead drunk.

"Oy, Pepeku! How can ye sleep at a party?!" Admiral Garara, also very drunk, began to violently shake Pepeku in an attempt to wake him up.

After participating in the war to defend the Empire of Baukis, Meruru felt she had learned what it truly meant to have companions. She swore once more that she would definitely go to the Rank S dungeon with the rest of the No-life Gamers.

Side Story 4: Unconquered

The young emperor of Giamut, Regalfaras von Giamut the Fifth, had been crowned after each of his older brothers met timely deaths. Because of this, there were those who called him the Bloody Emperor behind his back.

At the moment, Regalfaras was sitting at a heavy, luxurious-looking desk and glaring at the man and woman before him with disapproval. The pair remained standing instead of sitting down, either because they felt out of place or because they did not want to stay a moment longer than necessary, possibly both. Sitting next to the emperor was Hero Helmios.

"And that's basically just how Allen is," Helmios said. "I'm pretty sure the only thing he's got in his head is going to the Rank S dungeon."

"Is that so. And that is why he refused my summons?"

There was a reason for the emperor's bad mood. The man and woman before him were his foreign minister and one of the minister's envoys, respectively. And they had come together to deliver a certain report.

The report in question was an account of how the envoy had, on the emperor's direct order, approached Allen while on a magic ship and conveyed that the emperor wished to meet him when the ship landed in the capital of Giamut. However, Allen had turned her down in no uncertain terms.

"We are deeply sorry."

The foreign minister apologized on behalf of his subordinate, who had kept her head bowed the whole time. Before this audience, he had told her to stay quiet unless directly addressed and to leave all the talking to him.

"Allen is a former serf from a tiny country, is he not?" The emperor frowned. "He must have failed to understand just what you were saying. It appears the Academy's curriculum requires revision."

He apparently thought Allen had not comprehended the weight and meaning of the emperor of Giamut seeking his presence. A serf being granted an audience with the head of such a massive state was probably the first time such a thing had happened in history.

"That could well be the case," the foreign minister replied obsequiously while shooting glances at Helmios with upturned eyes. "It is unthinkable for someone to turn down an invitation from Your Imperial Highness."

The Hero sighed, lamenting the fact that he always happened to be around whenever the emperor received unwelcome news as of late. He had come here on a separate matter when the foreign minister and the envoy suddenly showed up.

"I'll ask Allen what he thinks," Helmios offered, despite already having a general sense of Allen's attitude toward royalty after spending time with him in Rohzenheim.

Logically speaking, there was no way that Allen, who had enrolled in the Academy with the highest entrance exam score of all time, would fail to grasp what a summons from an emperor meant. However, saying so at this moment would only prolong the conversation with no real benefit, so he chose to wrap things up while leaving the matter vague.

The foreign minister breathed a small sigh of relief and promptly led his subordinate out of the room.

"People seem to have forgotten how to show respect lately," Regalfaras growled. He was not stupid. He knew that his ministers and nobles were purposely putting off bringing him bad news until Helmios visited.

"I'm sure that's not—"

Knock, knock.

The two turned their eyes to the door. When the emperor granted permission to enter, the royal guard outside let two men in. One was an old man wearing expensive-looking clothing who did not look like a noble or government official. The other was a large middle-aged man who had a certain rough air to him like an adventurer.

Emperor Regalfaras narrowed his eyes. "There you are. Finally."

"I would never even think of ignoring a summons from Your Imperial Majesty." The old man walked over leisurely and took the seat in front of him and Helmios.

"What did I say? No respect," the emperor said, prompting a wry but noncommittal smile from Helmios.

"What are we talking about?" The old man raised an eyebrow.

"Nothing. Now, Guildmaster General Makkaron. The reason for today's summoning is Allen."

The man at the very top of the Adventurer's Guild hierarchy, Makkaron, nodded. "Hmm. Are you referring to the young man who managed to wound Hero Helmios?"

"That young man is said to be responsible for saving Rohzenheim from a Demon Lord Army force of several million. Is that even possible?"

"Interesting."

The country of elves had made an official announcement giving Hero Helmios much of the credit for their victory in the war that just ended. However, the emperor had heard from Helmios how Allen had been involved. Assuming it was true, the emperor wanted to know what abilities the boy had and how he had pulled it off.

"Helmios told me what Allen has done on the battlefield. I want you to explain how powerful he would have to be in a way that I can understand."

As a ruler, Regalfaras could not simply go, "Oh, someone strong showed up," and not do anything about it.

"I'll go over everything again," Helmios said. "Allen's achievements are beyond the powers he had when fighting me at his Academy's Martial Arts Tournament."

The Hero recounted how the No-life Gamers had landed on the southern tip of Rohzenheim and saved the queen of the elves, then won battle after battle until eventually defeating even a Demonic Deity. He let Guildmaster General Makkaron know everything he personally witnessed as well as what he had heard from the elven soldiers.

The man standing next to Makkaron listened with a skeptical frown.

When Helmios finished, Makkaron slowly replied, "I didn't expect him to be so powerful. If everything you said is true, it means Allen and his party killed millions of monsters all by themselves."

It was near the end of autumn last year when Guildmaster General Makkaron heard a student named Allen had managed to wound Hero Helmios during a Martial Arts Tournament at the Ratashian Academy.

"That's what it means, yes." The emperor nodded. "Is that possible?"

Makkaron turned to the Hero. "Helmios, could you pull it off?"

"Nuh-uh. Not even if I had my whole party with me."

"See? Curse the Ratashian king for trying to pull one over the world's eyes! I can't wait for the next Five Continent Alliance summit," Emperor Regalfaras spat, making no effort to hide his displeasure.

One of the articles of the Five Continent Alliance charter required signatory countries to announce whenever someone with a Talent of three or more stars was found within their citizenry. The fact that Helmios and his ten three-star Talented party members could not achieve what Allen's party supposedly had with even fewer members spoke volumes about just how powerful Allen should be. Not reporting this to the Alliance was a clear violation of the charter.

The Giamutan emperor was happy with the status quo where a Hero born in Giamut went around racking up miraculous feats. Someone from another country playing hero all over the place and hogging the spotlight was something the emperor very much wanted to deal with—even more so if that person refused his summons, therefore undermining his authority as an emperor. Emperor Regalfaras was looking forward to tearing the newly crowned King Invel of Ratash apart at the next Five Continent Alliance summit.

"Now, now, there's no need to be so hasty," Makkaron cautioned.

"What do you mean?" Regalfaras frowned.

"Helmios." The guildmaster general turned to the Hero. "If you were to fight Allen now, how would it turn out?"

"He *was* pretty strong during our fight with the Demonic Deity, but I believe I'm still much more powerful than him."

Allen had yet to level up his Summoning skill since his time in the Academy. And since he was dedicating Summons to helping his allies and the elves, his damage output was now even lower than when he fought Helmios.

"As I thought." Makkaron nodded. "It seems this Allen fellow's ability, 'Summoning,' is specialized for supporting other people."

Helmios nodded, recalling the elven soldiers who told him they felt more powerful than usual when fighting during the war. The reason Allen had brought Helmios along for the fight with Rehzel was because the boy fully understood his own strengths and weaknesses and had determined that he could not win in a one-on-one with the Demonic Deity.

"I see. Still, are you saying that he managed to repel a force of several millions with his party's help alone?"

"A certain country did splurge in hiring elven squads, effectively funding Rohzenheim with large amounts of money. Thanks to this, they have all the best equipment that money can buy. Their soldiers are also powerful enough to fight Rank B monsters one-on-one. Now, add all this with the buffs that Allen supposedly cast on them, and you can see what actually happened."

Makkaron's point was that the money that Rohzenheim received in turn for lending other countries elven healers had enabled them to outfit all their troops with mithril equipment. If the number of soldiers and monsters was around the same, then chances of the elves losing were low.

Even more so if they were fighting defensive battles from behind fortresses that gave them even more of an edge.

Of course, the Demon Lord Army had sent three million at the start, twice the size of the elven army. The elves did end up managing to beat them back, so the guildmaster general's interpretation of Helmios's account was that this result was not due solely to Allen's Summons but that the buffed soldiers themselves surely played a huge role.

"I see."

"Did Giamut not also receive a large number of elven elixirs? Perhaps the elves who could make these recovery items were also buffed, significantly increasing their production rate."

"I could see that happening. That would explain the elves giving Allen a title as grandiose as grand strategist. Securing him means being able to make as many recovery items as they want."

The news that Rohzenheim had installed Allen as grand strategist had reached Giamut as well. The emperor, being unable to imagine it was Allen himself making the so-called elven elixirs, felt Guildmaster General Makkaron's words made sense.

"So, is this all I can help you with today, Your Imperial Majesty?"

"No, there is more. This Allen is currently at the Rank S dungeon in Baukis. Helmios will be joining him there soon."

"With the war barely over! I sure envy the young 'uns for their energy!" Makkaron said with a laugh.

"I've heard that the Tower of Tribulation has never been cleared before. Exactly how difficult is it to do so?"

"There is a limit to how strong even the greatest heroes and champions can get. Many such champions who reached their limits have dashed themselves against the Tower."

This world had a leveling system, which meant everyone had a level cap. Those who reached this cap all invariably turned to the Rank S dungeon in search of orichalcum weapons and equipment.

"However, no one has cleared it yet?" the emperor asked again to clarify.

Makkaron nodded. "Indeed. A while back, the Rank S adventurer

Bask, also known as the King of Shura, also gave up when he reached the final floor. And if we're talking way back in the past, the champion Astel did the same."

"Now that's an old story," the emperor commented.

Gathering orichalcum equipment from the Rank S dungeon and actually clearing the dungeon were two very different things. To prove his point, Guildmaster General Makkaron even brought up a champion from thousands of years in the past. There were historic records, far before the birth of the Demon Lord, of champions who met tragic fates challenging the Rank S dungeon's last level. According to one account, one person who came back out alive had said, "That floor is Dungeon Master Dygragni's playground. It's no place for a mortal to step foot in!"

"So you confirm that clearing it is an impossible feat?"

"It is undoubtedly impossible."

"So it will remain unconquered?"

"This Allen character will learn the meaning of the term 'unconquered' the hard way."

The man in the highest position of the entire Adventurer's Guild confirmed with full certainty that the Rank S dungeon, the Tower of Tribulation, was insurmountable.

Side Story 5: Pelomas's Contract

Pelomas was Allen's childhood friend with the Merchant Talent who was currently attending a commercial school in the Ratashian capital. Previously, he had taken Allen's advice and established a trading company named Pelomas Whaling Company. At the moment, his company was headquartered in Granvelle City and mainly did business going between Granvelle City and the capital.

One morning, a government official came to Pelomas out of the blue and asked him to immediately head to the royal palace for a contract. His summons was very sudden, but the official was merely a messenger and did not know much else himself. However, he did seem especially anxious, almost as if this contract might decide the future of the Kingdom of Ratash.

Without ado, Pelomas hurried to the palace along with Raven, Milci, and Rita. These three were former adventurers who had been active in and around Granvelle City but found themselves practically out of work due to Allen annihilating the area's monster population. Pelomas had then approached them with an introduction from Allen, who was acquainted with them; Raven went, "I suppose this is better than working in the mithril mines," and agreed. And so they were now all working for Pelomas Whaling Company.

When Pelomas and the others arrived, they were taken to a parlor and given a change of clothes. Their guide asked Raven to remain there rather than join the others at the contract signing. Raven had a rough appearance, and there was a chance of him offending the other party.

Eventually Pelomas found himself in a heavily ornamented room. There was a table in the middle with chairs lining all four sides. Viscount Granvelle and a man with very sparse hair who was the Minister of Commerce sat on one side.

Pelomas was already acquainted with Viscount Granvelle thanks to Allen; in fact, the viscount was the source of much of Pelomas Whaling Company's business. Pelomas offered him a respectful greeting.

The seat between the viscount and the minister lay unoccupied. The minister indicated that Pelomas was to sit there. Taking his seat, Pelomas still did not know a single detail regarding the all-important contract.

"A-Are you gonna be okay, boss?" Rita asked while shifting uncomfortably in her expensive outfit. She and Milci were both uneasy thinking about how out of place they were in this extravagant room and, indeed, within the atmosphere of the entire palace.

"I, uh, think so?" Pelomas replied in an unsure tone.

"You *think so*?!"

"Silence!" the commerce minister thundered, the veins on his temple bulging. "Remember where you are!"

It was Pelomas's first time meeting this nearly balding man, and he felt cowed by the number of subordinates standing behind the minister as well as by all the documents spread out on the table before them.

Just as the young company president began apologizing with teary eyes, there were a few knocks at the door, prompting the minister to leap out of his chair. Seeing Viscount Granvelle also slowly getting to his feet, Pelomas gleaned that whoever it was required that he stand to greet them and so followed suit.

The door opened and several knights marched through. One of them said, "This way, my lord," before yielding the way to allow an elderly elf and his entourage through.

The minister of commerce gestured toward the empty seats on the other side of the table. "Welcome, welcome. Thank you for your willingness to discuss terms of the contract so soon."

"Ha ha ha!" the old elf chuckled. It turned out this was Elder Filamehl, the member of the Elder Council in charge of foreign affairs. "Speak nothing of it. I see we have kept all of you waiting for quite some time. Apologies."

One of the other elves, a diplomatic envoy, pulled out a chair for him. Filamehl sat with a grunt. Only after he was settled did Viscount Granvelle and the minister sit back down. Pelomas followed their lead.

The minister spoke first. "Sitting here with us is one of our merchants whom we have summoned to facilitate the signing of the contract detailing Ratash and Rohzenheim's official trade agreement. We are currently in the process of selecting more—"

Only now did Pelomas finally understand the situation. He had heard that Ratash and Rohzenheim had established formal diplomatic relations; they were now taking the next step to begin trading. And thanks to listening carefully in commercial school lectures, Pelomas knew exactly how important the elderly elf sitting before him was.

"Selecting more?" Elder Filamehl frowned. "That goes against what we agreed upon."

The minister looked alarmed. "Huh? M-My deepest apologies. We will hurry the process!" He paled at the thought of the massive amount of money that Ratash would be missing out on should this trade agreement fall through.

Not two days had passed since an elven diplomat showed up at the palace, announcing that Rohzenheim wanted to begin trading as soon as possible. Trade between countries was normally restricted to trading firms approved by both nations, but for some reason, Rohzenheim specified that it only wanted to do business with Pelomas Whaling Company. The minister of commerce had immediately investigated this nobody trader. Needless to say, he was very surprised to learn the company had only been in operation for a year.

However, there was no way around using Pelomas Whaling Company, not when Rohzenheim had named them specifically. As such, the minister had decided to first let Elder Filamehl meet Pelomas before recommending a few handpicked trading firms with established ties to Ratash. Indeed, the documents before him were profiles of such firms that met the royal standards.

"It appears there has been a slight misunderstanding," Elder Filamehl said. "We have no interest in any other trading firms. Rohzenheim is only interested in signing a trading agreement with Pelomas Whaling Company."

"*What?!* That is far too— Pelomas Whaling Company is but a newly established outfit that lacks experience, and President Pelomas himself is still a student!"

International trade normally involved many trading firms. Each firm could focus on handling the goods that it was best suited for, allowing for greater efficiency and higher profits. If a single firm were to take over everything, not only would it generate less profit handling items it was not equipped to, but it could stand to lose a fortune should it fail to react to market fluctuations.

In this particular case, the company president was still a student attending commercial school, and his company was barely a year old. Anyone with a mind could see that trading exclusively with Pelomas Whaling Company was a huge risk with potentially disastrous results for both countries.

"That is no issue. It was Grand Strategist Allen's request that we form this trade agreement. He informed us that President Pelomas is his good friend. As such, we have no interest in dealing with any other."

"I...see. So that is..." The minister of commerce shot a look at Viscount Granvelle and realized what was going on.

Viscount Granvelle was also here because Elder Filamehl had specifically requested him as a witness. The minister had believed this was because he was the lord of the realm where Pelomas was from and where Pelomas Whaling Company was based, but apparently the factor connecting everything here was Allen.

The elderly elf turned to Pelomas. "Now, Mister Pelomas. Grand

Strategist Allen said he is leaving it up to you whether we go through with this agreement. What do you think?"

The blood drained from the minister's face. "How can—?!"

"Minister," Filamehl interrupted. "Let Mister Pelomas speak."

If Pelomas refused this trade agreement, Ratash would lose an incalculable amount of revenue. The minister would rather accept Pelomas Whaling Company as the sole signatory rather than have the whole deal called off.

Without missing a beat, Pelomas said, "Thank you for choosing my company. We would be more than happy to sign a contract with Rohzenheim."

"No hesitation, I see." Filamehl raised an eyebrow.

"Naturally. I am aiming to grow my company as quickly as possible."

Pelomas was in love with Fiona, the daughter of Chester, the richest merchant in Granvelle City. When he asked Fiona's father for permission to court her, Pelomas was told that he would have to become a merchant that even Chester would acknowledge before he graduated.

There was only one year left until Pelomas graduated from the merchant school. He had been starting to think it was impossible for him to fulfill the condition in time, but if he succeeded in securing this deal, his firm would see enormous growth, and he would be that much closer to courting Fiona. He recognized this opportunity Allen was giving him.

"Hm. You don't look anything special, but you've got a spine, at least. That said, I'll have to test you before we actually discuss the terms of the contract."

"A test, my lord?"

"Rohzenheim does not mind losing a little money in this matter, so the test would be more to allay the worries of your minister of commerce here. We want you to prove that you have the ability to handle this."

The Elder signaled to his subordinates and they left the room. They returned pushing a cart loaded with several kinds of items, including weapons, armor, musical instruments, and medicine.

"What is this, my lord?"

"These are samples of products Rohzenheim is considering exporting to Ratash. What do you think? Do you see value in selling them?"

"May I use my skills?"

"Of course."

As the minister of commerce anxiously watched on with Rita and Milci, Pelomas activated Analyze to confirm each item's name, what it was made of, and what properties it possessed.

"These are all wonderful items. Do you have a specific selling price in mind, my lord?"

During his past two years at school, Pelomas had studied up and memorized everything he could on all kinds of goods, including weapons, armor, medicines, instruments, and even fine art. All of this effort was for the sake of making his love come true.

"Hmm..." Filamehl accepted a document from his subordinate and read from it. "This flute, for example, was made by one of Rohzenheim's prized craftsmen. We wish to sell it for ten gold." There were apparently two thousand of them in stock.

Pelomas activated his skill and turned the instrument over and over in his hands, studying it. He then set it down.

Next, he picked up a piece of armor. "This is very light. How much for it?"

"That would be twenty-five gold. We actually have many units of that armor. Around three million, in fact."

"Th-Three million, my lord? That is quite a lot indeed."

One of the elven envoys explained that this armor was actually crafted from the carapaces of insect monsters killed during the Demon Lord Army's assault on one of their major fortresses during the war. Allen's group had only wanted the magic stones and let the elves have the rest of the materials, which was why the elves had so many of these particular items.

"Which is why we hope you can accept as many as possible," the Elder finished.

It could be said that Rohzenheim's main reason for seeking a trade agreement with Ratash was to off-load its stock. A large number of elven cities had suffered significant damage in the war, and the country also had to make condolence payments to the families of those fallen in battle.

"As many as possible... I see," Pelomas murmured. He then activated his Extra Skill, Libra.

"Wha—?! Pelomas, what are you doing in a place such as this?!"

The sight of a heat haze springing up around Pelomas's body rattled the minister of commerce. Elder Filamehl and Viscount Granvelle directed their full attention toward Pelomas, wondering what the boy was up to.

After a thoughtful pause, Pelomas declared, "I will purchase your full stock of this armor—no, of all of the goods here."

The minister choked. "HUH?! Y-You must be out of your mind! *All* of— Do you know what you are saying?!" He barely held back the urge to pinch himself to awake from this nightmare.

"Minister, please don't interrupt our negotiations," the Elder warned.

"My head will fly!" the minister wailed. "Our country will go bankrupt!" He frantically tried to speak reason, but the elves half-heartedly reassured him as they led him a distance away.

At the end of the day, the Kingdom of Ratash was but a small country. Consequently, domestic demand for weapons, armor, and instruments was not very high. Expensive, valuable flutes made by skilled elven artisans might invoke some interest among the royal family and prominent merchant families, but trying to sell off a stock of two thousand was nigh impossible. Similarly, it could take a century to sell three million pieces of armor at twenty-five gold apiece. The responsibility for all this would fall on the Minister of Commerce, the person who greenlit this trade agreement.

Pelomas, however, shared none of the minister's anxiety. "Elder Filamehl, I wish to buy everything that Rohzenheim is willing to sell, including this armor. On three conditions, that is."

"Interesting. Let's hear them."

"First: allow me to negotiate the price."

"Of course, of course. Be forewarned—I am a formidable opponent."

"The second condition is related to payment. I would need a full year to arrange payment for the quantities mentioned."

"Interesting. So you mean to say you can sell everything within a year?"

The minister of commerce crumpled to his knees hearing this exchange between Pelomas and Filamehl.

"I can," Pelomas nodded. "There is more than enough demand if we include Giamut and Baukis."

"Hm? What do you mean by including Giamut and Baukis?"

The truth was Pelomas's plan was not to simply sell Rohzenheim's imports within Ratash. His Extra Skill, Libra, told him the worth of goods—not an absolute value, but the appropriate price for each part of the world. Flipped on its head, this meant that it also told him what the demand was in each place.

Specifically, he could get numbers for the global averages as well as narrow them down by continent, country, and even by realm or city. Thanks to his Extra Skill, Pelomas had just confirmed that demand for the elven armor was actually rising in Giamut and Baukis—Giamut needed to replenish its armory after the war with the Demon Lord Army, whereas Baukis had constant demand due to its large population and massive area.

This armor was lightweight and durable, making it suitable for anyone ranging from close-range fighters to scouts. Pelomas had no doubt he could sell all three million pieces in these two countries.

"I will introduce this armor to the market in Ratash, but I expect to sell most of these overseas," Pelomas concluded.

"I see." Filamehl stroked his chin thoughtfully. "What is your third condition?"

"I wish for trading rights in Giamut and Baukis. Would you be able to pull some strings for me?"

At the moment, Pelomas Whaling Company only had the authority to trade with Rohzenheim. Pelomas had determined that the Minister of

Commerce of Ratash did not have the pull to get him a license to trade in Giamut or Baukis and was therefore now asking Filamehl.

"Oh? You're asking me to use my connections?"

"It would make things significantly easier. I promise you will see a return on your investment within one year."

The look in Pelomas's eyes made Filamehl think he was negotiating with the emperor of Giamut for a split second. This gave him pause. However, he quickly told himself there was no need for the wariness. After all, this trade agreement was a request from Allen, the champion who saved Rohzenheim.

"Very well. Those two do owe me at least this much."

"Thank you, my lord. I look forward to doing business with you."

"Indeed. It appears we have ourselves a deal."

After this meeting, Filamehl secured Pelomas the rights to trade with both Giamut and Baukis within a month, marking a huge turning point in Pelomas Whaling Company's fate.

Side Story 6: Creating a Fortress City

Not long after Allen's group headed off for the Rank S dungeon, a large magic ship cruised through Granvelle City airspace. This was Viscount Granvelle's private ship. The large majority of magic ships were on rent from Baukis. But not this one—Allen had fronted the full ten thousand gold in one lump sum and bought it for the viscount.

Allen had always wanted to repay the viscount somehow, not only for everything that he had done for Allen during his manservant days but even after enrolling at the Academy, especially in the matter of restoring Keel's house. He did not mind simply handing over the money directly to the viscount, but when he tried thinking of something special that only he could procure, given the connections and prestige he had accumulated in Baukis, the idea of buying a magic ship occurred to him.

When gifting the viscount this ship, Allen had also asked him for a favor. Namely, he asked that the viscount allow the residents of his realm to use the ship too. This would give the people greater mobility and would consequently help promote economic growth within the realm.

Thanks to the viscount agreeing to this condition, the magic ship was currently transporting some knights of the realm and around a hundred households. The craft was heading for Rodin Village, the settlement where Allen's father served as chief. The households on board were hoping for work there.

Seated in a private room were two pairs of elderly passengers. One couple, Zohan and Jenica, were Allen's paternal grandparents.

"Is that true? Did that really happen?" Zohan asked incredulously.

"It is true, I assure you!" The Spirit B who was sitting with them replied. "His efforts saved an entire country!"

"My, oh my. What a wonderful child our Rodin has raised. Is our grandson really that incredible?"

"Of course, Lady Jenica. Lord Allen is more incredible than words can express!"

Theresia's parents were also in the room. However, this was their first experience riding a magic ship. They were so astonished that they had been pressed up against the window this whole time.

These four elders, all serfs by birth, had left their lands to their children so they could make this voyage. Quite some time ago, Allen had paid for anyone among his extended family who wished to become commoners.

"My, oh my! I do believe the village has come into view. My, it's so large!" Jenica, who had moved to a window of her own, exclaimed at the sight.

This prompted Zohan to do the same. "You're right, dear. Is this really a frontier village? It seems far too massive."

The pair had a good aerial view of the entirety of Rodin Village. The wooden fence that served as its perimeter marked out an area more than four times that of Krena Village, which they had stopped by earlier. Surrounding the fence was a wide moat. The drawbridge was currently up, giving the village near perfect protection from the monsters outside.

When the magic ship's shadow fell over the village, those aboard looking down could see that the moat was currently empty. Many people and boarlike beasts were inside, still working to expand it.

"Wh-What are those?! Are they not monsters?!"

"Please calm down, Lord Zohan. They are Lord Allen's Summons."

"S-Summons! So those are Summons too..."

Both Zohan and Jenica watched the construction work taking place down below with disbelieving looks.

Allen held his family's happiness above all else. During the war in Rohzenheim, he had seen the destruction wrought upon the citizens' lives when the Demon Lord Army got serious. To protect his family in case he ever died in battle, Allen had set in motion plans to turn Rodin Village into a fortress city capable of withstanding the onslaught of millions of monsters.

His Beast C Summons were doing most of the heavy lifting when it came to expanding the moat, but they were not good with the finer details. Allen needed villagers to help with fortifying the city during the months when there was no great boar hunting. However, if they were to do so, then there would be no one to tend the fields. And so Allen had consulted Viscount Granvelle and received permission to bring a hundred households to Rodin Village to do the farming.

Recruitment Details Posted in Granvelle City

- Each household will be paid a monthly salary of one gold (including travel time)
- The entire family is exempt from taxes
- Living quarters and three months of food will be provided
- Participation in great boar hunting is voluntary (in case of death, 300 gold to be paid out as consolation pay)
- When hunting great boars, weapons and armor will be lent out free of charge
- Period of employment of one year
- Limited to 100 households

The rate of employment was low in this world. Naturally, a large number of people applied for the opportunity. In the end, a lottery had to be held to decide who was accepted. The winners were now peering down at Rodin Village from the magic ship.

"Damn, impressive. So this is Rodin Village, where we can earn a gold a month working."

"It's a lot bigger than I thought. Can you even call this a village? It's more of a city, isn't it?"

"Are they really going to give us a place to live and food for a while?"

The great boars that would be hunted during the fall season never showed up in the vicinity of Granvelle City, so they had been described to the immigrants as merely "beasts that mess up the farmers' fields." During the hunting itself, weapons and armor would be provided, and apprentice knights would even come along, so the level of danger was no longer all that high.

Once one person joined in the hunt, word of the benefits of doing so would spread and the number of immigrants applying would shoot up the next time onward. Furthermore, keeping the period of employment to a year and constantly swapping out people was proving effective in raising the average level of the citizens in the realm. Those who returned to the city would have a much easier time finding new employment.

When the magic ship landed on the landing pad in Rodin Village, knights showed up to courteously escort Allen's grandparents.

"This way, sirs, madams."

"We have arrived? Thank you for being so kind."

The knights also led the newly arrived villagers to the open square in the center of the village. There, they found Rodin, the chief of the village, waiting for them.

The one leading the knights, Vice-Captain Leibrand, greeted Rodin. "Village Chief. I hope you are well. Here is the new batch of those who would be working here."

"Welcome, Vice-Captain Leibrand. Thank you for coming all this way." Rodin bowed respectfully. "We are currently preparing the usual welcoming feast. Please rest up in the meantime."

The residential area for the new immigrants was located close to the village square.

"I see. There are plenty of foodstuffs and alcohol loaded on the ship. Feel free to use them for the feast."

All of this food and alcohol had also been paid for by Allen.

* * *

Night fell, and the welcoming party for the new residents and the escorting knights began. A huge bonfire had been set up in the middle of the village square.

"Everyone, thank you for making the long journey to our village. I am Rodin, the village chief here. This is your welcoming party. I hope you enjoy yourselves."

When Rodin finished giving his speech in his best village chief voice, the feast kicked off in earnest. The meat being served was all fresh monster meat that Allen had his Summons carry from the White Dragon Mountains. Particularly attention-drawing was the five-meter-tall Rank B lizard-like monster that had been butchered and brought in.

"Myulla, dear, you're saying this meat was also brought in by one of Allen's Summons?" Jenica asked, gently stroking her granddaughter's head.

"Yep!" Myulla answered, her eyes sparkling. "It was like, thiiiiiiis big, and when the Summon let it down, it was like, *booooooooom*!" She spread her arms, trying her best to reenact the scene of a Dragon B bringing in a monster carcass in its mouth.

The old woman found herself wondering when was the last time she had been able to fill her stomach with as much meat as she wanted.

Close by, Zohan and Rodin were having a father-and-son moment. Rodin had founded Krena Village five years before Allen was born, meaning it had been twenty years since these two last saw each other.

"Look at you, being a proper village chief and all." Zohan thought back to when his son left at fifteen, saying that he wanted his own field. He had been a rascal who much rather preferred swinging his spear and playing pranks on others than helping out with farmwork.

"I can't believe it myself either. Though I suppose compared to Allen, I'm still no different from everyone else."

"Word of Boar Hunter Rodin reached even our village, you know? It made me happy."

"Pops..." Everything that had happened in the twenty years since Rodin arrived at Krena Village flashed through his mind.

Zohan turned to his grandson. "Mash, do you think Allen is cool?"

"Mm." Mash nodded shyly.

"When do you think he is coming home?"

"Beats me," Rodin shrugged. "He's gone to a different country. Maybe he'll be back after becoming a champion."

"A champion. Now that's something to look forward to." Zohan hoped he would get to meet Allen one day.

"In any case, you don't have to work the fields anymore, pops, mom. You can take it easy now and live however you want."

"You picking a fight?"

"What do you mean?! Do you know what age you are?!"

This house had more than enough space to accommodate both Rodin's and Theresia's parents. However...

"You went and became a big shot after becoming village chief, huh? You rascal. Of course I'll help out. How can I not after coming all the way here?"

His father's grin prompted Rodin to sigh as he remembered this was just what his father's personality was.

And so, with the arrival of the new villagers and Allen's grandparents, Rodin Village continued seeing even more growth than before.

Side Story 7: The Land of Spirits

Allen's group had left Baukis and returned to Rohzenheim. They were here because Sophie, who had received a class promotion the other day and become a Spirit User, needed to form contracts with spirits.

"That was fast. Are we gonna continue using this every time going forward?" Dogora asked as the party got off their magic ship at the landing pad in Fortenia, the capital of Rohzenheim.

"It sure was," Allen replied. "Baukis's superspeed magic ship really does live up to its name."

This time, the No-life Gamers had borrowed a superspeed magic ship, of which there was only a limited number even within Baukis. Being a *superspeed* magic ship, this vehicle was even faster than the high-speed magic ship that they had ridden when hurrying to Rohzenheim's aid when it was under attack by the Demon Lord Army.

Chartering this superspeed magic ship cost thousands of gold each day. Conversely, this went to show that in Baukis, it was literally possible to get anything as long as one paid enough money.

Two months had passed since the party first stepped foot in the Rank S dungeon. They had sold so many items worth several thousands of gold that now, time was far more precious to them than money. This was why Allen decided to charter a superspeed magic ship for this trip that involved them flying the entire length of the Central Continent to reach the opposite side of the world.

"Everyone, thank you very— My!"

Sophie was walking off the ship and thanking her friends for accompanying her on this trip when the cityscape of Fortenia leaped into sight and she exclaimed with surprise.

It had only been three months since the No-life Gamers fought Demonic Deity Rehzel here. However, the city had already begun reconstruction and was steadily regaining its previous look. The air was charged with the elves' resolute will to resume living under the canopy of the World Tree as soon as possible.

"This is incredible," Keel breathed, comparing what he was seeing with the scorched and flattened version of the city in his memory. "Did they do all this with their powers?"

"I'm sure they did." Sophie nodded. "We can call on the spirits of earth and wood and ask them to lend us their strength."

Thanks to the power of the spirits, homes, the grand temple, and the city walls were all going up at the same time.

"I see. When the restoration after the battle settles down a bit more, I might ask for help with my plan to fortify Rodin Village," Allen murmured.

A smile came over Sophie's face. "We would be more than happy to help."

Allen had seen many cities and settlements overrun by the Demon Lord Army and razed to the ground. He was currently working on fortifying Rodin Village, where his family lived, to prevent the same outcome there even if the Demon Lord Army attacked.

"Okay, guys, let's head out. Sophie, ride with me and guide me."

The party mounted their Bird Bs and headed out.

Sophie turned to the flying squirrel nestled at her chest. "Lord Rohzen, please show us the way."

"You got it, ha ha. You want to start with fire, right? We'll be heading to the mountains, then. This way."

Under the Spirit God's guidance, the party flew for a full day. The world was illuminated by the gentle light of the moon when they finally reached a giant mountain range. The barely visible, billowing clouds of smoke and the deep, red glow of surging magma flowing below made it clear this was a volcanic range.

A Bird E sent out to inspect one of the volcanic craters caught sight of a glowing red being within.

"Mm? There's something in the crater," Allen murmured.

"That's Salamander, the juvenile fire spirit you're looking for," Rohzen replied.

All the Bird Bs landed close to the crater, and the party approached what looked like a Japanese salamander. It was walking up to a crack between two rocks to lap at magma flowing out.

Allen's group recognized this spirit. Three months ago, when the elves held a feast celebrating the World Tree returning to their control, many spirits had gathered to join them. Salamander had been one of them, and Sophie had approached it in hopes of eventually contracting it when she became a Spirit User.

"*Au, au!*" the creature cried when it noticed Sophie. Apparently it also remembered her. It began lumbering over.

"Ha ha, this is a lively one," Rohzen chuckled. "So, let's do this. Sophie, approach Salamander to contract it."

Even though Rohzen almost never gave Allen advice, he proactively did so for Sophie. She obediently walked over to the juvenile fire spirit.

"*Auuuu! Au, au!*"

When Sophie held out her hand, the spirit reached for it with a front leg. The moment the two touched, they were enveloped in a bright light.

"And now the contract is complete. Ha ha."

"Thank you so much, Lord Rohzen!"

Just as Sophie was thanking the Spirit God she was cradling, her newly contracted juvenile fire spirit clambered onto her knees, happily crying "*Au, au!*" as it proceeded to climb up her front to settle on her shoulder.

"Um, please settle down." Sophie looked troubled by how lively Salamander was.

Allen asked, "Lord Rohzen, may I ask how powerful is Salamander? What rank would it be if it were a monster?"

"In terms of sheer fighting strength, a juvenile spirit is somewhere between Rank C and B."

The Spirit God had become quite generous with sharing information about spirits in general.

"Huh? What the hell. It's weak!" Dogora reached out to Salamander, who was rubbing its face against Sophie's, and gave the back of its head a few light pats.

"*Au!*" The juvenile spirit turned around and glared at him with sharp eyes as its body started glowing.

"What is— Salamander?! Ah..." Sophie had just noticed something was wrong when, the next moment, a wave of dizziness struck her, and she brought a hand to her forehead, wobbling on her feet.

"Princess Sophialohne!" Volmaar caught her in the nick of time.

WHOOOOSH!

That moment, a gigantic fireball dozens of meters in diameter appeared above Sophie and Volmaar, powerfully pushing back the dark of night.

"What on earth is that?!" Cecil exclaimed, shocked at the size of the attack. This was definitely beyond the scope of a Rank C or B monster's abilities.

"Salamander, calm down. You are absorbing your host's HP!" Rohzen said calmly in admonition.

The juvenile spirit, who had fallen to Sophie's feet, promptly curled up and quivered apologetically. The giant fireball disappeared as suddenly as it had appeared.

By checking his grimoire, Allen realized that Sophie's MP had been entirely drained, on top of which she had lost a bit of HP as well.

"Keel, heal Sophie up," Allen ordered before turning to Rohzen. "Lord Rohzen, what just happened?"

The Spirit God shot a side glance at Sophie stroking the juvenile fire spirit. "As Salamander only just contracted with Sophie, it doesn't yet have a good grasp on how much power to draw from her."

Spirits drew MP from their hosts to use their powers. After having gone through two class promotions, Sophie's max MP was greater than most elves. Furthermore, she was wearing equipment effective enough to help her in the Rank S dungeon. Put together, this meant she had a lot of MP. Salamander, who had only just contracted her and therefore had no idea how much power to draw, ended up taking all of it. This was how it managed to create the giant fireball from just now.

"You mean to say the strength of spirits' powers is proportional to the amount of MP expended?" Allen asked thoughtfully. "That sounds like Cecil's Petit Meteor."

"So that's how it is." Cecil knew that the power of her Extra Skill, Petit Meteor, was dependent on her Intelligence and Max MP. When she used it at max level and with all her equipment on, it could be incredibly destructive.

The rest of the No-life Gamers looked at the frolicking juvenile spirit and marveled at how much power it could wield despite how young it was.

With nothing else left to do for the day, the party then moved a ways off from the crater and pitched camp.

* * *

The next day, the party set off again in the morning. This time, they were headed for a flowing river.

"Hm, I'm glad you also managed to contract a juvenile water spirit without a hitch," Allen said.

"*Kee, kee!*" Kelpie, a juvenile spirit with the appearance of a baby dolphin with a blue back and white belly, squealed cutely. It was squirming in her arms like a fish on land and not listening to anything she was saying, likely because it had only just been contracted and was as yet unfamiliar with the experience.

"Aw, guess I didn't need this," Allen mumbled disappointedly, shifting the large fishing net thrown over his shoulder.

Cecil looked at him as if he was an idiot. "Just how were you imagining the encounter to go?" she asked.

This juvenile water spirit had also been among those who had gathered underneath the World Tree during the feast. It, too, vaguely remembered Allen's group.

Just as Salamander had been at an actual flowing stream of magma, Allen and Dogora had actually thought they would have to catch Kelpie like a fish swimming in a river. They were relieved this was not what actually happened.

"Lord Rohzen, is it possible for Sophie to keep Kelpie materialized along with Salamander at the same time?" Allen asked. He was wondering if Sophie could do the same thing with her spirits that he could with his Summons.

"Ha ha, that's generally not possible."

"Generally?" *That's not a flat-out no.*

"She might be able to when she becomes more used to materializing spirits. Also, when she has a lot more MP."

Allen realized this was similar to how he needed to increase his Intelligence in order to increase the number of Summons that he could Share with. At the same time, he also understood that Rohzen was indirectly telling him it was not yet time for this.

"I see. Thank you for answering my question, Lord Rohzen."

Keel peered into Allen's grimoire. "Damn, Sophie, you're getting a whole ton of XP. So, what's next? Wind, right?"

Every second that Kelpie was materialized, Sophie was losing MP and therefore earning skill XP. It felt like her class skill had reached Lvl. 3 merely yesterday when today she was already at Lvl. 4. Her skills had also shot from Lvl. 2 to Lvl. 4 in no time at all.

"I see, keeping a spirit materialized gives her skill XP. Sophie, I'll lend you this MP Recovery Ring. It should enable you to keep one of your spirits out at all times."

If Sophie was earning skill XP when she had her spirits around, then every moment was a precious opportunity to earn skill XP.

"Thank you, Lord Allen."

That same day, Sophie managed to contract with Éar, a juvenile air spirit. By then, however, the sun had set, so the party had to put off the last spirit for the next day. They therefore set up camp at a location close to where they had found Éar and spent the night.

On the last day, Sophie rode with Allen once again.

"The last one is earth, then. Did we meet one at the World Tree?"

A large variety of spirits had gathered at the World Tree during the feast, but Allen did not recall seeing a juvenile earth spirit.

"There probably were, but Sophie didn't manage to make a connection with any, ha ha," Rohzen replied.

"Lord Rohzen, do you know where we should be going?" Sophie asked.

"Well...all right. This way. It's quite a distance." The Spirit God proceeded to lead the party to a location farther south of Castle Lapolka.

Regarding Spirit Users and Spirits

- In terms of fighting strength, juvenile spirits are normally between Rank C to B
- The more MP a Spirit User has, the more powerful the contracted spirits become
- The higher a Spirit User's Intelligence, the easier they can communicate with their spirits
- High Intelligence is required to materialize multiple spirits at once
- Grand Spirit Users can easily materialize numerous juvenile spirits at the same time

During the flight, Allen wrote down everything that he had learned about Spirit Users and spirits over the past few days. Apparently Rohzen was willing to answer pretty much anything when it came to spirits. After asking the Spirit God many questions, Allen eventually worked out what he thought was the best way for Sophie to develop her abilities.

Put succinctly, he told her, "It seems that as a Spirit User, you should focus on increasing your MP first instead of forcefully boosting your

Intelligence. I suppose this does differentiate your role from Cecil's going forward."

For a Spirit User, both MP and Intelligence were important, but even if she became capable of calling out multiple spirits, she could lose MP so fast that even her HP might get drained and she might die. Given that, it seemed much smarter to continue materializing only one at a time but focus on making sure that they understood what Sophie wanted them to do.

"Understood, Lord Allen." Sophie nodded, then started. "What is that up ahead?"

"That is where your juvenile earth spirit is," Rohzen replied.

It turned out the Spirit God had been leading them to a crumbling ruin. They landed near the center and looked around. The weathered structures all around indicated that this used to be a city. However, most of the walls had fallen down, and little more than foundation stones were left of the houses, with only a few having a little bit of wall or a solitary pillar.

"This doesn't look related to the Demon Lord Army's invasion," Keel murmured.

"There's a juvenile earth spirit here?" Meruru started roaming around curiously.

Clatter, clatter.

It did not take long for the dwarf to find signs of movement. "Hey, something's here!" She indicated toward a boy who was shorter than even herself, the shortest member of the No-life Gamers. The boy was wearing a unique outfit that had a thick waist band and was lifting a piece of rubble as large as his own head, carrying it somewhere.

"That is Korpokkur, a juvenile earth spirit," Rohzen confirmed. For some reason, his voice was tinged with sadness.

"Sophie, go on and contract with it," Allen said.

Sophie nodded, dispelled Éar's materialization, then approached the earth spirit.

"Um, hello. Are you Korpokkur?"

However, the spirit did not respond in any way. It continued walking with its piece of rock. When it reached the only standing wall in a nearby house, it pushed its rock against it, grunting softly.

"Hng, hng. If I do this…like this…"

As Allen and the rest watched on, Sophie knelt down next to him, bringing her eye level to Korpokkur's. "What are you doing?"

"I'm fixing the town. Because everyone's gone somewhere."

"I see. This big city, all by yourself?"

"Mhm."

Korpokkur's facial expression did not change, but this only made Sophie sadder. With a lump in her throat, she asked, "Can I help somehow?"

"You would? Then please make up and be friends with the dark elves who left."

The party finally realized that this used to be a dark elf city. Perhaps this spirit had once contracted with someone who had lived here but was expelled from the continent as a result of the war between the elves and dark elves. Even worse, maybe his host had died in the fighting.

Either way, it would have happened more than a thousand, no, two thousand years ago. Korpokkur had probably been trying to rebuild this town all by himself ever since then. However, no matter how many stones he carried with his small hands, the city continued crumbling with the passage of time. It was way past the point where it could be restored.

Sophie blinked her tears away. "I am someone who will lead the elves."

"Mhm," Korpokkur replied, still pushing his rock.

"And I dream that one day, we will be walking along with the dark elves."

Hearing this, the earth spirit lifted his face and looked at Sophie for the first time. "Really? Thank you. It's a promise." He held out a hand.

His facial expression remained unchanged still, but Sophie thought his aura had gotten a little bit brighter. He gave her a hand.

"As the princess of the elves, I swear to fulfill my promise with you, Korpokkur."

When Sophie touched Korpokkur's tiny hand, the pair was enveloped in light and the contract was established.

Finally, Sophie had successfully contracted with four juvenile spirits and was ready to challenge the Rank S dungeon. On this day, she gained a strong motivation besides clearing the Tower of Tribulation.

Afterword

Thank you for purchasing this book! I am Hamuo, the author.

Hell Mode now has five volumes out. This was made possible thanks to everyone who picked up a copy and enjoyed reading it. I thank you from the bottom of my heart.

If you've been reading all the books so far, you'll know that this volume is the first one where we didn't manage to feature a full arc. I managed to do so for the frontier village arc, the manservant arc, the Academy arc, and the Rohzenheim war arc, but it was just not possible this time. I'm truly sorry. I got a bit too passionate about dungeon crawling.

The upside to splitting the arc into two volumes is that I got the space to write a few more side stories than usual. It became an opportunity for me to flesh out the world a bit more with events that I didn't get to include when writing the Rank S dungeon arc for the web novel version.

This is the afterword, so I suppose it's time to share something about the production process of the book itself. The truth is, when I was writing the second arc, I was considering ending the entire series by the fifth arc. However, Allen's adventures continued growing in scale. As of now, March 2022, we have five volumes out, but the story's only just beginning. I have every intention of continuing it beyond volume ten.

When volume six comes out, you'll get to read how this attempt by

Allen and his friends to clear the Rank S dungeon shakes out. And if you continue following the series, you'll find out the full scale of their grand adventure and how their story eventually ends.

This is about all I have to say about this volume and its side stories. Now, this is the part where I give out tidbits about my time growing up to meet my word count. I hope you stay with me.

In the afterword for volume four, I talked about how my family ended up building a house and settling down. That house was in the countryside and, although not too big, had a garden.

This was when my father took up a hobby—he started a two-by-one-meter field in the garden. He grew vegetables such as cucumbers and eggplants, and he was really into it. Honestly, there was no way his stuff could compare with the produce sold in the supermarket; I remember his oversize vegetables being served at our dinner table. When I commented on them, however, he never got angry. Or at least, I don't remember him getting angry.

Something else that happened back then was that, during my school days, I got a hamster from a friend. He said his had birthed too many babies, and he was looking for people to take them in, so I said yes.

The astute among you might think, "So this is where Hamuo got his name from!" I won't say it's entirely unrelated, but honestly, I just picked "Hamuo" as a pen name pretty much on a whim.

I've loved animals even since I was young, but the mood at my house always seemed like pets weren't welcome. So I decided to secretly raise the hamster in my room on the second floor. I thought that I could get away with it as long as I didn't get found out, but I got found out in two weeks.

Thankfully, I didn't have to get rid of it. Instead, my parents gave me permission to raise it, and so I began taking care of it with proper supervision. I put in what looked like shavings into a big plastic cage and installed a running wheel and a wooden nest. I remember this being one of the funnest times in my childhood.

When the shavings got dirty, I threw them away in a corner of my father's field, thinking it could become fertilizer.

Several months after I began keeping the hamster, when spring was turning into summer, something green bloomed in the field. Turns out a few leftover sunflower seeds that I had fed my hamster had taken root and were growing. When summer was in full swing, the entire field became filled with sunflowers. I remember being impressed with how much vitality sunflowers had.

Even so, my father did not get angry, and our house garden was decorated by sunflowers for a while.

That's about it for this story of how I spent my childhood in the home that my father built.

It appears I have reached the prescribed word count. *Hell Mode* is being published not only as a light novel but also as a manga serialization that's doing quite well—volume three is being released in the same month as this book. I hope you enjoy the story in a different way with the wonderful depictions of exciting action and interesting expressions.

Let's meet again in the next volume!

Thank you very much!
Mo

j-novel club

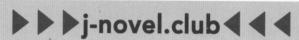